The Bitterest Enemy

by
Martin Hicks

Published by New Generation Publishing in 2013

Copyright © Martin Hicks 2013

First Edition

www.newgeneration-publishing.com

 New Generation **Publishing**

The Bitterest Enemy

Prologue

Another summer was moving into its final days in Virginia. The signs of it were still subtle, so far and maybe even unrecognised, at least by some, more likely the town or city dwellers, who, though a smaller proportion of the Army of Northern Virginia than that of their northern adversaries still filled a considerable number of the places in the ranks. To the many farmers and country boys however, who made up the greater part of the army, there was no mistaking them. While the days remained hot and many of the nights were still warm and sultry, the longer summer evenings were being gradually curtailed as the hours of darkness lengthened, and while the trees still retained their mantles of green those shades now had a look of faded tiredness about them, hinting that their days were numbered, as they proceeded on their steady, annual decline towards yellow and brown.

Harvesting, a further hallmark of this season of the year, was another though more pessimistic matter; for while, around the rolling hills and fields of Culpeper, Madison and Orange Counties, such cultivation as was still being undertaken had now reached ripeness, the occasion was but a pale shadow of its previous scale. A dismaying number of the Virginia piedmont's fields were now overgrown and neglected and many of its properties had fallen vacant, after yet another growing season that had been hamstrung and handicapped by the war. For the farmers who still laboured on their land, to have reached the point of harvesting another crop was a feat of some distinction, considering that the stragglers, not to mention the patrols and commissaries of both armies, had once more become regular visitors.

For the armies had returned, after their six week absence through the hot days of later June and most of an unusually wet July. They were back now in that region of Virginia between the Rapidan and upper Rappahannock Rivers, to continue their familiar routine, of probing and shifting, of

5

which the area had grown profoundly tired over the previous year. For the return of those endless hordes of soldiers, all of whom seemed to be constantly on the take, meant the prompt resumption of the dismal process of impoverishment, dispossession and destruction, with the life of any farmer whose barns and paddocks were within their reach returning to a grim battle for any sort of survival.

That familiar ritual of manoeuvring now had a feeling of laboured tedium about it, for it was an all too familiar pattern of events, to both the civilians and the soldiers of the area. Since re-crossing the Potomac River in the middle of July, in the wake of their three day confrontation up north in Pennsylvania, the armies had, after an initial few days of pretty urgent marching, taken to sparring their way slowly southwards, skirmishing repeatedly though without extending this to a further clash on anything like the scale of the battle that had taken place up at Gettysburg. There had been no larger fight since their return, but neither, so far, had there been any real break in contact which would allow the men a period of real recovery from the great battle and subsequent retreat to Virginia. Now, as a result of all of the manoeuvring, they were back almost to where they had been in the earliest days of summer. They had returned to a region where supplies were short and this threw both armies into an increased reliance upon the railroads to supply the bulk of what they needed to sustain their soldiers and animals, particularly since the campaigning was still in progress.

As for the farms, many of them that had been foraged too much for supplies by the men of either army, over the previous year, were now vacant. Their houses stood derelict, abandoned by their families and their fields lay overgrown and weed-strewn. They were a visible testimony to the piedmont's suffering and its weariness with this war, now almost at the mid-point of its third year. Worse still was the fact that there was, as yet, no tangible sign of it ending, of the victory that had been so taken for granted by both sides when the conflict had flared into life.

While there had been little in the way of rest and recuperation for the troops, the-after-the event analysis, in the Confederate Army of Northern Virginia, on their foray into Yankee territory, had already been extensive and it still continued. The army had begun its movement early in June in the wake of its victory at Chancellorsville a month previously. Three weeks had been spent sidling to the west and north initially along the upper reaches of the Rappahannock River, which had been the front line since the end of the previous autumn, into this very area to which they had now returned. The army had then moved north, most of it by way of the lower Shenandoah Valley, before finally crossing the Potomac into Maryland and advancing on into Pennsylvania during the final week of the month.

But for a variety of reasons, the bloody clash with the Union Army of the Potomac that had resulted had been a stuttering sequence of missed opportunities. Three days of fighting, at the start of July, had resulted in repulse and heavy losses, with the Confederate army unable to dislodge the Yankees from their defensive positions, and the Yankees disinclined to venture out of them. Finally, sorely weakened, short of ammunition, and unable to forage effectively in the presence of the enemy army, the southern troops had pulled back into Maryland. Delayed north of the Potomac River by heavy rains and a flooded river, they had been unable to return to the Virginia side till mid-July.

Unlike the previous autumn, when the return to Virginia had led to a six week period of recuperation, there had been no real pause in the campaigning, for the Yankees also had promptly forded the river, downstream from the southern army's crossing places. They had started south on a course that, if vigorously pursued, would quickly have threatened the southern capital city of Richmond and so the weakened and wearied Army of Northern Virginia had been compelled to manoeuvre southwards also, finally negotiating one of the Blue Ridge passes in order to block the enemy threat. The process of move and counter move had then been resumed and so the summer season of campaigning had laboured on, with this tedious routine of seemingly endless march and manoeuvre for the soldiers of both sides.

For the southern rank and file the tale of the season just ending had been the failure to gain that one final victory over the enemy, up on their own territory, that might have brought the war to an end, a chance which had fleetingly seemed to be within reach. That opportunity had passed by unexploited and frustration among many of the men over the failure was still pointed and acute, especially since the army had spent something near to a third of its strength on its Pennsylvanian adventure. All of this was exasperating enough, but what was even worse about the ill-fated campaign and battle up north was what had subsequently emerged, for unexpected things had gone wrong in the course of the invasion. Things to do with the transmission and execution of orders, which were not in the habit of going astray in the Army of Northern Virginia, had done so this time and the resulting stumbles had led to recriminations which still echoed around the camps and had been promptly picked up and loudly reported by the southern press.

For the first time among the enlisted men, serious and widespread complaints had been heard of the commanding general. Robert E. Lee had been appointed to command the army at the beginning of the previous summer and, once in place, had embarked upon a year of almost uninterrupted victories over the Union forces in Virginia. He had taken charge with the enemy army at the gates of the southern capital, Richmond and had, in a series of bold attacks and manoeuvres, relieved the city from threat and returned the seat of war to the northern part of the state. Each time since, when the numerically superior and much better equipped, Union Army of the Potomac had sought to renew its march south, he had delivered it a further bloody reverse.

The one negative feature in the story of the previous fifteen months had been the failure of the Confederate army to follow up its victories in Virginia with a successful invasion of the north, a stroke that could finally bring the Yankees to their senses, an end to their attempts at coercion and the war to a close. Now, with this latest disappointment, "Marse Robert," had come in for some pretty severe criticism from within the army and the carping was not yet done with. The more predatory of the southern newspapers had rounded on him also, blaming him for the lack of final success and the circulation of these editions around the army camps had fuelled the discussion and argument as to what had gone wrong and who was to blame for it having done so. Disillusionment had followed on from the failure in the north, particularly among the army's infantry and this was understandable, for it was the infantry who carried the heaviest burden of every significant battle and were therefore, by far, the worst affected by battle losses.

In that second week of August however word had begun to circulate that Lee had asked to be relieved of command and this news made the army sit up. Taking a verbal swipe at the general was one thing but, save for a thin scattering of men who would have welcomed his predecessor, Joe Johnston, back to the top command in Virginia at any time, there was no appetite for supplanting Lee. Johnston had his supporters to be sure, but also his critics, who were much more numerous. To many of the men in the camps, who recalled the mud-saturated campaign on the Virginia peninsula the previous spring, he was, "Retreatin' Joe," with his nickname maybe a little too close to fact for comfort. It was unkindly said of him that were he still in command, the Army of Northern Virginia might currently be defending a final toe hold of territory in southern Florida, while assembling boats to evacuate it to Cuba, or some such other Caribbean island. When it came down to it, whatever, "Marse Robert," had done or had not done over the summer, there were none whom the army as a whole would have preferred in his place. As for the just-ended campaign up north, there was enough blame and failure there to go around most of the high command.

The army's cavalry commander, "Jeb" Stuart had, after all, at the height of the campaign, absented himself for over a week, with his three best brigades of horsemen, depriving the army of its screen, of mounted, "eyes and ears," while he sought further fame and distinction by conducting a foray around the enemy army. The arrival of the Yankee main force in Pennsylvania had therefore gone unreported, leading to an unplanned collision, which had grown steadily into what was now being spoken of as the biggest battle of the war, thus far. But the faults among the army's generals had not ended with Stuart's antics. The two newly promoted Corps commanders, Ambrose Powell Hill and Dick Ewell, had not performed to expectations either. Hill had allowed a division of his men to blunder into the initial fighting and he had exerted no control over what had then taken place, letting the struggle develop, like an expanding accident, into full-scale battle, while much of the army was still miles from the field.

Ewell had also disappointed after a promising beginning in command of the Confederate vanguard on the way north. He had failed to press home the successful assaults of the first afternoon at Gettysburg, thereby allowing the Yankees to establish themselves on a ridge line that had proved impossible to take from them on successive days of further fighting. Powell Hill had then mismanaged his corps' part in these subsequent attacks, as had Ewell, yet again, leading many of the soldiers who now pondered over the abortive campaign to shake their heads and conclude that neither of the two was a real replacement for "Stonewall" Jackson, who had died in the wake of the spring fighting at Chancellorsville. No, was the collective wisdom of many, maybe the "Old Man" should have rode Ewell and Hill on a much tighter rein, at least until they proved themselves capable of the greater responsibility of Corps command.

Worst of all was the criticism of tardiness being levelled at James Longstreet, the experienced First Corps commander. "Old Pete" had been accused of balking and delaying in carrying out orders, which had compromised the attacks with which he had been charged and had led to their eventual failure. Longstreet was patient and deliberate, his soldiers knew that better than most, but the accusations now levelled at him by some, of dilatoriness to the point of sabotaging the "Old Man's" plans, was surely way in excess of whatever had taken place up north. There were plenty to blame for the failure of the campaign, but the upshot of the whole Pennsylvania adventure was that the army was back in war-ravaged Virginia. It had brought with it large amounts of captured supplies to be sure, but an opportunity had undoubtedly been fumbled and missed and thus the whole war in the east seemed, as a result, to be pretty well back to where it had been in the spring. It was not even as simple as that, for the returned army was now seriously weakened by its losses in men, animals and equipment and handicapped by its steadily diminishing means of replacing them.

It was bad enough to have lost so much of its strength as casualties of the fighting, but now a still more sinister force was at work. Instead of staying to wallow, like others, in the tide of criticism of its generals, a disturbing number of the enlisted men were indicating their views with their feet. Desertion, especially among the soldiers of those vital infantry formations, had, since the return to Virginia, reached a level previously unheard of in the Army of Northern Virginia. This put the whole criticism issue into a kind of perspective for it was the enlisted men of the army, especially its infantry, that were its fundamental strength. It was their valour that had won it its victories and their endurance that had kept it in the fight and, since it was here that the shadow of desertion stretched longest, here as a consequence, lay the greatest threat to the army.

Many of these same men had manipulated, or had sometimes been compelled to ignore, hunger and shortage among their families back at home, in order to stay with their regiments. Now, if such numbers of them were no longer willing to do this, then the army and the south as a whole had reached a pretty fundamental military crisis. It was indeed bad enough to have lost such a huge number of irreplaceable men in the late Pennsylvania campaign, but to be unable to retain the loyalty of so many of those who had survived that blood-letting added a further acute problem for the generals and the politicians, which, if it could not be tackled and resolved, promised ill for the future.

It was thanks to these men and their officers, that the Confederacy had pretty well held most of its own here in Virginia, but in the wide expanse of mountains and rivers to the west of the Alleghenies it had already forfeited great swathes of its territory. Important centres, like Memphis, Nashville, New Orleans and most recently, Vicksburg, had fallen to the enemy and none of them had ever been recaptured. Instead, out to the west, the Yankees now massed their apparently inexhaustible strength to continue their advance ever further south. At a time when it needed every man and gun to resist these threats, the southern armies could not countenance a further disaster of disillusionment among such of its strength that remained.

Daniel Ryan still served in that infantry, in Company B of the Ogeechee Volunteer Rifles in Major General LaFayette McLaws' First Corps division, fully aware, through the tide of camp gossip and the newspapers that circulated in the camps, of these larger issues that confronted the army and the south as a whole. He was painfully aware of the extent to which he and his comrades had wearied of this conflict, of its long periods of tedium and its periodic bloodbaths. It was now nearly two and a half years since most of them had enlisted and the mood of enthusiasm that had taken the bulk of them into the army at the start of the war had long since disappeared, to be replaced by, at best, a stubborn intent to see the struggle through. For the most part, Ryan, together with those who remained of his mess, occupied himself with the day to day routines of soldiering which had become second nature to them all since enlisting in Bryan County in Georgia, in the spring of 1861. As in messes throughout the regiment,

12

and indeed the army as a whole, their group shared duties and camp time, deeply trusting of each other, but that mess of closest comrades fully reflected the steady decline that the dismal attrition of war had imposed upon the company, the regiment, and the entire army.

Their group, which had begun the war with an almost impractical eleven members, was now reduced to five. In addition to Daniel himself, there was black-bearded Joseph Thompson, now a sergeant of almost a year's seniority and one of the company's natural leaders. Other survivors were the sardonic and sarcastic Otis Ballard, who had recently been confirmed as a corporal, Isaac Kane and Edwin Jones, both Eden Station boys with all of them, except Thompson, having been recruited there in Bryan County near Savannah.

The group had suffered particularly sorely over the season just concluding, losing two of its number to severe wounds with a further comrade killed at Gettysburg. It was dismally obvious that the war was wearing too many of them away and the main feature of the frustration that lurked in many men's minds was the fact that the struggle had now dragged grimly on for those two and a half years, with still no real sign of final victory.

The losses had inexorably mounted, but it seemed that every time that a chance had come to inflict a decisive blow on the enemy, some blunder or other circumstance had resulted in that chance being lost. The regiment, having already contracted from ten to eight companies the previous year had, due to the further depletion of its numbers, been further reduced from eight companies to six in the early days of the summer. As a result of its heavy spring and summer losses that had left well under two hundred men in its ranks, its officers were now being said to be contemplating a further reduction, to five companies or perhaps even four.

Losses of competent officers and experienced NCOs had been particularly dismaying, and twice since the return from Pennsylvania, Ryan had been approached by Thompson on the subject of promotion to corporal, only to decline both times.

"There's enough around here who would grab the stripes and the chance to tell other men what to do," he had told his friend on the most recent occasion, "without landin' the job on someone who doesn't want it." Thompson had shrugged.

"Fact that some want it don't mean that they'd be any good at it," he had growled, and there the exchange had ended.

All through the army, but especially among its infantry, regiments were struggling with similar manpower problems and, since there was no sign of an end to the bloody contest, those problems would likely only get worse. In spite of all of their beatings, the Yankees had kept coming back for more and although there was a grudging feeling of respect among the troops for this doggedness, it was more than counter-balanced by the men's frustration that, whether it was due to enemy doggedness or their own army's squandering of its opportunities, this dreary struggle of blood and suffering was dragging endlessly on, with ever more men crippled or dying as a result.

Perhaps, in the camps of the army at least, the talk would have remained inward looking and self-critical, had it not been for the intrusion of a further matter into their discussions, for, as August drew on, further stories began to circulate. These were nothing to do with their own army or its difficulties, but concerned the situation out to the west of those Allegheny Mountains, in Tennessee. Many in the Army of Northern Virginia had tended to regard the western struggle, waged on the far side of the mountains, as a poor relation. Everybody knew that out there things had begun to go wrong early on in the war, and had over the previous year gone from bad to worse. From early in 1862 the Yankees had gotten a twist on the Confederate forces and the blue-clad hordes had steadily encroached into southern territory along the various rivers, especially the Mississippi. It was also widely reckoned that the top southern commanders out there were not made in the mould of their Virginia counterparts, or so those in Virginia told each other, but there was undoubtedly more to it than that. Maybe many of the early setbacks came from the absence of any southern naval power on the western rivers, at least any that was able to look after itself, for that had proved a substantial handicap to the defenders.

Whatever the reasons, the Yankees had steadily gathered a head of steam, step by step overrunning the areas commanded by the Mississippi's various tributary rivers, until almost all of Missouri, much of Arkansas and portions of Louisiana and Mississippi also had been occupied. The western half of Tennessee had been lost too, in spite of profound effort and great expenditure of treasure and blood to prevent it and now, even as the Pennsylvania campaign had proceeded in the east, the Yankees had carried out a further push through the expanse of rivers, mountains and ridge lines that sprawled across the south eastern half of Tennessee, initiating a crisis that had steadily worsened over the final weeks of the summer.

That remaining Confederate foothold in the state had been lost as a result and this time without even a battle to try to save it. The Yankees had manoeuvred the southern Army of Tennessee from successive positions, driving steadily south east and, after a pause of several weeks to regroup and resupply, they had resumed their advance. They had pushed on until the armies now stood in the mountainous region around the rail junction town of Chattanooga, almost on the state line between Tennessee and Georgia. Hardly had this news been digested when still more word came, that Chattanooga too had been abandoned to the enemy and the Army of Tennessee had continued its retreat, crossing the state line into the northwest corner of Georgia.

For several reasons this amounted to a major threat to the integrity of the Confederate States that lay to the east of the Mississippi River. First was the danger that the Confederacy, already divided by the Yankee occupation of the valley of the

Mississippi, now ran the risk of being further sub-divided by this enemy advance, but there was more than just geography involved in the crisis. Georgia was a primary source of supplies for the southern armies, but it had also, over the previous two years, become a considerable manufacturing area, especially for war munitions, that must be held at all costs, even if it meant transferring additional troops from other marginally less threatened fronts to help defend it. Thus, as the seasons moved from late summer to early autumn, the southern strategists had been forced to consider a major redeployment of their already overstretched military strength in response to this further setback in the struggle in the west. Some more local reinforcements could be scraped together, from here or there out west, but it was clear to almost anybody in the government and the high command of the armies, that the prime source for any meaningful strengthening of the Army of Tennessee would have to be General Lee's Army of Northern Virginia.

This measure, of weakening the South's most successful army to stave off trouble elsewhere, was not new. Units had been taken from the Army of Northern Virginia the previous winter to defend southern Virginia, and part of North Carolina's coastal area. A similar troop transfer had been suggested in the springtime when the fortress city of Vicksburg, the last Confederate foothold on the Mississippi River, was coming under Yankee siege. For various reasons that step had not been taken back in May. The western theatre of war had been left to its own devices and as a result, on the very day that the retreat had begun from Gettysburg, far to the east, Vicksburg had fallen. A southern army of near to thirty thousand men had been forced to surrender, giving the Yankees control over the entire length of the big river.

Now the matter of the eastern army reinforcing the western one was being debated again and such hesitation, it was being said, should not be allowed to delay the prompt despatch of reinforcements this time. The thorn must be grasped, before crisis turned once again into disaster. Regardless of the

16

implications in Virginia, General Lee must send men from his army to northern Georgia. The option soon passed from rumour to expectation. A division, or more likely two, or maybe even a whole corps with a battalion of artillery for good measure, would be heading west and it soon became clear that, whatever trip and with whatever numbers might come to pass, "Old Pete" Longstreet's First Corps units, the great majority of whose units hailed from the deeper southern states anyway, would be the ones making it.

18

Chapter 1 A Farewell to Virginia

The idea of sending troops from Virginia, to help solve the crisis in Georgia, was all very fine, but the speed at which they could be gotten there was vital also. The heavily outnumbered southern armies could ill-afford to have a significant portion of their remaining soldiers hung up for a prolonged period of time on tortuous transit journeys, for that would only provide the more powerful armies of the enemy with further opportunity to press their advantages, in Virginia as well as in Tennessee. If this was allowed to happen especially out to the west, the situation could all too easily go from bad to worse, so, if reinforcements were to have the desired effect, whatever units were earmarked for transfer must get there quickly and this meant making the trip by the most direct rail route. Such a rail movement, for a force of this size, would require prodigious planning and the organising of a sizeable part of the worn and ramshackle southern railroad system, in order to assemble the rolling stock, to say nothing of the locomotives required to do the hauling. The movement would pose huge problems for the overworked and run-down lines, but, if all went well, even accepting the number of men, animals, vehicles and guns involved, the transfer, so the camp rumours suggested, could maybe be completed in something under a week.

But all did not go well. The operation was still in its discussion and planning stage in the first week of September, when still more bad news came from the west. The Confederate retreat from the central part of Tennessee had exposed the whole eastern portion of the state to Yankee incursions. The response to the Army of Tennessee's withdrawal had been an instinctive concentration of all remaining forces in the state to its south eastern corner, in order to assist in confronting the enemy advance on Chattanooga. This had included a detached force, employed in defending the city of Knoxville, a hundred and thirty miles to

19

the east in mountainous eastern Tennessee, which had journeyed west, to strengthen the army around Chattanooga, and also to prevent its own isolation. This had barely been accomplished when a further Yankee corps seized the opportunity thus created to advance south, from Cumberland Gap to the Holston River to occupy the city.

The loss of Knoxville, in an area of Tennessee known for the questionable Confederate loyalty of many of its people, was bad enough, but what made it worse was that the city stood on the East Tennessee and Virginia Railroad, which stretched from Chattanooga, eastwards through the mountains to Charlottesville in the Shenandoah Valley of Virginia, and then on to Gordonsville. This line was the only direct east to west railroad that the Confederate States possessed and was therefore critical to the proposed troop transfer. The occupation by the enemy of a portion of its length meant that any direct transfer of soldiers, from Virginia to south eastern Tennessee or northern Georgia by that route, was now out of the question. Troops going west would now have to follow an altogether different route, for they would be compelled to make a huge detour taking them over a sequence of as many as six different railroads. This revised route would carry them away on a great curve to the south, via Richmond and on through the Carolinas, before turning west into Georgia and then looping north again through Atlanta, to the threatened north western corner of the state.

The journey that had been originally estimated at a few days, would now be well over half as much further in miles and more than doubled in time. Further complexities would be experienced in the course of the transfer because of the lack of railroad interchanges and the different gauges of track used by the various companies whose lines would now have to be employed. It meant that the troops, with all their accompanying baggage, wagons and cannon, would have to disembark repeatedly from the cars of one railroad in order to transfer to those of another, in order to continue their journey. The means of reinforcing the embattled Army of Tennessee had hit a major setback. If a blow was to be struck at the advancing Yankees along the Georgia-Tennessee state line, it was in grave danger of being delayed, perhaps fatally, by the extra time that would now be required to get additional troops to the area.

Many of the officers and enlisted men in the Army of Northern Virginia had become experienced travellers on the Confederate rail system. Almost all of the non-Virginians in the army had come to the state by rail, at various times over the previous two years. Most of them had been transferred by rail from Richmond to the piedmont area, to which they had now returned, in the course of the campaigning of the previous summer. Some, including Daniel Ryan, had been involved in further rail travel in the course of detached duties, but, regardless of however many train journeys the various units had made, their experiences on the system had illustrated clearly to them all the drawbacks and pitfalls of southern rail transportation.

The men were thus no longer naïve enough to expect a smooth or efficient passage to wherever they might be bound on this latest rumoured move to the west, for the railroads suffered from a range of debilitating problems and most of these were common knowledge. Some of the routes, especially the north to south lines, were now seriously curtailed. In addition, many lines were now more limited in terms of connections to other places, and almost all of them were subject to periodic interruption from marauding groups of enemy cavalry or other irregulars.

But the process of decline in the railroad system involved much more than the loss of sections of the network to the enemy, or the activities of their horsemen. From the start of the war, the southern railroads, a substantial part of whose equipment had been produced in the northern states, had begun a slow but steady withering process, which had seen journeys along almost any part of them, become steadily slower and more tedious. There were several reasons for this, the first being that the locomotives and rolling stock that the

21

railroads still had, deprived of necessary repairs and maintenance, steadily wore down until they eventually went out of service. Almost all the locomotives had been individually designed and built and were therefore of such variety that they had little in the way of standardised parts. Thus out of service engines could seldom be cannibalised in order to keep others in use. Personnel problems also featured highly in the railroads' decline. Although the most skilled mechanics and railroad craftsmen were among the few who still remained exempt from service in the army, there were far too few of them and thus the neglected state of the railroad locomotives, and the rolling stock that they hauled, was made worse by the absence, in that army, of too many of the men who would, in normal circumstances, have helped to maintain them.

The same process of decline was true of the tracks themselves. The south had, prior to the war, produced only around half of the track that it required to replace its worn out rails, and there was simply not the industrial capacity, especially in the middle of a war, to increase this production. Replacement therefore was severely curtailed. The shortages of new track also meant that the construction of any additional routes to link existing parts of the network was almost totally out of the question. As if these problems were not enough, the track laid on some of the lines had been unsuitable from the start for the heavy demands of wartime traffic. Some of it was "U" track, a lighter type of rail, which wore out more quickly than the heavier duty "T" track. Even worse, some of the provincial lines were of, "strap", rail made from wood, with only a metal overlay, or strap, fastened on top.

Repairing, let alone replacing, the lines was becoming more and more difficult, since in addition to the state of the rails themselves, so many of the rail beds, the various points systems situated along them and the bridges that carried them over the gullies, rivers and ravines on their routes, were also in critical need of repair if not replacement. Here too the chronic scarcity of skilled labour, as well as materials, meant that repairs were delayed and abbreviated until the point of collapse was imminent and even then the work that was undertaken tended more often than not to be whatever minimum would eke out a further period of precarious service, rather than any thorough or comprehensive remedying of the problem.

Regardless of all this, as the first week of September came to its end, the First Corps divisions of LaFayette McLaws and Evander Law, the latter commanding in the absence of John B. Hood who had been badly wounded in Pennsylvania, received final orders to ready themselves for the trip west. Accompanying them would be a battalion of the corps artillery, but it was already being rumoured that the third division of the First Corps' under George Pickett, would not be making the journey to north Georgia. It had been detached from the army and was now stationed to the south of Richmond, still nursing its wounds after the grievous losses it had sustained at Gettysburg. For those who were earmarked to go however, every available railroad resource, it was being said reassuringly, would be utilised to facilitate their transfer.

Thus it came about that the men of the Ogeechee Volunteers were called upon to make preparations for the move, prior to heading for the Orange and Alexandria Railroad. The stories had been swilling around the camps for over a week, but, though the move to the west itself had been pretty well confirmed, most of the details of it still remained unofficial rumour to the enlisted men as they prepared for their departure. Their final day in Virginia was spent breaking camp, cooking rations, gathering the equipment that would be taken along and disposing of the baggage that would not go, mostly by burning. Even as they did all this, they remained unaware, officially at least, of where exactly they would be heading.

One person who would not be heading anywhere with the rest of the Ogeechee Volunteers was their chaplain. Jedediah Poulson had been with the regiment since it had been formed and, in spite of his advanced years, had soldiered on with his spiritual flock through all of the campaigns in which it had served, enduring hardship and shortages in common with the rest of the men. Poulson was popular, first and foremost because on that day seventeen months previously, back in Savannah, when the "Blues" had been adopted into Confederate service, he had not taken the easier option of staying, as some other officers had, in the relative comfort of home. He had come north to Virginia with the regiment and, having got there, as well as taking services and attending to the spiritual needs of the men, as chaplains customarily did, he had repeatedly shown that he was not afraid to get his hands dirty. Reverend Poulson had regularly taken a turn as an additional medical orderly when the regiment went into action, tending to the wounded in practical as well as spiritual ways, which had served to further confirm the enlisted men's regard for him.

But now he was absent having been accidentally injured, and seriously by all accounts, for in the course of the recent manoeuvring around Culpeper County: a piece of regimental baggage had seemingly fallen from a wagon, landing on the chaplain, in the course of its brief journey to the ground. The old man, who had ministered to many others over the previous eighteen months had, as a result, required some urgent ministering of his own and, having been treated by the Regimental Surgeon, a much less esteemed officer than himself, he had been promptly evacuated by ambulance and then by train to hospital in Richmond. Subsequent news of his condition had been sketchy, but the general conclusion seemed to be that he was unlikely to be returning any time soon.

"The ol' chaplain must a' strayed greatly from the path of righteousness," Ballard had declared, "if the good Lord don't even trouble to protect him from some damned officer's trunk."

24

The camps of the Ogeechee Volunteers were a mass of scurrying men that Sunday, all of them packing and dismantling, with the bustle of activity carried on in a fog of smoke which stank of burning baggage and frying bacon. In addition to the orders for departure , more orders had been issued restricting the belongings that each man could take to what he could carry on his person, and including in their details confirmation that the commissary and ammunition trains would not be going. This news was not welcomed by the men. They could readily see that, by reducing baggage, those changeovers at the various railroad depots might be simplified, but lacking a commissary train, or an ammunition one for that matter, would also mean that, once they had arrived in Tennessee, a huge question mark would hang over their various supply needs. If commissary arrangements in Tennessee were anything like the hand to mouth ones that regularly applied in Virginia, it was unlikely that much, if any, spare capacity for supplying extra soldiers would be available, meaning still more lean times for the arriving units. To many of the men, awaiting their turn to depart, the further the idea of this troop transfer went, the more tenuous it seemed to become, with more and more sanguine assumptions, rather than firm plans, featuring in its arrangements.

As for the regiment itself, there was still no official word on an additional consolidation of its numbers by the disbandment of any more of its companies and the distribution of their personnel among those that remained to bring them up to more practical complements. Among the soldiers of Company B however there was at least as much interest in this matter as there was in the larger prospect of heading off to Tennessee. One of the advantages of disbanding companies and posting their members to those that were retained, was that it allowed at least some of the officer and NCO vacancies in the remaining companies to be filled by experienced men. But Company F would predictably be next in line for disbandment and, if this was what eventually came to pass, the likely consequences for Company B seemed to please none of the men in its ranks.

Since the battle at Gettysburg, the company had been commanded by Lieutenant Benjamin Carson, a youthful officer of limited experience and it therefore followed that with two officer berths vacant, Company B would be one of the most likely destinations for the displaced officers of Company F. These would include a Lieutenant named Jefferson Gilby who, in addition to carrying an unenviable reputation in his own right, just happened to be the nephew of William Preston, the regiment's colonel.

The talk on this subject around the Company B camp, as the men busied themselves on their preparations, was almost universally scathing and resentful. Gilby had joined the regiment less than a year previously, in the aftermath of the Battle of Sharpsburg and the army's withdrawal from Maryland. He had been posted as a replacement lieutenant to Company H, but his high-handed arrogance had alienated many of its enlisted men from the start.

That situation had grown immeasurably worse with the death of John Ellis, a corporal in the company. Ellis had been placed under arrest, on Gilby's orders, after an exchange of angry words over the lieutenant's attempts to make barefooted men take duty watches in snow conditions. Gilby had, in the course of the arrest, made some further snide comment about Ellis' family, upon which Ellis had knocked him down. Preston had sustained his nephew in the matter and Ellis had been condemned to death, for striking a superior officer. The death penalty, in volunteer regiments, was rare, but the colonel had stuck to his decision and the execution, by firing squad, had taken place the day before the battle of Fredericksburg, souring Preston's standing with his men, and irrevocably alienating them towards his nephew. Since then, the soldiers of Company H, and Company F after its disbandment, had maintained a subdued hostility towards him and now there was every possibility that this man, together with his much put-upon black servant, would soon be on the roster of Company B.

As for the journey to the west, as they dismantled their camp the men finally learned a few more of its details. It seemed that the first of John Hood's brigades had already started their move. Having been stationed further east, these men had travelled south on the Richmond, Fredericksburg and Potomac Railroad, while the, "Blues" own brigade and others of their division, would start their journey on the Orange and Alexandria railroad the following day. They would board trains that would take them the relatively short distance south west to Gordonsville, which lay also on the Virginia Central line, journeying on from there to Richmond. The artillery battalion however would make the journey to the capital by road and then all three formations would continue southwards, to Petersburg initially and then on into North Carolina on the Petersburg and Weldon line. From Weldon, according to Thompson, there were alternative routes by which the journey might continue, south or southwest through North and South Carolina, before turning west towards Augusta in Georgia. All the men and guns would however have to travel through Augusta, to reach Atlanta, to begin the final leg of the transfer, to the far northwest of the state, where the armies now manoeuvred, in the mountains to the south of Chattanooga.

The journey would be further complicated by those differences between the connecting railroads. In addition to some of the tracks being of different gauges or widths to others, in most instances the rail lines did not exactly meet in their junction towns, but rather stretched only as far as their own company depots, which were usually located in different parts of those towns. Troops arriving on one line and intending to transfer to another one would therefore be required to disembark at the arrival depot and assemble there before making the trip across town on foot to a further depot, all the while trusting that trains would be on hand to embark upon for the next stage of their journey. It all added up to a first rate nightmare of organisation for whichever officers or railroad officials were in charge of the trip, especially if the railroads involved were still responsible for the transfer of vital ongoing shipments of food or ammunition for the armies, not to mention their routine passenger and freight services.

Nobody knew whether or not the Yankees would continue their advance towards Atlanta, which lay just over a hundred miles to the southeast of where they now manoeuvred. Atlanta too was being described as a vital railroad junction and was said to have a considerable share of war production also. In addition, just to the northwest of the city was the town of Rome, with its cannon foundry. Georgia, particularly that area of the state, was therefore a place that the Yankees must be kept out of at all costs, and time was against the Confederates, if the enemy pressed their advantage. As they now had to travel the long way there, Longstreet's reinforcements would take well over a week to make the journey, perhaps longer, if there were unforeseen delays at the various rail junctions along the way. By the time they got to Georgia, assembled and ready for battle, the situation, already bad, might have changed further, for the worse.

The final factors in the mix were the commanders of the Confederate Army of Tennessee. That army's commanding general, Braxton Bragg was known, by reputation at least, to the men of Lee's army. He was still another reason why they were glad, in spite of whatever had gone wrong over the summer in Pennsylvania, to keep "Marse Robert" as their commander. Bragg was reputed to be a cantankerous officer, who had feuded repeatedly with his lieutenants over the preceding year. A furious disciplinarian, he was said to have tried and executed men of his command for even modest breaches of military law, yet he had a name for indecision on the battlefield, which had wasted opportunities for success and cost men's lives, often to no good purpose. The loss of much of Tennessee was, rightly or wrongly, being laid at his door and, among the men who had been detailed to head west from Virginia, there was a considerable reluctance to serve under his command, but they were on their way now and there was nothing to be done about it.

It was the morning of the third Tuesday of September, the seventh day, it was being said, of the great troop movement. The weather was hot as the Ogeechee Volunteer Rifles waited at White Oak Station, on the Orange and Alexandria line, for their own rail journey to begin. The soldiers stood in long lines that stretched from the platform with its tiny depot building and on up the incline that flanked the railroad, while train masters' aides, clutching schedules and sheaves of further papers, scurried up and down those lines, sweating profusely, as they consulted with regimental officers. Occasionally, a file of waiting men was ordered into motion to head down towards the station, as the latest of a steady succession of trains pulled in, announcing their approach with wailing whistles, screeching air brakes and the noisy release of steam.

Some of the waiting units had been stood down, and the men from these lounged around on any piece of vacant ground that they could find around the station, with the cumulative buzz of their idle conversation filling the warm air and mixing with the multitude of train noises and the continuing shouts of command. After a short wait in their files, while officers hurried around requesting or bringing information or instructions, Company B was similarly dismissed. The men stacked their muskets in the customary pyramids of four or five, before seeking places to sit or lounge. A few women, local ladies, or volunteers from the neighbouring towns, were moving up and down the lines of idle men, dispensing lemonade and serving out corn bread or cookies, the staple food and drinks of so many of the hospitality committees in Virginia. As their turn came, the men clustered around the women to get their share, exhibiting extravagant gallantry and punctilious manners in spite of their dishevelled and infested state. Hats were doffed and elaborate bows offered to the women, especially those who were less than grand-mothering age, before the men returned to their places, balancing tin cup and cake in either hand. Back in their lines, some of them wolfed and gulped their way through their refreshments in a few brief mouthfuls, while others opted to savour them. These men nibbled and picked around the edges of their cakes and sipped their drinks slowly, making the each morsel and every drip last as long as possible, offsetting, as far as they were able, the tedium of their waiting time at the station.

With their refreshments long since consumed, the Ogeechee Volunteers were eventually summoned, something approaching two hours after their arrival. Stirred by their sergeants, they collected their muskets, reformed their column and began to shuffle down the last of the gradient and on up the brief incline to the station building, waved on by a succession of officers and railroad officials, towards the latest train. As they arrived at the track, the sergeants, on the direction of the train master, wheeled their sections and hustled them along the low wooden platform, past a pulsing locomotive and on past the first of a succession of cars.

As he came to the cars through the steam cloud, Daniel Ryan gaped in astonishment. These had undoubtedly started out as box cars, but they could scarcely now be recognised as such, for they were little more than remnants of what they had been designed and built as. All their sliding doors had been pulled from their mountings and the side and end planking had been prised away, by whatever means, leaving only their roofs perched upon the barest skeletons of their wooden frames. All of them, from the front of the train on down, were crowded with soldiers who shouted, cheered and yelled at the newly arriving troops, and whistled and called to any of the hospitality women who were within range. Most of them lounged on the floors of the cars, but still more had been precariously accommodated on the roofs, jostling each other as they attempted to arrange themselves as comfortably as the cramped and limited space permitted.

The arriving men of the "Blues" were given little time to scrutinise it all, as Thompson, Dellings and Bayfield yelled and pushed at them, shepherding them on down the train to where further cars were in the process of being loaded. More shouts finally halted them and they began scrambling on board the next vacant car, in a jumble of bodies, weapons and belongings. Daniel stepped forward to the track as the file in front finished embarking and pulled himself up onto the wagon, using the edge of the metal wheel guard as a step, before negotiating his way across the rough wooden planks of the floor, as Edwin Jones pushed aboard behind him. Those of their mess gathered at the front end of the car, as the arriving men of Dellings' section immediately occupied the space behind them. Daniel looked back past the confusion of limbs, weapons and blanket rolls, to see Bayfield hustling the remaining men of the company up, crowding them into the final scraps of space, until, with the floor area fully taken, the last of the men were directed up onto the roof. All of Company B were therefore now accommodated on this single railroad car, and he ruefully looked around at the men as they shifted and pushed themselves into the most comfortable places and poses, trading precious inches of space with those around them, almost all of them eventually getting themselves stretched out to lounge or lie on their unrolled blankets.

One car for the entire company was a forcible reminder, to any who cared to consider it, of how few remained of the near to a hundred who had journeyed north to Virginia by train those seventeen months previously. As for the rest, they were the cost of this continuing war and a lump came momentarily to Ryan's throat as the faces of some who were gone surfaced in his mind. He immediately banished the thought, forcing his attention back to the present, as still more of the following regiments pushed along the length of the train, passing within a foot or two of where he now lounged. The stink of body odour mixing with the steam and oil smells of the train was strong in his nostrils, as the successive groups of the following regiment were hustled by. Finally, after the briefest of further pauses, yet more files of men appeared, passing along beside the row of crowded cars to embark in their turn on the rearmost ones. All along its length, the train was now a mass of excited soldiers, skylarking, for the most part, like schoolboys on the final day of the school term.

Hardly had the last of the passengers been shepherded aboard, when the locomotive whistle screeched hoarsely from the front as the cars of the train jerked and shuddered successively into ungainly motion. They began their slow progress away from the station building to a chorus of further shouts and whistles from the departing soldiers. The straining locomotive began to build momentum as it drew away from the station and moved on into the rolling, still green woodlots and fields beyond.

Their initial journey took less than an hour, as Gordonsville lay only a short way down the Orange & Alexandria line. Gordonsville however was a junction town, where the Orange and Alexandria joined the Virginia Central which stretched on in its great south eastern curve to Richmond. The passage through the town and its crowded depot was conducted at a snail's pace, giving Wofford's men ample opportunity to exchange rude comments with some of the collection of troops who waited there for their own trains, and to wave and whistle to the crowds of local people who had come to witness the occasion. Clear at last of the town, and on the next stage of their journey, their train gathered a measure of speed, and the exuberance on the cars gradually subsided as most men settled themselves, at least until the next halt along the line was reached, where more civilians would very likely be assembled to cheer and wave. The whole thing was quickly gaining the appearance of a huge carnival as the jolting, vibrating train laboured on, with its screeching mix of noises and the occasional eddy of smoke or even a sprinkling of hot cinders arriving on the breeze from the locomotive's smoke stack, this prompting further excitement on the crowded cars.

Their train was held in a siding at Ashland for nearly half an hour, waiting, according to the story that circulated among the troops, for an ammunition train to pass, heading north with its vital cargo for those units remaining in Virginia. The men watched in near silence as the long procession of closed wagons clattered past, after which the troop train promptly resumed its southward journey, with still more cheering and waving crowds at the halts along the way. While their progress was slowed by the snails pace negotiation of some of the bridges that served the line, there were no more outright stoppages and Richmond was reached in the early evening.

The final blocks of the journey from Mansfield Hill in to the depot at Shockoe Bottom were marked by a substantial collection of people lining the track. These onlookers stood watching the trains pass, acknowledging this great military spectacle by their curious presence. Some of them waved and cheered to the passing men, with those on the cars returning the greetings, whistling and waving energetically in response to any sign of enthusiasm from the spectators. Others of the locals however were more restrained, or even muted, noting the passing of the soldiers rather than enthusing over it. Perhaps they had dallied too long in the heat of the day, Daniel Ryan thought as he watched the faces pass ever more slowly with the decreasing momentum of the train, or perhaps it was more profound than that. Maybe it was a deeper kind of weariness, based on disillusionment with this never-ending war. Price inflation was known to be high all over the south, but here in Richmond it was said to be steeper still. The men were aware of this from the variety of newspapers that circulated around their camps. They knew that even basic foodstuffs had continued to rise inexorably in cost over the previous two years, while shortages, often of those food staples on which the ordinary citizens and their families depended, imposed additional trials upon the city's people.

There had been unrest, even riots, in Richmond in recent months, with those involved protesting of their inability to afford even basic food at the inflated wartime prices. This too

33

had been reported in the army's camps. Richmond, for all of its frenetic, war-connected activity and industry, was feeling its own version of the cost of the struggle, the same as those counties further north were feeling theirs. Here was the consequence of so much of the productive land in the war-ravaged northern part of the state no longer producing food. The Confederacy's economy was creaking as a result, with starvation a real prospect for many of the poor when winter returned. This war had to be won before wholesale starvation afflicted large sections of the southern people, especially those poorer families, but, in spite of the efforts and sacrifices of the army, there was still no end in sight.

The train drew slowly in to the depot and shuddered eventually to a standstill. Hardly had it halted when the sergeants got to work, disembarking their sections and chivvying the laggards with shouted commands, as the men hobbled on stiff legs along the side of the train to assemble in their company groups. They were formed along the trackside and it was here that the final question regarding the company complement was answered. Waiting beside Lieutenant Carson were two other officers. The leading one was familiar to Daniel Ryan, as a result of his part in last winter's foraging expedition to Georgia. Lieutenant Morgan Jessop possessed a practical approach to soldiering, together with a widely acknowledged gift for varied profanity, and either because of that or in spite of it, he had apparently been promoted to acting Captain.

Whatever the reason, his arrival in Company B was something of a surprise to its enlisted men, for he was one of the few officers who had not featured particularly in the speculation, or the betting, as to who would take charge of the company. Along the newly formed ranks Daniel sensed a reaction of surprise, with the merest suggestion of a mutter audible, as the men took in the presence of the new captain. Jessop gave no reaction as he waited beside Carson with an inscrutable expression on his features, letting the men get a good look at him, while he cast his own gaze along the ranks,

34

as the faint mutters moved among the men. These while being their reaction to him as the new captain, were also a response to the man who stood on his other side and slightly behind him, a swarthy-complexioned lieutenant, impeccably dressed in a tailored uniform coat with the bars of his rank stitched in gold braid to his collar. Daniel Ryan felt himself stiffen involuntarily as he looked again on the features of Lieutenant Jefferson Gilby.

In view of the amount of speculation on the possibility of disbanding a further company of the regiment, the presence of Gilby was more of an unwelcome event than a surprise for the men of Company B. No disbandment had been officially announced, and Company F, with similar numbers to their own, stood in its ranks immediately to their right. Yet Gilby was here, having apparently been transferred while his previous company was still in being. There was clearly no accounting for what Preston might have deduced or connived in the interests of his kin, but here the little upstart was. and life, in Company B at least, would most likely be different as a result.

There was little further time for deliberation over the colonel's actions or motives however, as Jeffers stepped promptly forward.

"Company...!" He yelled, silencing the muttering as he called the men to order and, having done so, he stepped back, leaving the newly-appointed captain to address his command.

"We are to make our way now to the Petersburg depot to continue the journey," Jessop called. "I am informed that there will be an issue of replacement clothing, as well as of rations, at the depot." Daniel half-smiled to himself at the restraint of the captain's address. Jessop, for all of his command of profanity, had spoken in a measured, formal manner and this seemed a little uncharacteristic of the man, but then this was a formal parade of the company and his first acquaintance with the men as a body, so maybe even officers knew something about being on their best behaviour. Jessop

35

looked towards Jeffers, as Carson and Gilby waited silently behind him.

"First Sergeant!" he called, seemingly content to stick to formality, for the time being at least. Upon Jeffers' order, the company shouldered arms, before left turning into files to follow on after the rest of the regiment onto the street. To the surprise of some of the enlisted men, as the files left the depot and moved onto Seventeenth Street, ranks of uniformed militia appeared, with muskets shouldered, taking station on either side of the column, to escort the Army of Northern Virginia veterans on their way. This, Daniel Ryan reckoned, as he peered at the nearest of them, would most likely be a precaution against any who might try to take the opportunity to absent themselves and disappear among the watchers on the sidewalks. Ballard's voice came to him, as he peered across at the closest man, who had to be a grandfather, before nudging Daniel Ryan and gesturing with his head. Daniel glanced across, seeing what looked like a mere child with barely a suggestion of whiskers on his chin, almost abreast of the corporal. The boy paced nervously along in his place, gripping his musket with white-knuckled hands, looking to neither side, almost as though he feared to do so.

"If any of us want to skedaddle, then these damn, diapered kids and rheumaticky grandpaws ain't goin' t' stop us," the corporal growled. He looked at the boy for a second or two.

"Aarrrghhhh!" he growled and Daniel grinned as he saw the boy start with surprise.

"Have a care boy," Ballard grated, fixing his gaze on the boy's face. "We need meat and we ain't been fed yet."

They marched the three blocks downhill, wheeling to the right there onto Cary Street to head northwest for several more blocks, turning then onto Eleventh Street to continue towards the river, skirting the canal basin and crossing its spillway by the footbridge, before finally turning onto Byrd Street, where the Petersburg depot was situated. All along the journey between the depots, the sidewalks were busy with spectators, not in numbers on anything like the scale of the

"Blues" first arrival in the city the previous spring, but "enough to raise a holler," at least by Isaac Kane's estimation. They lined the way, although a few of them, like the previous spectators along the railroad line, were simply looking on. Many did wave and cheer however, and these greetings prompted an energetic response of waves, shouts and whistles from the passing soldiers.

Daniel Ryan's mind however was only partly on the exchange of enthusiasm, for he was mulling over the arrival of Jessop and Gilby. From his previous experience of the new acting captain, Daniel approved of the arrangement. Morgan Jessop had long since proved himself sensible and resourceful and he should make a good company commander, though it was a fact that not every good lieutenant made a good captain. The arrival of Gilby however, was another matter entirely. On the face of it, the company was now restored to a full complement of officers and could function routinely, with experienced men in charge. But with someone like Gilby in the mix, things would not be as simple as that. Time alone would reveal how he intended to fulfil his role in the company, but his reputation gave the broadest clues. As far as the enlisted men were concerned, there was little to be done but wait and see, but, if that previous service in the other companies was anything at all to go by, they would not have too long to wait for him to show his horns.

Above all else however, the regiment was heading for Georgia and an almost certain fight. Officers could buy the store in battle as easily as anybody else and indeed they sometimes were more likely to do so, especially if, like Gilby, they were dressed in distinctive uniform that drew attention to their rank. Company B had gone through a succession of officers over the previous seventeen months and there was at least a fair chance that the problem of the recently arrived lieutenant might solve itself, once the coming fight got under way. As far as Daniel Ryan was concerned he would be perfectly happy if the new lieutenant would be obliging enough to stop a bullet or something bigger, in the course of

37

whatever brawls awaited them out west, but that was in the hands of a higher authority than the army's.

The Richmond and Petersburg depot was just about as close to the James River as a building could get without those who used it getting their feet wet and, as the column finally approached the place around which still more crowds milled and soldiers waited, Daniel Ryan's mind began to turn to the replacement clothing of which Jessop had spoken. This depot too was familiar enough to him, for he had passed through it several times since first arriving here in Virginia. Today however, the scene was different from any of his previous visits, for in addition to the congestion around the building itself, there was a great deal of further activity on its far side. From that end of the building, out onto the vacant ground beyond it, makeshift tables had been set up. They stood there in rows, as lines of men passed along and, as at Savannah the previous year, they were piled high with uniforms.

The companies were halted and ordered into lines by their sergeants, promptly joining those who already waited, to shuffle forward towards the tables where busy orderlies were hard at work issuing clothing to the waiting men. As the line of Company B men shuffled closer to the tables, they were able to get increasing glimpses of what was on offer. There were pants, on the light blue side of grey in colour, but, unlike the Yankee version, these trousers were not made of coarse wool, which, while better than nothing , were a pretty uncomfortable option in the warmer seasons of the year. They were divided into small, medium and large sizes and laid out in separate piles, with signs painted with the respective letter, to indicate which was which. Beyond the pants lay further tables, these with stacks of tunics, similarly organised by size, but the men having moved along in lines on either side of the tables to receive their new pants, it was the tunics on the subsequent tables that were attracting a greater measure of their attention.

They were styled in the second Richmond tunic version, short in length like cavalry jackets, with side pockets and buttoned down shoulder straps. It was however, neither the cut, nor the style, but the colour, which was attracting the attention of the men, for even more than the pants, there was a positively blue shade to them. Men carrying their pants over one arm or a shoulder, gathered around the tables to prod and poke at the tunics as though there was something alien about them, hesitating to take one in case there was some mistake.

Blue pants had been worn by many in the army over the last two years, a considerable number of them plundered from the enemy. Yankee tunics had also been pressed into service, once their colour had been altered, usually by being turned into a darker shade of brown with improvised dye, but the issue of blue tunics, or even just tunics that looked blue like these did, was another matter altogether, as the talk along the rows of tables was making clear.

"Where in the hell did they git these?"

"They're goddam Yankee clothes!"

"We don't wear no damned blue."

"Did they git these from up north?"

"They'll be issuin' us with Yankee flags down the way," White growled.

The sergeants moved along the line as the chorus of complaint grew, chivvying at their men to get moving. Jeffers was there, with his own advice for those of Company B who hesitated.

"Gentlemen," he called profoundly, "either ya take a set o' these or ya stick with yore own duds, but, whichever way ya want it, git yore asses movin' along there." The muttering continued, but in response to the First Sergeant's words, the line began to shuffle into motion once more as, one by one, the men picked up tunics and moved along, though the comments and complaints continued to ripple among them. Beyond the tunic tables there were still further ones, with socks, also set out in piles, and these were taken with an absence of any fuss though, perhaps predictably, there were no shoes.

Having received their clothing the men moved away from the tables, following in their lines to where numbers of those already issued with new uniforms had gathered. Areas had been partitioned off, surrounded by canvas screens suspended on ropes and poles. Here buckets of water had been placed in rows and a smell of strong disinfectant soap was in the air. Men were stripping off their old uniforms, to wait in their turn for a place at one of the buckets, which were being continually replenished by relays of older men. The soldiers stripped off, in order of arrival, to wash themselves, pretty cursorily in some cases as far as Daniel Ryan could see, before drying themselves off with makeshift towels, and scrambling into their new clothing. Daniel looked up ahead, towards those who had finished their washing, drying and dressing. Their new tunics were indeed unfamiliar, not quite blue like the Yankee uniforms , but they were certainly neither grey nor butternut brown either. He was reminded, as he looked more closely at them, of the colour that some Yankee uniforms turned to when they were old and weather worn. They faded as the dye left them, until they were not really blue any more, but neither were they far enough away from blue to be called much else.

Around him the others of the company had stacked their muskets and piled their new uniforms, to begin stripping off shoes and socks and their ragged and infested clothing, leaving the latter in bundles as indicated by the sergeants, before moving forward to the wash area, where the contents of the buckets were being regularly splashed and spattered around in the course of the continuing ablutions. Daniel fixed his bayonet and settled his musket, hanging the strap of his haversack and his belt with his ammunition pouch over the bayonet. He folded his blanket roll and his newly acquired clothing, into a pile, which he balanced on top of his shoes, beside those of the others of the mess. He began to undress, feeling a shade self-conscious regarding the state of his underwear, as he did so, looking around at the others, as Ballard spoke.

"I ain't leavin' no shoes around here fer no orderly to take and sell," he growled. "Leave yours here and I'll watch 'em till one o' ya's done." The others did as he said without comment, and made their way on, to await a place at the buckets and begin their washing. Turnover was steady and Daniel, having been handed a fragment of the crude strong-smelling soap, a small square of rough cotton cloth and a larger piece for a towel, promptly got busy at the next vacant bucket. He soaked the cloth and began to work, coating the material with a lavish measure of the soap before beginning work on his hair. He rubbed the cloth across his head, scrubbing furiously with the fingers of his other hand, before working his way down across his face and neck, then moving on to his shoulders, torso and arms. The soap smelled strong and potent, though it likely wouldn't shift anything like all the lice, but perfection shouldn't be made the enemy of improvement, he reflected, as he stuck to it. He worked the lather that he had been able to produce, into his crutch and backside, pausing then, to apply still more soap to the cloth, before resuming his rubbing, as he worked his way down towards his legs and feet.

Dellings was pacing along the line of buckets, hurrying the toileting.

"Move yoreselves," he growled. "C'mon Daniel, ya ain't gittin' ready fer no damn dance."

Having finished his brief scrub, Daniel splashed his hands into the bucket in response, narrowly missing the sergeant with the water. Seeing and hearing the splash, Dellings wheeled towards him.

"I'll be gittin' my own damn turn," he growled.

"Cleanliness is next to Godliness, ain't it," Daniel told him, getting a profanity in reply as he returned to his rinsing down. The cold water tingled on his skin as, having concluded his brief rinse, he reached out for his towel, the somewhat larger square of the same rough cotton fabric as the washing cloth. He set to wiping and rubbing it across his face and hair, looking round then as Ballard arrived at the next bucket.

"They ain't as picky as you," he muttered, gesturing with his head towards where Jones, having finished his washing and drying, had been joined by Kane and Hale at the collection of clothing.

Ryan went on with his drying before moving across to join them, still working the damp towel around his legs as he did so. He knew there was a ragged set of underwear rolled in his blanket, as clean as they could reasonably be for a soldier on active service, and now was the time for them. He briefly inspected the equally ragged set he had been wearing, wrinkling his face as he did so. They were threadbare, to the point of hardly being worth keeping, but a spare set of drawers and a second pair of socks, at least gave a man the essentials of a change of clothes when on campaign.

Kane and Jones were almost dressed as he reached them.

"Least you got fresh drawers," Kane told him as, having retrieved them, Daniel lowered them with his right hand and deftly stepped his first foot into them. There was nothing to be done about his shirt however and, with it and the fresh drawers in place, he unfolded and donned the newly issued items of uniform.

The pants were a reasonable fit and the tunic slightly roomy, but he stepped around with those around him when he had finished dressing, scrutinising the result and comparing his own state to that of the others of the mess, before turning to the final job of drying his toes and feet and donning the new socks and his shoes. Ballard joined them, rubbing at his crutch with his square of towel.

"Maybe they ain't like the Yankees," he muttered, "but they're sure as hell close."

"Maybe they'll give us the same pay as the Yankees now," Jones observed, as he looked around at the others.

"How many months is it since they paid us anythin'," Kane snapped? "Thirteen dollars ain't no better'n eleven dollars if they don't show up to pay it to ya."

42

Around them, as Daniel tied the laces of his shoes, the company was beginning to re-assemble. The sergeants successively approached, each in his own new uniform. Jeffers arrived eventually and Kane, on seeing him approach, addressed him.

"Blue, First Sergeant, are ya losin' faith in final southern victory?"

"Lost faith in any kinda victory, first day I laid eyes on you boys," Jeffers growled in response.

The whole train trip, from Virginia down into the Carolinas and now on through Georgia itself, had fully lived up to Thompson's predictions. The journey steadily evolved into a masterpiece of cobbled- together travel, joining step by step into a disjointed sequence that got them all, in spite of the chaotic interludes that punctuated it, to each successive depot. Each time, upon their arrival, they were disembarked, assembled and then, more often than not, deposited in holding areas around the depots, before being assembled again, to be despatched on their way to the next depot, there to wait for the whole process to begin again.

At most of the junction towns the depots were well separated, being situated at the outskirts, rather than in the town or city centres. This, it was being said, was the custom of many towns, back when the railroads had first been proposed. Many municipal authorities had stipulated that rail lines and depots, be laid and built out near their limits, for fear that sparks or burning cinders, from the arriving or departing trains might present a fire hazard to buildings of the town. True or not, the practice imposed further delays, with the arriving men compelled to make their way across town after town in order to continue their journey. Such delays were often welcome, for in most places the locals distributed food to the soldiers and in some places the events took the form of gigantic picnics. Giant tables were improvised, around which the soldiers were seated, to be served platefuls of the local produce.

On leaving Virginia, strict orders had been issued that every man should retain on his person a four day supply of cooked rations. Each evening of the trip, rations had been issued to replace what had been consumed in the course of the day and these were cooked, mainly during the night if the men were not in actual transit, to be added to the supply in their haversacks. The trouble was that, with all the hospitality that was being lavished on the First Corps troops, the supply in many haversacks was scarcely diminishing. As a result, flour began to mould and meat to rot, resulting in supplies increasingly being thrown from the trains as the journey progressed.

That journey was a classic reworking of the army tradition of, "hurry, then wait," with the most bewildering of the delays, principally in those assembly areas, around the various depots at which they had arrived, followed by almighty rushes to the next one. Occasionally, as at Ashland and again at Petersburg, they had been held on rail cars waiting for other trains to use the line or, as in one case, until a locomotive arrived to haul their own cars. Such delays, whether spent in sidings or at depots, varied widely in length, ranging from less than an hour to, in once case, most of a day. Aside from the great picnics, at regular intervals through the days of the journey further food and drink were served at depots to the waiting men, showing that more than trains had been marshalled and organised, in preparation for the great troop transfer.

At every town, and also at the regular stations and watering halts along the lines, crowds had gathered to cheer and wave, and, better still, to offer further samples of baking or other refreshments that the local people had prepared. Some of the victualing had even included measures of whiskey, the spirit seemingly donated to strengthen the boys' fibre a touch. Company B needed little in the way of such revival, however, spending much of the time at the various halts on their feet, whistling and calling extravagant compliments to the ladies who arrived to serve, or to watch and cheer in the crowds along the way. As in Richmond, all the assembly areas and even the trains themselves were surrounded by cordons of local marshals, or by detachments of armed militia men. These latter came in for harsh barracking from the waiting First Corps soldiers for their continued presence here at home, while the real men were in the army, fighting real live Yankees.

William Wofford's brigade followed a route that, having led south from Petersburg on the line through Weldon, next took them to Goldsboro, before swinging down to Wilmington on the Cape Fear River, near the sea coast of North Carolina. Just ahead of them were Joe Kershaw's South Carolina soldiers, sometimes pulling out on their trains as Wofford's men arrived at a depot, and at other times waiting around, in the depot holding areas, for delayed trains to arrive. At Wilmington, part of Kershaw's brigade still dallied when the first of Wofford's men arrived and here more rumours abounded, as men of the two brigades fraternised. One asserted that their route to Georgia had been altered, or even closed, because some of the troops from the initial brigades of Hood's division had apparently caused such trouble in the course of their journey. The Company B men had grinned as some of the troublemakers were identified as "Old Rock" Benning's Georgians, their own former brigade.

Some men nodded gravely to each other, while others openly chuckled as they listened to the news. Bennings' men had reportedly wrecked the offices of a newspaper at Raleigh, and, in common with men of the Texas brigade, had fought with police and sheriffs at various points along the way, antagonising the local authorities to the point that Governor Vance of North Carolina was now threatening to close the state railroads to troop trains. Another story told how "Tige" Anderson's brigade of Georgia troops, also from Hood's division, had been diverted to join the garrison at the city of Charleston in South Carolina, since the generals had concluded that too many of its men would never be seen again if they were transported on into their home state.

This latter concern seemed to occupy the generals regarding several brigades, principally, it seemed, the ones that would be passing through their home states on the way west. There were numbers of Wofford's men also, who would need little in the way of invitation to "jump ship," on their home ground, or as near to it as they were able to get, if they got the slightest chance, but there was also, among most of them, a view that now, with the Yankees still not letting it be, and on the soil of Georgia itself, it was not the time to be going missing. There was a mood to stay with the colours, for the time being at least, especially when by doing so they would enjoy the attention, acclaim and hospitality of the local womenfolk in the towns that they were scheduled to pass through. There was a particular attraction in the food delicacies here, in this port city of Wilmington, rich on the proceeds of blockade-running and most men were prepared to continue on their way, content with the prospect that more such treats would continue to arrive.

From Wilmington the journey eventually proceeded inland, through Florence and then Kingsville, to the little town of Branchville, another junction town, where the men who had taken the coastal route met again with the units who had travelled inland via Raleigh and Columbia. Here a further extensive delay was encountered before they were eventually shepherded onto yet another near-dismantled box car which carried them westwards towards Augusta. From there, the talk said, they would proceed to Atlanta, before the final leg of the journey northwest to Dalton and Chattanooga where the western armies still manoeuvred and grappled, and the next big fight was awaiting them.

The soldiers saw relatively little of their officers while on the move, since they routinely travelled in passenger cars, separated from the enlisted men and NCOs, though in one or two cases they had been required to tolerate the inconvenience of a modified box car, with windows and bench seats improvised. At the depots they tended to re-appear to support, at least by their presence, the sergeants who shepherded their men around from place to place, but once arrived at depots, the train masters were left to allocate space on the cars, and customarily, when the embarking had begun, the officers adjourned to their cars once more, leaving the men to their own devices.

Having endured the mayhem and delays, the euphoria and the discomforts, the Ogeechee Volunteers arrived at last in Augusta in Georgia late on the Thursday, assembling there as successive companies disembarked from their cars. Still more rumours circulating here suggested that some of the troop trains had been run on the Charleston and Savannah lines to relieve the congestion on the other routes, but the men of Company B had been denied this flirtation with their home counties. To some of the boys there was a wistful element in all of this. They were back in their home state at last, some of them close to their homes for the first time in well over a year. Yet any feeling of home was illusory, for these depots were unfamiliar and impersonal places and, having come this far, the distance to their homes would now begin to increase again. The trains that they were to embark on would carry them away from the eastern counties of the state, on to the west and north towards Atlanta and Chattanooga. Some men spoke sentimentally of it, while others groused and complained. Still more stayed silent and subdued, though this in itself was a clear enough indication of how they felt.

The mood on the cars was different when they pulled out of Augusta, crammed on the remaining cars of a train carrying the last of Kershaw's regiments, even when they passed through the subsequent depots and halts. Some of the boys, whose reaction to the cheers and waves of the people along the trackside had, until now been enthusiastic and spirited, now seemed less enthused and frantic than they had previously been. Maybe they had become used to such scenes over the course of the journey, but Daniel Ryan reckoned that many had their minds still on those homes away to the east, in Bulloch, Liberty or Bryan Counties, with the thought of being

47

as close to them as they had recently been prompting further wistfulness and home-sickness among them.

Yet this very nearness to Liberty and Bryan Counties had been an ambivalent experience for Daniel himself for, in truth, he now felt less of a bond with the county and with the town of Eden Station itself than he had previously. He had lived there for something over two years, and had grown fond of the place while he had remained there, but the passage of time in Virginia was steadily proving that two years was a relatively short time in terms of a man's life, for he would soon have been away from the place for as long as he had spent there. He had no blood relations there, no more than anywhere else in America for that matter, and while he still felt a bond of gratitude towards the town, and in particular to Hal and Martha Bennett, who had given him a job and a home, many other links with the place had faded, or even disappeared. To Daniel Ryan it now represented a period of his life that was past. The army now was the present, and the foreseeable future also, at least until this war was finally won.

Chapter 2 Atlanta

The crowded troop trains chugged laboriously on, heading across the state towards the city of Atlanta, with every mile travelled further increasing the distance from the coastal counties, and, while some boys gazed longingly backwards, to Daniel Ryan it was what lay ahead, rather than what lay away to the south east, that was now the focus of his mind. He was sure however, as their train finally pulled in to Atlanta, with the sun sinking low in the sky, on the third Friday of the month, that he had never, on this or any previous rail journey, seen anything to compare with the crowds, or the chaos, which seemed to reign around the railroad depot that served the city. The building itself was mightily impressive, being a huge, brick structure, whose sides incorporated a succession of arches, presumably to help the smoke and steam from the trains to disperse from inside. It was situated in the centre of the city, with streets radiating away from it both to the north and south, an arrangement clearly at odds with the practice of other cities en route, with their peripheral depots.

The Atlanta building had a high curved roof, topped by a windowed gallery that ran its full length. It dominated the area, and was said to accommodate all the railroads that served the city, with multiple sets of tracks stretching through the building through tall, twin archways at either end, as well as stretching past it on either side. Trains, made up of every kind of cars, box cars, flat cars, even coal cars, were constantly coming and going, while still more wagons and car loads of reclining soldiers were parked in sidings which adjoined the further tracks that lay between the depot itself and the buildings and streets that flanked it on either side.

The whole area teemed with people, soldiers and civilians, with many of the former and most of the latter milling endlessly around, jostling and shouting to all those near at hand to make way. Lines of wagons waited at various places, along the margins between the town buildings and the depot.

Collections of them rattled across the wooden crossings that crossed the rails to either side of the building during the brief intervals between trains. More of them clogged the streets that stretched away to the north or south, with additional collections of them congregated in any vacant space around the depot itself. Crowds of civilians watched the proceedings, cheering and waving to the soldiers that arrived or departed on their trains, and to those who waited in their ranks or files for further trains to arrive. Between soldiers and civilians however there stood the inevitable companies of uniformed militia, armed with muskets, demonstrating once again that unofficial furloughs were not to be part of the proceedings here, any more than they had been at the previous towns and halts along the way.

Company B had little time, initially at least, to take in further details of their surroundings, being hurried from their places on the cars to assemble, before filing around the depot for a while and eventually being gathered in company groups to one side of it. The men settled to wait, exchanging rumours and comments with a nearby consignment of Alabama soldiers already embarked on a waiting procession of wagons. Now that they were at last in north Georgia, the talk was more of the fighting those few brief miles up the line, rather than any further gossip about the journey itself. The news however was not good. Bragg's army had apparently continued its retreat from Chattanooga, sidling around the north western counties of the state as it vainly tried to halt the Yankee advance.

There had been further fighting up there, the new arrivals were told, as the two armies sparred and manoeuvred in the mountains and valleys. As a result of all of this, the town of Dalton might no longer be the destination of the troop trains. They could be transported instead to one of the other stations up the Western and Atlantic Railroad, depending on where the Army of Tennessee eventually halted to assemble its strength. Once gathered and organised, they would see to giving these impudent western Yankees the licking they deserved.

Trains were regularly arriving, on the Western and Atlantic line from the north west as well as from the east on the Georgia Central line, the latter bringing their cargoes of cheering and whistling troops, while the former carried cargoes of wounded men, grim testimony to the continuing fighting up there at the Tennessee line. With the depot building itself occupied by the never-ending sequence of troop trains, some at least of the Western and Atlantic trains from up the line were pulling in on the tracks outside the depot, and hardly had the troop train, whose occupants had conversed so amiably just minutes previously, juddered into motion and departed, when a further train arrived from up the line, grinding to a screeching halt within yards of where the men of the Ogeechee Volunteers now waited. Orderlies and some female nurses quickly assembled and set to work, removing the first of a stream of groaning, crying soldiers, passing them down from the cars for a brief inspection, presumably to establish whether the hospital or the burial ground would be their most likely destination.

Most were then carried away from the cars, out through the seething crowds of soldiers in transit, on towards the lines of waiting ambulance wagons from which the leading vehicles shunted forward in turn to receive their cargoes of the afflicted, before turning tightly in the restricted space and lumbering away on their journey to the city's hospitals. Some of the passengers remained however, until the wounded had been dealt with, upon which they were loaded less ceremoniously onto further wagons, to begin their own dismal final journey to burial ground or undertakers, the manner of their going confirming the fact that they were beyond the point where any kind of medical care could help them.

As the orderlies and nurses finished their work the waiting soldiers were called to assemble, before being guided across the tracks on the wooden walkway. They were eventually halted on the far side of the depot, before being shepherded on to join an already waiting lines of soldiers, beginning a now familiar shuffle along towards where a set of large metal stoves billowed smoke into the air, with the smell of cooking food reaching the noses of the arriving soldiers. Plates were retrieved from haversacks and hurriedly wiped in readiness as they drew closer to the stoves, in front of which another row of trestle tables had been set up. The lines edged forward until the approaching men caught sight of the meal that awaited them. It was stew, and what was more it seemed to contain meat, not the fatty bacon or semi-digestible salted meat of standard army rations, but cubes of butchered meat, shining, luscious and smothered in gravy, with vegetables, and fragments of what looked like sweet potato mixed in. All the delicious smelling mix was making its way, in loaded ladles, from large iron pots to the waiting plates of those whose turn had come. The lines edged onwards, as more pans of steaming food were carried from the stoves, to be emptied into the serving pots, until finally it was Daniel Ryan who confronted one of them, with his plate extended towards a sweating orderly. The man loaded his ladle and splashed the food down onto the plate, before nodding briefly with his head to indicate that their business was completed. Daniel moved on, past where several other pots served similar steaming contents, to where a further man waited at another table, this one piled with squares of cornbread. The man lifted a square and deposited it on the top of Daniel's serving of stew, waving him brusquely on as he turned to Kane, who was next in line.

"Is that it," Daniel inquired?

"Thar's Trout House over thar, if ya kin pay what they're askin'," he was told as he started away, following Ballard to where the company group was re-assembling, some picking at morsels of food with their fingers even as they moved on. The meat was pork, well-cooked and of good quality, and the men cleared their plates in short order, wiping the last of the gravy from their plates with the cornbread and performing the customary ritual of licking whatever scraps remained before returning the plates and cutlery to their places in haversacks. Having finished, they sat back in the space they had been

allocated to eat, luxuriating in the feeling, once again, of having something tolerably close to a full stomach.

Night was coming and with the sunset the air grew steadily colder, while all around the endless coming and going continued. The interior of the depot was lit up as darkness fell by a succession of wall mounted gas lights which illuminated the area around it through the wall arches and the windows of the gallery that stretched along the apex of its curved roof. Around the building a succession of torches were also lit, shining their wavering yellow light and supplementing the lanterns and lights placed along the neighbouring streets. The whole depot area was brightly illuminated, while trains, men and supplies and stores of all kinds continued to come and go with the activity and noise only marginally diminished from its daylight level.

"Ain't no better chance fer a man to head off on a little furlough now than there was this afternoon when we got here," White muttered.

All around Daniel, the men of the company were now settling on their blankets to get such rest as they could in the only marginally diminished clamour around the depot. Daniel did likewise, but found that even brief dozes were rare, for the streets around the tracks and the depot building itself remained hives of activity on into the night, as the never-ending processions of trains and other traffic came and went. The nocturnal hours, as a result, consisted of a series of lurid, flickering images, emerging from whatever fleeting periods of rest he was able to manage.

All through those chilly hours of darkness further trains arrived and departed, with wailing whistles announcing their approach, and the hiss of steam their arrival, while above it all a large harvest moon lit the clear sky. Further units of the waiting men assembled, embarked and departed, though it seemed to Daniel, as he watched the continuing procession of locomotives and cars, that at least some of these overnight trains were carrying supplies, and above all ammunition, up the line to the beleaguered army.

Dawn finally came clear and still cold till the sun at length appeared, to begin the process of warming the day. Any who had slept this long now stirred, and men pushed themselves to their feet to stretch and yawn, while still the trains and other traffic came and went, until at last all of the men were awake and moving. It was Saturday, and today, surely, would see the final leg of their journey.

They were promptly called to assemble by the sergeants, and they clustered in their familiar groups, with their possessions gathered. They waited for a further time before being directed back across to where the stew had been served the previous evening, to join another established line of waiting men. Plates were produced again as they moved forward, to arrive once more at the same row of tables, to receive a measure of some kind of porridge, with a couple of hardtacks being issued, along with a small ration of cooked meat at the following tables. They made their way back to the impromptu bivouac, to settle there with this latest meal. Most initially devoured the porridge, upon which many also ate their meat and hardtacks. Daniel Ryan, mindful of the coming journey, opted to eat just one of his hardtacks, leaving the other and the small portion of bacon untouched in his haversack. If the journey continued up the line today, then there would likely be further local delicacies on offer and, even if there was not, the remaining hardtack and the bacon would make something of a supper.

Breakfast done and a period of restful digestion having been enjoyed in the growing warmth, they were assembled once again, this time with their weapons and equipment, to be guided past the depot building and halted along one of the tracks which snaked past the outside wall of the building. Even as they spread along its length, the tracks began to hum, announcing the approach of yet another train. A distant whistle wailed and the men watched the locomotive pull into view, slowing as it approached and releasing steam as it passed, engulfing them in the white driving clouds. Behind it the cars groaned and squealed as they slowed, and even before they had finally halted, the dismal smells that came to their nostrils had told the men that these cars too carried wounded men. The train finally ground to a standstill, for the by-now familiar procedure to commence, with nurses and orderlies appearing, the latter immediately clambering up into the cars to begin lifting the wounded men down to where further men waited with litters and carts. Nurses inspected their injuries briefly as before, with the groaning men being carried away following their inspection.

The process went on, working up the train, but hardly were the cars emptied of their final pathetic collection of corpses when more orderlies clambered up onto them, to begin sluicing them out with buckets of water passed up to them from a quickly formed chain at the trackside. The cars were then brushed out, a mixture of water, blood and some more disgusting debris spilling from them and splashing down onto the rail bed. Hardly was this done when the train was moving again, pulling out to execute its turn, while the soldiers waited.

On its return the train masters were immediately at work, signalling forward the first of the waiting columns of soldiers to climb onto the saturated boards and to settle themselves there. Daniel watched as companies of another regiment moved forward on the signal of their sergeants to clamber up into the cars. Finally they were all in place, jostling and moving as they settled in their spaces, whereupon the train master turned to the first files of the Ogeechee Volunteers. But despite his ordering, nodding and his gesturing, the leading companies made no move towards the train. Daniel stepped out of his place briefly to look up the waiting line, seeing Preston, in the midst of a group of other officers, engaged in an animated discussion with the train master, while all around numbers of the enlisted men closed up around those in front, inching closer, partly at least in anticipation of boarding, but undoubtedly also to hear what they could of the exchange. Daniel was aware of a movement beside him and he turned to see Ballard leave his place and start up the column, joining numbers of other men who were doing the same. On an impulse Daniel did likewise, joining his friend as they came up close to the front of the line, from where the raised voices of the officers at last coming to them above the confusion of other noises from all around the depot.

".....arrived here in pieces and bits, major, every step of the way from Virginia has seen us divided this way and that way, until my officers have hardly any idea about where anybody under their command is to be found" Daniel Ryan could just make out the colonel's words above the chaos of other sounds. "They are now going into battle and they will make the final part of this journey to contact with the enemy as a military unit sir, not as a succession of fragments." It promptly emerged however that the train master had other ideas.

"Colonel," he rasped, with what seemed to Daniel like barely controlled anger, "if I waited around here for every damned regiment that came in to get exactly the kind of transportation arrangements that it wanted, there'd be next to nobody headin' up this here line at all. You colonel are givin' me a man-sized pain in the neck. My orders are to fill the cars on these trains, and I ain't sendin' any train up that road haulin' empty ones. As long as your men are stayin' put here, this train full o' troops ain't goin' no place, not with empty space on it. If it don't go, it fouls up the whole damned movement, cuz other trains start to git held and delayed at the sidin's and yards along the line. A lot o' large sized generals, that are waitin' on this transfer, from Bragg on down, are gonna get pretty damned mad, when they find out that this whole thing's now bein' held up by one damned colonel, so, if you sir will not order your men to board, then I will find somebody in authority who will."

Preston however was not to be overruled quite so easily, for he ignored the man's words and continued to argue, until the train master seemed to weary of it. He turned away and gestured to his assistant, a lieutenant with spectacles.

56

"I've had jest about enough o' this!" he rapped. "Go get Colonel Jones, if you can find him and, if he ain't around, get Colonel Wright."

"And who might I ask are these people that I've got to wait around here for?" Preston inquired, though to Daniel Ryan, even at that distance, it sounded for the first time, that some at least of the note of belligerence had disappeared from the colonel's tone and manner.

"He is the officer detailed by General Bragg to head up this whole transfer," the major told him tartly. "Colonel Wright's the railroad commander, here in Atlanta, and both of them have got better things to do than come down here and play nurse maid for the loadin' up o' one damned regiment of infantry."

It took a few additional minutes for the situation to be resolved. A further colonel did indeed arrive and after a brief and frostily polite exchange of views on the matter, a fuming Preston withdrew, leaving his major, Henry Randolph, to see to the loading of those troops who would travel on the remaining trucks and cars of the waiting train. The crowd of spectators also withdrew, first and foremost to inform their companions, but also to gather their belongings, as the sergeants set to work once more, with the men quickly being assembled and moved up to form a line for embarking.

The railroad colonel had departed also, leaving the business in the hands of the train master and he, with the help of an assisting lieutenant, shepherded the lines on towards the remaining cars.

The lines finally shuffled forward, with men craning their necks to squint over the heads of those in front to see where they were headed. As far as those of Company B were concerned they need not have troubled. The shifting lines finally halted, with word filtering back that only the three leading companies had managed to find space on the train. The three who remained would have to wait for a further train and would be heading up the line as soon as places were

57

found for them, then to commence the job of finding and joining up with those who had already arrived.

It was as they waited there, having stacked their muskets and piled their belongings again, that a further officer arrived, another captain, this one sporting a patch on his right eye and an ugly scar down the same side of his face. He carried the seemingly mandatory sheaf of papers in his hand as he moved up the line, seeking out the major. The boys watched him approach Randolph who stood conversing with the three remaining company commanders. He immediately excused himself. Salutes were exchanged and a discussion followed, which was inaudible to the men in their ranks above the clamour of other noises, but the result of it was that the men were again called to order. They gathered their weapons and belongings once more and assembled, to be promptly moved away, following the one-eyed captain back along the outside of the depot itself through the crowds of soldiers. They reached the end of the building, crossing the line there between arriving and departing trains, there to mount and shuffle along and finally halt on a crowded platform inside the cavernous structure. Here, all the sounds of trains, voices and of milling humanity were vastly magnified, echoing under the high roof of the building into an almost deafening jumble of noise.

Randolph was at the front with the one-eyed captain, and he promptly waved the leading men on, with the following files once more commencing the same shuffling movement that took them forward towards another waiting train. Daniel Ryan stretched his neck to see, watching as the leading men reached where this further train had just finished loading its cargo of cheering, whistling soldiers on its sequence of flat cars. His eyes rested immediately on the line of occupied cars that stretched away from the front of the train, before scanning further along, finally to rest on several empty wagons at the rear.

Those in the approaching lines immediately recognised the occupants of the cars, for the shouts of recognition rose among both groups, echoing with the jumble of other noises, under the high roof as it became clear that they had once again overhauled some of the South Carolinians of Joseph Kershaw's brigade. These soldiers had shared the dangers of a succession of bloody battles with Wofford's men, most recently in Pennsylvania, and they acknowledged each other with a rising screeching yell that rose and reverberated around the building as the Georgians made their way along past the crowded cars, with the shouts and comments coming thick and fast as they moved along.

"No damn free-ridin' Georgians on a Palmetto train!"

"You damn fellers better have tickets fer this here trip."

"Git yore own damned train!"

The "Blues" soldiers ran something of a gauntlet along the platform, being subjected to the wit of each successive car in turn, finally reaching the vacant cars, there to be hastily shepherded aboard, while the chorus of hoots and further calls continued from the gamecocks on the neighbouring wagons. Those possessing blankets immediately spread them out on the rough, wet planks, still soaked with their dismal, sopping mix, presumably from the same sluicing down after delivering yet another cargo of wounded men. As the men settled, the sergeants continued to harangue and cajole, shifting them around to make space for more, until all were finally aboard, congesting the cars more than on almost any of the previous trains.

The officers had already departed, to join their gamecock counterparts in a carriage further up the train, their baggage being carried along behind them by a small detail of men. As he spread his own gum blanket, Daniel Ryan's nostrils were assailed by the dismally familiar combination of stenches that spoke of wounded men, blood and urine, vomit and human waste, with additional smell of disinfectant. Around him others also were reacting to the foul odours.

"Jesus what a stink!"

"Goddam smell'd choke ya!"

"Have we gotten this stink all the way up the line?" They would have it every inch of the way Daniel thought, remembering previous journeys, and the only thing that would diminish the dismal smells to any significant extent would be whatever momentum and draught that the train generated on its way north. The sooner therefore that this train got under way the better it would be. At this rate at least, he reflected, they would be up the line on the heels of the other companies, so it seemed that no lasting harm would have been done by once more dividing the regiment's soldiers to travel on two different trains.

These thoughts had barely registered when the locomotive gave a series of whoops on its whistle, the sounds near deafening in the depot building. The train jerked and juddered into motion, and with the initial puffing of the locomotive thundering and echoing in the confines of the building, the cars pulled successively out into the autumn sunshine. The depot and its surrounding streets still teemed with the same confusion of men and vehicles that had prevailed since their arrival, and the men cheered and waved in the direction of the watching crowds of onlookers, some of whom threw little salvoes of flowers, hardly any of which reached the slowly moving cars, though the occupants waved and clapped in reply. As the train drew clear of the depot area and laboured into a gradual curve that took them past the bulk of a large, round engine house and then on through the western portion of the city, the men had a chance to take in something more of Atlanta.

It seemed big to Daniel Ryan, though well short of the size of Richmond. All around there were mills and smoke spewing chimneys, demonstrating the value of the place to the war effort. It would surely not do to give the Yankees free passage to this place, he thought, hence this whole vast pilgrimage of the last eight days on which they had all been engaged. The train gathered pace as it left town until and with the increasing draught of moving air, the smell around the cars became less pervasive and the men shuffled around to finally settle themselves. The loud shouts and whoops that had been sustained as they passed through the city, turned gradually to more measured conversation, as Atlanta was left behind them and they headed, initially following a slow descent, away to the northwest, coming shortly to a town bearing the title of Bolton. The train slowed there to negotiate a covered wooden bridge that spanned the brown waters of a river and, having gathered a further measure of speed, they arrived, after a few more miles and further country halts where more onlookers waved and cheered, at another town, identified by its depot sign as Marietta, where still more crowds waited, applauding the troops and handing fruit and little bags of nuts up to the boys on the cars as they passed slowly by.

The journey proceeded in this vein through a succession of towns and further country halts, where still more of the local people had gathered to see the troops pass, generating further outbursts of feverish excitement. The town of Allatoona preceded a pass that wound through steep bluffs before a further river was forded, again by a covered bridge, before the town of Kingston was reached. Here the train stopped at a rail yard to take on wood and water and to wait until a further south bound train had passed. The troops on the cars were offered buckets of water also to replenish their canteens, with further little squares of corn bread being also passed up. The boys shouted and cheered and whistled to the watching waving locals, while the inevitable toileters disembarked, moving this way and that, through the civilian throngs, to find places to attend to the needs of their bladders or bowels.

Under way again, the journey gradually became much more of an ascent as the engine laboured up into more mountainous country. By now the sun was sinking and the air again began to grow progressively colder, as still they clanked and screeched and clattered on through darkening forests broken by stretches of cleared and cultivated fields, where, even at this late hour, clusters of local people still lined the track to cheer and wave. There were further crowds at the trackside towns of Cassville and Resaca, with still more standing in lines at the rural halts beyond, to wave to the men and clap them on, offering their own gifts of cold, fresh water and further little delicacies from their larders.

Dusk came and in spite of the rumours to the contrary, the train reached Dalton, where yet more crowds waited to cheer and wave. Onwards again and progress slowed as the train negotiated a succession of inclines, labouring upwards around a sequence of curves as higher mountains flanked the track. Eventually, its whistle screeched its hoarse metallic rasp as the mountains on either side converged in another gully, but, on hearing the shouts from those on the front wagons, men began to crane their necks to look. Daniel Ryan half rose also and squinted ahead into the smoke and dust, seeing that even straight ahead, the way now seemed blocked by the tree-lined vastness of the mountain. As the sides of the cutting ascended steadily higher on either side, more men stood up on the swaying cars to looks forward, finally seeing a cavernous opening approaching until, with a final whistle screech, the locomotive entered the bulk of the mountain, with its trail of ascending smoke vanishing in a second.

On the cars there was now consternation. Those who had risen to their feet to look hurriedly crouched down again, as the wagons in front successively disappeared from view in the darkness and smoke. The turn of the Company B car finally came and the men yelled as they entered the gloom of the tunnel, where the locomotive's labouring, the train wheels and all of the other noises were magnified in the confines of the mountain. The smoke from the stack, similarly confined within the restricted space, swept around in choking clouds, with occasional orange fragments of its cinders flying around the men, a few landing on clothing or even skin, all of which prompted another outburst of shouting and coughing, and an epidemic of scrambling around on the swaying cars. Nobody seemed to have seen anything like this before, a train line that went through a mountain. Inside the tunnel there was at first only blackness as the yells and exclamations of the boys mounted. As eyes began at last to adjust to the darkness, up ahead there were now glimpses of the distant orange glow from the locomotive fire, its dim light revealing snatches of the craggy stone walls and ceiling of the tunnel as they careered past before merging once more into the blackness.

The deafening passage of the tunnel went on and Daniel Ryan felt his heart pound ever harder in his chest at the thought of being marooned in the middle of this great hill, while the noise, the stink of smoke and the black gloom that surrounded them seemed to go on and on without an end. Then, suddenly, they were out into the colder, fresher air and the gathering gloom of the late evening. The echoing noises of the train faded instantly to their previous levels, as they emerged from the darkness while through a final drifting cloud of engine smoke, the rising moon could now be seen, shining through the trees to the east. Daniel felt his heart rate slow as all around him the boys relaxed and an excited jabber about this latest railroad experience began to course up and down amongst them.

The moon was above the trees and the night had already grown cold when the train finally slowed, with the cars jolting together and shuddering as they ground towards a halt, and a thick plume of white steam was expelled up ahead by the locomotive as it pulled in. The track was lined with waiting vehicles, and figures stood in rows between track and vehicles, their impassive faces lit by the flickering light of torches, passing within a couple of feet from where the soldiers watched from their places on the cars, before the train came to a screeching, hissing rest. A further shift of train masters was immediately in attendance, shouting instructions to the disembarking men, who, festooned with newly collected weapons, blankets and haversacks, clambered in swarms from the wagons and cars to collect and mill alongside the train.

Sergeants were already shouting to their sections and the men began to respond, moving along the track side on legs grown stiff through their cramped and prolonged inactivity, feeling the circulation returning only slowly as they hobbled forward beside the train, seeking to find their way into some kind of formation as still their sergeants yelled and badgered. All around was chaos as more men jumped or scrambled down from rail cars to begin seeking their sections and companies in the crowds that milled along beside the track. Ambulances waited in lines among the traffic that lay parked along the railroad, while their teams, nervous and fidgety in the congestion around the train, shifted and brayed. The sounds and the stink from the vehicles were clear indications that the fighting still continued up here, and in this line of wagons lay yet more of the human cost of it. That all too familiar combination of odours once again mixed into an unholy and near overpowering stink, while the cries from the sufferers mixed with the tide of other voices calling for companies and regiments, and the pulsing of the now stationary locomotive, all of it resounding in a distracting jumble of sound.

"15th Regiment assemble over here!"

"Company D, First Rifles, form on me!"

"For the love of Ch.... just let me die."

"8th South Carolina!"

"Oh God, God, God, the pain!"

"Water, somebody please."

"Company B, Ogeechee Blues!" That was Thompson, heard even in this chaos and those around Daniel turned at once and started towards the shout, finding others of their section as they went. They gathered into a group, as more men arrived and still more pushed past, responding to the shouts of their own NCOs.

Slowly the pandemonium along the tracks faded, as more and more men found their comrades and their places. As the space around the train cleared, the inevitable shift of orderlies began their work, lifting the men from the ambulances and carrying them across to the cars, where more had clambered up to receive the wounded, and, as the litters of blood-soaked sufferers were loaded onto the train, the cries of many of them became more harrowing still.

"Aaahhhh!"

"Leave me, for Jesus sake, leave me!"

"Oh mother of God!"

The space on the cars was steadily filled as more and more broken men were lifted across to begin the next chapter of their agony on the journey to the hospitals in Atlanta, while having collected into their company groups, the infantrymen began to push their way clear of the crowds around the train, seeking a place to form. As company B still waited, a grey-bearded orderly made to push past Daniel Ryan.

"What place is this," Ryan accosted him brusquely. "Where in the hell are we?"

"This here's Catoosa Platform," came the reply in a lazy mountain drawl. "Ringold's a mile or thereabout on up the line, but this is as far as you boys are goin'. They'll be headin' ya out thar across Pea Vine Creek over yonder and likely on over Chickamauga Creek." He gestured vaguely in the darkness. "Yankees're out there, west o' the creeks." The older man sniffed as he drew a further breath and continued. "Ain't no word about how the fightin's goin'," he went on. "Only thing we know fer sure is that they had a hell of a fight out there today," he nodded again, with his head this time gesturing towards the crowds of wounded men, "and there ain't no reason, that I kin think of, why there won't be another hell of a fight out there come mornin'."

He moved away, in response to a shout from further down the train, as the three "Blues" companies were called and promptly moved off in a series of irregular groups, with the men at last able to push their way through the continuing congestion around the train. Having trooped out in their groups onto the road that angled away from the tracks, they were halted on Thompson's shout, and ordered to assemble. The three companies quickly formed their ranks, and, in order at last, they were right faced and moved off, remaining in files of two, in order to negotiate their way past the jumble of vehicles along the way, where yet more ambulances, easily identifiable by the same combination of dismal smells, were lumbering up to add to the chaos around the station. Clear at last of the worst of the congestion and the doleful stink that accompanied it, the order came to march at ease and the men immediately broke ranks to gather in their mess groups as they continued along a still-busy road. An almost constant procession of ambulances still headed east, while the newly arrived units from the train pushed and picked their way around the west bound traffic of supply and ammunition wagons.

The track led on through stretches of woods and within minutes had brought the column to a creek. Without a pause the men were marched across, where in the deepest middle part the water reached up almost to Daniel Ryan's groin. Once across, the march continued without delay, with the men squelching their way along a road that, for the stretch nearest to the creek, was muddy from the water dripping from clothing and shoes. The trail wound on over undulating ground, but the Ogeechee Volunteers did not remain on it for long, being soon directed off by Jessop and the sergeants and on into the woods, there to bivouac.

The shivering men settled in their company groups as the half-expected, "no fires," order came around, spreading out their blankets on the carpet of pine needles, for in addition to being soaked from the waist down, the air around them was decidedly chilly. The nearness of the previous day's fight was now indicated by a persistent smell of powder smoke, whose drifting wisps gave the almost full moon a hazy, misty appearance. The wood soon quietened, with little in the way of talk, though the traffic out on the road continued without pause.

"Here at last," Winder muttered.

"Wherever the hell here is," Jones returned, as the men around them settled. Daniel Ryan, on hearing the comments, pondered only briefly as to where here was. Regardless of

66

that, it was where they went tomorrow that counted, but that would be up to the generals to arrange.

Whether the generals were still busy with their arranging, even in those chilly hours of darkness, never did emerge, but hardly were the men settled when they were being roused again by their sergeants to gather equipment and form, ready to move. The moon was now high and the night was bitterly cold as the gathering proceeded, accompanied by a chorus of curses and complaints. Blankets were rolled, looped and slung over shoulders along with haversacks, while the musket stacks promptly vanished and, within minutes of being called, the column was on the move. Above the files the breath of the marching men showed in brief, pulsing clouds in the chilly air as the huge moon illuminated such stretches of the landscape as the woods on either side of the road allowed. The 'march at ease' order was called again and the men gathered into their groups as the road began to ascend, speculating why a man couldn't get anything resembling a decent night's rest this side of the mountains.

"Joe says there was no orders," Ballard told them. The others were incredulous.

"Why in the hell are we marchin' around here in the middle of the night, if we got no orders to do it," Winder rasped?

"My God Eli," Kane said. "It jest takes one little thing to go wrong and the wheels come right off yore wagon don't they." There was a mutter of amusement as Daniel Ryan looked at Ballard.

"Do we know why we're out here and not in our blankets," he inquired?

"Why becuz our brothers in arms from the fair state of South Carolina are," was the corporal's response.

"Huh?" was the reaction from several voices at once? Ballard grinned at them, his teeth showing white in the moonlight.

"Seems like the rest o' the regiment never got out o' Atlanta ahead of us after all. Barnard says there's talk among the officers that they had some kinda train trouble back down the line so they've all got to git put on another train, which ain't gonna happen till the mornin'. They wired Randolph to tell him the news, so now we're orphans, at least fer tonight, the only part o' the whole damned brigade that ain't still in Atlanta. Joe says the Major's aimin' on stickin' with Kershaw's boys, cuz they're sayin' that he told the duty corporal to wake him up if the Gamecocks so much as moved," he paused then, as though for effect. "They did," he said at length. "Till the general gits here, Kershaw's in charge o' the division, cuz he's senior Brigadier, so where they go, we go." Jones sniffed.

"Division," he scoffed. "Right now, with, "Make Laws," still back there in Atlanta, the division is the Gamecocks 'n' us, unless they got more trains comin' in tonight like they said, but that ain't happened yet, cuz we'd a' heard 'em."

"The Gamecocks, us 'n' whoever o' Ben Humphries' Mississippians've come up," Ballard said, "but Bryan's boys are still in Atlanta as well as our own boys."

"Ain't exactly an army, up here then," Winder muttered, "but there's enough to do some damage to somebody, come mornin'." Jones snorted.

"In the mornin' we'll likely still be followin' the damn gamecocks around these here hills."

The road wound on, descending now until, at length, another creek was reached, the first evidence of it coming from the sound of water flow and sloshing feet, as whoever of the South Carolinians up ahead in the column forded it. Having arrived at the crossing place there was again no pause in the march to allow the removal of shoes or pants, and Company B splashed across in their turn, with the icy water at the middle stretch of the creek reaching up well past the men's knees. Once across, it was upwards again without any suggestion of a pause, climbing away from the creek valley with shoes now ungainly on the feet from their soaking, and

68

the shivering along the column only slowly subsiding. Eventually the road began to descend once more, with the moon now almost overhead, and talk, even the litany of complaints about the soaking and the lack of rest, having faded steadily away.

It was well past midnight, having crossed a further creek where the partly-wrecked remains of a wooden bridge this time spared the men another soaking, when the column was finally halted and moved off the road. The moon had begun to sink but it was still high enough in the sky to allow the men to see a little amongst the trees as they dispersed and sought places to settle, dim shapes moving here and there in their groups, selecting sleeping spaces. Smoke still hung under the branches, bitter and acrid in the nostrils, with thin tendrils of it wisping around on the moon beams that shone through the tree canopy, illuminating pockets of the ground below in a moving mysterious light.

At least the march had warmed them, Daniel Ryan thought as he unrolled his blankets and stretched out on the forest floor, cushioned by the debris of past seasons. He stretched out on the edge of his worn woollen blanket and rolled himself along its width to settle, with his hat beneath his head as a makeshift pillow. He lay for a time, looking up at the moon, feeling the first pinch of the cold on his cheeks, and was beginning to drowse when Thompson's voice came in a low subdued tone through the darkness.

"Barnard told me the name o' that creek we crossed back there, the last one." Daniel was aware of movements around the group as his companions stirred.

"Its name's Chickamauga Creek," Thompson added.

There was a pause, while the disturbed sleepers considered the sergeant's state of mind before responding.

"Orderly at the train told us that," Daniel Ryan muttered.

"What kind of a name's that," Jones grunted?

"Barnard says it's a Cherokee Indian word," Thompson resumed, "that means, "river of death." There was a further silence as the mess digested this. Then Ballard's voice came.

"I'm real happy ya told us that Joe, helluva happy in fact. I reckon I'd never a' gotten a wink o' sleep from worryin' about what in the hell the name meant."

"Jest thought I'd tell you boys," Thompson returned, "afore I went and forgot."

The replies were brief and profane as the group returned to the occupation of getting some rest in uniforms of which the pants at least were still wet from the creek crossings, but regardless of that, within minutes, save for the natural night sounds of the woods, there was almost complete silence around the bivouac.

Chapter 3 A Collection of Orphans

Another cloudless though misty dawn greeted the awakening men as, from camps all around them, the drum roll roused the various regiments of South Carolinians to assemble. Their own drums were silent or perhaps, Daniel Ryan drowsily speculated, they were still back in Atlanta, or maybe lost somewhere further down the line on a train. Around him others were moving, automatically observing the army's practice of rising with the daylight, drums or no. All around the camp men were starting the process of heading off to relieve themselves, or rolling blankets or rummaging through haversacks for something that would serve as breakfast. A few sauntered over to gape towards the nearest of the gamecocks camps, where the soldiers were forming into their long ranks, but still there was no call for the three orphan companies of the Ogeechee Volunteers.

Breakfast for the mess, the remains of the ration they had obtained in Atlanta, was almost eaten, when Jeffers and the other sergeants finally came around calling on their men to assemble. Plates were quickly emptied of anything that remained on them and, with many of their number still chewing on their final morsels, the men formed their ranks, all three companies, together with their officers, waiting in their places while the lines were dressed and called to attention. Major Randolph waited silently out in front, as the companies were successively called to order, and, once the ritual was complete, he flamboyantly summoned Lieutenant Carberry, the acting Adjutant to his side. The men strained to hear as the major began to speak, but since he made no attempt to keep his voice down they experienced no difficulty in understanding his words.

"Lieutenant," he intoned, "I would be obliged if you would report to Brigadier General Kershaw and inform him that our companies are formed and awaiting orders."

71

"Sir!" Carberry saluted and strode away, soon disappearing among the trees, while the men waited in their places and, out in front of the ranks, the major paced up and down, the sound of his boots, crunching on the decaying vegetation just audible among the other more distant sounds from the neighbouring camps.

The sun was now clear of the horizon, a sun coloured blood red by the mist of the morning and the remains of yesterday's battle smoke. It cast long fingers of alternating shade and dim light through the trees, and on across the sparse area of more lightly wooded ground where the ranks of the Ogeechee Volunteers waited, standing now at ease. Daniel Ryan looked across at that crimson sun, feeling a shudder of unease as he did so, sensing that perhaps it was all too clear a hint of what might well come today, in these dark valleys and woods.

In the camps around them the Carolinians could still be heard and glimpsed, forming into columns of march, but still the Ogeechee Volunteers waited. Finally there was movement among the trees and, along the waiting ranks, the heads of many of the men turned, almost imperceptibly, to see Carberry return. The lieutenant strode over to where Randolph waited. Salutes were exchanged and, with this formality completed, the lieutenant leaned forward slightly, as though to communicate his news in confidence. He had hardly begun to speak however when Randolph started away from him.

"I cannot hear you lieutenant," he boomed, "perhaps I have an ailment. You will have to speak much louder than that sir." Carberry looked at him as though he had taken leave of his senses.

"Louder sir," Randolph repeated, "much, much louder."

"Sir," Carberry nodded, and hurriedly composed himself, as he drew a deep breath.

"General Kershaw sends his compliments major," he called out, "but he says he has no orders to give to us, for we have not been placed under his command." Randolph nodded, as though to himself, and paused for several seconds, as though considering his options, before he spoke again.

"Lieutenant, I desire you to report again to Brigadier General Kershaw and tell him that Companies B, E and F of the Ogeechee Volunteer Rifles are formed and awaiting orders." Carberry almost started as he heard the words. Again he stared at Randolph, who met his gaze without blinking, crooking his head slightly to one side as he gazed straight into his face.

"Are you well sir," he inquired loudly? "Are you able to carry my message?" Carberry recovered himself once more and nodded.

"Indeed sir, I am perfectly well," he replied.

"I am most glad to hear that," Randolph told him, as the lines of men watched and listened. "Pray attend to your orders then sir," he added in a brusquer tone. Carberry saluted once more, before making his way again through the trees that separated their own camp from the nearest regiment of the Carolinians.

The ranks of men waited silently and the major resumed his pacing. The birds sang, while the sun inched higher above the trees, paling as it did so from the deep red hue it had displayed upon rising, while the straggling fingers of shadow that stretched across the ground began to change their pattern and shape. The camps around them were quieter now, with the South Carolinians having gone, leaving only servants and orderlies to busy themselves with dismantling and packing. Finally the sound of hoof beats came to their ears, the rhythm of a single animal, approaching the camp. The men again squinted to one side, this time to see the lean figure of Brigadier General Joseph Kershaw approaching through the trees. Kershaw rode on into the clearing, towards where the major waited, before reining in his horse, wheeling it sharply in front of where Randolph stood, sending a collection of dead leaves, and other debris flying around the first men of the front rank as he brought it to an untidy halt.

Salutes were punctiliously exchanged between the two officers, before the Brigadier spoke, while Carberry, hurrying as far as he seemed to deem it acceptable for an officer to do so, re-emerged from the trees once more.

"Major," Kershaw began sharply, "are you yourself today that you seem to understand neither a simple communication, nor the chain of command that exists in this army?" Watching and hearing it all, Daniel Ryan reflected that a man could be forgiven for concluding that none of these damned officers were themselves today and maybe the north Georgian or Tennessee mountain air was different after all from that in Virginia. Out in front the discussion was joined.

"Beg to inform you general," Randolph called. "Our companies are formed and awaiting orders."

The mounted Brigadier blinked as he heard the words.

"Major," he called again. "I have no orders for your command. You are not under my orders. Those who have been placed under my command are already on their way to meet the enemy. That sir, is where my presence is now required, rather than being occupied in having to borrow this broken down artillery horse, in order to attend to your persisting communications." He started to turn the animal, but Randolph was having none of this.

"With your permission, general," he called. "These men are Georgians and this ground that we are standing on is the soil of Georgia. The enemy is here sir, on the soil of our home and they shall hear from us about that. Having come this distance to meet them general, we will <u>not</u>," Ryan heard him stress the word, "skulk in our camps, while others go to join the fight. We too will go and meet the Yankees sir, with or without your help. We will not sit idly by, while the fight for Georgia's liberty goes on around us." Kershaw heard him out, while his borrowed horse fidgeted and turned, and, as he controlled the unfamiliar animal, the general allowed himself a second or two of further deliberation before replying.

"Your words are well spoken sir, but, since you are still not under my command, I can give you no orders. My own orders give me charge of my own brigade and that of General Humphries, but I have no authority over any part of General Wofford's brigade, because, your command excepted, it is still on the way from Atlanta." He paused and eyed Randolph briefly before resuming. "The brigades, that I have been placed in charge of, have been ordered to move on this road," he gestured with his hand, "westwards, towards the LaFayette Road, and that is where we will join the battle. If you are resolved to go to meet the invader sir, then that," he pointed along the road, "is the way that will take you there, but only you can issue such orders to these men, unless you can find General Longstreet or General Hood, for neither General McLaws, nor General Wofford, have yet arrived from Atlanta, and, while I would expect them to be here in the course of the coming day, it is impossible to say with certainty that they will not be further delayed."

Randolph pulled himself to attention before speaking again, and this time his voice was even louder than before.

"General Kershaw," he boomed, "Companies B, E and F, of the Ogeechee Volunteer Rifles, will presently take that road, ready for battle. I would be grateful sir, if arrangements could be made, before we join the fight, for our men to be supplied with an issue of ammunition, and if I could be kept informed of the orders issued by General Longstreet, so that I may best commit this command to action." Daniel saw a thin smile cross Kershaw's features as Randolph finished speaking.

"I will attend to all of that most willingly major," he returned, "and, if it would be of assistance, I shall detail a member of my own staff, to act as a guide, as far as he is able, in a country with which none of us are familiar, and to help with such communications as may be of service to you." The major bowed.

"I am indeed in your debt general," he called gravely.

Watching and hearing it all, as the pleasantries were extended and salutes were once again exchanged, Daniel Ryan marvelled anew at the minuet of exaggerated manners that seemed to be standard among so many Confederate officers. Even when they pointedly did not agree, they seemed to be able to wrangle and dispute with the utmost courtesy, as Kershaw and Randolph had just demonstrated. As the ranks of waiting soldiers watched, the brigadier finally turned his borrowed mount once more and put spurs to its flanks, departing in a further spray of debris and dust, leaving Companies B, E and F to come to terms with the thought that the major had now succeeded in getting them a place in whatever fight was planned for today.

Even as the watching men digested what had taken place before their eyes, from out to the northwest a scattering of distant musketry came to them, crackling disjointedly at first, but soon growing into a tide of noise that gave ample warning that somewhere out there the fighting was already under way. As they listened to the shooting grow, Daniel Ryan heard Ballard's voice, his words jerking the attention of the men around him from the departure of the Brigadier.

"What about that Randolph," he growled. "Can't let any ol' fight git started, without havin' t' land us in it, right up to our damned necks?" A series of subdued growls and snorts greeted this observation, as Kane answered him.

"What in the hell else were ya aimin' t' do today anyhow Otis?"

Out in front, the major was for wasting no more time.

"Companies will form column of march," he called. All around the little patch of cleared ground, the company officers took up the shout, relaying the orders on to their own commands that turned the three companies of men from a double rank parade formation into a column of files of four. On Randolph's further shouted order, that column stepped off, wheeling smartly to the left and making promptly for the road, kicking up its own collections of dust and debris and commencing immediately to compete, with the column of wagons, limbers and guns, for road space, as they wheeled out into the traffic.

The route remained generally west, though it zigzagged somewhat along country roads, placing the sun first on one shoulder and then on the other. The column tramped on through an increasing cloud of dust, generally following the traffic, making for this LaFayette Road that Kershaw had mentioned, to come to grips with whatever of these western Yankees were out there beyond those woods. Daniel Ryan pondered the prospective adversaries as the mess talk went on around him. The Yankees had been successful out here with these men that was for sure, especially when you compared things here with what had happened in Virginia. These western Yankees certainly had a reputation of being tougher opponents than the "paper collar" eastern army soldiers. Perhaps it was all to do with the Yankees having more farmers and country boys in the ranks of their western armies than they had in their eastern ones and this, together with many further stories about them, had all been discussed at some length on the trains, on the way here. Whatever way that might be, it was God's plain honest truth that now, before that yellow sun which was steadily adding its warmth and brightness to the morning, sank and disappeared again, all of that would likely have been put to the test.

Along the dirt road, flanked on either side by sequences of dense woods, the column moved, marching at ease, which greatly facilitated their ability to advance among the volume of other traffic around them. Ambulances continued to come from whatever battle waged out there to the west, while the artillery and ammunition wagons lurched from one side to the other in order to pass them on the rutted and congested road. All this compressed the files of infantry towards the verges, as they closed in on the fighting which had continued to grow in intensity and now raged in full intensity up ahead. The column moved in its cloud of dust, mixed still with a hanging remnant of the smoke, all of which softened the details of the landscape through which they passed to a vague jumble of greens and yellows, with only occasional breaks in the woods

77

on either side which marked where a confined patch of cultivation had been wrestled from nature's grasp.

They marched with the sun now almost behind them, following the road towards the fighting, with more and more evidence to be seen, not only by the continuing convoys of ambulances, of what had taken place the previous day. They began to pass the swollen bodies of dead men and the carcasses of dead horses on either side of the road, all of them covered by swarms of flies. Some were plastered with dirt or dust to the point that they were almost unrecognisable as men or animals, all testimony to the severity of whatever fight had raged over this ground yesterday, and to what was already shaping up for the day ahead.

Out in front that renewed battle still grew, as cannon now mixed with the continuous crackling roar of musketry, while on the road, the first injured men had appeared. These were walking wounded, able to proceed to the rear without help. Some walked, while others limped or shambled or shuffled, many of them clutching at blood-soaked tunics or improvised dressings, as they made their dismal journey to the aid posts. Then the more seriously injured began to appear, men who relied on comrades, many of them with lesser wounds themselves, to support them, as they sought the surgeons and help. All of it prompted the same familiar reactions in Daniel Ryan as he saw, once more within touching distance, these clearest of all signs of the nearness of the battle and, as the symptoms gathered within him once again, he tried not to look at the extent of the injuries as those bearing them shuffled by.

His mouth was already dry, while his heart pounded ever harder, thumping against the wall of his chest like a hammer as it always did at this time, and his throat felt as though he had swallowed a stone. It was all down to the knowledge that he could easily die here today, for many men undoubtedly would die today, before that sun went down behind the wooded ridges out to the west. Up there, where they were headed, the fight was already on, and the lives of some of the

78

men who had gone up there earlier this morning as this procession of wounded grimly indicated, would already have ended. All the men around him knew, as he did, that today could be their last day, for death on the battlefield made no distinctions. Most men however tried to be fatalists about it all, using a range of different ways of coping with the brutal gamble that soldiering compelled them to take.

Some of them habitually fell quiet, engrossing themselves with their own thoughts or fears. Others prayed quietly, their lips moving almost rhythmically, as though doing so might convince a merciful deity to spare them and take others. Still more grew loud, resorting to extravagant humour, or colourful comments, as to what they intended to seek in plunder, or what they would collectively do to the Yankees, if only the damned generals didn't foul things up, like they had back in Pennsylvania. Maybe some of these men really meant it, Daniel Ryan acknowledged, for it was a familiar reaction, and usually from the same men, that took place every time that a fight was imminent. But by now those around them knew well enough that for most of these voluble men, it was no more than their own way of handling their fears, now that the time was here again.

In late morning the column was halted, at the edge of a patch of cleared land, just short of a junction with another dirt road. Ranks of wagons were parked along the side road, on either side of the junction, and a further line, this of ammunition wagons, was parked up ahead between the road and the trees along the open ground that flanked the road and stretched away towards the junction. Long lines of Kershaw's South Carolinians snaked along the road from the row of vehicles, awaiting their ammunition issue, and their own column was now ushered off the road, on the same side, by their sergeants, to wait there as the turmoil on the road continued, while the activity at the wagons proceeded without pause. The men of the "Blues," waited as the heat from the sun rose, watching as the issue continued up ahead.

Eventually, having received their cartridges, the last of the South Carolinians were moving away, shepherded by their sergeants, but there was no sign yet, of any issue for the orphan companies of the Ogeechee Volunteers. Kane was scathing.

"Here's another damned line where we're last," he drawled. "Looks like we'll be last in every line out here." Thompson had just returned from consulting with Jeffers and heard the complaint.

"They are too," he growled, gesturing towards Kershaw's men, as they re-assembled near the road intersection. "They might be ahead o' us fer this, but they're behind everybody else around here. Kershaw's likely had enough trouble gittin' cartridges for his own boys, afore he even starts worryin' about us. They say these wagons're Hindman's, but this is only the start. Everythin' we need, everythin' that we ain't lugged out here from Virginia on our damn backs'll all have to be borrowed or begged from these Tennessee generals, from Bragg on down. Out here we're jest a collection o' orphans." Ballard turned at his words.

"So far, we surely ain't seen many o these western army boys, but any we have seen don't look too well fed to me, so it mubbee don't look like there'll be too much, in the way o' spare rations, or spare anythin' else, fer us around here." The men around him were still pondering the remarks when they were called on by Jeffers to make their way along the crowded roadside, between the passing wagons and artillery caissons, to form into lines at the now vacant ammunition vehicles.

A sergeant was in charge there at the wagon where Company B now began to assemble, and his expression darkened as the newcomers arrived.

"Who in the hell are you?" he growled at the leading men, as he cast a scowling look along the forming lines behind them. "There's six regiments in that there brigade that jest passed along here and there's four in the other one, so I bin told. Six 'n' four added up to ten, when I was gittin' schooled, so you boys're one regiment too many." He looked around suddenly, as a South Carolinian captain arrived on foot.

"Are you having trouble unloading the cartridges sergeant," he inquired, "or are you just naturally a slow and deliberate kind of person?" The sergeant looked around before replying.

"I already issued to ten regiments, like I wuz told sah," he said, though the aggression had disappeared from his voice like Preston's had done back at the depot, to be replaced by an aggrieved tone. The captain looked around at the waiting line of the Ogeechee Volunteers.

"Perhaps your counting is not as good as you thought sergeant," he said evenly, "or maybe you would rather keep all of these men from the fight, while you call everyone else back to count them again. I am sure that General Longstreet will be interested to know the reason why this division was delayed in reaching its position, and General Hindman also."

"Always us," Jones growled to those around him, "same as it was back at Fredericksburg, why in the hell don't anybody want to give us damn cartridges."

"Maybe they worry about who we'll decide to shoot them at," Daniel Ryan told him.

At the wagons, the sergeant had made his decision and was making the best of it.

"All o' ya got Enfields," he growled? Jeffers nodded.

"Reckon the ordnance sergeant's got a helluva easy job in yore outfit," the man snapped, "compared to our boys out here." He waved to his men on the other wagons and the line began to move forward, with the hands of the men reaching up to take the paper cartridge packs. Daniel Ryan immediately noticed that the cartridge bundles out here were wrapped in white paper, which most likely meant that they were from a different arsenal to the ones that had customarily supplied them back in Virginia.

"Forty rounds," Jeffers began to intone, from up at the front of the wagons, "save some o' yore wind fer the march gentlemen, forty rounds."

Daniel Ryan looked around at Ballard as they reached the wagon, while the wild clamour of battle continued in the woods up ahead. The corporal gave a brief shake of his head and, on seeing it, Daniel reached up and took a further bundle of ten from the one-armed man on the wagon, who grinned down at him as he pushed it into a pocket.

"Reckon if I was a goin' up thar, I'd want every piece o' lead that I could carry too," he drawled. Daniel nodded grimly and moved on.

As the men left the wagons they were directed across to the far side of the road and, on negotiating their way there, they were ordered to deploy, forming where the company officers stood in their customary pose with their arms and swords extended, to establish the line. The ranks quickly took shape, stretching out beyond the cleared ground, into a stretch of somewhat sparser woodland. Up ahead through the trees, the men could make out the long lines of South Carolinian regiments already deployed and waiting as they tore the wrapping from their cartridge bundles to begin arranging the paper cylinders in their ammunition pouches. Dead men lay in numbers here in the undergrowth, their bodies swelling and discolouring, while from up ahead, still more wounded straggled back, making their painful way through the woods, as they headed for the road that would take them to the rear.

Most ignored the ranks of waiting soldiers as they shambled or limped past, their eyes fixed ahead.

Some clutched their crude bandages to their wounds, as they tried to staunch the blood flow, but a few of the less seriously injured, or the indomitable spirits among them, sought eye contact with the men of Company B and called out to them as they went by.

"They're a breakin' up there boys."

"We're through their line and they're a runnin'."

"Y'all Bobby Lee's boys?"

"Ain't never seen no southern boys in blue afore."

"Give 'em hell when ya find 'em."

82

A further order came, this time for blanket rolls and haversacks to be stacked behind their formation. Men began to discard their possessions, but, as they did so a mutter of discontent began to move along the ranks. Leaving belongings and equipment behind when going into action was a familiar arrangement, but out here was different and most of the men, especially those who had heard Thompson's words, knew well enough what was likely to happen.

"How're we gonna git these back?"

"If we leave our stuff here we'll likely never see it agin."

"We ain't got no wagons t' bring our stuff back."

"Got a blanket now, won't have one by tonight if I leave the damned thing here." Gilby was the first of the officers to react.

"You heard the order," he yelled. "Carry it out." There was a momentary check in the complaints as men turned to look at the newcomer, but Jessop was by now alerted and he moved to take charge.

"Let's move it along boys," he called. "We got Yankees up there waitin' for us. Let's give them a good lickin' and we'll take what we need from them." The muttering grew more muted and gradually the piles of possessions grew, while Daniel Ryan, after some re-arranging of things that he was resolved to take on his person, stacked his haversack and blanket roll with the others of the mess. But he could sense the continuing resentment of those around him as they too transferred some of their more personal possessions from haversacks to pockets, before moving back to their places in the ranks.

Jeffers had meantime detailed two of the company to remain with the piles of possessions and Daniel noticed that Matty Weald was one of them. This made sense he reflected, for already Matty's chest had begun to trouble him and this with the Autumn hardly begun. He glanced at Weald and at Powell, his companion who still nursed the effects of his Gettysburg wounds, while the remainder of the company began to move back to their places. Daniel glanced behind, grimly acknowledging that no matter who Jessop left to guard the stacks of possessions, it was pretty unlikely that any of them would see their things again and this in a place where, as Thompson had reminded them, they would have to rely on others for everything.

Out ahead the gamecocks were moving in response to the shouts of their officers and NCOs, and hardly had they stepped away when they heard their own orders relaying along from where Randolph stood. Following the example of the South Carolinians to their front, the lines were dressed and bayonets fixed. More shouted orders then came, being promptly taken up by the sergeants and, guiding on their centre company, the ranks began to move, almost immediately into thicker woods where the task of preserving their line of battle, as they manoeuvred around the intervening trees, became steadily more difficult. This struggle with nature continued for a time until they were again halted, with the battle now a deafening roar out in front, while a great cloud of off-white smoke hung across the woods ahead of them, reducing the trees to vague shapes that drifted in and out of sight as the smoke eddied and shifted.

They waited in their ranks as the day grew still warmer, stood easy, which allowed them to rest their musket butts on the ground and to use their canteens. Daniel's mind however was still on the brief episode that had taken place back in the clearing where their possessions now lay, and from little snatches of talk that he could hear around him it was clear that the minds of some others of the Company were similarly occupied. On the face of it, what had happened back there was nothing more than had taken place before almost every fight. Blanket rolls and haversacks were an encumbrance to men going into battle, especially if they had to march or manoeuvre for any distance to do so. But this time, with new officers and in a situation where there was no apparent means of retrieving the things they left behind, there had clearly been additional reluctance to undertake what was a routine procedure.

Marching order and battle order were different things and that was all that there was to it. Or was it? Jessop had handled the men's display of reluctance with a measure of tact, but he had largely passed over the fact that they could well be in the process of losing the few possessions they had been able to bring here to Georgia. Autumn was here, as the chill of the previous nights had shown, and winter was coming near. Men who were forced to face it without blankets would remember with anger the way that they had lost them.

Yet it had to be acknowledged that Jessop's hands had been tied. The men were to advance in battle order and there was nothing that the captain could do about that. No, he thought, while Jessop might have earned some degree of resentment for what had happened, Gilby would have earned considerably more. The new lieutenant had quickly been removed from the situation when Jessop had spoken up, but his reaction to the men had been simple; an order had been given and nothing else mattered. He had a servant to retrieve his belongings, but his brief intervention had demonstrated to the enlisted men that the climate of discipline in Company B had changed. Jessop had a reputation for profanity and brusqueness as well as a reassuring streak of common sense and solid competence, but the new lieutenant had, in his own way, served notice on his men that they could expect little from him but rigid adherence to the letter of army regulations and ritual. As for the lost belongings, there was no help for it. With no wagon train, out here they would have to fend for themselves in different ways, and with the battle up ahead seemingly going well enough,   those that were able would tonight have to grasp whatever opportunity they could find to take what they could from the dead.

Around Daniel talk about the episode had faded away, replaced now by other comments, making their way along the line.

"Maybe they ain't got space fer us in this here fight."

"They'll find us a place, you betcha they will."

"Damn generals ain't brung us all this way, and gotten us all o' these cartridges, jest so we kin stand around 'n' watch."

"Be better if Marse Bob had come on out here with us instead o' bein' under that damn fool Bragg."

"We still got "Old Pete," White growled. "He won't take no shit from nobody like Bragg."

Daniel Ryan found himself wondering about it all as he waited. In addition to his other widely discussed traits, Bragg had a reputation for dithering on the battlefield. Whatever criticisms had been made of the "Old Man" back in Virginia, dithering was certainly not one of them, but now Virginia was far away. They were out here in north Georgia and today they would most likely find out at first hand whether Braxton Bragg's latest indecision would come in the course of this fight, and if its consequences would again be written in the blood of the men he commanded. The minutes continued to pass and the comments continued along the line, occasionally shooshed by the sergeants, while around the waiting ranks the stream of wounded men grew and somewhere not far up ahead the battle raged on, growing and approaching until it was roaring and crackling so close and so loud that it seemed that all that a man had to do was stretch out his hand to touch it.

It must have been near to noon, for the sun was high and shadows short when the waiting men were called to attention once again. Out ahead, the great cloud of battle smoke and the din of cannon and musketry had neither faded nor faltered. The muskets were promptly raised to the carry as, out in front, the "Gamecock" ranks stepped away. They were followed by the three companies of the "Blues" and the struggle with the trees was promptly resumed as the ranks went ploughing through a dense but brief stretch of woods, which ended abruptly at a further road junction. The ranks pushed across, gaining a brief respite from the whipping, scratching branches but only till they reached the far side of the road, where more woods loomed.

They moved back into the trees without delay to begin a further confusing struggle, enduring the thrashing branches and tripping on unseen obstacles for a further time. There were further, fleeting interludes, when cultivated plots or fields were encountered, and while the going at these times got briefly easier, the heat of the sun when they emerged from the tree shelter was now almost uncomfortably warm. From behind the struggling ranks, the sergeants cursed and threatened, but Daniel ignored their shouts, concentrating his attention on what lay ahead, while trying to negotiate his way, on legs that continued to tremble, to the point that he felt that he must inevitably stumble on the treacherous, obstructed ground. The air was filled with noise and the smoke of the battle continued to drift around them, irritating the eyes and catching in the throats and the noses of the gasping, breathless men.

They came, at length, upon a further dirt road. Beyond it, atop a small rise in the ground, sat a squat cabin of roughly dressed timbers, flanked by a barn and a couple of sheds. The ranks divided to negotiate this obstacle, to reassemble beyond the buildings, with the breathing of the men around Daniel Ryan laboured and heavy. His own breath came in harsh gasps and his heart still pounded in his throat, as the ranks passed from this further brief period in the sun back into the cooler dimness of the woods. The ground they were crossing now was strewn with fallen men, many of them hidden by the undergrowth, unseen, till a man was nearly on top of them. The men stepped around the visible ones with elaborate care, hearing the renewed anger of the sergeants behind them, as the line lurched and wavered.

For the first time today, artillery rounds began to land closer, exploding among the trees just ahead of where they advanced. The Yankee gunners must be firing blind, Daniel reasoned, for it would be impossible to see a target in these woods. So far, none of the shells was coming too close to the "Blues" line, but their arrival seemed to be serving notice to the struggling men that this fight was now reaching out for them.

Up ahead, Daniel began to catch glimpses of reddish brown through the trees, and he strained his eyes as they closed in upon it, finally recognising the form of an earthwork. All around it, the floor of the wood was covered with fallen men, lying thickest as they came up towards the wooden parapet that capped the stones and fence rails of the barrier. The ranks were halted and the men scrambled across, standing among the dying and the dead, as they reformed briefly on the far side. More shouted commands came and the ranks shuffled into motion again, moving on to arrive, almost immediately, at a small creek, upon which the formation dissolved again for the men to pick their way across, some of them being quick enough to balance muskets and grasp their canteens under the water to replenish their own supply, before reforming once more on the far bank, pursued by the shouts of the sergeants.

The casualties still lay thickly, sprawled in their grotesque poses or twitching and writhing, some stretching out pleading hands and entreating the passing Georgians, as they pushed and thrashed past, for that most profound of wants to afflict wounded men.

"Water!"

"Fer the love a' God, water."

"Please boys, water, jest a sip."

They pressed on, ignoring the cries, which, if answered, could have reduced the formation to confusion in seconds. Instead they concentrated on shifting and side-stepping which, while it spared most of the fallen men from being trampled on and most of the marchers from an ungainly tumble, did nothing for the composure of the file closers behind them.

Daniel Ryan turned his eyes away, as he customarily did, from the ghastly disfigurements that now lay all around him. The weakness in his legs persisted and they trembled involuntarily, while his chest still thumped with the frantic pounding of his heart against his ribs. Ahead they began to see lighter shades, the sure sign of a break in the woods, as more shells came whizzing in to land, closer this time, as the line finally emerged from the trees at a further dirt road, from which yet another road stretched on to the west. Dead and wounded men still covered the ground as the "Blues" ranks crossed the road, making an oblique turn on the shouts of the sergeants to move on along the further one. Company B now found themselves entering still more woods that flanked the road, though thankfully these were less dense, with little undergrowth, and fewer obstructing trees. The toiling men were thus able to see better where the fallen lay and thereby avoid them, and as a result the ranks were able to preserve somewhat better order as they pushed on through.

"Right wheel, guiding right into line." The latest order came relaying along and the ranks began to wheel, with the men of Company B hastening to execute the manoeuvre, aware that Company E, on the far side of the road, would be doing little more than marking time as they performed their much tighter turn to the right, while the other companies hastened to form on them.

In the course of the manoeuvre they left the woods to cross the dirt road and move into an area of cleared ground, swept with the smoke of battle, where a more substantial building stood, flanked by its own arrangement of barn and sheds, and the broken remains of further fencing. Artillery shells tore in, to detonate out on the field in front, as further shouts came, incomprehensible in the roar of battle, until they were relayed on by their own sergeants. The line was halted and dressed, with muskets now raised to right shoulder shift, as the men readied themselves, seeing the long lines of the South Carolinian regiments emerge from the smoke, standing motionless, maybe a hundred yards in front of them.

The Gamecocks had halted facing into what looked like a corn field, whose crop had clearly been ravaged in the course of the fighting, with many of the stalks trampled and flattened, and much of what remained standing being broken and damaged. Through the corn stalks and smoke more men had appeared, dressed in the same dull blue tunics as themselves; they straggled back, clearly in full retreat, towards the waiting Carolinians, pushing through their ranks which had been opened to allow their passage. More smoke drifted across from the latest salvoes of artillery shells which were arriving now at regular intervals, crashing into the field up ahead and sending cascades of dirt and fragments of corn stalks and leaves into the air.

The retreating men were close now, approaching the ranks of the Ogeechee Volunteers, and as they came they were revealed by their colours as the Alabamians of John Hood's division. The men of Company B gaped, for these were brave men, known for their tenacious fighting in successive struggles back in the east, but here they were skedaddling, from this their first taste of the war out here in Georgia. Along the ranks the men stared at the approaching fugitives. Were these western Yankees so different that even the veterans of the Army of Northern Virginia could not drive them? The order to open ranks was called along the line and each alternate man stepped behind his neighbours, creating a succession of man-sized gaps through which the retreating soldiers could pass. As they arrived, Jones was one of those who spoke.

"Move on boys," he called, "let the Georgians drive them." A dark-bearded soldier paused briefly on his way through the gap beside Jones and glared at him.

"Ya better save yore spit if yo're goin' up thar," he growled. "Ya'll find it's hotter'n hell, fer Georgians same as fer anybody else."

The last of the retreating Alabamians jostled their way through and the ranks of Company B were reformed to await the generals' pleasure. The men now had the heat of the midday sun on their backs as they waited in the open, while the artillery bombardment continued without let up, though Daniel Ryan was relieved to note that most of the shells were still landing amongst the corn up ahead. He felt anger and frustration rise within him, as still they waited. Here they all

90

were, having laboured through those tearing woods to reach this open ground, and now that they had gotten here they had been halted, seemingly in full view of whichever Yankees were out there, sitting targets for as many cannon as the enemy could range on them, standing still and almost inviting those Yankee gunners to take their time and shoot them to hell. Was this the first symptom, Daniel Ryan found himself thinking, of the indecision that seemingly plagued this western army?

"Load, but do not prime!" The order came relaying along and the men unfastened the flaps of their ammunition pouches and scrabbled cartridges from them, to commence biting, pouring and ramming: this done they resumed their waiting as still more shells plunged in to explode around them.

Mercifully, the waiting did not last. Out in front, the Carolinians shuffled into motion, moving away into the corn, though stretches of their line remained visible through the gun smoke, among the flattened and broken stalks. The order to advance now came relaying along their own ranks, to the outspoken relief of many of the men, and they too stuttered into motion, this time guiding on the centre company. Daniel looked ahead into the drifting smoke, catching fleeting sights of the Gamecocks again, as Company B entered the cornfield in its turn. Kershaw's men were advancing, those hundred yards or so ahead with their brigade line, crowned by its six waving regimental colours, now clear of the cornfield and stretching away to the left across an expanse of stubble. The double rank seemed to ripple as it negotiated the undulations of the ground, rising more pronouncedly on a shallow hogback near the middle of the field as they closed the distance towards still more woods at the far end of the field, vague smudges of green on the rising ground beyond that appeared and disappeared through the clouds of smoke.

The, "Blues" ranks had now emerged from the corn and, arriving at the remains of a further rail fence, they broke ranks to scramble across, reforming on the far side, and stepping off into the stubble that stretched away in front of them towards the higher ground and the tree line. Clear of the mess of corn stalks, they were able to see more of the litter of fallen men that stretched away across the field. Daniel gazed out in front, ignoring the sights and sounds around him, fixing his eyes on the waving colours of the Carolinians, as they swam into view through the drifting smoke. At least the shelling seemed to have ceased and the smoke now began to finally thin and drift away, allowing the advancing men to see something more of the field out ahead, covered with its litter of battle.

Dead and wounded men lay scattered across the stubble and several abandoned wagons lay, their animals absent from their traces, probably appropriated by fleeing soldiers to help them make their escape now their vehicles had been disabled or abandoned. From across to their left front, the chorus of battle still came, in a continuing maelstrom of noise, with its smoke cloud still risingand drifting away to the east. Out ahead, the far end of the field rose towards a partly wooded knoll, upon whose crest, bare of trees, were the Yankees. In the improving visibility, Daniel could make out the distant, rippling gleam of the sun on their bayonets and musket barrels and the drab blue tunics of the men who waited there, their flags fluttering gently above them. Those flags were waving now, in ever more elaborate swings and curves, but the men around them still waited, making no move to open fire. Daniel watched them intently, letting his eyes move only fleetingly down towards the ground in front to avoid stumbling on the broken, bloodied forms that lay there.

"Looks like them bluebellies can't wait t' git started," Kane growled.

"They ain't got long t' wait," Ballard grated in response.

On they pushed, still in their ranks, finding that moving was more difficult now, with the softer, uneven earth of the field compressing and moving beneath their feet. Still there was no sign of that Yankee line opening fire. The long lines plodded on, negotiating their way over and around the fallen, ignoring yet more pleas for water as they drew ever closer to the edge of the field, surely well within effective musket range of those Yankees up on the knoll. Daniel found himself reflecting uneasily that when that enemy line finally opened up, the Gamecocks, and their own companies also, would be so close that they could hardly miss.

The thought had hardly registered in his fevered mind when there was a movement up on that knoll, pulsing along the lines of glinting steel. The weapons moved almost as one, shifting and gleaming as they moved in unison. He watched intently but still no volley came, and now Kershaw's men were at the foot of the slope that led up the final hundred or so yards to the Yankee line. More smoke swept across, blotting out everything ahead, but Daniel Ryan still felt his skin creep from the knowledge that the enemy must fire and, at this range not only the South Carolinians, but also the following "Blues" line must be savaged by the hail of bullets.

The smoke began to eddy and drift and now faint glimpses could again be seen of the Gamecocks up ahead, halted and readying their weapons, though the shouted orders were lost to the following men in the deafening din of the battle. Daniel watched as the yellow flashes winked along the line out in front, though little of the sound of the volley penetrated the general din of firing. He watched as the muskets were lowered and then shouldered, with the lines pushing immediately forward in the wake of their fire.

Seconds later the Yankee return fire came, but the volley was disjointed and imprecise, with the balls coming through in a stuttering hail rather than the concerted impact of well-delivered fire. Few of the minie balls reached the "Blues," line, though some could be heard flying overhead, with their peculiar, whizzing buzz as, out in front, the ranks of South Carolina soldiers provided a substantial shield from the enemy fire.

A further bank of thick smoke cloud now swallowed up their own formation, making it impossible to see any further than the men on either side, and reducing the visibility ahead across the final portion of the field, to a few brief yards. Its foul stink irritated the eyes, noses and throats of the men as it eddied around them. Daniel's eyes stung and began to water, and a cluster of sniffles and coughs rose all around him as he tried to slow his breathing until the worst of the cloud had passed. At last a pale hint of sunlight illuminated the ground around him, and as the clouds thinned further it gradually became possible to see ahead, to where the ground sloped upwards to the woods beyond the field, leading on towards a ridge line.

The men moved on, adjusting their path and closing the gaps as they went, and now up ahead through the smoke, Kershaw's regiments could be seen, pushing on up the slope and scrambling over a further fence, to disappear into the trees beyond as another volley of musketry rippled along that higher ridge line. Much of the struggle ahead was now obscured by the trees, betrayed only by renewed plumes of dirty white smoke that mushroomed up among the tree foliage, adding to the earlier billows that seemed to hang there, dispersing only slowly through the woods. The Carolinians had disappeared into the trees and the edge of the field was upon them now. Lower down on the slope, the "Blues" now pushed up the first part of the ascent, encountering a scattering of fallen "Gamecocks" as they went. On up the slope they laboured, though there was little but smoke to be seen in the trees ahead.

Now they were closing on those woods and further commands came along, vague indecipherable shouts in the din of battle, until Thompson relayed them in his turn. The line shuddered to a halt and the muskets were brought down, from right shoulder shift to the ported position, being grasped diagonally across the body, more suited for moving through woods, but from which position it was also possible to promptly deliver fire. Another order came, relaying along as before, and the ranks lurched into motion again, pushing into the woods for the men to immediately resume their struggle with the trees and brush, manoeuvring around the larger trunks, jostling their neighbours as they did so, as they pushed on to the summit of the hill.

The shouts of the sergeants continued, ever more irate, as they laboured to maintain order among men, whose initial struggle was with the terrain, where rocks and broken ground as well as trees, now obstructed the advance. The woods remained thick with gun smoke, making it hard to see any significant distance in any direction and Daniel coughed repeatedly as it caught in his nose and throat. He felt his eyes sting and water as he moved on, trying to keep pace with Ballard to his right and Winder to his left. There were further shouts as the order to halt was relayed along again and he heard Thompson's booming voice take it up as he gratefully came to a standstill, wiping his right sleeve across his face. He looked around him and listened for the next order, hearing the buzz of more passing minie balls as he waited.

Up ahead the smoke was thicker still and only occasional moving shapes were to be seen in the shadows and the drifting smoke of the wood. The shouted order came and the "Blues" stepped away again, aware, as they advanced, from the volume of fire further up the slope that a full battle was raging there, sending a proportion of its bullets buzzing and zinging through the trees around them. As they came closer they began to hear the screeching yell of the southern troops just audible above the roar of musketry and the crashing boom of artillery. On they went, seeing the carpet of dead and wounded men growing ever thicker around their feet, where blue-clad Yankees now lay, mixed with the hardly less blue-clad Carolinians. Carson's voice came from just behind where Daniel Ryan vainly tried to keep his place while avoiding the wounded and dead.

"Move on boys," the lieutenant yelled. "The gamecocks must be drivin' them," while, from still closer by, he heard White's shout also.

"Ya see boys," he yelled, "these western Yankees ain't nothin' special after all," his words being promptly answered by a ragged yell from those around him.

Even as they moved across the higher part of the hill, they came under fire again. More minie balls began to buzz past, coming from what must be a further stretch of higher ground out in front, from which further tell-tale clouds of off-white smoke were drifting. The Yankees may have been pushed from their positions on this lower hill, but there must be more of them somewhere up there, who clearly were not going anywhere, for the southerners' position on this crest was attracting an increasingly heavy fire from them. Company B therefore needed no encouragement to push on from this exposed place, and they did so, labouring to keep their formation as they went, moving on into the protection of thicker woods. Further on, the trees briefly ended at the margin of a dirt road and as they reached it, further shouts came bellowing along to halt the ranks. More shouts came and the men briefly dressed their line.

The major tramped past behind the waiting men, accompanied by an unfamiliar officer, a lieutenant, who sported a palmetto emblem on his hat, most likely a messenger from Kershaw. He watched them disappear into the trees and smoke, as the thought came to him that maybe, with battle joined, the brigadier had decided that he had some orders for them after all. Still they waited, while up ahead the smoke drifted and the fighting raged. At length, further shouts came and the two ranks were turned to the left and moved off, with their battle line now transformed into a column of double files. They picked their way along the dried dirt and dust of the road with Company B now leading the formation. Somewhere to the rear, up the slope to their right, the hidden South Carolinians were exchanging volleys with an equally invisible enemy.

They moved on through the drifting banks of smoke for what seemed like a considerable time, but what could only in reality have been a minute or two, to be finally halted and right-turned into line once more. The order then came to prime muskets and the little copper caps were fingered from pockets to be pressed into place, then further shouts were relayed along and guiding now on the centre company, they started uphill, heading towards the fight that still raged there.

Daniel Ryan could feel the trembling sensation in his legs that had been with him since the ammunition issue, increasing still further, to the point that he felt certain that those around him must be able to see his weakness. On either side he could now hear heavy volleys of musketry, at last distinguishable from the general roar of gunfire that seemed to engulf the whole wood, while still denser clouds of smoke blanketed this higher part of the slope as he grimly grasped his musket across his chest and tried to keep his place in the thickening smoke.

The ground still ascended, but now the balls were coming through in numbers from somewhere to the left front. Men were beginning to fall from their places in the ranks around him, some of them crying out, while others cursed brutally, as they were hit. The command came, relaying along as usual, and the ranks shuffled once more to an untidy halt. More orders arrived and the muskets were at last brought up, to be aimed at some vague glimpses of movement and muzzle flashes in the smoke up ahead.

"Fire by ranks!" The order arrived, via Thompson's booming shout.

"Front rank, Fire!" Daniel Ryan squeezed the trigger, feeling the Enfield punch back into his shoulder. He began to cough again as the great bank of smoke swallowed the men around him, catching in his nose and throat and making his eyes water and smart once more. He had barely heard the report of his own weapon in the overpowering racket that now raged on in the wood, as battle with these western Yankees was at last joined. Along the line around him he was aware of men seeking cover among the trees and rocks, crouching, or edging to one side or the other, to gain at least some protection from the enemy fire. Many of them had been able to find places behind trees or rocks without moving significantly from their places in the line. Several, like Daniel himself, had moved a step or two forward to the shelter of a fallen tree. Daniel crouched behind the rotting wood, wiping the sweat from his face with his sleeve in a brief movement that hardly interrupted the biting and pouring of his next cartridge.

Long gone, he reflected as he hunched lower and felt for his ramrod, were the days when soldiers would stand boldly upright in their ranks to exchange volleys with the enemy.

"Rear rank, ready....Fire!" The deafening volley crashed out.

Standing boldly in the open had brought death and crippling wounds to far too many brave men. Now infantrymen had a well-established sense of self preservation and Daniel Ryan saw it confirmed repeatedly, as he finished his reloading and darted his eyes along the scant portions of the line that were visible on either side. The whole Company, as far as he could see, had taken cover, those who had been unable to find a tree or rock had dropped to one knee, to minimise the target they presented, seeking whatever additional help might be available from the slope or unevenness of the ground ahead of them.

"Front rank, ready!" He pulled the Enfield into his shoulder and aimed into the smoke cloud.

Fire!" The butt punched back into his shoulder as the smoke engulfed him, as the reloading began again. The enemy fire continued to come from up ahead in crackling volley each of which followed hard on the heels of the previous one, though, thankfully, many of the bullets were passing overhead in the dense smoke, where aiming could only be a "best guess" process.

All the while they kept up their volleying, reloading furiously to aim their shots into the smoke on the shouted commands, though with little idea of where the Yankees actually were save for fleeting, vague glimpses of the yellow flashes from their weapons. As they went on loading and firing, some men began to inch forward, cajoled by their sergeants, most of them attempting, as they did so, to move from one piece of sparse cover to another. Others were clearly delaying their movement from the places where they sheltered for as long as they could, before moving on again into the hail of musketry. Occasionally a man fell, though the smoke was thick, seeming to hang under the trees, so that they could only hear or sense that still much of the Yankee fire was going over their heads. On they edged, moving up the slope, but there was no slackening in the enemy fire, which was still coming in volleys with hardly anything of a pause for reloading between them. To either side, Daniel Ryan was aware of men halting, remaining in whatever cover they had found as the enemy fire continued in an almost unrelenting hail.

"Ain't goin' no place up there in this," Daniel heard the gist of Ballard's shout, even as Thompson's voice came.

"Fall back boys! Back we go, use the cover and serve 'em up some more as ya go." Along the line men began to move again, darting back through the enemy volleys, seeking the next tree or rock, or even the uneven places in the ground as they made their way downhill. Daniel went with them, feeling his skin cringe as still the enemy fire came, the Yankee bullets whizzing through the smoke, some of them to pass on through the trees, while others embedded themselves in nearby trunks or boughs, gouging out fragments of bark to reveal the lighter wood below. Downhill they went, till at last the dirt road was in view and the men began to collect in their groups as they reached it, seeking comrades in the drifting smoke on whom to form, as the hail of fire from uphill eased and finally ceased. Gradually the companies formed, as shouts came from along the line.

"They're comin' down!"

"Form ranks!"

"Git formed, and ready!"

Instantly the men were alert, forming ranks at the slight bank that flanked the road, ramming shots and fingering caps as they peered uphill through the smoke. A few darker shapes began to appear visible only faintly through the drifting clouds. He heard Thompson's voice.

"By ranks, front rank, ready!" The long barrels came up on either side of Daniel Ryan.

"Fire!" The musket punched back into his shoulder and he let the butt fall, grasping for a cartridge as he did so, biting and pouring frantically.

"Rear rank," More barrels appeared on either side of Ryan's head and he cringed, as he waited for the discharge.

"Fire!" The volley blasted out as Daniel Ryan rammed his shot home and replaced his ramrod, fumbling immediately for a cap. Then it was up to the present as Thompson's next bellow came.

"Front rank, ready....... Fire!" The Enfield punched back and the smoke billowed around, blotting out everything around Daniel Ryan as the sweat trickled into his eyes and the reloading began again.

At last the shouts came, again from Thompson.

"Cease fire! Load to the ready!"

The volleying stopped, though the smoke still hung densely along the dirt road and as it drifted around, Daniel was only vaguely aware of the men on either side, but some of them had begun to move as the shouts came.

"Now's the time boys!"

"Let's git on up there, while they're pullin' back!"

"Let's give 'em some more!" More men began to move, starting up the hill into the smoke, prompted by the movement of their comrades, till from out to their right there grew a succession of shouts, relaying along the ranks. The men came to a ragged halt, as their own sergeants took up the call, peering along the line as they waited, to see Kershaw emerge through the trees and smoke on the dirt road, followed by several officers, presumably of his staff. Jessop appeared from the left and, on seeing the general approach, pulled himself to something resembling erect and saluted. The brigadier briefly returned the respect as he came up behind the ranks of Company B.

"As you were captain," Kershaw snapped, and he waved towards the scattering of men who had started up the ascent, gesturing them back towards the dirt road.

100

"You must reform them here, captain," he shouted, trying to make himself heard in the din of gunfire. Randolph too had come across from the other direction, meeting the general's group. Kershaw turned to him as he caught sight of him through the smoke, standing almost level with where Thompson's section had resumed their places along the road. Salutes were again exchanged upon which Kershaw addressed the major.

"I trust that this is enough of a fight for your Georgians, and for you major," he called to him, "but you must break it off for the present, till we reform the line. Have your men remain here, until we can find the rest of my brigade, and then we will move on up to the top." He paced promptly away and as the other officers moved off in his wake, Daniel Ryan exchanged dismayed looks with his companions, while all around them a sequence of comments began.

It remained a widespread opinion, among enlisted men, that when facing a retreating enemy, the last thing to do was take the pressure off by failure to pursue them. Officers however were different. They seemed to nurse a more cautious set of obsessions about reforming lines and doing everything in close formation, suspending a pursuit in order to attend to this, thus giving any fleeing disorganised enemy the chance to do likewise, which was likely to result in whatever advantage had been gained over them being allowed to drip away. The enemy, once repulsed and going back, must be pushed and kept off balance, for the time taken to reform an advancing formation would be used at least as profitably by the pursued men as by their pursuers. This almost inevitably meant that the enemy would get away without further injury or would be ready for further fighting, costing more precious lives when the pursuing troops eventually went forward again. Along the line, as Kershaw's group disappeared into the smoke, the comments came.

"They're goin' back Cap'n, we should git up there after 'em afore they reform."

101

"Crazy to stop, when we had a foot on their damn neck," that was Jones' voice. The mutter of comment continued, audible in snatches through the gunfire, before being abruptly silenced by Gilby's shout.

"Enlisted men are here to obey orders," he yelled, "not question them." Daniel Ryan turned on the new lieutenant's shout, noting the tone and the implication of his words, for this reaction seemed to echo the sentiment of his earlier one.

Jessop's shout came next, above the clamour of shooting and the voices of the men, the captain also bellowing to make himself heard above the racket.

"Stay easy everybody," he yelled. "The brigadier says halt, so we halt and we stay here till we git told different, whatever kind o' sense that makes to all o' the spare time generals around here."

"He ain't in command o' us," White called, from close by. "He damn well said so hisself."

"It's goddam mule sense if ya ask me," Thorne growled, as those around him nodded grimly. Daniel Ryan said nothing. He looked towards Gilby, and then back to Jessop, as the new captain's voice came again, interrupting any further questioning or pondering still in progress.

"Get some o' those branches," he yelled, "and some rocks. They've already showed they're willin' to come down here and try their luck, so let's git a breastwork started, that side o' the road. Sergeant Thompson, take a detail back down to that fence line, and bring up some o' the rails. We want t' be ready, jest in case they decide not t' wait for us to come on up." Thompson turned to his own section and gestured to them.

"Ya heard him," he rasped, "move yore asses."

Chapter 4 An Uphill Struggle

They had returned to the fence, though they stayed to the right to avoid the barer summit of the knoll, eventually coming to the field margin. Navigating was difficult in the trees where the gun smoke hung under the branches, wisping in tendrils in some places, hanging in thicker clouds in others. Daniel noticed Thompson looking around several times on the way, as though seeking landmarks for the return trip. They picked their way back, carrying a load of fence rails which had just been added to the half-constructed barricade, when a louder commotion began through the woods to the right. All along that section of the line the musketry had never entirely ceased but now its intensity grew again, half-drowning the familiar, screeching yell of the southern troops that also echoed through the woods, both sounds rising steadily in volume. The men looked, but there was nothing to be seen in the trees and smoke. But as they peered into the gloom their own orders arrived, calling them to form in front of their barrier, so they left their labouring and assembled, grasping their weapons as they came.

Off to the right the yells and the firing grew still louder, drawing close enough to sound as if they must include the other companies of their own regiment, though still there was nothing to be seen in the smoke which stubbornly refused to clear, and hung under the trees in slowly drifting wreathes. Then more shouts of command came along, relaying in customary fashion, until they were taken up by the Company B officers and sergeants.

"Companies will move forward, guiding right on Company E!"

"Forward march!" Daniel Ryan moved off in his place in the rank, well aware that guiding on anywhere would be near to impossible in these dim, smoke-shrouded woods, but he discarded the thought, and focussed his mind on staying on his feet on the broken ground and in his place in the battle

103

line, as the involuntary trembling in his legs redoubled along with the pounding of his heart. Across the dirt road they went, their own screeching yell rising from their throats as they began to ascend the hill, only to find that it was less of a hill than a succession of hills, for they soon found themselves moving into the mouth of a gully, with the ground, while still ascending in front of them, rising much more steeply on either side.

"Guide right!" That was Jessop's yell, and Daniel began to sense the movement of the men to his left as, in response to the shouts of Carson, Thompson and Bayfield, that left section of the Company B line moved forward, commencing a gradual incline to the right which gradually brought them to the steeper slope on that side. On the men struggled, as the climb grew steadily more difficult, causing their yells to gradually diminish into a series of fragmented screeches. They began to pant and gasp as they laboured their way upwards over the tree-covered and debris strewn ground. Daniel Ryan's breath was again coming in gulps and gasps and the sweat was trickling down his face and body, making the back of his shirt stick to his skin, as he struggled to keep his place in the line, trampling ever upwards through the undergrowth, picking his way through the casualties that lay scattered in the woods around them.

The smoke remained thick though the trees grew sparser as they neared the top, but they were aware of its proximity only by a gradual easing of the slope. Then, from up ahead, the musketry abruptly resumed with a flickering ripple of faint yellow flashes visible through the smoke. Daniel dropped to the ground, aware that all around him his comrades were doing the same, again demonstrating their unwillingness to face the best-loaded volley of enemy fire while standing upright. But once the balls had whizzed past above them, they scrambled to their feet once again to continue their push towards the enemy line now revealed by its fire, as yet more musketry swept in from somewhere on their left flank. Another succession of faint, flickering flashes, but much

104

nearer, and this time the men did not drop for cover. When you got this close, having survived the opening enemy volley, the custom was to rush the Yankee line, attempting to spread confusion among the men who manned it and prise them away from their places, rather than check the momentum of the attack and endure a prolonged trial of a musketry duel, or worse still, invite a counter stroke from whichever Yankees were up ahead.

Now, as before, the general instinct to rush the enemy and dislodge them prevailed and the line lurched forward, hearing the bullets whiz and drone through as they went, bullets which brought a sequence of sickening, wet thuds, and grunts or cries, as some of them found targets among the advancing men. There was a momentary faltering in the advance, for, as before, the Yankee fire was unrelenting, with volleys following each other with intimidating rapidity as they thrashed through the ranks of Company B, reducing the lines to confusion as falling men cannoned into their comrades. The surviving men struggled to get clear of the casualties as they instinctively closed towards the centre, maintaining their forward rush. Still the enemy fire came, in an almost continuous pattern of yellow flashes up ahead, closer still, and the bullets whizzed through once more, bringing more men down and causing the line finally to convulse to a halt as the ranks dropped instinctively to one knee, seeking cover as they brought their own weapons up.On Jessop's shout, they primed and took aim.

"Fire!" The flash and smoke billow of their volley was accompanied by the thumping recoil of the muskets into their shoulders, and they immediately set to work on reloading, vainly competing with the enemy rate of fire. From whatever shelter they had found, they frantically readied their muskets, to send their own shots towards where they reckoned the Yankee line must be, aiming through the choking smoke at vague glimpses of muzzle flashes from the enemy weapons. With the advance stalled and the men under cover as far as it was possible to be, the enemy fire was less lethal, with many of the bullets splintering chunks from the trees rather than doing anything worse. The hillside was a maelstrom of noise and smoke as all along the company line men crouched and hunched, some of them still shuffling towards the nearest trees or rocks for better cover from the storm of bullets, as they reloaded again to continue their battle with their unseen foes.

"How could anybody reload that fast?" The thought hung in Daniel Ryan's mind even as he poured his next cartridge. "How many of them are up there? Unless it's..."

"Repeaters!" Ryan heard Ballard say the word as his own lips formed it. They had to be some kind of repeating weapons to fire that fast. He paused momentarily in his reloading as the thought came to him. They had seen repeaters among some of the Yankee cavalry back in Virginia earlier in the year, but were those Yankees up there cavalry, or did infantrymen out here get issued with these new weapons also?

The smoke cloud was now an off-white shifting gloom, reducing visibility to almost nothing, as still the fire fight continued. Along the line men laboured to maintain their place on the edge of the crest, firing independently from cover, for under such a barrage of enemy shots to stay in the open was to invite a quick death. For a time the unequal contest continued, but Daniel Ryan soon began to notice the men around him beginning to edge back, seeking further cover, loading and firing as they went. He followed suit, recognising the mute decision that the men of the company had made. They were not going to take this hill, not right now anyway, for the Yankee fire remained heavy and rapid, showing clearly enough that whatever kind of weapons they had, the Yankees up here were standing to their work and also using the advantage of their position. The southerners could sense this clearly enough without ever having laid eyes on their enemy, and they were tacitly acknowledging the fact by commencing another slow withdrawal and disengagement. Back they edged, moving from cover to cover, until the slope of the ground began to assist them, with the Yankee fire now going largely over their heads in the dense cloud of hanging smoke where no-one could possibly see a target. Around Daniel Ryan men were starting to turn away, making their way back downhill as the fire near the crest of the hill slackened, though most were reloading, and turning as they went to maintain fire on the enemy line and discourage any notion of a pursuit. On down the slope they went, crossing the dirt road and moving the final yards to reach their half-finished barricade and scramble across.

"Form!" That was Jeffers shout as he paced along the line, "and keep yore eyes on that hill."

"We ain't takin' no chances this time," Ballard grunted, as the section formed their line behind the parapet. Out in front the smoke eddied and drifted, but no warning shouts came and no darker shapes or figures were to be seen through the smoke.

"Looks like they thought better this time," Jones said.

Minutes passed and the firing along the front of Company B had died away almost completely.

"Pickets forward!" Jessop's voice came this time. "Sergeant Dellings, your section!" The men behind the breastwork began to relax. Daniel Ryan hunched downed to lean his forearms on the makeshift parapet.

"Hot around here," he said to Winder, as around them Dellings' men scrambled across the breastwork and started back up the first part of the slope, spreading out and pairing off as they went.

"Soon be hotter," Winder returned. "Linus says we're goin' up there agin. He reckons there's supports comin' up, Mississippi boys," he added, "a whole brigade of 'em back there, all fresh and ready fer a brawl, so we're all to git set to head on up there when they come up."

"Ain't no rest for the wicked neither," Daniel Ryan muttered as he wiped his wet sleeve across his face a further time before reaching around for his water canteen.

"They'll be sendin' us up with hardly anythin' t' shoot at them," Winder said. "I got less than ten shots left." He felt around in his pouch, "seven," he growled. "Ain't gonna send no Yankees packin' back up north with that."

"Best go look for some," Kane told him. "Honest t' God Eli," he added, with a wry grin, as others fingered their pouches, checking their own ammunition. "One little thing goes wrong..."

"I know," Winder returned, "the wheels come right off my wagon."

Jessop appeared, seeking out Thompson.

"Get your men down to whatever's left of that fence and git it up here," he rapped. "We've been lucky so far. Let's get a decent rampart here, at least so's any stray cows can't go trampin' over it."

Thompson was back from the barricade in seconds, waving his men away. Daniel Ryan pushed himself to his feet and moved off past the sergeant, starting down through the first of the trees with the others.

"Let's collect any cartridges we kin find while we're down there," Thompson called, getting a succession of nods from the section as they trooped away across ground that was growing almost familiar.

Their good fortune was that the Yankees who had originally defended this portion of the field, unlike those up on the ridge, had carried Enfield muskets, though the not so good part was that the fallen men who lay in the stretch of ground between the road and the field had only remains of ammunition remaining in their pouches. Thompson's detail moved across the shoulder of the smaller knoll to where the ground started downhill, inspecting the casualties of both sides as they went. As they descended the slope, they caught sight of a long double rank of brown-clad soldiers who had halted down in the initial portion of the wood just beyond the remains of the fence. Daniel eyed them as he approached, still seeking unused cartridges from pouches of the dead and wounded. The newcomers eyed them in return as they crouched in the shade or leaned against tree trunks. The men of the arriving detail nodded to them as they drew close and started work on the fence rails

"You fellers Bobby Lee's boys," one of them finally called, as Winder and Ryan hauled the first rails away from the tangle that remained?

"Sure are," Winder answered.

"Ya sure are dressed fancy," another called. "You boys git them blue-belly togs off a' Abe Lincoln hisself?"

"We just wear what we got issued," Daniel Ryan called. "We didn't make 'em."

"These are called grey back in Virginia," Ballard told the boy as he strolled down towards them with a couple of foraged paper cartridges between his fingers. "They mubbee jest look a mite on the blue side to you boys out here who don't know no different." Daniel followed him down, acknowledging that if they were going to talk, they might as well go closer to where they could maybe hold a conversation above the continuing gunfire.

They gathered in their respective groups, a few paces apart as the talk went on, with the Company B group still emptying the ammunition pouches of the fallen men while they exchanged comments with the newcomers.

"Hot work up thar," one of the fresh arrivals drawled. The words could have been a question or a comment.

"Hot enough," Ryan told him.

"Cain't you smart-ass Virginia boys shift them damn Yankees off that hill up thar, without needin' t' squawk fer help?" another boy wanted to know, his words too just audible above the unceasing racket of the battle.

"We're out here to lend a hand, not git you boys a furlough home," Ballard returned, his answer prompting jeers from a few of the waiting men.

"Who are you boys," Kane called to them.

"Seventh Mississippi, that's Patton Anderson's brigade," came the reply, "who're you?"

"Ogeechee Rifles, Wofford's brigade, that's Georgia boys, Longstreet's Corps, Army of Northern Virginia," Jones told him.

"Reckon you Georgia boys should'a stayed down here, t' fight in yore own back yard, instead o' headin' off up to Virginia to look fer more trouble," a Mississippian called.

"We got generals that decide them kind o' things," Kane answered.

"Maybe you got better generals than we got, but that surely wouldn't be hard," the boy said. They had moved still closer in the course of their exchanges, and were now gathered almost into a group, immediately in front of the Mississippians line, as the conversation went on.

"What's it like with this Bragg feller," Jones asked them?

"The major reckons he's a damned martinet," he was told. "Leastways that's what some o' the boys heard him say."

"He don't mess around with nobody that don't stick to army regulations," another boy told them. "He's had boys shot, fer leavin' the column, or fer sleepin' on the picket."

"Is he a fighter," Winder asked them. There were guffaws of ironic laughter at his question.

"Every time he's gotten us into a damned fight he's gotten us out of it on the wrong side," was the answer. "He done it up in Kentucky, up near Perryville, last fall. We whipped the Yankees up there and then Bragg ordered a retreat. Then he done it agin at Murfreesboro, at the start o' this year. We whipped the damn Yankees again up there, and what did Bragg do? He ordered a retreat."

"What's Longstreet like?" another boy inquired, seeming to tire of this depressing description of retreats. "Kin he do any better 'n ol' Bragg?"

"Old Pete knows what to do with Yankees," Jones said. "He surely knows his way around a brawl..." From further up the slope they heard Thompson's voice, carrying above the noise of the battle, and, on looking, saw him gesture them back. The Mississippians saw him too.

"Looks like yore supper's on the table up thar," one of them said.

"See you boys in hell," another called as they departed.

"On a damned cold day," Ballard returned, as they shouldered the poles they had gathered and started up the slope to where Thompson waited.

"Time t' git back," he told them, as they arrived. "Reckon we're gonna hit 'em again, at least they are," he added, gesturing down to where the Mississippians still waited. Daniel Ryan glanced back down at the group they had conversed with. He hardly knew them, for they had spoken for mere moments, but somehow the impending ordeal up on the hillside, in that torrent of Yankee fire that awaited those boys who stood down there still bantering, was prompting a tinge of regret and empathy in him.

"They might all be headin' up," he said, "but they surely won't all be comin' back down." He glanced down the shallow slope once more, towards the waiting Mississippians. Ballard looked across at him, with a resigned look on his face.

"It's the chance we all take in this here army," he growled, "and we all know it, them boys as well as anybody else."

"And their turn's come around again," Daniel replied.
They were back behind their improved breastwork when the Mississippians came up behind them and they stepped away, opening their rank for them to pass through and cross the barricade. A scattering of comments came as they passed.

"Give 'em hell boys."

"Drive 'em."

"Give 'em the steel." Daniel Ryan looked in vain for the boys they had spoken with, as the long lines halted and dressed just beyond the dirt road before moving on into the trees where the smoke eddies still drifted, heading on up towards where the pickets presumably still exchanged shots with the enemy, disappearing into the yellow-green gloom and the haze of hanging smoke. They waited, listening to the more distant shooting on either side, as they exchanged glances.

111

"Maybe they've halted to dress their line agin," Winder muttered.

"Mubbee they jest dug holes and hid in 'em," Jones returned.

The word had hardly registered when from further up the hill, an outbreak of louder, closer firing suddenly erupted, vaguely audible above the overall din, signifying that the Yankee pickets were being driven in. As more minutes passed, a cloud of thicker gun smoke began to drift down under the trees towards them, catching once more in eyes and throats as it enveloped the men at the barricade and moved slowly on through. They waited and watched, peering into the gloom out in front for some sign of how the attack might be progressing. Then a sudden, louder upsurge of firing came, a volley, clearly audible above the general battle noises. Another screeching, southern yell, harder to hear in the din of firing, came next to their ears, confirming that the Mississippians attack had begun. More volleys of musketry, and the smoke cloud grew still thicker as it drifted slowly downhill towards them, blotting out all sight of the trees further up the hill as the volleys continued in a steady sequence, indicating that the two sides up there were now slugging it out.

The fight went on, but gradually the shooting changed in character, becoming an almost unbroken volume of fire rather than separate volleys of musketry. The smoke bank now engulfed the whole of the wood, moving down the slope until it was all around the men at the barricade, making them sniffle and sneeze again, while along the barricade, men rubbed and wiped at their streaming eyes. Then dim figures began to appear through the cloud. They squinted hard at the shapes as they repeatedly vanished and re-appeared in the drifting smoke. The way they moved showed they were wounded men, as they came shuffling back down the gentler, final part of the slope, clutching at their injuries, staring wildly at bloody uniforms and injuries as they came up to the barrier. Carson's voice came, calling out to those nearest him.

112

"Some of you get across and help these men over!" Daniel was aware of movement around him and he leaned his musket against the barricade before stretching out to help a man who had been assisted onto it from the other side. The process went on as more and more wounded appeared, while still the crashing racket of fire continued from up towards the crest. Jessop appeared and shouted to Thompson.

"Get a man out to the picket line sergeant, pickets in. Let's be ready for the b...... if they come on down again."

Daniel heard Thompson call and saw him gesture to Winder.

"You heard that, go tell Jim Dellings to get his boys back here." Winder scrambled across the top rail of the barricade, jogging away across the dirt road and vanishing almost immediately into the smoke, as Daniel grappled another wounded man across the barrier. More and more of them were arriving and almost all of the men of Company B were now engaged in assisting them across as the men of their picket appeared among them. Finally, as yet more men emerged through the smoke, Daniel Ryan got a glimpse of Dellings, his face covered with sweat and powder stains, as he reached the barrier and the tide of wounded at last began to slacken. Dellings eyes sought out Jeffers as he pushed through the waiting men and clambered across.

"Barnard!" he yelled. Jeffers appeared promptly from along the line.

"Whar's the cap'n," Dellings roared. "Reckon he ought t' know that they're comin' back and the Yankees are on their tails." Daniel Ryan grasped his musket at the sergeant's words as he gazed across the dirt road into the denser smoke cloud beyond. In the wake of their own pickets many more figures were now appearing, emerging from the smoke just a matter of yards away, as the main body of the Mississippians moved back steadily to swamp the space between the barricade and the dirt road.

"They're comin'," the first of them shouted as they arrived.

"They're comin' down." Jessop was immediately there, whether from Dellings' warning, or from what he was now seeing with his own eyes. He strode up to the barricade, waving his sword.

"Open ranks," he yelled. "Get across you boys and clear our damned front. Move your damned asses or we'll fire through you." All along the barricade there was now a scene of confusion. The remaining wounded men still struggled weakly to cross while the retreating men milled around them, waiting their turn, some of them glancing nervously behind them and a few actually pushing their way past the wounded in their haste to get across.

Jessop was growing frantic as the Mississippi officers yelled and cajoled at their men, their shouts becoming more and more shrill and urgent as still the jam of men in front of the barricade remained.

"Git across and move on down."

"Shift yourselves, move!" For a few further moments it seemed that the confusion would simply go on and on, but gradually the Mississippians cleared away, many of them manhandling their groaning wounded comrades bodily across the barrier and away to the rear with them. Company B formed their ranks at the barricade again as the last of the retreating men pushed past, fingering caps into place while the smoke out in front still drifted to reveal a scattering of dark shapes among the trees. Not a rank or formation of men, was the thought that came to Daniel Ryan's mind, but, whoever they were, whether the impetuous or the stupid, if they came on down they were about to learn a hard lesson. All along the barrier, having primed their weapons, the men of Company B leaned forward resting elbows or musket barrels on their makeshift, uneven parapet.

"By ranks, front rank ready!" Thompson's voice relayed the orders "Aim!" and the muskets came up, the hammers were pulled back to full cock by the right thumb of each man as the weapon was briefly sighted..

114

"Fire!" The blast of the volley could be felt along the line as the weapons lurched back. The smoke billowed around the men once more, stinging eyes and irritating noses. The race to reload began, with ramrods beginning to clang on musket barrels, as Thompson's shout came again.

"Rear rank ready.... aim.... Fire!" The men worked furiously, each of them knowing only too well that speed in delivering volleys of fire was crucial in an infantry engagement, and in this one, with the Yankees likely armed with something more than single shot muskets, it was still more vital. If the enemy knew that your volleys were coming regularly, that knowledge, especially if he had no cover, would eat away at his resolve to stay and fight it out. Bite, pour spit, ram, replace ramrod, replace cap, ready.... It all took maybe something just under twenty seconds for well-trained, experienced men and that could make the difference, for Company B would stick to their work, and that could be the thing that helped them to prevail. But here the southern ranks also had the cover of their barricade, while those Yankees, even with their smart-ass repeating weapons, were out in the open, exposed and vulnerable.

The smoke billowed around the barricade as the volleying went on, each one followed by another episode of frantic reloading. The smoke was now so thick that there was once more nothing at all to be seen out in front, and the men, firing in their ranks, were again aiming by best guess. Even the muzzle flashes from the enemy muskets were now invisible in the dense cloud. The volleys were crashing out from the barricade with grim regularity and it was simply a matter of sticking to the loading and firing until the ammunition ran out or the Yankees faltered, or your luck ran short.

It seemed to last for a long time. Daniel Ryan had no idea of how long, but soon, from the fragments of noise that could be heard between their own volleys, the firing out in front seemed to be fading. He gradually became aware that fewer whizzing balls were now crashing into the wood and stones of the barrier or buzzing past their heads, but the smoke hid everything and there was no way that a man could be certain that the enemy had been repulsed. Then the shouts came, almost inaudible in the din of musketry as they relayed along the line. Thompson took it up.

"Cease firing! Load to the ready!" The musketry declined to a spattering of single shots, before fading away completely. Daniel Ryan reached into his cartridge pouch, feeling around for his next shot, noticing as he grasped the cartridge that only a few paper cylinders remained in the pouch. Out in front the smoke was at last thinning, as he rammed the bullet and wadding home and the call came along the line.

"Pickets forward!" Jessop's voice came to them again as he moved along the line. He sought out Thompson. "Your section this time sergeant." There was a brief pause before the shuffling and scrambling began, as men crossed the barrier and made their way forward into the thinning smoke, pairing off as they went. The fallen of both sides lay out here so there would be ammunition to be gathered, necessary because the few shots that remained to him would be of little use if this fight went on, and with plenty of daylight remaining, there was no reason to think that it would not. His eyes sought out Ballard and the corporal nodded to him as they moved towards each other, making use of the trees for cover. They advanced up the slope, settling into skirmish order and drill, each of them moving alternately, while the other paused with his musket at the ready, altering course towards the dead and wounded men as they went to inspect their cartridge pouches. Ryan and Eli Winder came up towards the body of a fallen Yankee and as he closed on the man, Daniel's eyes went immediately to the weapon. It was the length of a standard musket, but the lock was unlike anything he had seen before on a long arm, for it resembled the mechanism of a revolver, though the only revolvers that Daniel had ever seen or heard of were pistols. Winder stopped, and resting the butt of his own musket on the ground, bent to grasp the weapon, lifting it from where it lay to gaze at it. His eyes sought out Thompson and he whistled, seeing the others of the section look along as

116

he raised the rifle higher. A few moved a step or two towards him as they looked.

"I'll be damned," Jones said. Thompson waved them forward with a snap.

"Reckoned it had to be somethin' like that," he added to those nearest to him. "Eli, take it back down and make sure the captain sees it, then git yore ass back up here." Winder grinned and lowered the rifle, before starting back down through the trees. On the hillside the others returned their eyes to the front and resumed their cautious advance and the quest for ammunition.

They halted just short of the gully, unwilling to approach too close to its commanding slope, for without sufficient men to cover both sides of it, closing on one side would make them vulnerable to anyone on the higher ground on the other side. Thompson waved them to a halt and they paused there in a ragged uneven line that stretched along the slope, each man waiting in a place where he could see as much of the slope as possible, but still communicate with his partner.

Daniel looked carefully up the hill. They were there sure enough. Even though the smoke still hung thickly he could see movements as dark shapes flitted among the trees up there. Then the first shots came, dimly audible in the continuing sounds of battle along the line, but real enough as the bullets began thudding into nearby trees, or went buzzing on past with their own distinctive, whizzing sound. The southerners dived for cover behind whatever lay nearest, though some of them, Daniel Ryan included, were too far from sizeable trees or rocks and simply flung themselves flat among the dead leaves and sparse undergrowth as the Yankee bullets whizzed past. Daniel Ryan looked up, assessing the ground around him for cover, and seeing a sizeable fallen branch a few yards to his left, slightly to the rear of where he lay.

"Let 'em know we're here to stay boys," Thompson called, and at that a succession of shots rang out, returning the enemy fire, while the ravine and its surrounding woods became further obscured by the smoke from the firing. *Now*, Ryan's mind told him, while the smoke from those shots was thickest. He jerked himself onto his knees and crawled furiously for the branch, levering himself the last couple of feet to lie prone behind the scant protection that it offered. Around him, the Company B skirmishers moved carefully, acknowledging that the Yankees, higher up on the top of the gully, again had the advantage of position, and with those revolver muskets could fire repeatedly at any target that they saw.

Daniel Ryan remained where he was, spread-eagled on the more open ground behind the fallen tree bough as the initial exchange of fire continued, making no attempt to take part. Instead he laid his musket alongside and looked around him: he realised that he lay in a gentle swale, where the ground formed a minor fold in front of him. It was nothing like enough to protect him from the Yankee bullets, particularly from a higher position, but it was a help. The main weakness of this place was that the branch itself lay a foot or so above the ground, cradled there by its smaller branches, leaving a gap between the thickest part of the branch and the ground below sufficiently large for an alert enemy to aim for.

He reached out with both his hands, feeling the sharp scratch of thorns and prickles on the skin of his fingers and palms as he scraped the dead growths away, and began pulling handfuls of earth into the gap just in front of where he lay. A fragment of a branch thumped onto the ground near his arm: having been provided by Ballard, who crouched behind a nearby tree. Daniel reached for it and pulled it round in front as the scattering of picket fire went on around him, settling it into his modest mound of earth before stretching farther out to grasp at a further piece of rotting branch, pulling it towards him to fix it on top of his earth pile, half on top of the other piece, closing the gap to a few inches.

The smoke cloud all around him shifted and eddied, but he still felt exposed and vulnerable and he knew that he would need more than the cover provided by the earth and the branch fragments if this exchange was going to continue for any length of time. If only he could find some stones, he thought feverishly as he continued to work at blocking the gap between limb and ground, they would add some substance to what he had already gathered, for a branch on its own, particularly a rotting one, would barely deflect a minie ball. He burrowed his hands still deeper into the earth on either side of him, pulling more handfuls of it across to wedge it below the pieces he had settled in place. Loosened earth would not stop a bullet either, it would scarcely slow it, but it provided a bonding into which more substantial protection like branches, or best of all rocks, could be embedded.

Thompson crouched a few yards to Daniel Ryan's left, behind a more substantial tree, his eyes flitting from his men up to the higher ground, where the Yankees lurked, their presence periodically revealed by those distant yellow flashes and plumes of powder smoke. They were sending their shots down the slope in a steady spatter, to buzz past or thunk into nearby tree trunks, dislodging further fragments of bark to reveal still more of the yellow-white wood beneath. Thankfully, in this smoky gloom, aimed shots would be near to impossible, but there was always the random factor of luck. A man could just as easily die from a, "to whom it may concern," bullet as from any that was aimed at him personally. There was a movement on his left side and Daniel turned his gaze to see the sergeant briefly aim his musket on the near side of his tree and squeeze off a shot, the smoke from it immediately billowing around him and hiding him for several seconds from his men, before it started to drift and thin.

"Let's give 'em a shot or two boys," he called along. "Don't want 'em thinkin' we ain't up fer a fight." Daniel paused in his burrowing to look up the hill, as a largish stone thumped down, arriving in the carpet of forest debris beside him, where Ballard still crouched. He grasped it gratefully and manoeuvred it around in front of him, working it into his makeshift cover. He squinted uphill again. The Yankees were

119

still there alright, as the continuing flashes and smoke clouds showed, but in this continuing smoke neither side could possibly have a clear sight of the other. As though to emphasise their presence, the main branch of his barrier jerked and moved as a bullet struck it. Daniel winced as he saw the shard of bark fly off from a point a couple of feet from where he lay.

Along the southern line there still seemed to be something of a hesitation in maintaining fire, with men whose cover was less secure understandably reluctant, even in the smoke, to reveal their positions to a better-positioned enemy. Daniel Ryan again mopped the sweat from his face with his sleeve before returning to his fortifying, finding a further couple of reasonable sized stones which he added to his barrier, pushing them into place before returning to work again on earth gathering. Finally he pulled up the Enfield and laid the barrel across the limb, groping for a cap with his right hand as he steadied the weapon with his left. He pressed the little copper thimble into place with his finger and pushed the musket forward, settling the butt into his shoulder and resting his arm on the limb at its junction with a smaller branch. He squinted along the barrel, to sight on where he thought the crest of the ridge would be, watching for a yellow muzzle flash before he squeezed the trigger feeling the punch of the recoil as the weapon discharged. It looked like this was how this particular skirmish line duty was going to continue, he mused as he withdrew the musket, a potentially deadly ritual of outpost firing, where shots came and went, though neither side could possibly get anything resembling a clear view of what they were aiming at.

Time passed and Daniel Ryan had assembled a reasonable barrier, supplementing the branch just in front of where he lay. He had kept up his occasional shots at the Yankee pickets, rolling onto his back to reload each time. Loading was a more awkward process this way, taking more time than when kneeling or standing, but this was no place for a man to rise to his knees in order to do it more quickly. As he

120

continued to fire he could feel his musket recoil increasing on each shot as the barrel and lock steadily fouled from the clogging residue of the black powder.

It was a process that got inexorably worse, especially after anything more than a dozen or so shots, though it could be less or more than that, depending on the quality of the powder in the cartridges. There were cleaner bullets available, these generally having been scavenged from dead or wounded Yankees, distinctive by the blue or pink paper in which they were wrapped. They looked like minie balls, but were distinguished by a larger metal washer fixed at their base. Daniel kept those that he had scavenged in his tunic pocket along with the bottle cork that he used as a muzzle stopper, and his pricker. There were two of them there now and they could be used to scour some of the black grime from the barrel upon firing, but the benefits of this measure were limited and the process did nothing at all to clear the lock. The weapon would eventually risk misfiring if the mess was not cleaned, ideally with an acidic fluid, or failing that, by thorough washing and polishing, but at times like this, only by making the best use one could of a cloth and the metal pricker.

He rubbed at the nipple of the lock with his finger, pausing to blow the residue away before repeating the process on the hammer cavity. He reached down into his pants pocket to pull out the grubby utility cloth that he kept there, using it to wipe the messy black residue from the lock. Next he fumbled his fingers back to his tunic pocket and grasped the pricker, hauling it from its place and inserting the fine metal spike into the nipple hole, before rotating and twisting it to and fro, so as to dislodge as much of the residue as he could. He withdrew the tool and blew hard into the nipple to clear away the debris, repeating the process and using the cloth to clean the lock as far as he could. He paused to wipe his face once more with his now-soaking sleeve before replacing the pricker and selecting one of the cleaners. He rolled onto his back as he bit the pink paper flap, poured the powder and inserted the peculiarly shaped bullet before reaching for his ramrod.

The Enfield punched forcefully back into his shoulder as he fired the cleaner, and the smoke cloud engulfed him as he pulled the weapon back and reached into his pouch for his next regular cartridge, before rolling onto his back once more. The cleaning he had attempted would help, he reflected briefly, as he spat the bullet and reached for the ramrod, but the fouling would soon build up again, with every shot adding a little further deposit to whatever remained from the earlier firing. The ball rammed home, he replaced the metal rod in its channel and rolled onto his stomach once more, laying the musket beside him before taking a further turn at reaching and scratching, ever further away, for more earth or debris. Another piece of dead wood was just about within reach and he waited for one of those nearby to shoot, taking advantage of the smoke cloud to raise himself up and lunge to the side, grabbing at one of its twigs to pull it towards him, and on securing it he pushed it into his rampart and jammed it into place, beneath the main limb, with more handfuls of earth. Another shot now, perhaps, and he fumbled for a cap, flicking the spent one away from the musket nipple, before setting the fresh one in its place, as sweat continued to dribble down his face and drip from his chin.

The exchanges continued, not controlled firing, but a continuing stutter of independent shots, with each man loading before peering into the smoke for any vague suggestion of a movement, before firing, all at a deliberate pace. Failing any sort of sighting, they sent their shots towards the faint yellow flashes from the top of the ravine or, when these could not be seen, at the smoke plumes from the enemy weapons. There seemed to be no suggestion of any further advance from the Yankees. Instead a gradual decline in their fire became evident and the smoke cloud began to shift and thin. Soon the section of the trees in front of the Company B line was quiet, save for isolated shots, though the racket of battle still continued along the hillside to the west.

Whether this reduction in fire meant that the Yankees had withdrawn, or were simply saving ammunition, it was impossible to say, but this was no time to get careless, for if the visibility continued to improve, the risk of aimed shots would increase. The men settled to watch, some scrutinising the crest of the ravine which was now vaguely visible, while their partners began the task of rubbing and scraping to clear and clean their muskets. If the Yankees were not advancing that was well and good, but neither were the southerners, and this meant that the Confederate attack, on this part of the field at least, had come to a halt. Stalemate would surely not be to the liking of the generals, but it remained to be seen what they would decide to do about it.

The skirmishing dragged on, punctuated by further rock and branch gathering. These protections, spaced among the larger trees or rocks, gave the men who sheltered behind them, a vital survival edge. Stones and tree stumps would stop bullets, and the thicker wooden branches could deflect them, so a man behind any barrier, even ones as makeshift as these, could continue the fight with a measure of confidence that would be absent if he was out in the open. Thankfully the smoke had not completely cleared, continuing instead to drift in wisps around them, still making proper observation and aiming difficult for both sides. The drifting cloud denied the Yankees the full advantage of their position, and kept the exchange between the pickets of both sides a matter of best guess so far as sighting was concerned.

Eventually the men on the firing line were relieved by others of the company. Those along the line became aware of their comrades arrival behind them, as they manoeuvred forward, using trees and brush for cover. Once a comrade was close enough, he called to the man being relieved, who nodded around to him, before firing a final shot and moving immediately, to take advantage of the cover offered by the smoke cloud from the discharge of his musket to change places with the arriving man, who took his place in whatever cover struck him as best, before readying for his own shot. In this way Daniel Ryan changed places with Jack Milton, of Henry Bayfield's section, diving behind the same tree as Ballard, to await the next shots before moving on back, while Milton, ignoring Daniel's fallen branch position, settled behind a neighbouring tree. Away from cover, makeshift though it had been, his heart pounded harder and his legs again felt weak as he crouched, watching others move back and forward around him, before lunging away himself to the next vacant tree as more shots rang out along the nearer part of the skirmish line. He repeated the strategy several times more, using further trees and a stump for shelter before he deemed it sufficiently safe to make his way back to the main position beyond the dirt road, knowing that there was just a single cartridge remaining in his pouch, and a single bullet loaded in is musket.

Back at the barricade, a detail from the company was formed to seek water. These men, including Ryan and Hale, collected canteens from the others and moved back down the hill, picking their way in turn among the wounded and dead of both sides from the earlier fighting. There also were those who had become detached from the formations that had waged that battle to the west; they now roamed or squatted in groups to the rear of the battle lines. The Company B detail finally reached the gully that ran to the west, where, it was being said, a stream was to be found. It did not take long to see the tell-tale signs, a crowd of men along the length of where the watercourse ran, some of them waiting while others crouched for water.

Daniel Ryan looked around them as he and his companions joined the crowd that was coming and going, seeing the sweat-stained, hollow-eyed, powder-blackened faces of the men stare back at him, worn faces, on whom the strain of these long hours of battle and danger was clearly etched, as they waited for their turn at what remained of the water. Finally, as still more men moved away, gaps began to

124

appear along the stream and the first of Ryan's companions were able to push their way through to crouch among those who were already at work on their canteens.

The water was by now a mere trickle, whatever its previous flow had been, and the water that remained was cloudy and discoloured, but thirst made men a great deal less particular and finally, with their canteens at least partly replenished, they gathered again to start back up the hill, prowling through the drifting smoke in the woods to find some recognisable landmark or sign that would lead them back to the company. It was the dirt road itself that eventually guided them back to distribute the canteens to their owners. Up along the ridge the firing still remained as only spatters of outpost shooting, leaving more distant gunfire to tell of where the battle still raged. But with its decline on their own front, those other, more harrowing battlefield noises grew in intensity, as the cries and screams of the legion of wounded men who lay along those hillsides and in those gullies, began to shred the nerves of their comrades.

The afternoon was gone and the angle of the sun's rays shining through the trees told of it nearing the western horizon over to the left, when the ammunition wagon laboured up along the dirt road. The brigades along the lower ground, between the hillock and the main ridge, had adjusted their positions, with each taking over a section of the main line, while the outpost screen in front of the three companies of the Ogeechee Volunteers had been reinforced more or less along its previous line, with half of the remaining men now spaced along the forward position. Those who now remained at the main barricade had occupied themselves, in between working on their fouled muskets, with further strengthening of their rampart. Details of them had headed back around the shoulder of the hillock, seeking fallen branches to add to the barrier, while those remaining collected more earth and stones and piled them into it. With the arrival of the wagons the work was briefly suspended, allowing those in the main line to assemble and receive a reduced thirty round issue of cartridges. This done they were promptly sent forward once again to man the picket line, enabling the men up there to return in order to replenish their own ammunition supply.

There was no word of a further advance, so far at least, Daniel Ryan reflected as he settled behind a tree on an altogether quieter picket line, though smoke still drifted through the trees. There were only occasional shots now being exchanged, most likely through a shortage of ammunition among the Yankees, he reckoned, though the more distant firing told that fighting still raged on other parts of the field. Perhaps, he thought, this battle, like Sharpsburg almost exactly a year ago, would grind to a halt, due to the lateness of the hour and the sheer exhaustion of the participants. But the cartridge issue, this close to dusk, was a broad enough hint that the generals had not done and a further advance on this front was a pretty likely prospect.

The sun was near to setting but the noise of battle had still not ceased, when word was sent up to the picket line that another attack was imminent. Fresh brigades of soldiers would advance on the left, while a mixed brigade was deploying to the rear of their line and would advance shortly. The word was passed along the pickets to expect these men, and they settled to await their approach. It came within minutes, a growing thrashing noise of many feet on the floor of the woods, of men pushing through the trees, breaking the smaller branches in a continuing crackling chorus as they came, the noise gradually imposing itself over the more distant musketry.

The pickets looked back down the slope and immediately made out a double rank of advancing brown figures, endeavouring to hold their formation on the broken ground of the slope, as their sergeants shouted a continuing stream of invective. The pickets scrambled to their feet as spaces opened in the newcomers' ranks to let them pass. Daniel stepped through one of these gaps, catching a strong smell of body odour as the men passed, their faces set and tense. A few calls of encouragement followed the men as they moved away up the slope.

"Give 'em hell up thar."

"Shift their blue belly asses off o' that damned ridge."

"Skirmishers forward!" At this shout a scattering of brown figures detached themselves from the main body, quickly jogging forward into the gully to vanish among the trees and smoke of the darkening woods. The battle line pushed on behind them, followed by sergeants and officers, at the same steady pace, until they too were almost out of sight. A further crackle of musketry began to grow from up nearer the crest, telling that skirmishers were now in action. More noises came, shouts of command and the steady tramp of more formations from further down the slope, where another sparser rank of men was now in view, advancing through the trees, blue clad men, their own comrades. Ballard swore as he saw them.

"Looks like we ain't done yet," he growled to those nearest him.

Ahead, up towards the crest of the ridge, the firing was quickly growing into the full clamour of battle, as yet another screaming yell rose from the throats of the attacking troops, while the remainder of the three, "Blues" companies came up to the picket. Jessop was out ahead of the ranks of Company B and he raised his sword as they covered the final few yards.

"Gentlemen," he called, the word just audible above the crash of battle up the slope, "take your places." He gestured towards the ranks with the sword as he called the order, bringing them to a halt. The waiting pickets moved into the line, turning quickly as they arrived in their places, with Jessop now moving to take up his own station to the rear. He looked briefly along the waiting line before again raising his sword, a signal to the watching sergeants that the next order was pending.

"Guiding right," the call came from along the line, for the Company B officers to take it up.

"Forward march!" The ranks shuffled into motion, even as the sergeants were still relaying the final order, with the men immediately having to begin adjusting their path around the intervening trees, then to hurry back to their places, pursued as always by the growls of their NCOs. At other places they had to break ranks and divert past fires burning in the undergrowth, their smoke drifting across to join the lingering battle smoke, while flames crackled and hissed as they spread through parts of the wood.

They started the steeper, harder portion of the climb, with the ranks still wriggling and distorting as men dodged the various obstructions. Many of them were panting and blowing again with the effort of the ascent, and now the sound of the musketry ahead increased in volume as they approached the top of the ridge. Their route had this time taken them to the right of the now familiar gully and they scrambled up the steepest part of the slope, hearing a crashing barrage of fire from further on, as the battle now raged in full force at the top.

At last, through the smoke, a dim collection of images came into view: a formation of men, deployed obliquely to the right of their own advance, and as they came up towards them a bellowed order came relaying along, wheeling their ranks to form upon the troops already there. More orders, and they were moving again straight up the slope, while still the battle raged to their right and left. The slope was now levelling and they were advancing through a dense cloud of smoke with a litter of dead and wounded men lying in the grass, many of whom groaned, screamed or cried out their familiar litany to the passing soldiers. Their pleas and entreaties were almost lost in the din of musketry, their lips still moved but only snatches of their words could be heard.

"Water boys, fer Jesus sake, water."

"Finish me off, for god's sake."

"Just a little drink, please!"

"Water."

The advancing men ignored the cries, and the grasping hands that pulled at the legs of their pants or their ankles, trying only to avoid stepping on the fallen men as they passed. Now there was shooting coming from up ahead and bullets began to buzz past, mercifully high thus far, as their own ranks were finally halted and their weapons prepared. To their left, through the drifting smoke, must be the right flank of some at least of the other brigade, but in the clouds of stinking smoke, there was no sign of any other formations. With their weapons loaded and primed the orders came, barely audible in the din of battle. Deafening volleys of musketry were crashing out at regular intervals, but the intervals between them were so brief that it sounded like an unbroken crescendo of gunfire all across the summit of the hill.

"Prepare to fire by ranks, front rank, ready...." Already the men were moving, to wherever would bring them to the shelter of some kind of cover.

"Fire!" Even as the Enfield punched back into his shoulder, Daniel Ryan knew that opening fire would attract a much heavier response than anything that had so far come their way, from whatever Yankees were ahead on the crest of the ridge. The enemy up there would now sight on the muzzle flashes of the incoming volley, thus making their replies much more dangerous than they had so far been. He set his face grimly and manoeuvred himself into place behind a tree trunk, as he frantically bit and poured his next cartridge. As he worked he was aware of yet another wounded man grasping at his ankle, as he too cried out water.

"Water, jest a sip...," the voice implored. Ryan ignored the entreaty, concentrating on his reloading, but the tugs and the pleas continued as he fired his second shot and grabbed for his next cartridge.

"Jesus," the voice at his feet pleaded, as Ryan bit the cartridge open and made to pour it. "Ain't ya got an ounce o' pity? Jest a sip, jest a little sip."

Daniel spat the bullet into the muzzle and stuffed the paper after it.

"I got other things to do right now," he snapped, as he furiously rammed home the charge, returning his ramrod to its channel as the volley from the rear rank crashed out. His ears cringed from the concussion of the blast, as he grasped at a cap and flicked the spent one away, pressing the fresh one into place, while still the voice entreated, faint and scarcely discernible in the din of the firing.

"Jest a little water, for Chr.....'s sake." Daniel glanced down, seeing through the drifting smoke cloud, the staring eyes of the wounded man standing out in his face, blackened as it was with smoke and smeared with what must be dried blood. How long had this boy lain up here, with the bullets from successive attacks whizzing past mere inches from where he lay? Daniel caught the gleam of the badge that was pinned to his tattered hat lying on the ground beside him, recognising the palmetto tree emblem on it, just as he heard Thompson's shout "Front rank, aim...... fire!" the musket bucked again and immediately he was reaching for a cartridge, biting and pouring while still the Carolina boy at his feet pleaded.

"Jest a little water." Daniel cursed and paused with his reloading for a brief few seconds to grasp the strap of his canteen and swing it over his head, pulling his musket into his body to prevent it obstructing the movement. He loosened the screw cap in a single movement and let the canteen drop to the ground, returning immediately to his loading. He rammed the shot, moving almost frantically to be ready, this time sticking the end of the ramrod into the ground, to save those vital seconds as he reached for a cap.

"Front rank, aim......" He pressed the cap into place and swung the weapon up.

"Fire!" His own shot was a split second late and he swung the musket down, grasping for his next cartridge as, once more, he heard the croak of the voice at his feet.

"God bless ya, feller." Daniel put the words from his mind, as he worked on his reloading, this time pulling the ramrod from the ground to ram the shot, feeling the resistance grow

130

as the barrel gradually fouled again, before returning it to its channel and reaching for a cap. Around him he could hear grunts and cries as the enemy fire whizzed through, felling those whose luck had not held this time from their places with the sickening impact of lead on flesh or bone. The rear rank volley blasted out again as he reached for a cap and his ears throbbed once more.

In a fight there was never a way to measure the passage of time. The drills of loading and firing were too frantic, the sounds of men on either side close enough to reach out and touch, being struck by the brutal thuds of heavy lead slugs too intimidating, and the all-consuming fear of suffering the same fate was too terrifying. Yet there was a madness in battle that could dull the desperate horror of the experience. In the course of it a man could almost detach himself from the reality of what he was doing and what was happening all around him, letting the drills, so often practiced that they were virtually automatic, take over. But simple things, like the episode with the water canteen, could jerk reality back into focus, beginning the insidious process of sapping morale and resolve.

The trembling of the legs would get still worse, till a man felt that he must surely stumble. The heart, already pounding like a hammer in the chest, would feel as though it would burst through the ribs, while the throat would seem to be on the verge of choking from the lump that had settled in it. These deadly battle experiences were maelstroms of frantic movement, choking smoke and intimidating noise, in the course of which time was impossible to estimate. But time in a fight was not the real issue: what mattered most of all was to keep up your fire and pray to God, while you did so, that somehow he would notice, just enough to keep those whizzing, death-dealing, lead slugs away.

The end, when it came, arrived gradually, with a falling off in the volume of fire to their left and, probably as a result of this, their own order came along shortly after.

"Company will withdraw by..." the rest of the shout was lost to Daniel Ryan as a further ear-splitting volley from the rear rank blotted out Jeffers' voice.

"Keep up your fire boys." That was Thompson, his shout immediately following that of the First Sergeant. Daniel sensed rather than saw the rear rank move back, concentrating as he was on reloading, but as he replaced the cap he heard Thompson shout again.

"Front rank, back you go, form on the rear rank." Daniel moved back, feeling exposed and vulnerable as he left the shelter of the tree, immediately seeing the muskets of the rear rank appear through the smoke, coming up as the men commenced their brief aim. He moved quickly into place between two of the gently swaying muzzles, catching a glimpse of the black powder deposits on them as he took his place.

"Fire!" The explosion of smoke and flame came again on either side of his head and his ears buzzed and sang with the concussion. The barrels disappeared from view as they were withdrawn for reloading and Daniel was aware of the men behind him moving away once more as he levelled his own musket on Thompson's shout.

"Front rank, aim..... fire!" The musket butt punched cruelly back into his shoulder and then it was down and he was reaching for his next cartridge, as still the bullets buzzed past through the dense, dirty white cloud.

The withdrawal continued, gradually taking them back down the slope until they were below the enemy volleys. Daniel could hear them whizzing overhead again, as the slope increasingly extended its protection to the withdrawing soldiers. The order came, to cease firing and load to the ready, and he felt the barrel scorch his hand as he let the butt of the musket drop to the ground once more. His fingers automatically reached for the next cartridge and he went through the process of reloading for a final time, grasping the cloth from his pocket to protect them from the fierce heat of the barrel.

All around them the firing was dying down, declining till it was an untidy spatter of shooting, more like an overgrown outbreak of skirmishing rather than anything more substantial. Reloading done, he reached around for his canteen, cursing as he remembered that he had forgotten to retrieve it. It must be up near the crest, where that South Carolina boy still lay. He looked to his left at Winder, who had just taken a drink from his own canteen. The black man caught his gaze and immediately extended the canteen towards Daniel.

"I saw what you did up there," he said. "Reckon you didn't think that your water was wasted on that gamecock boy?" Daniel nodded briefly as he took the canteen, rinsing his mouth with a small amount of water, then spitting it out before taking a deeper draught to swallow.

"Didn't mean to give him all of the damned stuff," he grunted, as he handed the canteen back to Winder. He looked around, noticing for the first time that Hale was no longer with the mess group.

"Matthew?" he said gently.

"He took a ball in the shoulder," Winder told him. "I ain't sure how bad. Couple o' the rear rank boys helped him on down and he's on his way back. He's a tough cuss. Take more'n a ball in the shoulder to git him."

They did not withdraw all the way down the slope into the gully. Instead they waited just below the brow of the ridge where the trees were more numerous, as the smoke drifted and thinned, the fires still burned around them and the skirmish firing went endlessly on. More orders came and were passed along the line. There was to be a further general advance up the slope once more, not in formation this time but in open skirmish order. The advance began, with the men moving from cover to cover as they went until, as the slope began to lessen under their feet, the firing began once more. Not full-blooded volleys, but an augmented episode of skirmishing, with men seeking targets of some kind before firing. Evening was coming, with the sun now almost behind the trees, shining through the woods out in front and making observation, when the smoke had thinned sufficiently to attempt any, still more difficult.

As time passed even this firing began to fade and decline as all across the summit of the hill the final rays of sunlight shone in long fingers through the trees ahead of them, illuminating the smoke that still drifted in clouds under the canopy, until the last rim of its yellow orb that had risen blood red over their morning bivouac was gone, and, in the woods, the light began to turn towards dusk. The firing had now died away almost completely, allowing the cries and screams of the wounded to dominate the hillside. They waited, until finally talk began to move along the ranks.

"They've gone."

"They've pulled back up there."

"The bluebellies've skedaddled." Still they waited, as rumours and comments circulated until, as the last of the smoke drifted away and the brow of the slope hardened in front of them, the shouts came, calling the weary men to order once more.

"Skirmishers forward!" A succession of figures moved away and Daniel, having felt Thompson's tap on his shoulder, went with them, seeing the others of the section pairing as they went forward. There was no sign of Ballard, so he looked towards Jenkins, seeing the boy nod as he came to a halt, allowing Daniel to pull ahead, before he too halted, crouching down into the grass as he peered up the brief remainder of the slope, through the eddying smoke, to seek any sign of movement. He scanned across the ridge, half-seeking any sign in the landscape or among the carpet of fallen men that might tell him where his canteen lay, but he pushed the notion from his mind. There was little chance of recognising anything, especially since their time up here had been spent in a dense smoke cloud, and besides there were more important things to do right now. He looked briefly up as Jenkins moved past, stooping as he advanced a further short distance before dropping to a crouch once more. Daniel watched intently, looking past the boy and on through the trees and undergrowth.

Skirmishing was all about keeping your eyes peeled, seeing your enemy a second before he saw you, and it therefore did not do to allow other thoughts to divert your concentration. He straightened up and began to move, passing by where Jenkins crouched, treading gently forward, fixing his eyes on the ground that was now starting to open up beyond the forward crest of the ridge. A second's hesitation or inattention could cost a man his life out here and, even though the Yankees seemed to have gone, they would almost certainly have left a rearguard, or at least a screen of skirmishers to fall back more deliberately, discouraging any pursuers with aimed shots.... As though to confirm his thoughts Daniel caught the briefest glimpse of a puff of gun smoke and heard a crack ring out, then the ball approach with its curious whirr as he crossed the top of the ridge. He dropped down immediately as the shot passed, sensing the others on either side of him doing likewise. He waited before scrambling a few feet to one side to gain the cover of a tree, hearing footsteps in the grass behind him as he settled there. He looked around and saw Jenkins coming up level and making to move on over the crest.

"Don't be in such a damned hurry," he snapped, seeing the boy drop into cover a few yards ahead of him at the words. "Give them time to get goin'" he told him. "They ain't stayin', if they were they'd never have left the highest ground here. All they're doin' is tellin' us not to crowd them."

They waited, as the light around them continued to slowly diminish. He became aware of men moving forward around them and he pushed himself to his feet and did likewise, making his way past where Jenkins still crouched. He crossed the ridge crest and gazed out at the ground beyond. The details were beginning to fade as the evening advanced and dusk came. The greens and yellows of the trees and scrub were disappearing, merging into darker shades and shadows and presently the word came along for them to halt and hold

135

where they were. In the darkness, the risks of continuing to manoeuvre became even greater and, largely for that reason, night almost always brought an end to fighting, however fierce the day had been.

Chapter 5 Dead Men's Shoes

It was almost completely dark when the remainder of the company came up, Daniel heard them coming, recognising the sounds even above the chorus of screams and cries that seemed to come from all around him, as the line halted just at the crest of the ridge. He looked back, seeing parts of the woods still illuminated by the fires which silhouetted some of the arriving men as they moved. Presently a relief came forward and the skirmishers moved back to join the remainder of the company. They waited until finally the word was passed to stand down and the men collected into their groups in the gloom.

"Are they goin' to let us have fires," Jones growled?

"Go ahead and build 'em," the voice was that of Jeffers. "Half the damned woods're on fire, so a few more ain't goin' to make no difference." Wood was promptly collected and fires were kindled below the brow of the ridge, though with their haversacks in the rear and most likely lost for good, the fires meant warmth and nothing more.

Night brought more mist to mingle with the smoke from the fires and the drifting, smoky remains of the battle. They squatted or sat, savouring the spreading warmth of the fire, for the evening had brought renewed cold. Their rest however was brief, as scarcely had they gathered and settled when Ballard appeared, gesturing to the others of the mess to gather.

"Time to git out there," he told them as they assembled around him. "We got near to no chance o' seein' our own stuff agin, so the sooner we git goin the better, cuz if we don't get started now the best o' any pickin's'll be gone." The men got to their feet without comment and moved forward onto the smoke-wreathed ridge. Those of the enemy dead lay nearest to the bivouac, had already been plundered, and a scattering of men remained at work here, picking over what remained. Ryan and his companions did not delay, moving past them and on over the ridge, to descend a shallower slope on the farther side into still more wooded ground, seeing more men, similarly engaged, emerge from the smoke, which remained thick from the many fires that still burned in the trampled and shot ravaged undergrowth, illuminated in places by the flickering glow of the flames.

They passed through the picket line after Ballard had exchanged a few muttered words with Linus Cooper. From all around there came the cries and groans of wounded men, many of them unseen in the smoky fog, while others loomed into view in the white gloom, their hands raised in entreaty. These men were Yankees, but several times the Company B men came to where the fallen soldiers lay close to the fires, and regardless of their uniforms, they paused to drag men from the worst of the flames, saving them at least from burning to death, though their appeals for water or for other help, were still ignored.

"If we start givin' 'em all water, we'll never git up there," Daniel heard Ballard telling Jenkins. "Time enough fer that kinda thing when we've seen to our own needs." Along the slope the men moved on, continuing their trek through the drifting smoke from the fires. This part of the woods was quieter, though by Daniel Ryan's reckoning they had now passed a good way from their own lines and only a few now probed among the fallen Yankees here. Ballard however seemed unimpressed.

"Let's keep goin' fer a stretch more and see what we kin see," he said. They moved on, now making their way through a thin scattering of plunderers, pushing through woods where lurid gleams of smoky moonlight cast their pale gleams of illumination through the gaps in the trees. They began to ascend again, following the slope of the ground as it rose to the north and west. Here there were very few dead and the plunderers had vanished, but still Ryan and his companions passed on, skirting an open field before veering to the left into a further stretch of trees where no fires burned, and only the fleeting barbs of moonlight, dimmed by the endless drifting eddies of smoke, gave any suggestion of light.

Daniel was now beginning to feel a sense of apprehension at their position, a sentiment shared by some of his comrades, to judge from from the whispered comments that were starting to circulate.

"Are we headin' all the way up to Chattanooga?"

"Where in the hell are ya takin' us Otis?"

"Ain't no point foragin' where there ain't no dead men." Those words came from Jones, but along the line and slightly out in front, Ballard's step did not alter.

"Go on back if ya ain't up fer it," he growled, but no further whispers came.

Daniel watched his friend pushing on through the trees, seeing the set of his shoulders in the pale gleams of moonlight as he concentrated on the woods ahead, but behind him the apprehension still grew. They were far in advance of their own positions, acting on an assumption that the enemy had finally left the field and headed back towards Chattanooga. Maybe they had done so, but there was also the possibility that they had halted, awaiting daylight, in order to conduct a more orderly withdrawal. But even if the Yankees main forces were still skedaddling there was every chance that they had left a rearguard behind to discourage pursuit.

"Over there!" The voice of Eli Winder came to them and they stopped and turned to see him point out to the left of where they had halted. Daniel Ryan strained his eyes to see, but at first could make out nothing but darkness and shadows stretching away under the trees. Kane appeared beside him. Then there were movements showing that others had already reached whatever lay there.

"Looks like we struck lucky," he murmured, pointing further to the left. "That there looks to me like a company assembly area." Ryan nodded, seeing the clearer space at last with its stacks of belongings, where a few southerners already worked. They both headed towards the place, following on after Winder and the others who had been closer. The first of their number reached the place and Daniel saw them stoop to examine what they had come upon. Jones was just ahead of them.

"Glory be," they heard him say, as he slung his musket on its strap and moved on to begin to prowl.

"The lord helps them that's ready t' help themselves," Kane intoned, repeating the longstanding company plunderers saying, as he and Ryan reached the place. Daniel slung his own weapon, as he moved to begin his own search among what now lay all around.

All kinds of belongings lay there, some of them stacked in groups or rows while others were scattered around, with the contents of haversacks and knapsacks littering parts of the ground, though from what the smoke-dimmed moonlight revealed, this was a wide area to be plundered. and even counting the men who were already here, there seemed to be plenty to go around. They spaced out and set to work, searching through the haversacks and knapsacks, which, by their groupings, presumably marked where individual sections or squads had left their belongings. This must have been the assembly area of a company at the very least, Daniel Ryan thought as he heard the chorus of little whoops and exclamations all around him, announcing his companions' glee at what they had found. He peered around the litter of belongings, searching first for a haversack, preferably a heavy, well-stocked one, noting even in the dim, smoky light of the wood, that those that lay here were the water-proofed versions, with their off-white canvas coated in dark-coloured paint. He hauled at one by its strap, noting its weight appreciatively as he dragged it clear of the rest of the pile, and steadying it against his hip with his left hand, he pulled at the strap, releasing the tin cup suspended there, and groped around the contents.

The first item he pulled from where it was pushed down beside a tin plate in the smaller section, was a cloth bag. This must be coffee, he thought, and this was confirmed by the aroma as soon as he unfolded the flap. He felt again to find a smaller bag which he discovered was more than half full of sugar. A knife, which also doubled as a fork and a spoon, completed the contents of this section. The larger compartment of the haversack initially revealed several hardtacks and then a wrapping cloth which yielded a generous piece of meat. He rummaged on, pulling out several of the vegetable cubes, so prized by Isaac Kane, before pushing his hand back inside, feeling cold metal with his groping fingers which closed around what turned out to be a can, filled, according to its label, with sardines.

All around him his companions were unearthing similar prizes from the haversacks. Ryan slung his own booty over his shoulder by its strap before turning to the nearest knapsack. He loosened its straps in turn and thrust his hand inside inwardly gloating over the value of the haul. First to emerge was a shirt of a light colour, which he held up in the dim moonlight, stretching it across his chest to check its fit before dropping it to the ground beside him and reaching further into the packed knapsack. Next came a pair of thick woollen socks which he deposited with the shirt. Strapped to the top of the knapsack was an almost new waterproof blanket, not the plain version, but a revised type with tapes attached along its length, enabling it to be more easily combined with another of its type to form a simple ridge tent. He turned the knapsack over in order to unfasten its lower section, finding inside a tightly-folded woollen blanket. He moved his fingers appreciatively among the almost new pile of its fabric: why, this was looking like the best haul ever. He pushed the socks into his tunic pocket and with the blankets and shirt under his arm, moved on to pick up a further haversack and pull it open. Inside were more hardtacks and salt pork, some of which he was able to jam into the haversack that he had already taken.

This was proving to be a priceless haul, but there would be no canteens here and he knew that he must forage further to procure a replacement for his own. All around him others were gathering to compare their finds. Ballard had laid out a

141

gum blanket and on it the others were piling the food they had collected. Ryan walked across to where the corporal stood, with his own haul laid out in front of him.

"Is this why you moved on this far from the pickets?" he inquired quietly. Ballard turned and winked at him in reply.

"Reckoned there'd be somethin' better up here," he said. "I reckoned there'd be southern boys prowlin' through our stuff by now, so we needed somethin' more'n jest a few hardtacks. I figured that the Yankees would most likely ha' used the woods t' deploy 'n' come up, but they'd a' used the roads to skedaddle. We'd a fair chance o' comin' across some o' the stuff they'd mubbee left on their way up, if we pushed on a stretch," he gestured around, "same as these other boys did." He looked around the clearing. "This is good enough," he added, "ain't it? But I'll tell ya Daniel," he said in a lower tone of voice. "I was jest about to turn back and own up to bein' a damned fool when Eli saw this place."

Kane approached to deposit the rations he had found on the blanket before crouching to examine the things that already lay there.

"I tell you boys there's some damned good eatin' here," he told them, as he fingered several tins of the sardines, including Ryan's. In the darkness, Winder's teeth showed as he grinned across at him.

"We ain't finished yet," he said. "There's another whole set over there that we ain't even gotten to yet.

Reckon there's more here than we kin take." Ballard took a step towards them.

"That'll do some other boys," he said. "We can't carry no more'n a little o' what's here." He pointed farther into the trees. "Edwin says there's a creek over thar," he said, "so we kin fill up our canteens, afore we divide up what we got and head back." He looked down at the haul of food. "Let's take what we kin fer some o' the others. I reckon we could use a wagon up here, or maybe more'n one, if they wurn't all back in Virginia."

Daniel had taken the tin cup from the haversack strap, noting appreciatively the hanging ring secured around its rim, before starting after Winder, pushing his way through a stretch of ferns and long grass, to where the creek lay. He knelt there, laid his musket beside him on the bank and stretched the newly acquired cup into the freezing water, and drank the contents greedily. He repeated the process several times, feeling the chill of the water gradually numbing his throat before he paused, pushed himself up onto his knees and re-attached the cup to the haversack strap. He bent again, briefly rinsing his hands before splashing handfuls of water into his face, rubbing it into his eyes and around his neck with his fingers, though it seemed to make little difference to his feeling of unkemptness.

"Let's move out," Ballard's voice came to him, "we're a mite far from home here." Daniel retrieved his musket and stood up, making his way over to where the others were assembling at their supply of foraged food.

Having pooled the haul of food, they began to divide and pack what they could carry. All of them now sported woollen blankets rolled inside water-proofed ones and most had foraged additional ones which now lay next to the food blanket. Inside his own blanket set Daniel Ryan had rolled the shirt, socks, and a set of drawers that he had subsequently discovered in another knapsack. With the night already cold and winter on the way, spare clothing would be worth its extra weight and bulk. His new haversack, re-adorned with its tin cup, was soon filled with food to the point that he, like his companions, had furnished himself with a second one, likewise packed with still more rations. These could be eaten as far as possible when they got back to their bivouac, and there was maybe even enough for some items to be given away along with with the spare haversacks and blankets, to others of the company, though that would be a matter for the whole mess to decide. With both haversacks packed near to capacity and the additional set of blankets slung over his right shoulder, he stepped away, aware that there was a further

143

excess of food that still lay on the blanket. What remained, together with everything else that lay all around these woods, would be someone else's windfall.

"Good night's work," Jenkins said to nobody in particular. Daniel Ryan did not answer. It was a good night's work and much of it was due to Ballard's shrewdness, but his mind was now moving onto other things as his eyes wandered around the dimly lit expanse of the glade and at the belongings that lay scattered among the grass.

Having satisfied his needs, he was starting to see this place differently, maybe more like what it really was, for each of the piles of belongings that they had just finished going through, represented a man. Daniel fingered the strap of the first haversack. He was a Yankee certainly, but even Yankees were people. The possessions of this man had now been rifled through here where he had left them. Perhaps the man and the others who had assembled here were now out on a road that led across the ridge to the city of Chattanooga, embroiled in the confusion of the retreat, with his possessions simply lost and irretrievable, as Company B's were also, a windfall to those who found them. But, on the other hand, it might not be like that. That Yankee, whoever he was, could equally be somewhere not so far from here, clutching at a wound as he pleaded for help, or for water, or maybe he was lying, still and cold, his body slowly stiffening somewhere up there on the ridge top.

Daniel had seen this many times before. Each time the men of Company B had left their own belongings before going into battle it had been the same. Everyone had left their possessions, most often neatly piled, to be recovered later when the fight was done. Sometimes, like today, they had been unable to return to claim their possessions. On other occasions, like back on the peninsula last summer, they had returned to find them plundered. But most times when they had come back and had recovered what they had left, there had been those other piles, the ones that remained, each of them representing a man, a comrade, someone whose face

144

could be so readily pictured who had not returned for his things.

It was no different for these Yankees, Daniel reflected, as he turned away with his companions. They had not returned, but each of these piles that he and his comrades had gone through with something akin to glee, was a man, and who knew where those men were now, or whether or not they still lived and breathed? Even Yankees were maybe worth such a thought, but then he forced his mind back to reality. It did not do to think like that. Those woods and hills all around were littered with men of both armies who had left their belongings in piles this morning, believing they would be back to claim them. It did not do to ponder on how many of them would never return and how their existence was therefore reduced to nothing, save for these pathetic bundles of possessions which would be rifled through by others, whether their enemies or those of their own side. It made little difference, but when it happened and his scant belongings were scattered or taken by another, a further part of each man's fragile footprint on God's earth was gone forever.

It had all added up to a feast of considerable proportions back at the temporary bivouac, with most of the company benefitting in some way from it. The hillside had been less busy on their return, with only a few late-starting scavengers still at work on the dead around the crest. It would be good to get hold of some shoes, Daniel had reflected, since his own were entering that critical margin between worn and disintegrating. There had however been few left, and what had remained had been the smallest sizes, of no use to most men. They paused only briefly among the dead whose bare feet and naked limbs now gleamed dully white in the pale rays of light from the sinking moon that brightened and dimmed in the still drifting smoke in the interior of the wood. The cries and groans of the many wounded had still rung out in a continuing chorus of misery, though they seemed to have faded at least to some degree, as the more gravely injured men weakened or died. Many of the fires too had now dwindled to smouldering, smoky clumps, and only subdued glows of orange could be seen across the whole area, down the hill into the gully below, which still stank of smoke from the guns as well as from the fires.

They had built up their bivouac fires and then feasted lavishly, firstly on sardine fish in salty oil speared from a succession of tins by the prongs of their forks, while Kane worked on the main substance of the meal assisted by Daniel Ryan and Eli Winder, all of whom dipped rather less frequently into the sardine tins as a result. The consensus among them was to pass on the surplus plunder, the additional haversacks and blankets at least, though they had resolved to keep most of the rations. The excess had been passed on to some of the others, and as a result of the foraging by various groups of its men, the company was now not far short in terms of equipment of where it had been that morning.

"The lord taketh away and the lord giveth," Elmer Bentley had said and Ryan had found the saying rather appropriate. He had used his newly acquired combination knife and fork for the meal, examining it in more detail while Kane began dishing the main part of the mix, a concoction of pork, hardtacks and a number of those little dried vegetable cubes, all cooked in their own fat onto the waiting plates, At one end the thing was a spoon, while at the other it was a fork, but with the outside prong of the latter widened and sharpened to form a miniature knife blade. It was maybe typical of the Yankees he thought, as he turned it over in his hand. They seemed to have a liking for such gadgetry, even with the simplest of things.

The food was promptly dispatched, with everything washed down by the luxury of real coffee sweetened with sugar. The mess had eaten well, but still had a healthy enough supply of food, coffee and sugar for tomorrow, and this was packed away into haversacks. All of it finally done, Daniel had settled himself to rest, pleasantly full and wrapped in his new woollen blanket, with the oilskin wrapped around it as a

146

groundsheet and cover. Perhaps this day had been one of the worst, he reflected, for the battle just finished had been waged with a brutal intensity that matched the struggles back in Virginia. The thought swam lazily across his dulling mind that these western boys, it had turned out, surely knew how to set about a fight, but the foraging expedition had been just about the most profitable they had known. It, and the supper that had followed, had occupied them since the fight had ended. Maybe that had helped them but now, rolled in his blankets in the smoky darkness, there was time to think, even though he was dog-tired and his body was still in the process of recovering from two days and a night with little rest.

His mind still raced with the tensions and the horrors of the day just past, whose dismal harvest of suffering and death still surrounded them. At least their own mess, save for Hale's wounding, had survived the day, though Elkins, Bryant, Petersen and Green, the latter another conscript, were missing from their sections. The images continued to crowd into his mind, but exhaustion was at last overcoming them and he felt the jumble of thoughts finally slowing as he drifted towards sleep.

He had hardly seemed to close his eyes before he felt his shoulder being shaken by a hand that turned out to be Thompson's.

"We got work to do," his friend growled, "Git yoreself ready."

"Damn the man," Daniel's tired mind told him. Thompson had feasted with the rest of them on the captured rations. He had gained a replacement haversack from the spares in which they had carried the excess food back, and had even been provided with a set of Yankee blankets, thanks to the efforts of Winder and Jenkins, but he still couldn't leave his benefactors to a decent rest.

Daniel sat up and looked around the camp. It was still dark, but the first gleams of the new day were coming away to the east. All around him the others of the group had felt Thompson's hand or heard his words, and were rising to their

147

feet almost as one, moving to retrieve their weapons. They rolled their new blankets, looping and donning them, together with the haversacks, unwilling to run the risk of their being plundered in their turn by others. All this done, they made their way forward to where the sergeant now waited, wearing his own new possessions, in company with Lieutenant Carson. Daniel saw in the dull flickering of the nearest fires, that all of Thompson's section, who still remained on their feet, and also a few of Dellings' men, were gathering around him, and as they came together into a group, Carson addressed them.

"The generals reckon that the Yankees are half way to Chattanooga by now, or maybe they jest hope that they are but, since they ain't certain of any o' that, they want patrols out along the line to see who's there and who ain't there no more. We're moving up over the ridge and then pushing on a stretch, to see if they've all moved back like they think and gone as far as the generals maybe hope they have." Nobody spoke of how far forward their mess had already gone in search of plunder, collectively concluding that what the lieutenant didn't know wouldn't hurt him, or them either, but if he had eyes in his head he would notice the finery in which they now assembled and would know that equipment like this had not come from the battlefield itself. Carson, for whatever reasons, chose to say nothing on the matter and, having concluded his briefing, he turned towards Thompson.

"Let's get started sergeant." Thompson gestured the group forward.

"Spread out," he said, "skirmish order, but stay in contact." They started forward, moving across the width of the plateau, separating to cover a larger area of the more open ground. The ridge, with its litter of dead and wounded, was starting to change with the coming of the first of the light, and grisly and surreal sights were now emerging from the darkness. Scattered around the summit, a few men still rummaged among the fallen, and Daniel Ryan watched them work as he moved among them.

Some men, but by no means all, would not plunder those who remained alive, he could see them doing it, moving on past those who still moved, instead to concentrate their attention on what remained on the bodies of the dead or the unconscious. Daniel himself had always been one of these. There was something disconcerting about taking from a man who still moved and breathed, and often such treatment would inflict further agony on those who had already suffered much. The thought made his teeth grind and his blood turn. Up here, he reflected, there were plenty who were past any kind of help, but there could be nothing of value left on the great majority of them, though still these most persistent foragers prowled and rummaged.

Numbers of the wounded were still conscious, some stretching out their hands even now, as the detail drew close, crying and entreating for help. A few of the Company B men halted and fingered their canteens, but on Thompson's brief growl, this abruptly ceased and they moved on without further pause. Daniel Ryan, and likely some others also, gazed straight ahead, shutting out the pathetic cries, the weakly grasping fingers and the ghastly sights that littered the ground all around them. They left the hilltop to descend its farther, gentler slope, where the trees grew a shade sparser. There were fewer dead and wounded here, though the smoke seemed to hang thicker as they moved down into the lower ground, where some of those who lay here had clearly crawled after being injured up on the summit.

The Company B group passed through them, moving on into a further belt of thicker wood which led on to end abruptly at the edge of an open field. They started across, and before having gone very far, came to a dirt road. Carson waved them to the left to follow its path, back into the trees that bordered the field. They pushed through the obstructions once more and it was after they had been doing this for some time that Daniel Ryan began to hear faint noises. Coming to him, among the renewed cries and calls of yet more wounded, were the sounds of voices, not those of injured men but more measured talk, as though orders or advice of some kind were being given, distinguishable even among the accompanying litany of cries and groans from suffering men. Daniel looked across towards Winder, who was out to his left beyond Jenkins.

"I hear it," he told him softly. He turned towards Ballard, who was out to his right, seeing him nod also. They grasped their weapons, feeling in pouches and pockets for caps as they moved stealthily on, starting to see signs of movement beyond the next thicket. A crude path, little more than a trampled-down way, led from the dirt road around and through more trees and brush, and the men gathered towards it, moving along it stealthily as it curved away to the right through the woods. Daniel Ryan held the cap he had selected between his thumb and forefinger as he pulled the hammer of the Enfield back to half-cock, hearing the others successively doing likewise as they continued along the rough path. He felt his heart rate increasing as they followed the tracks, for already there were signs of what lay ahead, significant among them being the increasing groans and screams of the wounded men and presence of many more flies swarming around the approaching detail.

But it was the cries themselves that had awakened a memory in Daniel Ryan, for they were not the calls for help of wounded men who lay on the field. Rather, these were the shouts and shrieks of men in renewed torment and he had heard such cries before. Up ahead, Carson raised his hand to halt them.

"Bayonets," he said, as they closed upon him, his voice little more than a whisper, "and no noise." The steel blades scraped from their scabbards, some of them clinking or scraping gently as they were fitted over the musket muzzles and twisted into place. As the sounds continued Carson waved them forward again and the group moved off, following the curve of the track as it led onwards, still to the right, but Ryan knew already what they were about to come upon. At last the way ahead began to widen as it veered around the next clump

150

of trees and undergrowth to reveal the beginnings of a clearing, as the increasing smells of blood and death came to them. There were movements ahead through the branches and leaves and then the first of a series of tents came into view, stretching away in a row. Even though he already knew, Daniel Ryan stiffened as he once again saw the sights, heard the sounds and, above all, smelled the overpowering stink of a field hospital in the aftermath of a battle.

Day had almost come, but the first grey light was softened by the remains of the mist and smoke that gave the scene a surreal appearance, softening its images, though there was no diminishing of the noises or the smells. A succession of tables stretched along in front of the tents and at each of them laboured a surgeon and his helpers, clad in blood-stained aprons. The nearest of them looked around towards the group of southerners as they approached around that final bend, half-deploying across the open ground as they came, without pausing for so much as an instant in what he was doing.

"Reckoned you boys'd be along," he growled, as the Company B men moved past his table.

"We ain't stayin' around here," Thompson immediately snapped, as some of the detail began to make for where a pile of equipment lay. "Git whatever ya need and be ready to move on."

At one side of the clearing lay the dead. Long lines of them, some more clothed than others and it was there some of the detail headed towards, seeking the things they lacked. Daniel Ryan went with them, seeing a pile of shoes near one end of the lines of dead. White and Thorne were already there and he joined them, immediately reaching down, seeking shoes that looked like some kind of a fit. He lifted a shoe, turning it over in his right hand as he balanced the Enfield with his left. It was in pretty good condition, he reflected as he dropped it beside his foot to confirm the size. Satisfied, he pulled the knot in the lace of his own right shoe before straightening up and helping it off with his left foot. He stepped into the replacement, using his finger to lever the heel

151

into place, before moving his foot around inside as he tested the fit. It was slightly large, but the thick woollen socks he had plundered earlier would help that. He sought out the left shoe and repeated the process before crouching to lace them both, balancing his musket on the inside of his shoulder as he did so. All the while at the tables, little more than touching distance from where he straightened up, the cutting and the screams continued without let up, grinding on the senses and searing the mind.

The Company B men learned, from brief snatches of talk with some of the orderlies, that the Yankee army had indeed retreated in the direction of Chattanooga. Most of it had seemingly been driven from the field early on in the fight, some time around noon the previous day, they were told. The remainder, who had gathered to defend this northern portion of the enemy line, had followed them in the course of the evening. The Yankees had shown some interest in the fact that they were from Virginia, and in the succeeding minutes, as word went around, several of them had made their way over when their work had brought them closer, to exchange brief comments with the arrivals.

"You boys from Lee's army?"

"You Virginia boys sure enough?"

"They told us a whole mess o' Lee's boys were on their way out here."

"Has Old Man Lee come out here hisself?" As the light grew, the inevitable question followed.

"How come you reb's got blue duds?"

Daniel Ryan having outfitted himself over the previous hours now lacked only a water canteen. He moved across to a further equipment pile, flexing his feet in the unfamiliar shoes, where a group of his companions were already going through the contents, seeking a canteen. They were there in plenty and Daniel helped himself to a fabric-covered one, feeling by its weight that it was almost empty.

Jenkins had arrived at the shoe pile, prowling through what remained, and Daniel glanced at him before starting across, casting his eyes around the remaining shoes, and seeing almost immediately that only excessively small or large sizes, or badly worn footwear still remained. The boy straightened up and shrugged across at Daniel.

"Nothin' that looks like my size," he said.

"Check on the dead Yankees then," Daniel told him, but he could see immediately by the boy's manner, a reluctance to take this option. Maybe it was the idea of plundering under the eyes of the surgeons and orderlies who had tended these men that was discouraging the boy, who was after all still relatively inexperienced in the realities of soldiering. Ballard also had come across and Daniel was aware of him watching Jenkins as he hesitated.

"You can let your scruples stop you if you want," Daniel told the boy, "and maybe that'll make you feel all righteous for a while. But come winter, in a few more weeks, and your feet are in the ice and mud, you'll wish you hadn't done that." Beside him Ballard grunted in agreement. The corporal shrugged and turned to go and then, turned back briefly to Jenkins.

"If yo're doin' it'," he growled, "you better git on with it cuz we'll be gone soon." Daniel looked back at the boy, seeing doubt in his expression. Here in this place, it probably seemed worse than out on the field, but need was greater than delicacy.

Jenkins nodded finally and turned away, starting across the clearing, stepping carefully as he went among the rows of suffering men and hurrying orderlies, coming at last to the rows of those who had not survived, their numbers still increasing as orderlies brought yet more dead men to lengthen the already long rows. Daniel saw the boy start along the first line, noting that some of these men's shoes had already been taken, for their bare feet protruded prominently, white, as those of the dead always did. Jenkins moved along the first rank, peering at the shoes that remained, but it was not until he had started along the next row that he stopped, having probably come across a pair of shoes on a dead soldier that

153

seemed to suit him. Daniel saw him bend to pull them from the Yankee's feet, placing the first shoe on the ground beside his own foot to take a rough measurement. Daniel started towards him as he bent to take the other shoe, just as the two orderlies arrived with yet another body. Daniel looked around at them as he approached, seeing their faces as they laid the corpse in place and turned towards Jenkins.

They looked for only a second or so before they moved away, saying nothing, but, Jenkins had seen them also. He stopped what he was doing until they had turned away before returning to the shoes, his face flushed in embarrassment. He pulled the remaining shoe from the dead man's foot before loosening his laces, removing his own shoes and stepping into the newly acquired ones. They were good, being near enough new, and as close to a proper fit as made no difference. He laced them and turned to Daniel.

"I ain't never done anythin' like that before," he said, "and them two made it worse, like it weren't right."

"Ignore them," Daniel told him. "If you waited for the likes o' them to agree you'd never get anything. D'you think shoes're any use to him," He gestured towards the dead man as he spoke, and it was as he glanced at the corpse that he noticed, protruding from the man's shirt pocket, the leather thong that had previously been hidden by his tunic.

He stepped across, bent over the man and reached out his fingers to yank on it, revealing a little bag of brown leather. Resting his musket on the crook of his elbow, he grasped the bag and, as Jenkins watched, he pulled the drawstring loose before emptying the contents into his other hand, peering at them as they tumbled from the bag. He recognised the pricker and the bullet worm immediately, though the former was obviously manufactured, unlike the improvised versions carried by most in Company B. They made do with any sort of a spike, a nail fashioned to a sharper point, with, at best, its other end also sharpened, to aid in embedding it into some kind of improvised handle. This one however was a cast tool, with its spike at right angles to its shaft and the handle fashioned from the same piece of steel.

The worm also was cast from steel, with its base having a worked socket to fit over and screw onto the end of the musket ramrod.

Daniel peered at it briefly before turning the contents over in his hand to examine the remaining items that had lain obscured by the two most familiar tools. The links of a chain moved in his hand, with a split ring at one end and what must be a nipple cover at the other. Daniel had heard of these, but had never come across one before, since like so many other things, they were improvised in the southern army. They fitted between the hammer and the musket nipple, keeping the latter dry in wet weather, with the ring capable of insertion around the trigger guard to keep the cover safe. He picked it up and showed it to Jenkins, seeing the boy peer at it.

"If you'd been more thorough, you'd've gotten these," he told him.

The last of the bag's contents was a barrel plug, but again it was of a type that Daniel had never seen before. Most southern soldiers made do with either scraps of cloth or bottle corks, with the latter sometimes bored through to accommodate a piece of string or rawhide which could be tied through the musket sling for safe keeping. This however was, like its companions, a much more cultured piece of equipment, consisting of a wooden plug, embedded into a ringed, steel handle. The plug itself was quartered, to allow it to compress when being inserted into the barrel, holding its place there and sealing the muzzle by expanding to grip the inside.

Daniel looked at it, admiring the simplicity and the utility of the thing, holding it up for Jenkins to see as the thought came to him. Didn't this latest find simply emphasise the way things were and had always been in this war? While the Confederate troops largely made do with improvised and make-do tools and equipment, the damned Yankees, with all those factories up north that could manufacture just about

155

anything that their soldiers needed, producing these kinds of things by the thousand. Wasn't this just a typical instance of their enemies' abundance of everything needed to fight a war? It was like the combination cutlery piece that he had foraged earlier and, even more pointedly, those damned repeater rifles that they had been faced with the previous afternoon. Their supplies of all kinds were so plentiful, while their southern opponents laboured under shortages of so many things. Daniel shook his head briefly as he returned the tools to the bag and pulled the drawstring tight again before pushing the bag into his pants pocket.

"What's plain stealin' back home is different when you're soldierin'," he told Jenkins. "There ain't any ten commandments around here, especially when the winter comes. You should know by now that loyalty and honest dealin' is for them in your mess and maybe the company, as far as the rest go, you take what you need when you get the chance. If you don't learn that, you'll only make things tougher on yourself."

He slid his musket down the inside of his forearm, gripping the stock with his left hand and kicking the butt up with his foot for his right hand to grasp, and started back to where Ballard still waited, aware that Jenkins was following. Ballard grinned briefly at him and shook his head.

"Schoolin' done fer now?" he muttered. Daniel nodded, as Thompson's voice called on them to assemble and they made to where the sergeant waited with Carson, and then formed in a rough line in front of them.

"Time to git goin'," Thompson told them. "We got more important things t' do than stay around here and plunder Yankees, so let's git to it."

"How far are we goin' Joe?" Abe White inquired of the sergeant. "We know the Yankees have gone now and we know where."

"As far as he says," Thompson told him, indicating towards Carson with his thumb.

"Thought we had cavalry fer reconoiterin' and sech," Thorne commented.

"Maybe ya want to transfer then," Thompson told him. "That way ya might git a horse to bitch at and maybe give me a rest."

The morning was wearing on and the sun had some time since burned away the remaining wisps of mist as they ascended, following a road that led up into what appeared to be a gap in the higher ridge that dominated the north western skyline. Two detachments of Forrest's cavalry had passed in the course of the ascent and Carson had conferred briefly with the officers of each, as the men clattered by on their lean looking horses which Daniel Ryan reckoned would have benefitted from a few more decent feeds. The way was littered with abandoned equipment; clothing, hats, muskets and loose cartridges, with the inevitable scraps of paper blowing around on the wisps of breeze.

All along this stretch of the road, there lay a succession of abandoned wagons. Some of them had been burned and their ashes lay, identifiable only by some part, wheel rims or part of the frame that the flames had not completely destroyed. Others simply stood with their loads intact, while still more had been rifled and plundered, with the contents of broached boxes of ammunition and rations mixing with the general litter along the road. The vehicles without exception had been rendered immovable, with the spokes of their wheels splintered and broken. The teams of some were missing, but others, with just one exception, had been shot dead. They lay surrounded by swarms of flies, their blood dried in pools on the dirt of the road. For the mules of that one wagon however, the ordeal was worse than the brief impact of a bullet. These animals had instead been hamstrung and death had not yet released them from their torment. They remained in their harness just alive, with their sad eyes resting accusingly on this latest passing procession of men whose cruel insanity had inflicted this fate upon them. Thompson waited as the file of

157

his men moved past, having borrowed Carson's pistol and he dispatched each animal in turn, with the shots echoing flatly in the early morning air.

The Company B men helped themselves to as much of the abandoned food as they were able to carry, getting a supply of salted beef and a collection of hardtacks, which was packed away into haversacks.

"Helluva place this," Jones declared. "More plunder'n a man kin carry. I tell ya, out here's nothin' like it is back in Virginia."

Occasional bodies also lay along the sides of the road, their presence marked by further swarms of flies, and as the Company B patrol moved steadily up towards the shoulder of the ridge, Daniel Ryan began to wonder just how much had been achieved the previous day. Not even in the aftermath of Second Manassas had they seen sights like this in the wake of an enemy skedaddle, for this now had all the appearances of a rout about it. The scenes along this road spoke not of a mere retreat, but of much large scale disorganisation, suggesting wild haste or maybe even panic, among the withdrawing enemy, and if this was so, it clearly indicated the scale of the opportunity that now beckoned to the southern army. Ballard summed it up when, having stared this way and that at the debris along the road, he pronounced on it to those around him.

"There's a dozen o' us headin' up this here road, when the whole god-damned army should be along here on these Yankees' tails. They are there for the takin' and all Bragg has t' do is give the damned order." Some of his companions paid little heed to his words, though others glanced around at him as they continued up the road.

"But will he," Winder growled at length?

"If he don't," Kane replied, "then he ain't worth a shit as a general."

Whether it was Carson's inexperience, as White and Thorne had suggested, or some deeper military reason that he had overlooked to share with his men, the hike to the north continued. They reached the top of the gap near noon, and with the shoulder of the ridge still ascending on either side, came upon a cavalry picket, Forrest's men again, who had more information about the enemy.

"That there's Rossville. Chattanooga's on a piece and whatever o' the Yankees ain't there a'ready are on their way there," a grizzled sergeant told them. "The last o' them's pullin' back across the valley yonder, but they ain't overly keen t' go. You boys'd be better plantin' yore asses hereabout, at least till the ginrals git organised about what they want to do about it." Carson, as a result had detached Thorne and White to wait at the roadside while the remainder of the detail accompanied him on a further ascent of the ridge to the northward.

The ascent took a further half hour, but the effort was rewarded when they reached the ridge crest. From there it was possible for the Company B detail to look out over the whole of the area that stretched away to the north and west, towards where a considerable river, the Tennessee, so Carson announced, looped its way across the landscape, with a city, Chattanooga presumably, situated on its near bank. Out in front they could see a picket of cavalry, presumably more of Forrest's men, at the beginning of the descent, while lower down on an expanse of flatter land between the bottom of the ridge and the city, there were still formations of Yankees, rearguards most likely, making their way on towards the fortifications that surrounded the city.

For Daniel Ryan, by far the most striking feature of the scene, more than anything that the Yankees were doing, was its sheer grandeur, for nature had spared little in its efforts to impress. The land that stretched from the foot of the ridge where they now stood, was relatively flat as it extended away towards the river, but over to the west this expanse of lower ground was enclosed by an imposing mountain, higher by a considerable margin, than the ridge line that they had just ascended, which loomed from over to their left on towards the river, some way to the west of the city. The ridge on which they stood seemed to stretch from almost the southernmost shoulder of the mountain away north eastwards, closing towards the river as it went, and framing Chattanooga and the area of flatter ground around it, into something of an irregular triangle. The Tennessee River itself formed the northern side of that triangle, but it was far from straight in its progress to the west. It first appeared beyond the northern extremity of the ridge line, flowing west, but soon its route veered almost at right angles, moving southwards for a stretch, only to turn to the west once more as it came up to the city, the only man made feature of this valley.

Chattanooga lay on the south bank of this portion of the river, where its westward flow had been resumed, but this direction too continued only briefly, for hardly had the Tennessee passed the city when it changed direction once more, commencing a giant hairpin loop that saw it flow south again for maybe a mile, only to virtually retrace its progress by means of a tight further loop that turned it back northwards, leaving a peninsula of land confined within it. Having enclosed this finger of land, the portion of it nearest to the hairpin bend covered with scrubby woods, the river continued northwards, vanishing between the finger of land to the east and the imposing mountain to the west.

The city of Chattanooga was, to Daniel Ryan's eye, the least impressive part of the whole scene, dwarfed as it was in size and grandeur by the river and the mountains. It was also not that much of a city, being no more than a town of pretty modest proportions, smaller than Richmond, or even Atlanta. South of the town, a railroad depot could be made out, into which several railroads fed their tracks and this, along with the buildings of the town, lay within a great arc of earthworks clearly visible from their elevated position. Spaced along the fortifications were the Yankees. Daniel Ryan squinted as he gazed at the scene. It was as the hospital orderlies had said. The enemy retreat had brought them this far only, for here they were clearly settling, occupying the defensive lines

160

around the city, where strong points and minor forts linked the trench lines that had been dug to enclose and protect it. The reddish-brown trench lines stretched southwards from the river bank to the west of Chattanooga, flanking a further sizeable hill that rose beyond the western margin of the town, then moving gradually around to the east in a curve that took them to a strongpoint which guarded the south east approach to the town. From there they zig-zagged their way back northwards, ending at the river above Chattanooga. Yes, the Yankees were still there, Ryan reflected, and from the positions that they had already occupied, it certainly didn't look like they intended leaving anytime soon.

Having scrutinised the scene at some length, the lieutenant summoned Linus Cooper, and dispatched him, together with Norton and Bentley, to take word of this development back to the major, for having skedaddled as far as the city and the river, the main bulk of the enemy now seemed disinclined to go any further. There was traffic on the distant bridge across the river, but the great majority of the troops down there were going nowhere, instead being engaged in setting up camps all around the city. It therefore remained to be seen, having driven the Yankees from the field yesterday, what Bragg and the rest of the generals would do in order to take advantage of that success.

Chapter 6 A Stuck Up Prideful Little Son of a Bitch

The men of the detail were organised into duty watches by Thompson, while they waited for orders from Randolph. Those orders arrived late that evening with the return of Cooper and his companions. The instructions came from Preston, who, Cooper confirmed, had finally arrived with the balance of the regiment, and the colonel's message was simple. Carson and his wayward detail should stay put, observe the enemy and await the brigade's arrival. The lieutenant ordered the off watch men to set up a bivouac camp, away from the road but overlooking the southern approach, which would enable them to observe the arrival of further friendly formations, while reducing the distance that the men heading for the ridge crest to take their turn on watch, had to climb to reach their station. Fires were kindled, water collected and the Yankee rations were produced for cooking, going into a stirabout stew for Ryan's mess, which was promptly dispatched, while around them the evening turned to darkness.

Late the following morning the first infantry began to arrive, proving to be men of their own division. Kershaw's brigade led, and the Company B men watched as its regiments filed successively past, with Humphries and Bryan's men following. As a result it was the afternoon when Wofford's troops arrived, including the Ogeechee Volunteers, with their separated companies reunited at last. They plodded up the road to where Carson's men were still camped below the crest of the long ridge, and on being informed of their approach, the lieutenant descended in person to meet them, accompanied by Cooper, Norton and Bentley. The regiment was halted, and after consultations, the men set up camp, having brought with them a welter of further rumours to be passed on to those in camp and on watch by the returning

Cooper and his companions, as to what was most likely to happen next on the heels of Sunday's great victory.

Bragg, the newly arrived men had said, had ordered the army forward across the Tennessee, to the east of Chattanooga, aiming to force the Yankees from their fortifications around the city and make them fight again before they could recover from the licking they had already received. This was welcome enough news, but having come this far along the road that led directly towards the city, their own column was now halted here on the ridge just short of Chattanooga, facing the Yankee positions. This led to much more gossip among the men, for it was immediately clear to those of both the advance detail and no doubt also to the arriving men, that their own division, having been moved up towards the defences of Chattanooga itself, would have great difficulty in being part of any advance across the river.

As night fell the lights of the city together with a great curve of twinkling campfires around it, marked where the enemy were and where they seemed intent on remaining. Could their own presence here signify that Bragg no longer intended pressing that enemy into a further fight to complete Sunday's victory, or was their own division simply not to be included in that fight? The talk coursed up and down the bivouacs. What kind of a general detached the most recently arrived division of his reinforcements from the main body if a fight was pending, especially when half of that division had not been in action at all on Sunday? Things were certainly different out here in Tennessee, the men of Company B repeatedly told each other.

The pause on the ridge lasted only until the following morning, which dawned misty and cold again. The regiment was roused at first light, and with those of Carson's detail having breakfasted on more of their foraged rations, the company was assembled in marching order, ready to step off as the sun began to burn the mist away. The road descended from the ridge, moving steadily down onto the flatter land,

163

with the departing mist revealing more and more of the landscape and the approaches to the city. As they closed on the fortifications they heard a crackle of musketry from ahead, soon followed by the heavier boom of artillery, as the leading formations, Kershaw's men presumably, pushed any remaining Yankees into the Chattanooga defence lines.

The shooting slowly subsided as they crossed a further creek before following the regimental column off the road to the west, finally setting up camp near to midday in the fields between the creek and a large but neglected house. Pickets were ordered forward while the remaining men were stood down. Weapons were stacked and belongings piled and this done, details immediately set out, with water parties heading back to the creek, while those seeking firewood dispersed to scour sections of the woods that were scattered across the area. There was no rations issue, so the mess was left to make the best it could of what remained from their foraging on the road. The talk was still of the next move and already the rumours were circulating. The Yankees would go, once the army was across the river and threatening their rear. It therefore only remained for the men of their own division to get their camps set up and await developments.

But things did not go as the rumours had predicted. Over the succeeding days, instead of having crossed the river to force the Yankees into another fight, unit by unit, the rest of the army began to appear on the approaches to the city of Chattanooga. The mountains and ridges all around the city were successively occupied by the southern army, though along the "Blues" portion of the line, which lay to the south of the Chattanooga, the battle lines were closer to the city. To their left were the brigades of Hood's division, now commanded by Micah Jenkins, said to be a favourite of Longstreet's, especially since "Old Pete" was, for whatever reason, not disposed to confirm Evander Law in the command he had held since Gettysburg. To the right of their own division, on the other side of the creek which formed the boundary between the two commands, the men of Stewart's

164

Army of Tennessee division had now arrived to take station. "Old Straight", for so the general was referred to by his men, commanded brigades of Louisiana and Alabama boys, with some Tennessee and Georgia regiments for good measure. Contact was made between the pickets and with the water details, who made their way to the creek with their bundles of canteens, but there seemed to be little expectation among Stewart's men of anything happening in any sort of hurry.

"That's Bragg fer ya," they told the Virginia contingent. "He gits the Yankees set up fer a real lickin' and then sits on his butt, watchin' them reinforce or git away, while he argues with the bishop and the other generals. We'll be sittin' around here till the Yankees are too strong to shift out o' there. That's jest the way ol' Braxton Bragg does things." Perhaps it was supporting evidence for these depressing predictions that there was no word yet of anything, other than establishing camp, setting out outposts and organising duty details for the various regiments and brigades, and as this proceeded growing misgivings spread among the men. Doing nothing, when an already beaten enemy lay straight out in front, did not seem to be any sort of a way to follow up a victory, and while nobody was in any great hurry to see an immediate repeat of Sunday's bloodbath, simply sitting seemed to be handing that enemy a welcome gift of time which he was likely use as profitably, and maybe even more usefully, than his southern besiegers so far seemed inclined to do. With the army now stationing itself on the great arc of high ground that hemmed Chattanooga in on the south side of the Tennessee River, numbers of its enlisted men were now openly questioning the tactics of Braxton Bragg. Having spent a dismal forfeit of blood in driving the Yankee army from the battlefield down on Chickamauga Creek, he was apparently now content to sit on the top of this ridge line, as Stewart's men had said, and watch them recover.

Nothing more had been heard of the thrust across the Tennessee to force another fight, and with the substance of his army now camped around Chattanooga, the idea seemed to be little more than that intended by the general. It was being said that no southern troops, save for elements of the cavalry, had crossed to the northern side of the Tennessee, and the upshot of this was that the Yankees, having already been given near to a week since the battle to recover, were being left to their own devices in the city. Having chased them into Chattanooga, Bragg was leaving them in comparative peace there, opting for a siege instead of anything more aggressive.

The enlisted men were immediately sceptical. What kind of a siege was this, they asked, where only the routes on the southern side of the river were closed to the enemy? Many heads were being shaken in disapproval. It surely was not the way that "Marse Bob" would have handled things, the Virginia contingent assured each other. At best, what Bragg was settling for was a gentle squeeze on the Yankee windpipe, way short of the full-blooded throttling of the enemy that the situation required. By allowing the Yankees to stay in the city, Bragg was inviting them to recover their organisation, send for reinforcements and generally get themselves back into fighting trim before the next brawl. While they did that however, the Army of Tennessee, having already been reinforced from Virginia, Mississippi and Eastern Tennessee, could expect no further help. It was as strong as it was going to get, while the Yankees, if permitted to hang on in Chattanooga, however beleaguered they might be there for the next while, would almost certainly be the focus for all kinds of reinforcements from all across the mid-west and likely from further afield also.

There were plenty more Yankees, or so Stewart's men told them. The powerful enemy army that had that very summer captured the fortress of Vicksburg and occupied the last part of the Mississippi valley, was reportedly inactive. Would the Yankee high command not now be galvanised into activity, dispatching at least some of these men immediately, to assist the defeated and besieged troops on the Tennessee? Once they gathered their ample strength, the enemy would inevitably outnumber and outgun the Confederate force facing them. All that these defeated Yankees had to do was hang on in

Chattanooga and help would come to them. By simply sitting his army on the hills and ridges around the city, Bragg was letting this happen, and the consequences of it all would likely be serious for both him and his men. Inactivity now, while the enemy got started on their recovery, was as good as throwing away the fruits of the victory that had been won at such cost last week. The sentiments, and also the words that Kane had used about Bragg back on the road near Rossville, were therefore now being heard from many men in the newly set up camps.

"He ain't worth a shit as a general."

With McLaws' division established in its place in the siege lines between the eastern shoulder of the imposing Lookout Mountain and Chattanooga Creek, Company B found their allotted camp space along the bank of one of the smaller streams that fed eastwards into the creek and while this made the collecting of water a pretty simple exercise, it imposed problems on the men in other ways. The Confederate picket line was thrown forward not quite to the main creek itself, and with the meandering course that the waterway followed, the pickets had the creek on three sides in the sector held by their units. As the days passed, all along the line the strategy seemed to be little more than sitting and waiting for the Yankees to starve themselves, rather than tackling the job of getting it done with any degree of energy.

Chattanooga Creek wriggled northwards along the eastern flank of the division's positions, flowing towards the city before abruptly turning westwards, to meander its way between the picket lines of the two armies as it zig-zagged on its final stretch to empty into the Tennessee River at the northern foot of the great bulk of Lookout Mountain. In places its banks formed tall gullies on either or both sides of the stream, while in others it flowed along almost level with its banks, allowing a man to see for some distance out across to where the enemy positions were set up, while the Yankees undoubtedly did likewise.

Looking out across the flatter portions of the creek towards the river beyond, McLaws' pickets could see portions of the enemy lines, to the north of which lay the city itself and those railroads that passed just to the south of Chattanooga. Immediately to the west of the city lay the bulk of Cameron Hill, obscuring the view of that portion of the river. Stretching south west from Chattanooga was the Chattanooga and Nashville Railroad, which crossed Chattanooga Creek almost at its junction with the river and in company with the road west from the city, traced a route along the tiny margin of land that lay wedged between the foot of Lookout Mountain and the southerly loop of the river. Up at Chattanooga itself, the Tennessee was now spanned by pontoon bridges, connecting the city with the northern bank of the river, over which a trickle of supplies were rumoured to be reaching both the Yankee defenders and such of the civilian population that remained there. What was arriving was said to be well short of what was required to sustain them indefinitely but, in spite of the activities of Brigadier General Joe Wheeler's southern cavalry up to the north of the river, it was clearly sufficient to enable them to hold out in the Chattanooga lines, thus prolonging the siege and allowing the Yankee high command to figure out how best to relieve the place and then to get on and do it.

As the days passed the enemy lines grew visibly stronger, with much more digging and fortifying going on, and by common consent, were now well past the stage at which they might have been assaulted with any prospect of success. If not attack, the men told each other, then why not manoeuvre the Yankees out of the place? Push across the river, upstream or downstream, and block off their final links with any source of help. Sitting and waiting for slow starvation to work was, at best, a risky business.

Everyone knew that the Yankees had endless resources of men as well as everything else that they needed in order to fight, and there persisted a feeling that the southern army had now allowed itself to become involved a process of

168

reinforcement and re-supply that it could not win. The Yankees, with all of their manufacturing and transportation resources, would pour whatever was needed into Chattanooga, both men and munitions, that would eventually break this passive siege. Already there were rumours that Army of the Potomac units were being sent from Virginia, while further divisions were said to have started from the Mississippi River. Even if only parts of these stories were true, the time to finally crush these obstinate blue-bellies was finite and the opportunity would steadily decline until at length, sometime in the pretty near future, it would vanish altogether.

Duty watches were along the forward positions near the creek, from which the men on watch could see across the river to the city of Chattanooga itself. The place was not particularly large, nor was it particularly impressive, Daniel Ryan reflected in the course of one of his own watches. There was more of the frontier town character about it when compared with places like Williamsburg or Fredericksburg. As in other places that he had seen back in Virginia and had heard of out here to the west, the importance of Chattanooga seemed to be more in the railroads which met here, rather than with the city itself. The direct east to west line from Gordonsville in Virginia passed through Chattanooga, though it had seemingly been built in several different sections and was therefore called several different names in the course of its journey through the south west of Virginia and the eastern section of Tennessee. Up that rail line, a stretch to the east, was Knoxville, the place whose occupation by the Yankees had led to the journey of their own detachment from Virginia becoming diverted and prolonged, to the point that nearly half the infantry and all the artillery sent from the Army of Northern Virginia had missed the recent battle.

No, Chattanooga was nothing to write home about, but the Yankees still had it. The campaign that had been launched with all of those reinforcements, sent from different places to drive them away from it and back up into middle Tennessee, had succeeded only in driving them into the place. They sat across there behind their defensive trench lines, but they were starving slowly, so the rumours said. Perhaps, some men reckoned, Bragg and the generals might be right. Perhaps it might after all be only a matter of waiting, allowing hunger to work its course, and the place could fall without further bloodshed. This was the strategy that Bragg had seemingly adopted and it sounded simple when it was talked about in camp, but sometimes waiting could seem more like inaction and hesitancy, and Daniel regularly found himself wondering which of all these terms really applied to what the general was doing.

As for rations, the misgivings, voiced by Thompson and others, were soon proved correct. Back in Virginia, the food staples had mainly consisted of a beef or bacon meat ration, with flour for bread and periodic issues of hardtacks and seasonal vegetables. Tennessee quickly proved to be different in this respect. The standard ration turned out to be corn, almost always unparched, with only a small bacon ration accompanying it. To make matters worse, the ration was even less regular than in Virginia, which threw the men into the practice of bargaining for extra food at local homes and farms. Since leaving Virginia the men had been under orders to maintain four days cooked rations. This soon proved utterly impractical and as time began to pass the amount of food held in the men's possession steadily dwindled until by the final days of September, most men were engaged in a hand to mouth existence, with nothing at all in reserve.

Those initial days in the lines around Chattanooga saw a continuation of the dry weather, but it also saw an undesirable practice quickly establish itself, one that had become decidedly uncommon over the previous year along the Rappahannock River in Virginia. Outpost shooting was, to many, particularly those who had come from Virginia, a pointless exercise that killed and crippled good men for no good reason. Having begun on their arrival in front of the enemy positions, it reduced picket line duties to tense, nervy episodes, and as the days began to pass and there was no cessation in the sniping, talk among the messes of Company B began to focus on the problem and on what, if anything, could be done about it.

It was on Ballard's watch that Kane and Ryan, tiring like everyone else in the company of crawling around the bottom land like moles, asked him for permission to try to make contact with the nearest Yankees, to arrange with them to put a stop to the damned foolishness of outpost firing, at least on their own section of the lines. The corporal looked at them, with an unconvinced expression on his face, before answering.

"If that's the way you want to spend yore damned time out here," he said, "then I ain't gonna stop ya, but, if either one o' ya finishes up with an extra hole or two in his hide, then don't say I didn't warn ya." Kane and Ryan nodded and promptly moved away, heading out to where they knew Jones and Jenkins were already on watch. They crawled the last part of the way, as was now common practice, due to the risk of attracting a shot, and moved along a route which used the uneven ground and features like particular trees and brush patches for cover, finally reaching the picket point where Jones sat, in the lee of a small rise in the ground. He turned as they approached, while beyond him the figure of Jenkins came into view.

Along the Confederate line, a succession of "gopher hole" trenches had been dug, except in those places where the ground itself could be adapted by a breastwork, and this was the option taken up here by Company B. The little rise where they had set up their picket position, and where Jenkins now lay almost prone, had a shovelled earth and stones parapet, with a top log for good measure.

"Surely ain't time yet," Jones said softly, "not by a ways." A few feet away at the top of the rise, Jenkins looked around as he heard the words. Kane put his finger to his lips as the

171

two newcomers moved up to settle beside the boy and briefly peer out across the top log.

"We're gonna try and do somethin' about this," Kane told him, in a tone that was a little more than a whisper.

"Somethin' about what," was the response from Jenkins from his place at the parapet, "the war, or this here siege or what?"

"This stupid sharp-shootin'," Ryan said. "We're goin' to try and talk to the Yankees out there and see if they'll see sense." Jones was sceptical.

"The Yankees?" he retorted "Strikes me that these western boys do it cuz they like it. Either that or they ain't as smart as the other boys back east are."

"Maybe we'll try anyhow," Kane replied. "Can't make things much worse than they are a'ready. A man ain't safe out here." Jones shrugged, while Jenkins still watched from his place.

"You're goin' out there," he said, as the other two moved up beside him in turn, to scrutinise the enemy positions?

"If it's OK with you," Ryan replied, as he settled himself at the little parapet. "It's maybe more reliable than throwin' a message over, wrapped around a rock." Jenkins said nothing, contenting himself with shaking his head. Jones had moved up last and he too settled himself in beside the boy, before raising his head slightly, to squint out towards the enemy line.

"Where are they today?" Kane inquired, of nobody in particular.

"Same as before," was the reply from Jenkins, "past the tree a ways, the one on the far bank, that bigger one." He pointed, though Kane was still looking out towards the Yankees.

"Who's out on either flank?" he inquired eventually.

"Eli and Silas to the right, Abe and Charlie're on the other side." Kane looked around at them.

"Edwin, Daniel, maybe you boys could head over and tell 'em what's happenin' so they don't open up while we're out there."

172

"I'll go," Jenkins said quickly, sliding down the slope of the rise. He looked at them both a little sheepishly, as he straightened up into something between crouching and kneeling. "You two kin get yourselves ready, if you're serious about this," he added. Then he and Jones were gone, disappearing quickly into the brush in their respective directions.

"Let's give 'em a little while to git that done," Kane said. Daniel looked at him doubtfully.

"Let's wait till they git back," he returned. Kane grinned wryly at him.

"Don't have no sense of adventure, do ya Daniel?"

"Don't have any desire to catch a bullet if I don't need to," Daniel Ryan retorted.

"Shouldn't be out here at all then," his companion replied.

Jones was back within minutes, with Jenkins following after a further brief interval. Kane waited, looking around them all in turn, before raising himself up slowly onto his elbows.

"Hey Billy," he called. They all hunched down as he shouted, waiting for a response, be it a call or a shot, but there was nothing. They waited for some time, before Kane looked at Daniel.

"Your turn," he said. Daniel had expected it, but hardly welcomed the thought of shouting next, especially since the Yankees might already be drawing a bead on where the first shout came from. He moved back down the bank and along behind Jones, moving several yards to the left before pushing up the rise again. He raised himself slightly, taking a deep breath as he did so.

"Billy," he called, "Billy Yank!" He ducked down again, listening for a return shout, or worse.

Time passed, but then a distant voice finally came back.

"Whadya want reb?" Daniel Ryan looked across at Kane and the two of them exchanged conspiratorial smirks. Daniel pointed towards him and silently mouthed the words "Your turn!" Kane turned and looked out towards the Yankee picket line.

"Want to talk," he called, "got a message."

"Message from who?" came the eventual response?

"Message from the Governor o' Georgia," Kane replied, almost at once.

"That right," came the faint answer, though this time it came more promptly, "what does he want?" Daniel Ryan smiled briefly at this, for they were talking, not shooting, and there was now at least a chance that this might lead to something better. He looked over at Kane.

"Might as well get on with it," he said. His companion nodded.

"We wanna come across," he called, "if you boys'll hold your fire." There was a further pause at that, before the reply came back.

"Why in the hell d'ya wanna do that?" the voice called, with its northern twang clearly recognisable.

"Reckon we're jest naturally sociable, southern boys," Kane answered. There was a pause, which seemed long to Daniel Ryan but in reality could only have been seconds. He lay and looked at Kane.

"Maybe they ain't as sociable as you are," he muttered, but then the next shout came across.

"Come ahead! We won't shoot, but don't bring no weapons." Jenkins looked at them.

"You're goin' over there unarmed?" he said. Daniel shook his head.

"Why the hell not," he retorted. "We want to talk to them, not shoot them and even if we took a couple of damned cannon, what chance would we have if they decided to shoot us or keep us over there?" He looked again at Kane.

"Let's get on with it," he said, rising to his feet and passing his musket to Jones as his heart began to thump in his chest. Kane did likewise, and with a final glance at each other, they stepped across the top log and started towards the enemy line.

Daniel Ryan could feel his heart pounding and his legs trembling as he walked, with his feet pulling and swishing in the long grass. Why this was as bad as the prospect of any fight? What had seemed like a good idea back at the grand post, and had even seemed clever enough out here on the outpost line, had suddenly become extremely serious. If any of these Yankees was in a mood to shoot them, or if any had simply not heard the brief shouted exchange, then each of them, out in the open and unarmed, was a sitting duck. The slightest move that the enemy pickets didn't like and the shot could come, and at this range with no cover, that would be the end of it all. Maybe these western Yankees were simply more set on fighting and killing than the Potomac boys back in Virginia were, but it was too late to worry about that now. If they hesitated or made to go back, that could well be the move that would bring the bullet, for right now they would be squarely in the sights of any number of the enemy. Daniel inwardly thanked providence that neither of them was wearing any foraged Yankee clothing, for that could be the thing that could end any prospect of a safe return.

They reached the bank of the creek and moved slowly along for a short way, seeking a place to cross without having to wade too much. Eventually they came upon a place where the watercourse widened, shallowing as a result. He nodded to Kane and they picked their way over, using rocks as far as possible. Near the middle however they had to settle for wading a short stretch, with the water midway up their lower legs as they sloshed over. Having reached the far bank they squelched on through the long grass, trying to catch a sight of the tree that Jenkins had pointed out as a marker.

As they drew closer Daniel Ryan looked more closely at the ground beyond. Eventually his eyes caught a movement, out ahead and to their left and he became aware of a figure dressed in drab, faded blue, rising from the ground and waving them forward. He looked at Kane and they both altered their course towards the man, stepping slowly and deliberately as they approached where he stood.

175

"Well, ain't that somethin'," the Yankee said gently as they came up to him. "Reb's in blue." He looked at them again as he slung his musket, a Springfield, Daniel Ryan noticed, rather than any sort of repeater, on its strap. "Ain't our blue, reb', his voice hardened, "or is it?" Daniel looked back at him.

"It's grey," he said. "This is what grey looks like in Richmond these days." A faint shadow of humour crossed the Yankee's face as he pointed on to his left rear.

"Mick reb's too," he added, allowing himself a slightly wider grin as they passed.

"Down there," he said. "Must be a hell of a message you got, if it's worth riskin' yore damn necks for." Ryan and Kane moved on past the man, coming almost immediately to a crude breastwork which they stepped across before dropping down to the trench beyond. It was more of a barrier than a trench for it had no rear, consisting of a thrown up earth and stone wall several yards in length, with a parapet of logs set on top. Three other Yankees, one of them wearing a corporal's stripes, waited to the rear of the breastwork, scrutinising their arrival keenly as they moved away from the barrier. The Yankee who had guided them in arrived behind them, stepping down in turn.

"Look at these Richmond uniforms," he said. "These ain't no ornery reb's, these're Bobby Lee's boys. Reckon we got ourselves some real important visitors today." The corporal eyed them briefly before speaking.

"Now what's so important today that makes a bullet or a berth in the stockade worth the risk?" he eventually growled.

"We ain't been out here long," Daniel Ryan told them, "but we're already sick and tired of the way things are around here." The Yankees exchanged looks.

"Why, what could be the problem," the corporal said, with exaggerated punctiliousness, while around him, the other three exchanged smirks. Encouraged, Daniel Ryan steeled himself, moved across to an ammunition box and sat down on it.

176

"Maybe you boys all like doin' things different out here," he said, "but bein' visitors from the east, we surely ain't used to it. When we go on outpost duty, we look forward to the chance of some peace and quiet and maybe even to catch up on a wink or two of sleep, but out here all that you western boys seem to think of is wastin' bullets on keepin' everybody else awake." He watched as more grins formed on the faces of the four Yankees. So far all of them had remained standing, but now the corporal laughed again and scratched his head as he moved across to sit down on another box. He waved towards Kane to do likewise.

"I'll be damned," he said. "You'd risk a bullet to come over here and tell us that. You surely ain't no ornery cuss reb'. Don't know nothin' much about ol' Bobby Lee, but you Virginia boys are maybe somethin' different right enough."

"We ain't Virginia boys," Isaac Kane told them, "We're from the Army of Northern Virginia, but we're Georgia boys. Where're you boys from?"

"We're Ohio boys," one of the Yankees replied, "Franklin County, that's up near Columbus," he added. Daniel nodded in acknowledgement, though while he had certainly heard of Ohio, neither Franklin County nor Columbus meant anything to him. The corporal however seemed more interested in getting back to the subject that had brought the southerners across the lines in the first place.

"So what about this outpost stuff," he said, bringing the talk back to business.

"It's about holdin' fire out here," Kane told them. "It surely makes sense to us. It's bad enough havin' duty out here in this damned mud hole, without havin' to crawl around in it from mornin' till night because some boys got itchy trigger fingers, or some general, who don't have to come crawlin' around out here himself, reckons we oughta go on takin' shots at each other."

"Ain't jest us that shoot, reb'," one of the Yankees said, in a slightly hostile tone.

177

"Everybody does it out here," Daniel Ryan nodded as he spoke, "but it doesn't make any sense. If we all keep on with this sort o' stupidity, any of us sittin' here now could be in a pine box or a hole in the ground by this time tomorrow or next week and for what? It's bad enough gettin' shot in a real fight and we all take our chances with that, but shootin' each other on an outpost line's just plain stupid, at least it is to our way o' thinkin'." The Yankees looked at them.

"We are havin' a war," one of them said at length. It was Isaac Kane's turn to nod in agreement.

"We surely are," he said, "but that don't mean we have to be mean or ornery about it." There was more looking around at each other, for a few further seconds, till the corporal spoke again.

"Even if we don't fire and you don't fire, when we're on watch," he said, "there's plenty o' other boys that might not like the idea. It only takes one o' them to shoot and then all of us're back where we were at the start."

"If we don't try it, it won't work," Daniel Ryan told him. "If we do try it, it might. Let's at least pass the word around and maybe give it a chance. Would you boys rather go on crawlin' around the muck around here, or would you like to be able to take a crap, without havin' to sit in it to avoid a bullet?" There was a silence before anyone else spoke, but at length the corporal scratched his head yet again, pushing his hat onto the back of his skull this time in order to do so.

"OK," he said at length, "so maybe jest about everybody would prefer some peace and quiet out here, like ya say, but everybody's got t' do it or it jest don't work. We've had truces before but they only lasted till some trigger-happy son of a bitch took advantage and then that was the end of it."

"We kin spread the word back over on our side," Kane said, "'n' you kin do the same over here. If it ain't gonna work then we just finish up like it is now, with more boys gittin' killed for no good reason, but we held fire the whole o' last winter, back on the Rappahannock River in Virginia and the Potomac Yankees did the same. We're only joinin' in out

178

here cuz you boys started shootin' when we got here last week." The corporal scratched his head yet again.

"OK, so we won't fire as long as you boys don't and we kin all figure out what we say to any damned officers that don't like it." Daniel Ryan had his answer ready.

"You've dug in here," he said. "We're diggin' in over there," he added. "There just ain't the same targets as there were before."

"Suppose the colonel or somebody comes around and tells us to git back on with it?" another soldier said.

"If there ain't no way of avoidin' it, then you kin call across and tell us," Kane replied.

"How many times do you see your colonel on the outpost line in any week," Daniel Ryan added?

They all grinned at that and Daniel looked around the group of Yankees.

"Does anybody really want to go out of their way to keep this stupidity goin'?"

"Not me," one of them answered immediately, and the others nodded in turn.

"Well it looks to me like we've maybe got a deal," the corporal said.

"So we'll shake on it," Isaac Kane said, and a solemn sequence of hand grasping followed.

"Give us time to spread the word," the corporal said. "Suppose we start this from nightfall? Don't mean we'll be aimin' to shoot today, but some boys might if they ain't heard."

"Fair enough with us," Kane replied.

"We'd offer ya coffee," one of the Yankees said, "but we're a mite short on one or two things these days."

"It goes around and comes around," Daniel Ryan returned. He and Kane got to their feet and made to go, but were halted by one of the Yankees.

"What about the Governor of Georgia," he inquired?

"Oh yeah," Kane answered. "Governor Brown says you're all to pack up and head back up north and stop makin' him

179

mad." The remark brought a further bout of outright laughter from the group.

"Reckon you better tell him that ain't goin' to happen," the corporal told them.

This time they did go, stepping up onto the top log and down onto the turned earth beyond, dallying there momentarily to get their bearings, before setting off on their way back. Kane looked at Ryan.

"It all looks different from this side," he said. Daniel took a deep breath.

"Edwin!" he yelled the name loudly and after a pause they saw a ragged cloth raised in the air on a bayoneted musket.

"That way," Daniel said, grinning briefly at his companion. As they moved off, Daniel Ryan heard a couple of further remarks from the Yankees they had left behind.

"Reb's in blue," one of them said. "Surely never saw that afore."

"Maybe things are different back east," another voice returned, the words just audible before distance and the tramping of their feet through the grass of the muddy bottom-land drowned out anything further.

The word was promptly passed along the Company B outposts, and somewhat at variance with what the Yankee corporal had said, from midday on there was no further shooting along that portion of the line. Along the other companies' fronts also, as the afternoon hours passed, the firing steadily faded, indicating that the news was continuing to spread until by the time that dusk came the shooting had stopped completely along the entire regimental sector. Conversely, it started to become simpler to keep track on where the Yankees were and on what they were doing, since now they were already beginning to go about their business with a lesser degree of concern about concealing themselves. As a result, little glimpses of their dark, drab tunics began to appear, over in the direction of their positions.

180

The matter did not end there however for in the course of the following day, with the silence along the Company B portion of the forward positions markedly noticeable, Bayfield appeared, during an off-duty time for their mess, with an ominous message.

"Lieutenant wants you two," he growled, gesturing Towards Ryan and Kane. "You too Otis," he added. Daniel exchanged a glance with Isaac Kane.

"Which lieutenant would that be," Ryan inquired?

"Who in the hell d'ya think," Bayfield rasped in reply?

"What could he possibly want with us?" Kane exclaimed in an innocent tone of voice.

"I surely haven't an idea in the world," Daniel returned, with his tone matching Kane's.

"That right," Bayfield growled. "Move yore asses," he snapped as he turned to go, while behind him the three of them got to their feet and started after him.

"Quiet today ain't it," the sergeant tossed the remark over his shoulder as they went, making a certainty of what they had already suspected.

They reached the company tents and Bayfield took a coin from his pocket and rattled it twice on the awning pole. From inside the already familiar call came, half-pompous, half-irritated in tone.

"Enter!" Bayfield stepped across and drew the tent flap to one side.

"The boys ya wanted to see are waitin' outside, sah," they heard him say.

"Send them in," again the pompous tone and Henry promptly re-emerged.

"Detail, harn!" It was most always the same, Daniel Ryan reflected briefly as he stiffened to attention. When Henry called men to attention the grunt was almost always incomprehensible as a word, but the tone left no doubt as to what was required. He had no time to dwell further on this however, for the sergeant's next command followed promptly and they were marched into the tent, halted abruptly there, left

181

turned into line and stood at ease. Gilby was sitting on a folding stool at the captain's camp table, which was littered with papers.

Bayfield straightened up and saluted.

"Detail as ordered sah," he rapped, formally. Gilby rose from his stool, giving a gesture of a salute in return.

"You are dismissed, sergeant," he intoned. Daniel Ryan saw the sergeant blink as the lieutenant shifted his gaze along the three who waited in their line in front of the table, but he obeyed the order without comment. Gilby remained silent until he had left the tent.

"You two," he began, as he eyed Ryan and Kane, "are in serious disciplinary trouble." His gaze shifted to Ballard.

"You, as corporal of the guard when the offences took place, are in worse."

"Beggin' the Lieutenant's pardon.....," Kane began.

"Silence!" Gilby snapped. "You will speak when you are told to speak. Until that time you will hold your damned tongue." Kane fell silent, helped by a slight prod from Ballard's elbow that Daniel Ryan sensed rather than saw. Gilby stood there, with his face now flushed with annoyance, drawing breath before continuing.

"You two enlisted men, Kane and Ryan, crossed the picket lines and communicated with the enemy."

"How in the hell d'ya think ya git yore Yankee papers?" Ballard growled. Gilby's mouth dropped open as he turned to face the corporal.

"You damned insubordinate trash," he shouted. "I'll have your stripes for that." Daniel Ryan thought quickly. If Gilby was allowed to focus all his anger on Ballard only, then the consequences might be grave for his friend, who was likely to answer in kind. He took a quick breath and spoke.

"Are you goin' to spend the day tellin' us how much trouble we're in," he said evenly, "or do you want to know what happened..... sir?"

182

"What?" Gilby turned in his direction with a further yell. He stepped over towards Daniel Ryan and squared up in front of him.

"With the Lieutenant's permission," Daniel Ryan said, trying to instil a calmness in his voice that he did not feel. Gilby hesitated and Daniel caught a hint of something in his face. Was it uncertainty? He could not tell, but then the Lieutenant paused and his breath steadied. A slow smirk crossed his face.

"So go on," he said in a condescending tone, "so tell me what happened."

"Private Kane and me were out in the picket position," Daniel began, knowing it would be best to keep any changes to what had actually happened to a minimum. "The Yankees were callin' across and we did too. We asked 'em how much ammunition they were goin' to waste afore they learned to shoot, and they shouted back tellin' us to try standin' up and make a target? We said it was a waste of time anyway and they shouted back askin' if we thought we had a better idea on how to spend our time. We told 'em we did and then, when we told them what a damn fool thing it was, to go on takin' shots at each other for no good reason. They called over that, if we didn't like things the way they were, we should go across and talk it over. We reckoned that they didn't think we'd do it, but we said we would and so we went over, once they said they wouldn't shoot. We had a talk with 'em and the result of it was that everybody figured it was a waste o' time, and of men's lives too, with all o' the pot-shot shootin' out on the picket. They said they'd stop if we did, so we left it at that with the word bein' spread along on both sides. Corporal Ballard was at the grand post for all of the time this was bein' done and knew nothing of what had happened." Gilby looked at Kane.

"I suppose you can confirm all of that garbage," he said.

"I kin and I do," Isaac Kane told him. A brief silence followed in the tent and in it Daniel Ryan could hear the breathing of his companions as they waited for the officer's

183

next words. Gilby turned and moved along in front of them, turning as he reached as far as the height of the tent would allow.

"Rogues stick together," he said, "but I could have guessed as much." He resumed pacing, moving along in front of them while Daniel continued to watch him intently, almost afraid to identify what he was seeing as indecision on the lieutenant's part. Maybe he really was uncertain as to how far he could push this, but they were surely about to find out.

"By your own admission, you two have left your posts and fraternised with the enemy," he snapped, "in a deliberate and serious breach of army regulations." He turned to Ballard. "You permitted this to happen, so all of you are placed on the captain's report. You will be detained, under open arrest, until the offences are dealt with." He turned and called out.

"Sergeant Bayfield!"

"Sah!" The response sounded somewhat distant, but within seconds Henry had pushed the flap aside and entered the tent, but in those brief seconds the thought firmed in Daniel Ryan's mind that by passing the matter on to Jessop, Gilby had stepped back from the confrontation he had engineered. Maybe this was a clue as to how he should be handled. Maybe, when it came down to it, the little shit really did lack a measure of courage. His deliberations were interrupted by Gilby's abrupt response to Bayfield's arrival.

"These three men are under open arrest. They are to be detained in camp with extra duties, until further notice. Take charge of them."

"Sah! Bayfield shouted. "Detail.... harn," Ryan, Ballard and Kane came languidly to attention.

Seeing the gesture, Gilby stepped towards them.

"Your insubordination and insolence has been noted," he told them, "and it will not be forgotten." He turned to Bayfield.

"Carry on sergeant."

"Sah!" The three of them were promptly left-turned and marched from the tent. As they moved away Bayfield spoke up.

"You boys better learn two things," he said. "Firstly, that little shit don't give a damn how many boys die out on the picket, or about how many might see out today and tomorrow and next week neither, becuz o' what you two did. The second thing is that you crossed him today, with yore smart-ass back talk, and he ain't gonna let that pass. You three jest made a real enemy back there cuz you took him on. That insulted his pride and if there's one thing he is it's a stuck up, prideful little son of a bitch."

"Enemy!" Daniel Ryan exclaimed. "I reckon he ain't short o' them around here. It's friends he's most likely short of."

"Don't matter whether that's so, or whether it ain't," Bayfield retorted, with a tone of increasing irritation in his voice. "The three o' you crossed him back there and his eye is on ya now. He'll go outa his way to land on you boys, even if you ain't got the damn horse sense to see that. You three better go real careful around him, or you got hard times comin'."

"Stuck up or not," Ballard answered, "he ain't cleanin' up none of his shit with my damned shirt tail."

Being under open arrest turned out to be no great hardship for Ryan, Kane and Ballard, for it simply meant a substituting of chores and fatigues for picket line duty, and even that was only for the remainder of the day, since Captain's report cases were routinely due to be dealt with the following morning. What did emerge however was that throughout their labour on sinks and other camp drudgery, a sequence of men came up to speak in support of what they had done, as they carried on with such business as they were in need of.

"Ya did right out thar," Silas Norton told them. Others were equally supportive.

185

"Don't let that little b........ worry ya," was White's comment. Charlie Thorne also made a point of speaking out, as he buttoned his pants flap.

"Tell that ornery little shit t' go t' hell," he told them. Daniel Ryan smiled ruefully at that for, by Bayfield's reasoning at least, they had come tolerably close to doing that and had likely got themselves in deeper trouble as a result.

Captain's report had, since arriving before the Chattanooga lines, become a more significant part of Company B life, due mainly to the fact that Gilby made certain that there were plenty of customers for it, though on that Saturday morning there was only one further man, Jeff Gant, in addition to Ryan, Ballard and Kane awaiting Morgan Jessop's attention. Gant was dealt with first, for a minor transgression in camp, with the complaint again having been brought by Gilby. This being concluded, with further fatigue duties, the three waiting miscreants were marched into Jessop's tent by Jeffers, to confront the captain. Gilby was standing beside the littered table this time, while Morgan Jessop now sat on the folding stool. Jeffers halted the brief file and left-turned them into line. Jessop looked up.

"Not quite our usual transgressors today, lieutenant," he murmured. Gilby reddened visibly.

"No sir," he said.

"Well, tell me the story," Jessop continued. Gilby produced a paper, only to return it to his pocket when Jessop's attention focussed on it.

"These enlisted men," he began, "Kane and Ryan, have admitted to leaving their posts on the picket line unmanned and to crossing the lines and communicating with the enemy, in serious breach of army regulations, which forbid any truce with the enemy, unless sanctioned by superior officers."

"Did you two leave your post unmanned," Jessop snapped?

"No sir," Daniel Ryan replied. "We were relievin' Privates Jones and Jenkins, but they stayed on while we were across."

186

"Did you ask for a truce with the Yankees," Jessop interrupted?

"No sa," Kane answered. "We jest went across."

"Who went across," Jessop snapped?

"We did," Daniel Ryan answered, "that is Private Kane did and I did, sir." Jessop turned to Gilby before returning his gaze to the three miscreants with a loud sigh.

"Will somebody tell me what Corporal Ballard is doin' here then?" Gilby again looked uncomfortable as he made to reply.

"Corporal Ballard was corporal of the guard at the time that these offences took place."

"Were you aware corporal that two of your watch had gone across the lines without orders," Jessop inquired?

"He was back at the grand post and didn't know nothin'," Kane interrupted.

"Silence!" Jeffers roared. "The captain's question was addressed to Corporal Ballard," he added in a somewhat more measured tone.

"Thank you First Sergeant," Jessop drawled. "Well corporal, where were you when all o' this this took place?"

"At the grand post, like he said," Ballard replied.

"So, if you were in the rear and they were on the line, why are you here?"

"I ain't sartin sure myself," Ballard returned. Jessop sighed again.

"We want to deal out some military justice to whatever guilty parties we got here," he said, "not line half the damned company up in here when it was jest two men that did the deed, whatever the hell it was. Corporal!" he looked at Ballard directly.

"Sa!"

"You are dismissed."

"Left turn," Jeffers took over and marched Ballard from the tent. Jessop then looked at Gilby and Daniel Ryan saw the lieutenant's features flush as he watched Ballard go.

"My apologies lieutenant," he said, as the tent flap swung back into place. "Pray continue."

"In addition," Gilby resumed his account, "the same two entered into an agreement with the enemy, to withhold picket line fire, when no authorisation for such a step had been given by their superiors."

"Ah!" Again Jessop intervened, breaking in on Gilby's monologue.

"Sir?" Gilby looked across, with a look of something close to exasperation on his face, which was reddening further at this latest interruption.

"There is a difficulty here," Jessop said, in an almost absent-minded tone. "These two men are here on report for arrangin' an outpost cease-fire on our company front. This is awkward, for I understand that the commandin' general has last evenin' approved a proposal, from the Yankee commander no less, for an outpost cease-fire all along the whole line. These two have only preceded the whole army by a day, or maybe less than a day, or hours or thereabouts. When they got started, on whatever it was they did, the Yankee letter was likely already on the general's desk, so I ain't sure how much I should be punishin' them for doing something that the whole army's doin', as of today." Gilby looked at Jessop and then at Ryan and Kane.

"They did what they did without orders sir," he said tartly, "in breach of army regulations."

"Men do a hell of a lot without orders in this here army," Jessop answered. "If the Yankees come this way, we expect 'em t' shoot 'em without any orders. Picket lines ain't places where orders can get issued for everythin' that happens." He turned back to Ryan and Kane.

"Did you two communicate with the enemy?"

"Yes sah," Ryan and Kane replied almost in unison. Jessop eyed them severely.

"I am well aware, like I say, that a lot o' this goes on," he said. "I am also aware that plenty o' useful information, as well as coffee and other things, can be gotten from doin' it,

188

but what in the hell made you two think that you could jest go ahead and set up a damned prayer meetin' on your own account?"

"They were callin' across and we called back," Daniel Ryan told him. "We got to callin' about the bullets they were wastin' learnin' to shoot and after that one thing kinda led on to another." Jessop shook his head and shuffled a few of the papers on the table. He looked around at Gilby.

"Storm in a damned coffee cup," he muttered, though Ryan could clearly see, by the expression on the lieutenant's face and the deep flush that coloured it, that he did not agree in the slightest with Jessop's view.

"There is the matter of their insubordination and insolence also Captain," he intoned icily.

"Ah yes," Jessop returned, replacing the papers on the table. "They were insolent to yourself, lieutenant."

"They were sir, and Ballard also." Jessop looked around at Gilby.

"Corporal Ballard too," Jessop raised his eyebrows. "Reckon I should'a kept him here instead o' sendin' him off. We better have him back in here then," he replied. He looked at Jeffers.

"First Sergeant, get Corporal Ballard back in here."

"Sah!" Jeffers stepped away out of the tent and was absent for what seemed like a considerable time. He returned eventually.

"Sergeant Thompson has gone fer Corporal Ballard sah," he intoned.

"Thank you First Sergeant," Jessop murmured.

He had hardly fallen silent when the tent pole was rattled and on Jessop's summons, Thompson's face appeared around the tent flap.

"Corporal Ballard, sah," he called. Ballard strode into the tent and resumed his place.

"Thank you sergeant," Jessop dismissed Thompson and the tent flap closed.

"Private's Kane and Ryan," Jessop began. "I will delay punishment on the matter of you communicating with the enemy, but I formally remind you both of army regulations and caution you that punishment must be expected for breaches of them and that more serious punishment will follow any further actions of this kind. But what the whole army is settin' up t' do today is something that I am damned if I kin see how I kin punish you two overmuch, jest because you got around to doin' it a mite early. As for the insolence and insubordination towards Lieutenant Gilby, who were the witnesses of the insolence and insubordination Lieutenant?" Gilby's face was by now almost purple.

"I was!"

"You were? Well yes of course you were lieutenant, but was nobody else present?" Jessop inquired, again raising his eyebrows inquisitively.

"They were," Gilby gestured towards the three miscreants.

"Only the three of them and you?"

"Yes........" Jessop looked around at the lieutenant.

"They are not witnesses, they are the um..... accused men. Where was the duty sergeant?"

"He was gone, I dismissed him." At that Jessop tutted and drummed his fingers briefly on the paper-strewn table. He looked again at Gilby, but said nothing as he turned to face Ryan, Ballard and Kane.

"On any such matter I will always take the word of an officer, even though it may be uncorroborated. You three've been in this army plenty long enough to know that insubordination towards a superior officer will not be tolerated. You will therefore be given extra duties for the next seven days, as a punishment for your conduct and you are cautioned as to your subsequent behaviour towards your superiors. You Corporal Ballard are reminded that a corporal can lose those stripes jest as easily as he got them and you jest did." He glared at them. "The three of you are dismissed."

"Shun!" Jeffers voice rang out again almost before the captain had finished speaking, and on his further shouted orders, the three were marched from the tent.

It was after dark and the camp had settled when Thompson came looking for Ballard, Ryan and Kane as, with the others of their watch, they were gathering their weapons for a further picket duty.

"Barnard wants ya," he said briefly.

"Where is he?" Ballard inquired.

"The First Sergeant has been inspectin' the outposts," was the reply. They got to their feet and moved quietly through the resting camp, starting out northwards once more towards the outpost line. The sky was cloudy, though that cloud was broken, allowing fitful periods of moonlight to occasionally illuminate the landscape with dim light. One such spell had just commenced when they saw Jeffers approaching, his gait unmistakable in the moonlight. He strode up closer before gesturing to the three of them to step from the trail to where a further track diverted to the left, following them along it for a few yards to the shade of a large bush.

"It is my understandin'," he began, "that the captain would be grateful if you three, and maybe sartin others around here, could maybe try figurin' out for yourselves how the land lies in this company now and act like ya had some measure o' brains in yore thick skulls. That way he, and others, won't have to spend no more time diggin' you out of any more holes that yore damned stupidity has gotten you into. Are we clear on this?" he finished.

"First Sergeant," the three of them answered, almost in unison.

"Well get out of my damned sight and from now on see to keepin' yoreselves out of trouble, instead o' everybody else around here havin t' do it for ya."

Thompson was still at the mess fire when they returned from the outpost duty.

"You boys were lucky ya didn't lose some o' the skin off o' yore asses," he said, as they settled themselves, "and not just a damned set o' stripes."

"That little shit don't scare me none," Ballard rasped in return. Thompson shook his head.

"Maybe ya need t' think a mite more on what Barnard, and Henry, told ya," he growled. "What happened today could've finished up a sight worse than it did. Jessop went out on a limb to keep you boys from real punishment. When he did that, he was tellin' Gilby to lay off o' the reliable men in this company, but if you keep showin' up on report then there ain't gonna be much more that he kin do. If it was Boyce he'd carry more punch, but he ain't here. Jessop's only an actin' captain and when he crosses that little shit Gilby, he's goin' up agin the colonel's damn kin. Maybe you three wanted less to happen today, but you kin bet on it that Gilby wanted a helluva lot more. He couldn't make no dereliction charge stick, cuz Edwin and Sam Jenkins stayed on watch, but he wanted you done good fer crossin' the lines and extra good fer sassin' him. The main reason why he never got that was cuz he dismissed Henry and Jessop made good use o' that mistake. You boys got a favour from him today, fer whatever reason. Maybe it was somethin' to do with you two bein' with him on that detail to Georgia, at the turn o' the year, but crossin' Gilby ain't clever, cuz, when ya do it, there's a good chance that you finish up crossin' Preston as well. Jessop knows that, but he still dug you outa yore hole this mornin', but you kin bet that he ain't gonna do that more'n once. If you three got any brains at all, ya'll walk careful around Gilby from now on, little shit or not, cuz Jessop ain't gonna lift no spade on yore account agin."

"Why's he after our hides at all?" Daniel Ryan growled. "We're supposed to be fightin' on the same side in this here war."

"Reckon John Ellis wondered about that too," Ballard interjected.

192

"Ain't nobody fightin' on the same side as Gilby," Thompson retorted, "except his kin. To him enlisted men are no accounts. They ain't no better than blacks, cuz they ain't "quality," like he is. That's how he sees it. We're all jest cannon fodder, only useful fer keepin' things the way they are back home, fer him and his like. If he could, he'd deal out company justice around here like he does to that boy o' his. A set o' stripes was jest about the least that he was goin' t' git outa today's business, but stripes kin be gotten back."

A silence followed Thompson's lecture, after which the conversation, mainly under Eli Winder and Edwin Jones' guidance, was diverted to other things before the mess turned in.

Daniel Ryan had returned to the subject with Thompson the following day, though in his heart he knew that what was done was done and no intercession would restore Ballard's stripes. He felt obliged to raise the matter on behalf of his friend at least once more with the sergeant, but what he got in return, fairly predictably, was a brief reiteration of the previous advice.

"At the end of it, what me and Isaac did was nothin' to do with Otis," he had concluded. "So it ain't fair that he gets punished for it."

"Since when were things fair around here," Thompson had snapped, clearly tiring of the subject? "It's all gotten to do with responsibility. It was his watch it happened on and he told me that he knew what you boys were doin' anyhow. Like I told ya, stripes kin be gotten back. Will ya git it straight Daniel, the biggest problem you boys got is nothin' to do with corporal's stripes. It's cuz you decided to sass Gilby. That insulted his pride and he don't forgive nothin' like that."

"That's what Henry said," Ryan had said, "but by then it had happened."

"Well if ya couldn't see sense afore it all, at least see it now," Thompson had affirmed testily and there the matter had finally rested.

Chapter 7 A Kind of a Siege

As October came, the weather had turned decidedly more autumnal. The winds grew increasingly cold and penetrating, and days of heavy and persistent rain saw the ground on either side of the creek gradually flood as the accumulating rainfall on the mountains and higher ground drained down towards the river. The "Blues" camp ground also became sodden, since it lay at the bottom of a gradual slope, which made it a natural draining area for rain water from anywhere higher up. As conditions steadily worsened, the whole state of affairs became increasingly exasperating to the waiting southern troops, for as far as they could see the indecision and hesitation in their commanders meant that the victorious army, rather than pressing on into Tennessee, languished instead in these muddy camps, short of rations and almost everything else that they needed to sustain themselves.

The opportunity to strike the Yankees again, when they were disorganised and weakened by their defeat, had by now been pretty well thrown away. They were still out there, organised and busy, almost inviting an attack on their improved defences. The results of the campaign thus far had therefore been nothing, beyond the driving of the enemy army into the very place that had been their objective since the spring.

For the southern army there seemed that little was now to be done but wait in their camps and their waterlogged outpost lines for something to happen. Rumours circulated, as they always did, but most of them were of what the Yankees were doing, rather than anything of note regarding their own army.

The establishment of these regular camps however had given the new lieutenant the opportunity that everyone had fully expected him to grasp at, to impose himself upon the men of the company and on one of them in particular. It was no surprise to anyone that he came down heaviest on Eli Winder, picking on any minor matter to place him on report, or award extra duties off his own hook. Jessop, undoubtedly seeing how the land lay, had immediately altered the platoon arrangement, so that Thompson's section, which included Ryan's mess, was placed under Carson rather than Gilby, but the latter was nothing if not industrious and he promptly set to the task of getting around the Acting Captain's arrangements by finding further fault in any situation in camp that he could contrive.

As for routine fatigues, as opposed to punishment details, those placed on them were customarily rotated by the sergeants and all four of them from the outset began to apply their own sense of justice to whatever they were compelled, by Gilby's actions, to give at least lip service to. Where they were presented with any scope to bypass or minimise the severity of the new lieutenant's more vindictive wishes they largely did so, and, when they were not Winder tended to find himself on a lot of details where he was detached to do something else of a less onerous nature by the NCO in charge, which blunted, or at least diverted, whatever sanction that Gilby may have intended. Not that he was spared his share of the menial and unpopular tasks and fatigues in the day to day running of the camp, but there quickly emerged a level of army justice that continued to operate outside the influence of the lieutenant, administered by the sergeants in an even-handed if bad-tempered, way.

It all had to be done with a degree of tact and delicacy, since the lieutenant was not stupid and if the discarding or undermining of the spirit of his orders was done too obviously or too openly, disciplinary trouble could easily land upon many more than Winder. The one redeeming feature in it all, as far as Winder in particular was concerned, was that Gilby, while clearly down on him, regularly found plenty of others in Company B who fell short of his military standards and therefore required their own doses of extra duties or company punishment to improve their soldierly qualities, and he did not hesitate to administer either when the need for them arose as, in his eyes at least, it regularly did.

195

Since being demoted, Ballard had said little on the subject of Gilby, until after a spiteful beating of his servant boy Josiah, the lieutenant had been thoroughly discussed by the mess and thereafter, on outpost duty with Daniel Ryan, he had commented further on the matter.

"As fer that little shit," he told Daniel, "Joe still reckons we got off light and we was lucky and maybe he was right about that as far as it goes. But takin' care not to give him another chance at us don't mean I'm aimin' to start likin' him, or ticklin' his ass either." His expression had hardened as he continued. "He might be an officer and all, but the hair and skin he got last time was mine. I ain't forgittin' that any more than ev'body else says he will. From now on, any chance I git to show him up fer the cheap little shit that he is and make him sweat a little, you kin bet I'll be takin' it."

"You know the chance you're takin' if you do that Otis," Ryan told him. Ballard did not reply. "Then I hope you're good at walkin' on a thin rail," Daniel finished.

"Well whatever balancin' it takes, he ain't gettin' no nice, front parlor manners from me, that's fer damned sure," his friend had replied grimly.

Ironically, while Gilby was now an increasing trial to the men of Company B, his black servant Josiah was the opposite. The boy had a diffident manner, which at first seemed to indicate slowness, but the men quickly discovered that nothing could be further from the truth. Far from adopting anything of his master's supercilious attitude towards the enlisted men of the company, Josiah became something of a benefactor. It was one of the boy's jobs to organise his master's ration and to cook it and he was known to be pretty adept at doing this. As time passed in the depressing, under-supplied camps, Josiah established a practice of routing little extra measures towards the enlisted men. Sometimes it was small portions of food, while on other occasions it was as simple as salt, or mustard, or any other spices that added taste to the mundane rations of corn and bacon that most often arrived.

196

His generosity was aimed most pointedly towards company messes where he perceived particular hardship. He somehow procured mustard plasters from Thomas Sterling's stock for Matty Weald's chest, and came up with some lemon juice to treat symptoms of scurvy in Bryant. As the weeks began to pass, an increasing number of the company found good reason to be grateful to the boy. Nobody questioned his sources and he chose not to divulge them, but Ballard was only one of those who commented that, had he chosen to charge for his unofficial supplies, the boy could have made a small fortune. Disdaining that, he seemed content to steadily ingratiate himself with the company, becoming a favourite among most of these hard-bitten men, a position traditionally difficult to earn and even more difficult to keep.

One of the most exasperating things about those wet and chilly days that extended into the month of October was the dark suspicion that the minds of the generals were far from the matters of greatest importance, such as how to go about turning the Yankees out of Chattanooga. This was repeatedly indicated by a succession of stories that circulated around the camps, indicating that instead of concentrating their attention on the enemy, the Army of Tennessee high command had reverted to its previous custom of internal division and enmity. Bragg was said to be accusing his lieutenants of disloyalty and sedition, while they, if the stories passing around were true, were accusing him of incompetence. There was certainly plenty of incompetence around in this here army, the Company B men told each other, when all along the lines the men were surviving on painfully short rations as they waited for the move that would decide this campaign and get them out of these wet bottom lands.

In addition to what was taking place among the army's commanders here in Tennessee, a letter, so one story said, had been sent to President Jefferson Davis in Richmond, signed by almost all of the senior generals, calling for Bragg's removal. There was disbelief at that rumour, especially among the Army of Northern Virginia soldiers, unused as they were to such goings on among their superiors. Their neighbours of Stewart's division however remained unmoved.

"They'll take it in turns like they did afore," they told the disbelieving newcomers. "Generals'll try and get Bragg relieved, and then he'll try and git them run outa here on a damned rail. Happened after Perryville last fall and agin after Murfreesboro at the turn o' the year. That's the way Bragg runs this here army." The men of Company B nodded their heads in understanding, but a kernel of disbelief lingered in at least some of their minds. Surely the generals, having spent their men's lives on chasing those Yankees out of Georgia last month, would see first to the task of following up on that success? And if it was too late now to force the surrender of the Yankee army, they would at least see to pushing them on back up through Tennessee before indulging themselves with such bickering?

"Not so," Stewart's men told them. "You boys wait and see. This ain't the first time by far that this kinda thing's gone on around here. If they've written to Jeff Davis about all of this, like we hear they have, then he'll be out here soon, same as he was back in December. He come out here back then and talked, like only a damned politician can and in the end, nothin' happened. Bragg was confirmed and everybody else was shuffled around some, but nothin' that needed changin' got changed and plenty that didn't need changin' got changed. That'll be the measure of it all. Davis is Bragg's bosom buddy, even if nobody else in the whole damned southern Confederacy is and Davis knows what's gone on around here before. Reckon he'll be out here t' scratch Bragg's ass afore long. If he shows up here that'll be as close to proof as you kin git about how things stand around here."

They had agreed that they would indeed wait and see, after all there was little else to do with the time, but the second week of October had just arrived when, with his coming preceded by still more rumour, the President arrived on the Western and Atlantic Railroad. Ryan's mess were as near to

198

speechless as they had ever been when the word spread of Davis' arrival.

"Things surely are different out here," Jones said, when he heard the news.

"Looks like we was wrong," Ballard told them. "Looks like these western generals don't let anythin' stand in the way of a good ruckuss, not even the damned war."

The President was indeed with the army and it was virtually impossible to be ignorant of that fact. A series of reviews and inspections subsequently took place, letting the great man get a look at the soldiers and likewise letting the soldiers get to look at him. McLaws' brigades were no exception and Daniel Ryan, who like others of the regiment had never seen a real live president before, scrutinised the chief executive closely as he passed by, getting an impression of a pale, thin face, surmounting a goatee beard. Davis' eyes, Daniel concluded, were his most striking feature, for while one seemed to be affected by some kind of infection, covered as it was by a moist film of some kind, the other gleamed like that of a bird of prey.

The President had clearly come to this last corner of Tennessee to do his best to encourage and inspire his soldiers and he undertook this task with a series of speeches, in the course of which he compared the Yankees to biblical villains, exhorting the men with stern determination to hold firm and resist the foe, who were laying waste their lands and communities. While this may have been fine as far as it went with the army's rank and file, everyone knew that it was the ill-concealed discord in its high command that had brought the harassed executive here to the lines around Chattanooga, and while the soldiers listened politely to the president's words, interest was more closely focussed on any news of how the real crisis was to be resolved.

The majority of the men, even among the recent arrivals from Virginia, reckoned that Davis must surely remove Bragg from command, though who he would replace him with was a matter of guess and conjecture and there was no end to the suggestions as to whom it might be. The senior generals included Leonidas Polk, Lieutenant General and Episcopal Bishop, also known as one of Bragg's most critical lieutenants, but another long-time friend of the president's. William Hardee was a further Lieutenant General serving in the west, who had written books on military matters. Joe Johnston's name did the rounds also. He had been the original commander in Virginia, whose wounding back at the battle of Seven Pines, eighteen months previously, had brought Robert E. Lee to command and who had, on his recovery, been transferred to the west. All three names were being touted around the camps, as possible replacements for Bragg. Less fancied, but still on hand if chosen, were Daniel Harvey Hill, a hard fighting if sometimes too outspoken veteran campaigner who had served his own term in the Army of Northern Virginia, and, almost surprisingly to some men, "Old Pete" Longstreet himself.

There were some among the army's enlisted men who were quick to take advantage of the interest in the subject and took bets on who the new commander would be, with odds being offered on each of the possible replacements. Polk, as the arch-conspirator and principal critic of Bragg, would surely not get the job and Joe Johnston too was not favoured, having sustained a long-standing feud with the President on his own account. Hardee was generally seen as the most likely successor, but did he have the required killer instinct to get after the Yankees, before it was too late to do so? The rumours went back and forth for several days, while the president met with the various generals, but the army's collective jaw dropped when, after concluding his process of consulting and conferring, President Davis departed for Richmond on the train, having done no more than confirm Bragg in his post and firmly overrule those who wished to see him removed.

"What did we tell ya all," Stewart's cynical veterans had trumpeted? "Ol' Bragg'll still be in command around here when the Good Lord arrives, to judge the whole damned lot o' them."

As more days passed and October advanced, the command dust began to settle. Further steps, approved apparently by Davis, also emerged. Polk, the long-time critic of Bragg's, departed to a command in Mississippi, being replaced by Hardee as corps commander. This, so Stewart's observers reckoned, was a simple swapping of jobs, undertaken to get the annoying Bishop out of Bragg's hair. The services of Harvey Hill were also dispensed with. He was dispatched from the army, returning, it was being said, to his native North Carolina, apparently too outspoken for high command in this highly political army. Bragg, having been supported by the president, promptly set about re-organising his army, switching a succession of regiments from one brigade to another and brigades from one division to another, with only Longstreet's Virginia command completely escaping the transferring epidemic. It was Otis Ballard, inevitably, who found the telling comment on it all.

"They've got themselves a different kind o' war out here," the deposed corporal pronounced, sharing his latest observation on this much-aired subject with the off-duty mess. "They got a whole set o' generals who're so damned set on fightin' each other, that they ain't got no time to think about goin' after the Yankees."

There was another rumour that first appeared in those middle days of October, though this concerned the Yankees instead of the southern high-command. "Sam" Grant, that western general who had captured the western Tennessee forts last year and Vicksburg on the Mississippi during the summer just ended, was rumoured to be getting the top command at Chattanooga. Coming with him would be at least some of his Mississippi army. Men shook their heads at this story, knowing only too well that if this was allowed to happen, it would make the job of pushing the Yankees out of the city and on up into Tennessee all but impossible.

As time passed, Sam Jenkins had become fully integrated into the mess. It was not that there had been any kind of formal step in the process, instead it had rather evolved, for since the arrival of the company in Tennessee he had been included for meals and had been contributing his ration as a result. Daniel still nursed reservations about the boy, but in view of the fact that the others, especially Ballard and Thompson had accepted him as a member of their group, he went along with it, keeping any more critical thoughts to himself. Jenkins had shown pluck in two successive battles now and, whatever else might be seen as faults in him, he had in addition to a measure of gumption, proved at least an initial level of stickability, the lack of which, above most other things, was the most frequent criticism aimed at conscripts. They too often tended not to stay with the colours, in many cases absconding at the first real opportunity, and how could a man rely on someone who would quite likely be gone by tomorrow or the day after?

For the first week or two after the lines around Chattanooga were established, Daniel had maintained a measure of distance, allowing himself to be paired only occasionally with Jenkins for picket duty, but as October stretched on through its second week and the weather continued chilly and damp, he had finally consented to a further pairings and a night picket had been the result, with Linus Cooper being corporal of the guard. Ryan and Jenkins had pushed forward towards the creek for their first duty, relieving Winder and Kane in the process, before settling to their watch. Jenkins had stayed relatively quiet throughout that first hour, saying no more than a few words about anything. In due course Winder and Kane had returned to take their next turn on duty, upon which Ryan and Jenkins had made their way back to the grand post for their off-watch time at the fire there. Ballard, restored to the mundane chore of outpost duty, had been on watch, though he too had returned after the change of pickets to settle himself by the concealed

202

fire, once Jenkins had shifted along a log to make space for him.

"My ass can't be that big," Ballard grunted, eyeing the space that Jenkins had vacated, "ain't enough vittles issued around here fer that."

"Boy knows his place," Jones had observed, "doesn't want no trouble in the mess."

"If ya still want to make a good impression on everybody around here, you farm boys better jest git busy on writin' home fer extra vittles," Ballard had told the boy, "that'd be a hell of a good way of helpin' yore store credit around here." Jenkins hesitated before saying anything in reply.

"Times're pretty hard back home now," he eventually said, in a subdued tone.

"Aint yo're folks got no relatives t' help out," White wanted to know, "now yo're off soldierin'?"

Jenkins hesitated again before answering, as though embarrassed at being the centre of attention of the others of the picket.

"There's jest m' two sisters at home with my ma now," he eventually said.

"Most families got uncles or cousins, hell, there must be at least a grandpaw, or some kind o' family that kin help out at times like this," Cooper said, and Daniel Ryan noticed that Jenkins again delayed before answering.

"Got a cousin, who's older than me," he said, "but Bart went off and enlisted, back at the start of the war." Daniel Ryan felt his ears almost prick up at the boy's words and his eyes immediately fixed on him as he finished speaking.

"Bart," he said abruptly? Jenkins looked back at him.

"He's a cousin on my pa's side," he answered. Ryan still gazed at him.

"Was he the only one in your family who enlisted back then?" Daniel almost snapped the question back at him. Once more there was a pause and by now Jenkins seemed downright reluctant to continue the conversation. Maybe it was all just a bit too much attention and scrutiny for him, in

203

front of the others of the mess, but Ryan still had his eyes fixed on him.

"Caleb," he finally said, "what was Caleb to you?" It was now Jenkins turn to show surprise on his features and again he hesitated before answering.

"Caleb was my brother," he said at last, "but how do you know about him?"

"Your brother," Ryan said, shaking his head. "Well, I'll be damned, your brother?" He looked at Jenkins again. "I met Caleb, back at the start of the war. It was the week that Lincoln called for Yankee volunteers to invade the south. I came across him on the road, when he was on his way to the railroad to catch the train into Savannah. I gave him a ride into Eden Station." Jenkins looked at Daniel.

"Caleb was near two years older'n me," he said. "When the war looked like it was comin', he went off and I stayed home. Ruth 'n' Lizbeth are a lot younger'n me. They was too young to be much of a help, so ma kept me home, at least till I got drafted." Daniel Ryan shook his head again, feeling himself redden, though glad that the others would see little of that in the glare of the fire. He should have seen it, he told himself: apart from the surname, the Christian names should have been a clue. Caleb, Samuel and even the two sisters Ruth and Elizabeth for that matter, all were names from the Bible, as many of the poorer white families tended to have.

He should have seen it, and if he had done so, it would all have been easier for this boy, Sam Jenkins in particular. He tried to recall the appearance of the boy from his now vague recollection of his features and build, but could not think of any obvious resemblance between the two of them. He struggled vainly to picture Caleb Jenkins as his mind went over it all, and his attention returned at length to the conversation. There was still more to it, for he knew that it had not ended there. He turned again to Jenkins and nodded across to Ballard also.

"Back down at Richmond, Otis, last year at Malvern Hill," he said. He turned again to Jenkins. "That was the last time I saw your brother. We came across him after he'd been hit. He was layin' in a swale in the ground, with a whole crowd of other boys. Some o' them had been hit like him, but others had ducked on down there like we did, out of the way of the fire the Yankees were layin' down. Maybe your brother had managed to crawl there after he'd been wounded, but by the time we got there, it was gettin' dark." He looked again at Ballard. "Remember him Otis," he said, as Caleb Jenkins' features finally swam once more into his mind? "That wounded boy, the one that spoke to me back there, the one that I wanted to bring back in." He saw Ballard nod as his eyes flitted between him and Jenkins.

"We had to wait till it was dark," he went on, "till the Yankee cannon and musketry had stopped. It wasn't even that long, only minutes, but it was too long for your brother because he was dead by the time we were able to move." It was Ballard's turn to speak now as Daniel Ryan fell silent.

"I remember the boy," he said. "He'd gotten a shell fragment in his chest, weren't no hope fer him."

He addressed the comment to Jenkins rather than to the others around the fire. Daniel Ryan looked at Jenkins.

"Why didn't you join your brother's, your cousin's, outfit when you got drafted?" he asked, though his tone was now more even and measured.

"Weren't no point," was the boy's reply. "Bart was back home by then. He got hit in the leg at Second Manassas and the wound infected, so he finished up losin' the leg."

This time it was Daniel Ryan's turn to hesitate in replying.

"If I'd known you were his brother," he said at length, but then he grunted in annoyance. "I should've seen it...." The silence resumed, as though nobody quite knew what they should say next, until Cooper eventually spoke.

"Small damned world ain't it," he said?

"Surely is," Jones added, and after a further short pause, the talk around the fire moved on.

As they moved on up to take their next watch, Jenkins remained silent. Daniel Ryan walked slightly behind the boy and he looked several times at his dim outline as he followed, wondering what he must be thinking. More than that, he was still annoyed with himself. He was annoyed at not making the connection between the two boys: after all how many Jenkins families were there in Bryan or Liberty Counties? The silence persisted as they moved on, lasting until they came up to where Isaac Kane sat on the same fragment of rotting tree trunk, at the foot of the same shallow rise in the ground topped by its little rampart from where they routinely watched. Winder was there, at the parapet, stretched out on his stomach as he gazed out towards the Yankee positions with his musket in his hands. Kane grinned at them as they arrived, showing his teeth in the darkness.

"Relief time at last," he said. "Ain't nothin' stirrin' out here." Jenkins moved on past and, dropping to a crouch, he moved up and took his position beside Winder.

"Go get yore time at the fire," he said softly. Winder looked at him briefly and then shuffled back, prodding Jenkins in the ribs as he went and straightening up as he came to the bottom of the rise where Kane now stood.

"Reckon the Yankees are all tucked up in their blankets," he said, "or maybe they've evacuated, 'n' Bragg ain't found out yet."

"Well tonight it's our job to tell him Eli," Daniel said, "ain't it?" Kane snorted.

"Let him go look for himself," he growled.

"Don't reckon he would figure out what was happenin'," Winder retorted, "even if he did go and look, he most likely wouldn't git it figured out even if he got run down by one o' their wagons," he added, as the two of them started away to the rear.

Daniel Ryan sat down on the section of rotting wood that Kane had vacated. He looked again at Jenkins' vague form, in the darkness just ahead of where he sat, feeling that he should say something but at something of a loss as to what. He had

206

been short-sighted, at the very least and stubborn and opinionated and prejudiced. He had not given the boy a chance until he had been virtually forced to. Now, as a result of all of the talk and the finding out, he was confronted with the extent of his own worse side and it was a far from comfortable feeling.

"If I'd known, I'd 've acted different," he said, keeping his voice low. A muttered grunt came eventually from Jenkins.

"Reckon that's all past and done now," he said, "so there ain't none of it' goin' to be no better fer chawin' it over again." Daniel pondered the reply, knowing that it did not make him feel any better about any of it. He sat in silence for a further time, before pushing himself from his seat and starting up the little rise, crouching and then stretching forward until he was beside where Jenkins watched a few feet to his left, with the boy still just a dim shape in the darkness. He looked across as Daniel arrived.

"We kin take turns at this," he said, with a hint of irony in his words. "'spect I know what a Yankee looks like by now." There was silence for a brief time before Daniel spoke again.

"I should've given you more of a chance," he said, "sooner than I have done. What I said to you about friends, in Virginia back in the summer, was true. People like us have to be careful about friends, cuz we lose them too easy in this line of work, but that doesn't change the fact that I haven't been fair to you." Jenkins still looked out ahead and said nothing. Ryan looked at him, knowing that he wanted to conclude this episode and leave Jenkins to his watch, but he knew also he should not do that just yet. He gritted his teeth and drew a further breath.

"I'm sorry I treated you the way I did," he said. Jenkins looked around at last.

"I reckon I understand now what you meant, about friends and conscripts and all," he said. "Look at them boys who arrived with me. Three of 'em ain't around here no more, so I reckon that proves you were right. But I'm here still and I'm aimin' to soldier the best I kin. Reckon a part o' that's because o' Caleb gittin' killed like he did." He fell silent for a few further moments before resuming.

"Maybe boys around here, even the ones like you, kin see by now that I ain't a quitter and I'll be stayin' around here, till we lick the Yankees good and proper." Daniel nodded in response, though in the darkness Jenkins might well have seen nothing of the gesture. He made to move back down the little rise.

"That's fair with me," he said. "Reckon even I can see that by now." Jenkins looked around at him as he moved away.

"What d'ya mean?" he inquired softly.

"You're still here, ain't you?" was Daniel's reply.

October's days passed, in a climate of comparative boredom as well as hardship, while the weather grew gradually colder and the supply of firewood grew harder and harder to replenish. Rations remained a fraught subject, with supplies, mainly of poor bacon and corn and an occasional ration of onions and Confederate coffee, arriving in quantities that were seldom enough to last more than a day, or at most into a second. This presented a problem since those meagre supplies tended to arrive on a very irregular basis, often only twice, or three times at most, in a week. This left anything up to half of the days of a week to be supplied by whatever could be gleaned from the local area which, with the whole army stationed along the line of the river and therefore competing for whatever was available, was not much.

The essence of the trouble was the absence of a proper commissary train to supply Longstreet's men, their own having remained in Virginia. This meant, as Thompson and others had predicted, that they were forced to rely largely on the wagons of other formations, whose trains had, by all accounts, been insufficient for the job before a single hungry mouth had arrived from Virginia. The railroad brought much of what the army consumed up from Atlanta and trains arrived daily, but what they delivered was never enough to supply such a large force. The problems did not end there however, for even when the provisions got up to Ringold or Catoosa, the shortage of wagons and teams meant that there were never enough vehicles to haul them promptly to the camps that now formed a great arc around Chattanooga.

The trains made their return journeys to Atlanta, carrying the sick and wounded to the hospitals in the city. As the autumn drew on the warm weather illnesses declined, but cold weather ailments increased and few of the trains departed with empty cars.

There was something of an irony in the fact that one of the passengers on one of those trains in middle October, was the Ogeechee Volunteers' own Regimental Surgeon, for Thomas Sterling had contracted pneumonia. God knew how he had managed it, some of the men commented, considering how little contact he customarily had with the sick men of the regiment. With Jeremiah Yorke, his assistant, gone last year to another regiment, it meant that the "Blues" now had no surgeon, but Sterling's absence, the same sarcastic observers commented, might even lead to an improvement in the men's state of health. Other men came up on the trains, including a scattering of the army's returning wounded. Among these were Matthew Hale and Luke Petersen who arrived from Atlanta within days of each other, late in October. Hale seemed little changed, quiet and serious as before, and with his return the picket pairings were quietly adjusted to allow him to pair with Winder once more, though Daniel Ryan, to the surprise of some in the mess, declined any change to his pairing with Jenkins.

The siege went on, with the whole of the army's infantry stationed along the mountains and ridges along the southern bank of the Tennessee River. With the additional divisions as well as its own complement in place, the line frontage for a brigade sized body of men was comparatively narrow. This meant that duty periods on the outpost line, with successive regiments taking turns, was periodic, and much of the men's time was therefore spent in camp, where discomfort and boredom were common. Camp vices grew and flourished, with gambling becoming increasingly prevalent among officers as well as enlisted men. Prostitutes too had begun to arrive in the locality, following the armies as they had habitually done over the previous two years when the troops settled in one place for any length of time. They set up in tents or in derelict buildings that soon attracted business. Some men disdained to patronise these women, but there were still plenty who did, frequenting their premises during off-duty times when they had the money to do so, often having to stand in line, awaiting their turn.

The men of Company B, like many others in the wider army, responded to the advancing seasons as they had the previous year. Most of those who had stayed clean shaven through the warmer months ceased to shave, and beards generally grew progressively longer, in many cases extending down towards the owner's chest. These men resorted to additional facial hair principally for its warmth, even though it served also to provide a further breeding ground for their infestations and gave all an even wilder and more unkempt appearance than before. As for duties, aside from periodic outpost watches and standard camp fatigues, there were few, with even drills limited for many units by a lack of sufficient space where they could be undertaken. Details were set out daily to procure firewood, which in the absence of sufficient transportation, had to be carried back to the camps in bundles. The distances involved grew steadily greater, with an increasing portion of the day being spent on the chore, but many men still regarded it as something to occupy their time, and volunteered to serve on such details in preference to remaining idle around the camp.

The siege was proceeding, much as it had done for near to a month. Longstreet's two divisions held the left or western flank of the army's positions around Chattanooga, which was, the men told each other, where any real man's work would most likely be required. It was from the west after all that more substantial Yankee reinforcements would approach the city, since the south and eastward approaches were

Confederate territory and held by their army. The northerly approaches to the Tennessee River consisted of a succession of mountains and plateaux, which were difficult to cross in any event and were being periodically ranged over by Southern cavalry, making reinforcement or resupply along the inadequate roads that crossed such barren expanses an unlikely option.

The camps abounded, as they always did, with rumours on every possible angle of the campaign. It was being said that the Yankees in Chattanooga were eating leather and that rats or horsemeat were now delicacies in the beleaguered city. Another story said that reinforcements from, of all places, the Army of the Potomac back in Virginia, had finally been sent west and that Joe Hooker, the Yankee general soundly whipped by Robert E. Lee at Chancellorsville back in the spring, had been placed in command of them. Other rumours said that the western general Grant would soon, as previously predicted, be showing up at Chattanooga and a large part of the army that he had led through the summer along the Mississippi River would be arriving too, commanded by that other western Yankee, Sherman. Another thing that had been reported and then confirmed was the activities of the Chattanooga Yankees on the western end of that hairpin loop of the river to the northwest of the city. Stories had circulated of enemy troops establishing a lodgement on the Confederate side of the river and of pontoon boats being floated down to transport them across before being used to bridge the river. Maybe, some men suggested, the Yankees were trying to set up a supply line to the west, for it was hard to think of why else they should be interested in such a manoeuvre.

To some men all of this had the appearance of a gathering storm, as the enemy assembled his strength, but to others it was no great problem. If the rumours were correct, then the Potomac Army reinforcements consisted of the Eleventh and Twelfth Corps, and they were formations that the Army of Northern Virginia had regularly chastised back east. As for the western generals and their troops, last month had shown

211

what they could expect when they came up against the south's best formations, and this would happen again when and if the rumoured reinforcements arrived. The left flank of the Confederate line moreover, from where all of these reinforcing Yankees must approach, was held by John Hood's old division, including Jerome Robertson's Texans, Evander Law's Alabamians and the redoubtable Georgians of "Tige" Anderson and "Rock" Benning. If, the men around the fires told anyone who wanted reassurance, any Yankees came up on that flank, they would get a damned warm reception from men who knew exactly how to see to such things.

The final days of the month had arrived when the fight occurred, out to the west on the far side of Lookout Mountain. It began well after dusk, when with the moon having risen among broken clouds, a distant scattering of musketry awoke the sleeping camps. The drowsy men looked at each other, initially exchanging only brief comments on the outbreak.

"Somebody surely couldn't sleep over thar."

"Reckon they either got up early, or forgot to turn in?"

The initial outbreak was brief however, though the period of comparative quiet that followed it was also, lasting not even as far as midnight, then being broken again by further shooting, outpost firing again, though this time it did not fade, but grew steadily in volume until it had reached the pitch and intensity of a real fight. By now thicker cloud had gathered, hiding the moon, save for a brief occasional shaft of its pale light shining through. The men stirred again, acknowledging that further sleep was now unlikely, at least until whatever fighting was going on out there was resolved. Aware of all of the rumours, they began to gather around the remains of their fires only to be interrupted by the call to arms.

The company paraded in the darkness, waiting in their ranks for word, but after almost an hour with nothing in the way of news or orders arriving, they were dismissed to their fires, though the men kept their arms and equipment with them. Further precious wood was thrown upon the fires to revive the flames and, wrapping themselves in their blankets,

212

the men sat around, listening to the shooting which raged on in near to full scale battle proportions out beyond the mountain's bulk, passing an occasional comment on what they were hearing.

For some time there had been those rumours of Yankee reinforcements advancing on Chattanooga from the west. Their own First Corps comrades were positioned out on that western flank and surely they would have kept an eye on any approach routes, particularly with such commanding heights as Lookout Mountain and Raccoon Mountain beyond it from which to do their watching. The musketry crackled on through most of the hours of darkness, while the awakened men to the east of the mountain listened and speculated. As the dawn drew closer, the firing declined and finally ceased, but the talk around the fires did not for, whatever had taken place out there to the west had taken a fight of substantial proportions to get it done.

Morning brought damp, cloudy weather, but with it came news that astonished many of those in the camps, for more Yankees had indeed made an advance up the Wauhatchie Valley, between Lookout and Raccoon Mountains, pushing along the road that snaked up to link with the pontoon bridge on the west bank of the river. They had been met by elements of Jenkins' command, but following the overnight fire-fight the southerners had pulled back, leaving the whole valley route in Yankee hands. This meant that a route was now opened for supplies in quantity to begin reaching the besieged army in Chattanooga. The Confederate grip on the enemy throat, however passive or ineffective it had previously been, had now been prised loose. The dark fears that many men had expressed over the previous month had come to pass. While Bragg and his generals had done next to nothing, other than argue among themselves, the Yankees had used the time to advantage and now the position along the Tennessee River had changed and it was the enemy who had grasped the initiative.

213

The early news and the cascade of rumours that followed brought still more unwelcome details, for it was being said that the Yankees, who had forced their way up that valley to the west overnight, had been none other than Joe Hooker's Eleventh and Twelfth Corps men, those despised arrivals from Virginia, who had been hard luck outfits back in the east. It was being said that they were the men who had forced back Jenkins' soldiers, who had for a long time been counted among the best soldiers in the Army of Northern Virginia' and by doing so those half-baked eastern Yankees had changed the whole situation out here at Chattanooga. Around the southern camps men were at first disbelieving of this news and of what it meant. Howard's "Dutchmen" and Slocum's garrison rejects, had been looked down on, even by the rest of the Army of the Potomac Yankees, yet here they were getting the better of John Hood's old command. How could such a thing have happened? What kind of fumbling or mismanagement of Bragg's had led to this and, all in all, what in the hell was this whole business out here in Tennessee coming to?

Chapter 8 A Mission or a Mercy

The succeeding days brought more rumour. It was being said that Longstreet and Bragg were now on such bad terms that the Army of Northern Virginia divisions would soon be leaving the army. They would shortly be gone, heading eastwards by the railroad, making their way back to Virginia. On the way they would be occupying the city of Knoxville and pushing back the Yankee force that had advanced down into the eastern region of Tennessee when the Confederate force stationed there had been withdrawn, prior to Chickamauga, to reinforce Bragg's army. Almost all the men welcomed this news, for they had grown heartily tired of campaigning out here, where jealousy and discord reigned and the ordinary soldiers' efforts seemed to be cynically wasted. What was worse, away from the influence of General Lee even the officers of their own corps seemed to have entered into this culture of jealous rivalry.

Longstreet had been on poor terms with Bragg, according to the stories around camp, since the battle in September, but just about everybody seemed to be on poor terms with Bragg. Even worse, was the persistent rumour that a previous rivalry between Evander Law and Micah Jenkins, both men commanding brigades in John Hood's old division, had festered into something more like outright dislike, especially after that confused affair along the Wauhatchie valley the previous week, where each had blamed the other for whatever had gone wrong. Longstreet had, maybe predictably, taken the part of Jenkins, whose promotion to temporary divisional command, had been engineered by him, but with one of the pair in acting command of the division and the other still commanding its largest brigade, it seemed that their continuing enmity would bring nothing but trouble for the enlisted men caught in the middle of their feud.

On the Tuesday word began to circulate that the rumoured departure was imminent, and sure enough that afternoon the company was paraded to be told the news. They would withdraw that night and make their way eastwards to a station on the railroad where trains were being assembled to take them east. Rations were to be cooked prior to the departure, but these failed to arrive and the men were forced to make do with the scant remnants of the previous days' issue. After dusk, men from Stewart's division arrived on the line to occupy the positions that "Blues" had held.

"You boys had a belly full of ol' Bragg a'ready?" they inquired.

"Heard yo're all high tailin' it off back east and leavin' Bragg to it out here," one had said.

"Wish we could head off someplace and leave him to it too," another had added.

The Company B duty detail promptly drew back to their camps, joining the remainder of the men already assembled to leave. There was no moon as the files stepped off, with a guide it was said, at the front of the column. Although the rains had ceased, the roads remained muddy and the men sloshed their way south east, though with the 'march at ease' order given, they were able at least to form their customary groups and avoid the worst of the lying water and mud on the road. The sergeants continued to badger their sections however and repeated muttered complaints were to be heard as they continued their march.

"Close up, fer Ch...... sake!"

"Will ya git a damned shift on?"

"Move yore damned asses!" As the night progressed a drizzling rain began which gradually soaked the tramping soldiers, and first light found them with the great bulk of Missionary Ridge off to their left as they laboured on through the mud of the road. With the daylight, a brief halt was allowed and the men left the road to gather in their groups in the woods that flanked it to avoid the rain, crouching or sitting in the wet grass until the assembly order came along for the column to resume its trek.

216

The march to the rail halt at East Chattanooga that Wednesday morning continued to be tedious, conducted as it was on quagmire roads, with the drizzling rain spattering down on the column. Predictably, on their arrival they found the place surrounded by idle soldiers. The column was halted and eventually stood down, with little in prospect but a considerable wait, in the company of the many who had preceded them, for their turn with the trains.

East Chattanooga station lay on the East Tennessee and Georgia Railroad some distance to the east of the city and it presented a picture of run-down neglect. The station itself was little more than a country halt on the line and was maybe flattered by the term "station." It was surrounded by columns and groups of soldiers as various units of McLaws' division waited all around it for trains to arrive to transport them up the line to God knew where. Supplies too, typically, seemed to be in short supply, a situation undoubtedly made worse by the inability of the local munitions and commissary trains to furnish the corps' needs, especially now that its men were on the move once more.

Rubber blankets were employed by their Company B owners to set up shelters while trains came and went, and Ryan joined with Ballard and Jenkins for this purpose. With time now on their hands the former had employed himself in commenting upon the efforts of others to escape the rain and to note the arrival of still more columns of bedraggled men. His gift of sarcasm was repeatedly used on whatever aspect of the scene that took his attention, though Daniel Ryan was by now paying only passing attention, finding his mind dwelling more on the prospect that now faced them.

Perhaps it had been the nature of this whole Tennessee business. At first it had been talked of as a relatively brief episode, coming out here to see to the business of giving Rosecrans' Yankee army the licking it needed, chasing the Yankees back through Tennessee, and that done, heading back east to where they belonged. It had turned out to be nowhere near as simple as that, but then with the army, such

217

things never were. Plans would be made to do this thing or that thing, but they seldom ran their course without a sequence of problems, or snags of one kind or another cropping up. The battle, those six weeks ago, had illustrated this. The Yankees had been licked and sent packing, but far from re-establishing the Confederate cause in southern Tennessee, the retreating enemy had finished up taking refuge in the very city from which they were supposed to have been driven away Then there had been the siege, which had not been that much of a siege at all, for Bragg's army had never seemed to get around to closing off all the ways of supplying the city. The Yankees in Chattanooga were supposed to be starving, but they had shown no inclination to quit the place or to surrender, and now, as a result of that crazy fight last week they had received reinforcements, and a regular trail of supplies would now be reaching them. Considering the shortages in supply on the Confederate side, it was maybe unclear as to who was now starving the most, and for that matter whether it was the Yankees who were trapped around the city, or the Confederates that were pinned down on the adjacent hills and ridges.

Their own part in that particular episode was seemingly now at an end, but it was beginning to look like they might not be heading straight back to Virginia after all. Instead, if the latest rumours were true, although they were to be carried north east on the East Tennessee and Virginia Railroad, they would not be travelling anything like as far as Virginia. It was now being said that Knoxville, the city that sat astride the railroads, was their destination. The place was something over a hundred miles up the line and now the First Corps divisions were said to be on their way there to whip the Yankees who occupied it.

But it was increasingly apparent that this might be no simple matter. Knoxville was now said to be occupied by a large Yankee force, and recapturing the place might well involve a fight of some proportion before their journey back to Virginia could be continued. Their role here in Tennessee

218

therefore seemed to be extending ever further into the future, as though having got themselves entangled out here they were now stuck with it. This region had already shown how cold, wet and miserable it could be and for Company B, and indeed the whole regiment, with winter drawing on, the future seemed to hold little but the continuation of this dismal kind of campaigning, with no certainty of either a return to Virginia, or even of more comfortable winter quarters being set up here in Tennessee.

Late in the afternoon, the call to assemble came. The men stirred themselves, collecting their possessions and weapons, wishing to be gone from here, but reluctant to trust the news that they were finally going until they saw some evidence that it was actually about to happen. Trains were still arriving, but the number of cars that they hauled seemed to accommodate precious few of the waiting soldiers, while still more men, vehicles and guns were arriving around the station, promptly occupying whatever spaces had been vacated by those who had departed up the line. Having formed their files they were shepherded across to the railroad, where yet another locomotive was grinding in having executed its turn on the "Y" of track beyond the depot building.

The engine that had just arrived presented a sorry spectacle, with its boiler plates scarred and rusted. Steam leaked from a variety of places along it, though as it noisily drew to a halt, Daniel Ryan quickly concluded that much more than the boiler was in urgent need of attention. As though to confirm this, the moment the locomotive had stopped a burly black man dressed in stained dungarees promptly jumped down from the footplate with a large oil can in his hand, to begin squirting the contents liberally onto the bearings that connected the various pistons, flanges and drive wheels.

The cars that the locomotive had delivered were of the same standard set by the engine and continued the southern railroad tradition of being worn down and dilapidated. Virtually none of the railroad cars that the Company B travellers had seen, since way back in the opening weeks of the war, had been in anything resembling good condition, but as far as Daniel Ryan was concerned, these trucks and cars seemed to take the idea of "worn" to a new level. Sections of the flooring were missing from the flatcars, and though the worst of these holes had been patched with green lumber, there were still many places where a man could look through the boards onto the wheels and frame below. The box cars were no better, some being mere frames, planked with more unseasoned wood which, as the sergeants hustled their men on board, bent and sprang alarmingly as significant weight was placed on them.

"Be goddam safer walkin'," Norton called.

"We already tried that," Dellings told him. "Git yore asses on board and let's see if this is any better." The men arranged themselves tentatively on the cars, many of them moving gingerly to avoid finishing up on the rail bed below, with the sergeants hurrying them into some sort of order. Eventually the train was as ready as it was going to get and the locomotive gave a hoarse blast of its whistle. It began to puff, and then to pull, jerking the cars into an uncertain and protesting motion which faltered several times as the engine laboured and strained, before finally establishing something that resembled a continuing, if juddering, momentum. They began to pass trees on either side, though at a pace that was so far little faster than that which they had recently managed on foot.

"War'll be over by the time we get anywhere," Matthew Hale commented, in one of his comparatively rare contributions to the mess discussions.

"I surely hope so," Kane told him. "Right now we got more chance o' trouble from wood splinters in the butt than from anythin' the Yankees are doin'."

The train journey was indeed like no other that they had previously experienced. The cars screeched and groaned every yard of the way, the sounds preying brutally upon the hearing of those on board, who periodically gritted their teeth and screwed up their faces in response. The majority of the men, being on open cars and wagons, were subjected to regular soakings from the successive showers of rain that fell throughout the evening and on into the night, though the Company B gum blankets saved their owners from the worst of these. For all however, when the rain came it was a matter of sitting through the downpour as stoically as possible and doing what could be done to dry blankets and clothing once the shower had passed.

As if the weather was not enough of an ordeal, on several occasions, when the train was faced with any steeper kind of climb, the locomotive faltered to a screeching, steam-blowing halt, upon which the passengers were ordered to disembark and walk alongside their wagons and cars till the top of the gradient was reached. On two of these occasions, the locomotive resorted to the tactic of backing up for a stretch after the soldiers had disembarked, to give itself a chance to build sufficient momentum to manage the climb on its renewed approach. This done, the train screeched to a further halt and the toiling men were ordered back on board, for the laborious haul to recommence.

Towns were passed, each of them marking their progress to the north east. Cleveland came and went, followed by Charleston. The little Hiwassee River was crossed by a neglected wooden bridge, with a further town named Athens being reached shortly after. Up ahead lay their destination, a place by the name of Sweetwater, where rumour said the divisions would assemble before commencing their advance upon Knoxville. Ambrose Burnside, that same general who had been in command of the eastern Army of the Potomac at Fredericksburg last winter, was said to be in command of these Yankees up ahead and some of the men on the train looked upon this as a good omen. He had not been much of a tactician back then, they told each other, for he had marched a large part of his army up to an almost impregnable position only to be shot down in hordes and maybe he would be equally obliging this time around. It was being said that he had pushed his forces westwards from fortified positions around Knoxville itself to the Holston River, to meet the Confederate advance there where the railroad crossed, just upstream from its junction with the Little Tennessee River.

What emerged also was that William Wofford, the brigade commander, would not be leading them in this campaign. The general was absent in Georgia, on sick leave some men said, while others maintained that the general had instead gone home to bury his daughter, who had succumbed to illness. The brigade was, for the time being, under the command of Colonel Solon Ruff of the Eighteenth Georgia, a man regarded as a brave leader and a good soldier, even though he was only in his twenties. Ruff was a professor of some kind and must therefore be a clever man. His military qualities would now, with brigade command, be put to the test.

The Ogeecheee Volunteers arrived at Sweetwater on the Sunday to find that although plentiful rations had been gathered and stored there, what was available was in the process of being loaded onto the trains from which Longstreet's troops had just disembarked, to be shipped back down to Chattanooga to Bragg's army. The following days were therefore spent foraging and requisitioning to build up sufficient of a supply of provisions to allow the advance towards Knoxville to commence once the remaining division of infantry and the artillery had arrived.

Tied to the railroad by their shortage of transportation, McLaws' troops undertook the march from Sweetwater towards the railroad bridge, a distance of maybe fifteen miles, anticipating a fight in getting across to the north bank. A pontoon bridge was on the way up the railroad, this being why the troops could no longer travel by train, and therefore once the pontoons and other equipment had arrived the real trouble could begin. The weather remained disagreeable with rain on almost every day, and a great deal of it on some of them as they tramped the muddy road from Sweetwater eastwards on that wet Wednesday, some of them enthusiastically anticipating what was to come. Burnside's Yankees, they told each other, would have the usual abundance of equipment and supplies and here therefore was the chance for the First Corps soldiers to make up some of their many shortages.

Their initial destination was the settlement of Loudon, near to where the Railroad crossed the river, lying on one of those hairpin bends which the river had a habit of making. The column halted short of the town and the men set up camp to await the next move. Details were immediately dispatched to forage the area until, with sufficient rations collected, to provide provisions for at least the immediate future, the units were re-assembled. There was however no word of bridging pontoons, which condemned the men to spending their time in dismal, soaking camps and then, when the bridging equipment all finally arrived on a succession of trains, there were no wagons to haul it anywhere else.

On the Wednesday afternoon, shortly after their arrival at Loudon, the men were finally given notice of a pending move, a night march and sure enough, almost immediately after darkness fell, they were roused and assembled, leaving camp fires banked up with extra wood to fool any watching enemy. The destination was said to be a place on the river where a ferry had previously run, and by the Thursday morning the destination had been reached and the pontoons, having been manhandled the distance from the railroad to the river, were being assembled for the bridging to begin.

The bridge, so McLaws' men heard, was promptly enough laid and the men of Jenkins' division were the first to cross. The unwelcome part of the exercise was that McLaws' brigades were not present to take their turn, having been detached by Longstreet to foray along the southern bank of the river in an effort to divert enemy attention from the crossing downstream. Eventually they had returned to the bridge at Hough's Ferry to find that it was a crude and makeshift structure, precariously anchored to the banks of the river. Pulled and distorted by the current, it executed its

223

crossing in the shape of an inverted "S," rather than in anything resembling a straight line.

The troops promptly began to cross, with the waiting brigades able to observe the instability of the structure as the leading regiments negotiated it. The pontoons strained and creaked, pulling against their supporting ropes, as the men approached to take their turn. To Company B, it all seemed too reminiscent of that similar crossing of the swollen Potomac the previous summer. The Holsten River was high, as the Potomac had been, carrying the autumn rains of the previous weeks downstream on its strong current, but the crossing proceeded regardless of that. The orders, the same ones as previously, went along the files, reformed in their fours for the crossing.

"Don't march boys, ya know damn well by now, jest walk across."

"Same as last summer, walk across and it keeps the thing steadier." Daniel looked out across the crowded pontoons as he came up to the approach. This bridge, even more than the one last summer, had a precarious look to it, with the pontoons having been improvised from a variety of different timbers. Some of them had settled, flooding almost to their gunwales in the river, confirming that they were far from watertight, and men all along the column looked on the prospect of trusting their safety to such a structure with grave misgivings.

The previous summer crossing of the Potomac had been made in darkness, an eerie and troubling experience, but now, as he looked out at the swaying walk way and wallowing pontoons, Daniel began to reflect that maybe darkness was better, for much of that experience had been invisible, hidden from view by the blackness of the night. Here everything was out there, in plain sight, and as he stepped onto the first of the timbers and felt it lurch and tremble under his feet, Daniel began to wish that darkness could obscure the hazards of this crossing as it had in July. The files linked arms, as they had done the previous time and set out along the shifting boards, making elaborate efforts not to synchronise their steps, an awkward thing for veteran soldiers to do since marching in time with their comrades was an ingrained instinct and hard to overcome unless a man concentrated his attention on doing so.

The journey across the Holsten was, if anything, more unnerving than the Potomac crossing had been. The men grasped each other's arms grimly as they negotiated the shuddering walkway in their files, some of them scarcely daring to breathe as they crossed. Daniel Ryan resolved to concentrate his gaze on the man straight ahead who happened to be Charlie Thorne and he stuck rigidly to this, pointedly ignoring the succession of shifts and shudders on the way across. The relief was obvious among many of them when they reached the far side, with outbreaks of cheering and chatter erupting along their files as they scrambled up the muddy bank. Ballard, as always, had a comment for the occasion.

"I declare to ya'all," he said. "If I ever try t' tell you boys to climb on another o' those goddam death traps jest shoot me." Jones was not to be outdone on this occasion.

"With yore smart mouth," he said, "thar's some days I'd be happy enough to shoot ya, without needin' no bridge fer a reason." The men tramped on, marching at ease once more on another quagmire road.

Up ahead, the latest stories said, the river turned yet another hairpin bend and the Yankees had been sighted by the cavalry on the far side of the one that their own column was beginning to traverse They had, it seemed, not gone far and maybe a fight was on the way after all.

Not content with negotiating just one of those river bends as the long columns of men, guns and wagons started eastwards, they came upon another of them and then another, where the road stretched on within sight of the river, before turning further inland on its north easterly course. The Saturday afternoon wore on, with the rain falling more heavily than it had earlier in the day and the road becoming steadily more treacherous as a consequence. They reached a village, said to rejoice in the title of Lenoir Station, but there was little to be seen of it in the gathering dusk, as the rain still fell and the men toiled onwards. Beyond the village they were at last halted and moved off the road for a fleeting episode of huddling without fires, in wet woollen blankets beneath their waterproof shelters. If the Yankees were as close as they had been reported, then maybe the fight which had been anticipated for the day just past, had been delayed rather than postponed.

Chapter 9 Pursuit

The men of Company B were roused, in the darkness of the Sunday morning, as still more heavy rain fell, driven on a freshening wind. Daniel Ryan stirred and looked around at the glistening black cocoons as they began to move in response to the calls. With the routine complaints of their sergeants in their ears, they gathered equipment and belongings before forming their ranks, with gum blankets serving again as ponchos for those men fortunate enough to possess them. The step off came promptly and as they sloshed down the road, awaiting the march at ease order, fragments of gossip soon began to percolate down the column. Burnside's Yankees were over towards the river, marching on an almost parallel road just a mile or two off there to the south east. With any sort of luck they could catch the Yankees, pin them against the river, and give them the licking that would end at a stroke the campaign that had only just begun.

This rumour was reinforced pretty promptly after setting out, when a dismounted trooper from Wheeler's cavalry was encountered at the roadside. He sat under a roadside tree, with his carbine, saddle and other possessions around him and the remains of a gum blanket around his shoulders. The taunts from the column began as soon as he came into view.

"Hey mister, whadya do with yore mule?"

"You sittin' this whole war out now boy?"

"Seen any Yankees this mornin'?"

"Reckon his horse's run off." The man ignored the insults, preferring to answer the more serious queries as to where the Yankees were.

"They're skedaddlin'," he called to the passing infantry. "They're headin' back t' Knoxville, but they gotta pass a crossroads up thar," he gestured with his free hand. "We could bushwhack 'em, if you boys kin git there ahead o' them." As they left the man behind and moved on, Daniel Ryan heard him repeating his news to the files behind, till his voice faded, drowned by the noises of the weather and those from the passing column.

A pulse of something resembling anticipation began to run along the files, as men digested the cavalryman's words. Maybe that chance of a fight was closer than they had thought and the men reacted to the news in their own characteristic ways, some loudly anticipating a chance to whip these damned blue-bellies, others remaining more thoughtful and restrained at the prospect. The column splashed on as still the rain fell, driven on what was now a stiff wind which swept it into the faces of the marching men, but that pulse of anticipation sparked by the trooper's news, still motivated them. If the Yankees were as close as the cavalryman had said, they could likely expect a fight today after all and, as the talk went along the column, the first faint sounds of gunfire came to their ears from off to the southeast.

With any sort of good fortune the Yankees could be intercepted, or even beaten to the crossroads of which the soldier had spoken before they had the chance to get back to Knoxville and shelter behind its defences. If the march could just be pushed enough, till this place up ahead was reached, the enemy could maybe be cut off and bagged like rats in a barrel. If Wheeler's cavalry were up there, harassing the enemy as it seemed from the faint crackle of musketry over to the south, they could surely delay them and fix them until the infantry arrived and finished the job on them.

The buzz that ran through the company, as signs of the fight grew, was almost visible. The enemy were over to the south and they could be defeated here, miles from their base, if the southern troops at the head of the column could just get to that road junction first. If this could be done, then the day would then become a matter of hunkering down and letting the Yankees come at them, and everyone knew well enough that this was the best way to fight a battle. In the meantime the march must be pushed and the crossroads reached, and maybe this was the turning point in their fortunes that had seemed to languish since the fight at Chickamauga more than seven weeks previously. The roads were deteriorating in the continuing rain, which if anything was getting heavier, with all the men now plastered up to the waist or even beyond in chilling, liquid mud, but they were away from that damned fool Bragg, and with their own officers in charge they could do it, with any sort of luck they could do it.

Hardly had they resumed their progress on the execrable road, when orders came relaying down and the mud-plastered Company B column was briefly halted, before being wheeled from the road to the left into a dripping, soggy wood. They were moved on, further from the road and they pushed ahead through the trees and undergrowth, trying to protect themselves from the whipping, tearing branches that in addition to snagging at clothing and scratching at skin, was dislodging further cascades of water onto them.

Eventually the column was halted again and the shouted orders came along to right face into line of battle. The men pushed their way into ranks, forming on the group of bedraggled officers and sergeants, who had positioned themselves among the tree trunks and bushes that obstructed their deployment. If they were going to advance in line of battle, the thought raced through Daniel Ryan's mind, his heart pounded like a hammer in his chest and throat, then the Yankees must have reached the junction first, so it was now a pursuit rather than an attempt to entrap the enemy. Then more orders came, interrupting his thoughts, shouted along by the officers and relayed by the sergeants, jerking the lines into ungainly motion across a saturated landscape.

The morning passed with the men labouring on across broken country, negotiating ravines and thickets, fields and fences, gullies and woods, soaked to the skin and scratched and scoured by brambles and briars. Weapons began the hike at the port, but after a time the ranks were halted and the muskets were slung, allowing the men, at least to an extent, to use their hands to aid their progress over the difficult ground. Eventually the lines reached a more open stretch of country, but as they continued their advance, they soon came under fire. Artillery shells began to tear in, their progress virtually invisible in the rain and low cloud, landing in the soggy ground up ahead, sending fountains of mud into the air as they exploded. After a while, the dull thuds of the cannon and the blasts of exploding shells were joined by musketry. Away to the right, towards the road, there came the scattered crackling of what was most likely a skirmishers' exchange, all but confirming that whatever else had transpired this morning the Yankees were out ahead and had therefore not, after all the labouring in the mud, been overtaken and cut off by the southern advance.

They plodded on eastwards, making for a place that so far existed only by the stranded cavalryman's words. The gusting of the wind, the tinkling of equipment, the bellows and curses of the sergeants and the endless slopping of feet in the mud were the prevailing sounds of the advance, with the wheezing breath of all but the closest of the men lost among the other noises. Any talk along the ranks in the early part of the morning had died away and the advance now continued in a determined silence, save for the occasional shouts of the company officers, taken up promptly by the sergeants.

"Push on, men!"

"Hold yore damned places boys!"

But coping with the conditions was a seemingly endless trial. They were having to virtually flounder their way forward over a sodden near-flooded countryside, extracting each foot from the mud in order to transfer it forward and plant it down into the treacherous muck again, repeating the whole process with every step, while the shells continued to arrive, sending their geysers of mud into the air and always presenting the threat that the next salvo, or maybe the one after, would land in their midst, scattering their showers of splinters and fragments among the harassed men. As Company B continued to labour they began to hear other familiar sounds of still more firing, musketry this time, from up ahead that quickly grew, drowning out the more desultory outbreaks of skirmishing away to the right. These latest outbreaks seemed to announce that out in front somewhere, the race against the retreating Yankees might well be in the process of being decided.

The lines were eventually halted and most of the initial hour of the afternoon was spent with the men standing in their places, while up ahead, beyond another stretch of woods, a heavy skirmish dragged on. As the firing continued and their own ranks remained motionless, comments began to make their way among the sodden, mud-plastered men.

"That must be Wheeler's boys," Abe White called. "Reckon they've gotten them by the ass up there." Others around him however were more sceptical.

"Too damn soon t' tell anythin' like that," Jones retorted. Around them most men kept their own council on who was doing what in whatever fight had gotten under way out in front. So far, whatever it was, it did not involve them directly, and the daylight hours of the brief late autumn day were passing.

Out ahead the firing was growing and a further mutter went along the lines. As the prospect of a fight returned, the tell-tale signs of battle began to spread among the men. Daniel Ryan felt his body shuddering, though whether that was due to the cold and his saturated clothing or to those familiar tensions on the approach of another fight, he could not tell. In addition to the shuddering of his limbs, his heart was pounding increasingly hard, while his stomach felt its customary nausea and his throat seemed almost blocked by the lump that no amount of swallowing ever seemed able to dislodge. These thoughts were still coursing through his mind when the next orders came.

"Recover..., arms!" The muskets were retrieved from where they rested by their slings on the shoulder, and manoeuvred around for the butts to be placed firmly on the wet ground.

"Fix Bayonets!" The right hand of each man reached immediately around, to grasp the socket of the bayonet where it rested behind him. Daniel withdrew his own weapon, hearing and feeling the slight scraping sound and sensation that spoke of the beginnings of rust in the scabbard, for the rain in this damned country would rust just about anything. He tightened his muddy fingers around the hollow socket as he brought the weapon around and fitted it over the muzzle of his grounded musket, sliding it briefly along the barrel till it reached its place with the muzzle foresight settled in the "L" shaped cavity in the socket. The bayonets were then rotated that quarter turn to the right so that the blade rested to the right of the barrel. This done, the locking ring on the bayonet socket was twisted, tightening until the blade was locked in its place to the right of the barrel. Daniel tried to relax momentarily as he waited for the next command.

"Ready muskets!" Stoppers were withdrawn from the barrel muzzles.

"Load, but do not prime!" On either side of him hands fumbled under the flaps of cartridge pouches, Daniel's fingers did likewise, gripping around a paper cartridge, and he pulled it out, shielding it from the rain with his hand as he pushed the flap between his teeth to bite the paper and tear the thing open. Retaining the heavy lead bullet in his teeth, he pushed the cartridge immediately to the muzzle of the Enfield, still holding the fingers of his other hand over it to save the pouring black powder from the worst of the weather. He leaned forward to spit the bullet into the muzzle, guiding it in with his fingers, before stuffing the paper wrapping into the barrel after it. He reached for the ramrod, grasping it in his right hand and pulling it from its channel, before twirling it in the air and inserting the button into the muzzle, pushing it down in one smooth movement. A couple of firm thrusts and the steel rod was withdrawn and twirled again, before being pushed firmly back into its channel, thus completing the loading. It was all done in a smooth sequence of activity: for there was no need, in a veteran formation such as this, to separate each stage into the separate commands that were detailed in regulations. All along the line the men replaced

232

their muzzle stoppers as they waited for the anticipated further shouts of command.

"Skirmishers forward!" The distant shouts came along and Daniel watched the sprinkling of dark figures leave from further along the line, jogging forward in their pairs, to zigzag away among the trees, until most of them were out of sight.

"Carry arms!" Up the muskets went, with the trigger guards now resting on the fingers of the right hand and the barrel of the weapon steadied against the right shoulder.

"Guiding right, forward march!" and at last the line shuffled into awkward motion, suffering again the familiar difficulties of advancing through woods, with men having repeatedly to leave their places to dodge around trees and bushes, while the shouts and profanities of the sergeants showed that they were taking their usual impatient view of such deviations.

The line lurched on, over rough and uneven ground, until finally they came up towards the crest of a shallow rise with the edge of the woods at last in view and they emerged from the dripping trees to hear the order to halt come relaying along. The line shuddered to a standstill and the men shuffled back into their places, dressing their ranks and adjusting their muskets, then gazed ahead, as still the rain drove across the fields, coming now in a diagonal from their left. In front lay a muddy pasture which on reaching a wooden rail fence, changed to a wider expanse of even muddier stubble that stretched away into the distance towards the drifting cloud of smoke which covered the ground out in front, alternately obscuring and revealing a substantial brick property over to their right front. Beyond it, at the distant margin of a further field, was a lighter blue smudge, the overcoats of an enemy line of battle, surmounted by its dully gleaming hedgehog of musket barrels and bayonets.

Out ahead they could see the men of their own skirmish line, almost at the fence that separated the pasture from the stubble, with the first of them now reaching and clambering across the rails, being greeted, almost immediately, by a stutter of shots marked by puffs of distant gun smoke.

"Reckon Joe Wheeler's boys couldn't a' got that much of a twist on 'em after all," Ballard announced, "but what d'ya expect from the damned cavalry?" There was a brief snigger of acknowledgement from a few of those around him, as more shouts came to them from the right announcing the arrival of the step off order. Along the line it came, just audible above the distant skirmish fire until closer voices took it up.

"Shoulder arms!" Up the muskets went with the butt plates now supported by the right hand.

"Forward march!" The line was moving again, shuffling untidily forward at first, until a rhythm of march was established and the movement became somewhat more even-paced and orderly. The mud of the grass field was treacherous, causing a few of the men to slither and slide as they headed on towards the fence labouring to preserve their formation. From behind them, Jeffers shouted an order and a detail of men promptly left their places to double time forward and set to work attacking the posts and rails until, in a matter of seconds, the obstacle was no more. The battle line came plodding up to the tangle of wooden debris, crossing it with exaggerated care, being halted briefly on the far side to reform the line before stepping away again.

If the pasture had been treacherous, the softer mud of the stubble field was worse, for it allowed the men's feet to sink further, making movement even more difficult, especially since feet emerged from each successive step with an ever-increasing clod of mud attached to each shoe. Daniel Ryan stumbled on in his place in the front rank, concentrating on trying to keep step and pace with the men on either side and squinting only occasionally through the rain and mist towards where the enemy line lay, now hidden in the drifting smoke of the skirmishers' encounter. Then, heavier firing erupted from somewhere off to their right, while out in front, as the smoke momentarily cleared away, there was a movement along that distant blue line, as those men brought the weapons down from their shoulders to present them.

"Too far," the thought went through Ryan's mind in an instant, for even assuming that they were rifled weapons, many of the soldiers who carried and used them could not be relied upon to hit much at anything over a couple of hundred yards. The distance between the two lines, though closing steadily, was way further than that and, seeing the movement, a hint of relief soared through his brain. If they fired now they would be discharging their best loaded volley, at a distance where few of the shots would logically find a target. He watched the enemy line intently now, listening for the slightest hint of a distant shout of command. Around him some of his comrades were scathing.

"They ain't openin' up," that was Winder's voice, "are they?"

"Let 'em open up all they want," Jones snapped back. "They won't hit nothin' at that range." The distant blue line remained there motionless, just visible through the mist and the downpour, with muskets still presented.

Ryan began to think that perhaps they would wait after all, but then a ripple of off-white smoke began moving along the enemy formation, hiding it from view as it spread, with the crackle of the volley coming to them a second or so after the discharge had been seen. Daniel braced himself, reacting in spite of the distance, for it was always unnerving when an enemy line opened fire. Their own ranks sloshed on through the mud, but this time there was almost nothing. A few of those buzzes peculiar to minie balls came to the ears as the closest shots went past, but along the Company B part of the line there was nothing more. None of the sickening smacks or crunching thuds as heavy lead slugs hit flesh or bone; nor any gasps, curses or shouts of shock or pain, as men realised that they had been hit. There was only the continuing more distant firing to be heard from somewhere else along the line and the close-by noises of laboured breathing and those wet, sucking sounds of many feet in the dragging mud.

Up ahead, the smoke was drifting clear again to reveal the enemy line, closer now and hurriedly reloading, fumbling with ramrods and caps. Then came the distant order and the enemy muskets were levelled again, but it was not the same uniform motion that had preceded the first volley. This movement was more ragged, with not all of the enemy soldiers having completed their reloading, maybe through having to take additional care in the driving rain. They were rushing now, Daniel Ryan could see it in their frantic attempts to catch up, as they pushed against those on either side in their haste to level their weapons before the order came.

"Fire!" They heard the command this time and again the dirty white smoke billow engulfed the Yankee line, with the crash of the volley coming closer on the heels of the smoke cloud. This time however the noise of the volley was more ragged, like a brief stutter rather than a single, crashing noise. This time there were more buzzing bullets audible as they whizzed past and now there were one or two of those thuds and a single shout of pain from along the line. Daniel felt a push on his left side and he almost slipped in the mud, keeping his balance by stamping his raised foot immediately back down into the gripping mud. He pushed on, shifting his arm to re-balance his musket and hurrying the step or two that took him back into his place. The smoke out there was clearing again, but now they were descending slightly, down into a shallow dip that was beginning to hide the Yankee line. They heard the command and saw the muskets come up, followed by that pause as they aimed and waited for the laggards.

"Fire!" Again the order came clearly and this time the volley came through the wisping strands of smoke from the one that had preceded it. The shots came buzzing through and again Daniel heard a couple of those squelching wet thuds as bullets found vulnerable limbs. The line heaved and buckled momentarily, but steadied itself as the men pushed on, ascending out of the dip as the smoke began to thin again. The Yankee line was close now. Daniel could see the buttons on the light blue overcoats emerging from the smoke, seeming so much closer than they had previously been to the point that,

236

even through the driving rain, the features of individual men could almost be made out, as they rammed furiously and fumbled in hip pouches for caps. But now it was the turn of Company B as the order came bellowing along to halt the line.

"Ready muskets!" That was Thompson, whose shout could be heard anywhere. The weapons were balanced, while stoppers were removed from the muzzles to be stuffed into pockets.

"Prime!" Daniel's fingers were pushing into the cap pouch on his belt to grasp a tiny cap, feeling its sharp edges against his fingertips as he withdrew it. He reached up with his fingers still grasping the cap and pulled the hammer back to half cock with the heel of his hand, before pressing the cap down onto the metal nipple and squeezing its sides inwards as he pulled his hand away, fixing his thumb onto the top of the hammer while his finger reached underneath to the trigger. He eased the hammer down gently resting it on the cap.

"Aim!" Thompson again and all along the line Daniel Ryan caught glimpses of the long barrels coming up to present towards the enemy. He settled the butt of his own weapon into his shoulder, pulling the hammer back to fully cocked and simultaneously squinting along the barrel to briefly sight the tip of the muzzle button into the groove of the rear sight, as he swung the weapon towards the enemy line.

"Fire!" He squeezed the trigger as smoothly as he could, sensing the flash of the cap near his face, more prominent in the cloud and rain, and feeling the kick of the Enfield as the recoil from its discharge punched the butt back into his shoulder. The smoke cloud swirled all around, harsh and acrid in the nose and eyes as Thompson's voice came again.

"Charge 'em boys, forward and let's get at 'em!" All around Daniel Ryan the muskets were being levelled as another Yankee volley tore through. Daniel sensed rather than saw men stumbling as the bullets took them, but this was a ragged volley delivered in the wake of their own fire. He tightened his grip on his own musket, thrusting it forward at hip height and pushed clumsily forward into the smoke, feeling his feet slip and slide as he attempted to accelerate and hearing the shrill yell rise along the line as he advanced. He gasped an inward breath before adding his own voice to the screeching shout as he stumbled forward through the treacherous mud and the slowly thinning cloud of choking smoke.

"They're pullin' back!" Daniel heard the shouts from around him as they emerged from the dispersing cloud, catching his first glimpse of the enemy line moving back, as yet more artillery shells began to approach, tearing overhead to burst just behind where the ranks of Company B advanced.

They pushed forward, seeing the Yankees moving away, still in a rough rank but going nevertheless, with only individual soldiers pausing to fire at their assailants. Then came the tearing paper noise of more arriving shells, a whole salvo of them, suggesting that more guns were now deployed on those ridge lines up ahead. These explosions came just ahead of where they advanced, splashing more ugly fountains of mud into the air as they scattered their deadly rain of fragments around in front of the advancing infantry. Men went down while others faltered, coming to a slithering halt in the mud. Ahead Daniel Ryan heard a ragged cheer rise along the Yankee line as they saw their pursuers hesitate. More deep thuds came from somewhere behind them giving notice that southern guns had also begun to fire, sending their projectiles over, to cross paths with the next Yankee salvoes. Daniel looked upwards, finding he was just able to distinguish a few of the smoky trails of the shells, almost white against the greyer overcast of the sky and the lancing rain. He grimaced towards Winder, getting a brief shake of the head in return.

"Bad place to be right now," Winder said and Daniel nodded half to himself. Much of the Confederate artillery ammunition was so damned unreliable that it was just about as likely to explode above their own men as the enemy or sometimes, it was said, even before it cleared the barrel of the

238

cannon. He could hear the shouts of the sergeants around him as still more shells tore overhead.

"Form boys! Form!" Daniel turned and moved towards where Thompson stood beside Carson and Bayfield, all of them with their arms extended to either side, to guide the men of the company back into line. They began to assemble, slithering and shuffling in the mud as they took their places. Daniel saw Ballard and Winder and then Jenkins, Hale and Jones and finally Kane appeared, with blood on his face. They jostled into the line as Kane's voice came, in the midst of the continuing firing.

"It ain't mine." He looked out in front as still more of the company jostled their way into their places. The Yankees were some distance away now. They too were gathering their men and forming a more cohesive line as they went, but in truth the fact that they were out there in front at all was the main disappointment. The day, Daniel reflected, had begun all those hours ago in the pre-dawn darkness with the prospect of cutting these Yankees off from their base at Knoxville, but the presence of this rearguard on the Kingston road that led on to the north east in the direction of the city, was clear enough proof as to who had won the race for the crossroads. As the line was called to order, Daniel looked away from the retiring enemy, casting his eyes around him and seeing away to the rear the pathetic brown shapes twitching or prostrate in the mud of the fields. There were not many of them, the thought came to him almost at once, but here was the real cost of the day and even as the sights registered, into his mind came the notion that these men, like those who had spent their blood back down around Chattanooga, had likely died for nothing.

The pursuit was resumed almost immediately, but pursuit was a flattering notion of what took place in the final daylight hours of that brief late Autumn day as the rain at last began to ease. The artillery exchanges continued, but as the time passed and the Confederate line moved carefully forward once more, the gunners appeared to be engaging in counter-battery fire and were content, for the meantime at least, to leave the infantry be. They came up towards the enemy again, as the light of the brief, overcast evening had already begun to fade. This time however the advance never approached the enemy rearguard to the extent that they had been able to earlier in the day, for the simple reason that the Yankees now seemed content to check the Confederate approach with a few volleys of musketry before pulling back again, covering the withdrawal with their artillery.

The men in the Company B ranks were growing increasingly angry with it all. Perhaps it was frustration at being balked after a long day of endurance in the wind and rain when they had believed that they had a chance to trap their foe, but their comments now showed an exasperation at the way the day had gone. There was not the slightest reason to spend any more men's lives, when the opportunity had clearly passed and the Yankees had shown that they had no intention of staying around to fight. As dusk fell, the pursuit was finally halted and the men were dismissed to seek shelter, thankful that they had not divested themselves of their blanket rolls, haversacks and other possessions before starting their advance.

The rain had passed when Daniel Ryan awoke, after a sound enough sleep in his wet clothing and blankets. Fires had been forbidden the previous evening, which reduced the men to gnawing on what remnants of food, whether cooked or raw, that they carried with them. Word began to circulate of a Yankee supply train having been abandoned during the forced marches of the previous day, but Company B saw nothing of this as they gathered in groups to share such warmth as they could mutually generate. The cavalry and maybe some of Jenkins' men, who had been over on that flank yesterday to press and harry the Yankees, would be the most likely beneficiaries of whatever had been captured. Their own lot had been to try for whatever rest could be gained in a saturated bivouac, through which a stiff wind still gusted. As for today, fires were being kindled, many of them generating much more smoke than warmth, in an effort to get some kind of drying and maybe to heat something to eat or drink before the march was resumed. Knoxville was said to be upwards of ten miles distant over flooded roads, and with the enemy making for the city, their own arrival there, as hard on their heels as possible, might make the capture of the place somewhat less difficult. The generals would surely therefore be keen to get their men on the road to resume as much of a pursuit as might be feasible.

Chapter 10 Knoxville

They came up towards the outer defences of Knoxville late on the Monday, finding that the cavalry were already there, but with the daylight already fading they were bivouacked along the roadsides to wait till morning before attempting to invest the place. Tuesday morning brought fog, and having assembled at dawn, the troops waited by the roadside for the weather to improve. The fog gradually thinned, clearing finally in the late morning and the brigade column was set in motion, to the north of the railroad, ascending onto a plateau of higher ground, with Wofford's men eventually deployed, facing east, to the rear of Humphries' Mississippians. Kershaw's regiments were already pushing forward to the south of the railroad, which was flanked by a creek. The South Carolinians were deployed in front of what looked like a hastily erected breastwork of fence rails, set on the crest of a hill, marked by two tall trees. To the north of the hill lay the creek and to the south flowed the river. If this was the position that Longstreet intended to attack, there was only one way to do so and that was straight towards it, for with its flanks anchored as they were, there were no other options.

Afternoon had come and, save for some sharpshooting and cannon fire, the lines remained as they had been since morning. Finally as evening approached, a brief cannonade was opened, shattering portions of the barricade. The men on the opposite ridge watched as fragments of fence rails flew into the air, waiting in their ranks while the South Carolinians advanced, steadily increasing the pressure on the Yankee positions until, after a brief but bitter fight, they finally crested the ridge and overran the enemy line.

The whole southern line then moved forward as the evening drew on, moving north-eastwards with Wofford's men staying to the north of the railroad, and finally deploying into line, facing south on either side of a further road that stretched from the city to the northwest. The main positions

242

were established on a ridge line which descended southwards into a valley where the railroad line ran, with the division's right flank extending away from the road towards the bank of a creek. Beyond the railroad a forward picket line was established where the ground began to rise more steeply towards a further ridge line, and along its crest the enemy works were situated. Substantial entrenching had taken place and this was continuing, with turned earth much in evidence, and even as Company B worked on laying out their own positions, distant labouring figures could be seen along the enemy line. Beyond the front edge of that ridge the forward enemy trench line was also being strengthened, with sections of abbatis beginning to appear along its length, protecting the earthworks behind. The main enemy positions were anchored at their north western point by a more substantial earthwork, where a Union flag fluttered on a pole and what even at this distance looked like a parapet of rawhide-covered cotton bales with cannon embrasures placed at intervals along its length.

Whatever the generals decided to do about Knoxville, a view of the defences, even one as limited as the one available to Company B, showed that there was not the slightest chance of the southern troops simply walking into the place. The mood among the men was therefore far from cheerful, for here lurked the prospect of another version of what they had just left down at Chattanooga. Unless "Old Pete" showed himself to be a damned sight better general than Bragg and had gotten over the "Tennessee slows" as some of the men had taken to referring to it, the same kind of stalemate could develop here at Knoxville as had happened back downriver. Delay and indecision among the generals could soon fritter away whatever chance there was of capturing the place without making a major campaign of it. The men of Company B had seen that once and they did not want to see it again.

Camps were established beyond what remained of the belt of woods that separated the main lines from the railroad and the land beyond. The days began to pass and more rain fell. Porter Alexander's artillery batteries, having arrived and been initially placed in the course of the first couple of days, were promptly dug into emplacements. In one sense this was routine, for it allowed the gunners to go about their work and service their pieces with less chance of counter-battery fire or sharp-shooting inflicting needless casualties among them. The other benefit of their presence was that artillery units carried a range of tools, some of which the neighbouring infantrymen were able to borrow, to help with their own digging and entrenching.

The trouble with it all was that emplacements were most usually dug when guns were deployed in the positions where they were intended to stay and this likely hinted at more delay and maybe even a siege, like the one they had just left. This would provide still more time for the Yankees up there to shift a lot more earth, and site more cannon of their own. Since southern troops, short of proper tools, could at best dig at just about the same rate as Yankees could, the whole thing smacked of stalemate, which was bad news for the Confederate infantry.

Although word was spreading around the camps that these Yankees were mostly locally recruited militia who would skedaddle at the first sign of trouble, the more reflective men did not quite view it in that way. Militia or not, at the end of whatever ritual of preparation took place here, all that those Yankees ultimately had to do when they finished digging, was sit. It was the Southern troops who sooner or later would either have to admit failure and leave, or cross that open ground out in front from which most of the trees and brush had been systematically cleared, to reach those enemy works. The longer that attack was delayed, the stronger those works would be and since the Confederate force had neither the numbers nor sufficiently large calibres of cannon to reduce the city by bombardment, it would come down to the infantry to capture it by storming some part or another of its defences. Sooner or later, when all the preliminaries of digging and bombarding had been gone through, the Southern infantrymen would have to leave their own lines and negotiate their way across that cleared killing zone, and if practical experience on the matter of attacking fortified positions meant anything, considerable numbers of them would likely not survive the experience.

So far there was no word of an attack, but up on their higher ground the Yankees still dug and shifted, but then on the Wednesday evening word began to circulate that an assault was being prepared, an initial stroke to capture the trenches of the enemy outpost line. This was progress of a sort, but while such a move was a necessary first step, capturing a section of enemy trenches would also announce to them, in pretty obvious terms, where any further attack would subsequently be made. The brigades selected for the attack were prepared, with Kershaw's men again leading the assault. Wofford's regiments were not included, which maybe gave a grim hint, the men muttered to each other, that at some not too distant date theirs might instead be the task of assaulting the main enemy line.

The Thursday came and the story regarding the attack was finally confirmed. Their own role would be to support the advance and go forward only if the South Carolinians failed to carry the trench line. The men were dismissed to breakfast, a scant ration of corn pounded into flour with musket butts and baked up into ramrod rolls and washed down by a cup of substitute coffee. The hours of the morning then passed by without major incident until shortly after noon, when under a brighter sky the regiment was assembled, as outpost firing to the front began to rise to a level that gave clear indication that it was no longer just outposts.

The engagement went on, within earshot but out of sight of the waiting men of Company B until later in the afternoon when, as the firing declined and the sky began to cloud, word arrived that the enemy forward trenches had been taken. The men braced themselves. Would the main assault now go forward, capitalising on whatever confusion existed among the defending Yankees after the loss of their positions? Time passed and dusk came early under the greying skies, but still

245

no word came of further orders. As darkness gathered the men were stood down. Whatever was being planned for the main attack it would not be today, which gave the Yankees a gift of further time to dig new forward trenches and generally repair whatever damage had been done by today's proceedings.

As the changeable weather continued, the troops waited in their muddy camps and still more days passed. It was now being rumoured that the further delay was due to the fact that reinforcements had been requested and that Bragg was actually sending them. As for the capture of the skirmish trenches, the additional delay had, as had been predicted, given the Yankees ample opportunity to recover and they had made the most of it. They had promptly laid out a new line and were hard at work improving it. It was closer to their main defence perimeter to be sure, but a significant obstacle nevertheless, with its establishment and strengthening steadily nullifying the efforts that Kershaw's men had expended in capturing the previous one.

On the Tuesday, almost a week after the initial advance, there came more trouble. Daniel Ryan's section was off duty, with dusk having not long faded into darkness, when firing erupted from the direction of the lines. The off-duty men were immediately assembled and moved forward, seeing the flashes of musketry from up ahead as they cleared the tree belt that flanked the railroad. A shouted order came along and the files were halted and deployed into line. The muskets were promptly loaded and bayonets fixed before the ranks were moved off once more with a line of skirmishers out in front. Men peered into the gloom ahead, seeing plenty of muzzle flashes out on the valley that faced them, with the whole scene being faintly illuminated by the rising moon. Daniel Ryan felt his heart pounding as the ranks moved on picking their way carefully in the strange light.

Night actions remained very rare occurrences. It was too easy for soldiers to blunder aimlessly around in the dark and find nobody to shoot at, or worse still, being unable to see

246

whom they were approaching, they could finish up blazing away at anyone who came within range, with friends just as likely to be on the receiving end of their volleys as foes. Daniel's mind went back to the fighting at Salem Church the previous spring, when the brigade had been ordered forward at dusk only to spend much of the darkness floundering through gullies and thickets, to briefly exchange volleys with a mysterious formation which they took to be Yankees, though to this day he had not learned for certain who they were. At least here the area where the fight was taking place, on the ground off beyond the railroad where a forward trench had been established, could be made out, but the area was now covered by a cloud of gun smoke through which only an occasional muzzle flash could be seen, though the crackling symphony of small arms fire went on without pause. Ahead in that smoke and darkness, their own skirmishers, not to mention those from the rest of the brigade, were floundering or fighting in between their advancing main lines and the enemy. How it would be possible to get the regiment into action without firing into the backs of their own men would be a fine problem for Henry Randolph or some other officer, and a pretty fatal one for the skirmishers if any mistakes were made.

Wounded men were coming back now, grim, shuffling figures that appeared out of the darkness to push their way through the ranks before disappearing just as quickly into the night. Some of them muttered or spoke as they went, responding to the questions levelled by the advancing troops, giving some word as to what was taking place up ahead.

"What gives up thar?"

"What in the hell is goin' on?"

"Damn Yankees came outa nowhere."

"Never saw them till they wuz near on top of us."

They were across the rail tracks now and closing on the fight. The men grasped their muskets more firmly as they drew ever closer to the shooting, with the line being finally halted while more men were pushed forward, likely to figure out where the enemy were and how the ranks should move to come to grips with them. The orders finally came and the men shuffled into motion once more, starting on the upward slope until the firing seemed to be almost right in front of them. They could hear bullets whizzing past, almost all of them passing overhead, to the relief of those in the ranks.

A succession of shouts then came from up ahead, audible in fragments as the firing ebbed and flowed, but soon there were dim figures emerging from the smoke and gloom, calling as they came. Daniel Ryan saw muskets around him raised in aim and heard the faintest of clicks from the closest of them as the hammers were cocked.

"Friends!"

"Don't shoot!"

"Don't fire boys!" Around them their own officers and NCOs took up the shout.

"They're friends!" Then Thompson's voice rang out, dispelling any further uncertainty.

"Hold your fire!" The approaching men reached the line, pushing through as the men opened their ranks. More appeared, ghostly shapes that loomed from the darkness and drifting smoke, and now more shots from up ahead were coming, whizzing past closer than before, and the men in the ranks began to call out to those who still approached.

"Shift yore damned asses!"

"Clear the goddam front!"

"Git the hell outa the way!" Hands were raised in acknowledgement as their own skirmishers jogged the final yards to push their way through to safety. At last they were gone, but the first men in the ranks were now beginning to fall as some of those bullets began to find targets. Jessop's shout came, obscured by the continuing musketry, but quickly taken up by Thompson and Dellings.

"Ready muskets!" The men who had not already done so reached immediately for caps, with a succession of clicks telling of hammers being cocked to enable them to be placed in position.

"Aim low, boys!"

"Company will fire by ranks! Front rank, ready... fire!" The volley crashed out, with its cloud of smoke smothering everything, stinging eyes and irritating noses. Daniel felt the recoil punch the butt of the Enfield into his shoulder and he immediately let it drop to the ground, steadying the stock with his left hand as he reached around to his pouch for the next cartridge. Already the shouts were coming.

"Rear rank, aim!" He was aware of the long barrels appearing over each of his shoulders as he bit and poured his own cartridge.

"Fire!" The roar was deafening and the smoke swirled all around him. His eyes were watering as he rammed his own shot home and returned the rammer deftly to its place, immediately reaching for a cap to then flick the spent one away and place the fresh one in almost a single movement.

"Front rank, ready!" Thompson's voice again, with the timing almost perfect.

"Aim!" There was nothing to aim at in the smoke cloud and the darkness, but the barrels swung into place, varying a little in their angles as the men applied their best guesses.

"Fire!" The roar crashed out again and the smoke billowed all around, further tormenting already streaming eyes and noses. Hands reached again for cartridges as the musket butts dropped to the ground, and it all began again as the orders came for the rear rank and the barrels swam into view on either side of the reloading front rank men.

In those fleeting seconds as the men of both ranks frantically reloaded, the crackle of further musketry came to them from either side where other formations were also clearly at work. From out in front the fire still persisted, but this was indicated more by the passage of whizzing bullets rather than by the sound of the musketry itself. As he loaded and fired, Daniel Ryan found himself analysing the character of this crazy fight being waged in almost pitch darkness with an enemy that they had not so much as glimpsed. They were here on this muddy slope, littered with the stumps of felled

249

trees, firing their volleys of bullets into the night and trusting to almighty God that whoever was out there was not creeping closer or flanking them, for in the darkness and smoke there was not the slightest chance of seeing them. It all struck him as a most unnerving experience, with all the disadvantages and none of the benefits of a daytime fight.

All battles were numbing, terrifying ordeals, but somehow this one, in the dark, seemed to be preying on his mind more than the daytime brawls did. On the Company B front, the orders came bellowing along at regular intervals. The successive volleys went crashing out, each of them illuminating the ground and the smoke cloud where the ranks stood for a split-second, upon which the fumbling process of reloading was feverishly recommenced, while all along the line the muskets of the other rank were readied again waiting for Thompson's unerring shout, which came as before and as always, at exactly the right moment.

"Front rank, ready!" The barrels went up to the present position, but Daniel Ryan gave only the most cursory glance along the sights, still able to see nothing but smoke ahead of him, but even as they heard the rear rank men reach for further cartridges, he was aware that out in front there was now nothing coming in return.

"Cease firing, load to the ready!" The reloading went on, with ramrods now clattering audibly as they were inserted into musket muzzles and returned to their places with a couple of firm downward thrusts, with more rattling and scraping as they found their channels. Out in front the smoke was beginning to thin and clear. Slowly it drifted, eddied, and dispersed, until at last the peering men in the ranks could make out, in the dim light of the moon, something of what lay out in front. From behind them there came a shouted order.

"Skirmishers forward!" A brief pause followed and then along the ranks there was a shuffling movement, as those detailed for the duty pushed their way through and started forward to vanish quickly into the gloom as the moon went behind cloud. Out in front they could hear those other battlefield sounds, the cries and the groans of men who had been hit and wanted others to come to their aid.

The battle line waited and watched as the moonlight came and went in shifting cloud, and the comments passed around in low half-whispers.

"Looks like they've skedaddled."

"Reckon we showed 'em agin."

"Didn't have no real stomach fer it did they?"

"Damn western bluebellies can't stick to it no more'n their eastern boys did." As he listened to the talk, Daniel Ryan heard a mutter of other voices behind him. The moon emerged again, then there was a movement to their rear and Thompson was immediately there just behind the men of his section where they stood in the ranks.

"Git forward," he rapped out. "Skirmish order."

"Thar's boys gone forward a'ready," Jones growled.

"Well let's go find 'em," Thompson snapped back. Daniel Ryan was aware of Jenkins edging towards him as they left the ranks behind and started forward on the muddy slope. He nodded the boy ahead as he came to a halt and crouched down, cradling his musket in his hands with a cap in his right palm ready to prime at the first sign of trouble. His heart began to pound again after having briefly slackened to something closer to normal, as he strained his eyes into the gloom ahead.

"Thank god for the moon." The thought flashed across his mind as the cloudy wisps moved away from its white luminescence, giving a measure of form to what lay around them. He saw Jenkins a short way ahead and slightly to the right, while Kane moved up on the left. Daniel saw him pause and then crouch and his eyes flickered back towards Jenkins, barely visible up ahead. Surely the boy will know by now to stop at a reasonable interval and not go wandering off into the darkness. The night was cold, but, as always in a fight, Daniel was almost soaked with perspiration. He could feel the sweat dribbling down his back and chest, growing quickly cold against his skin in the chilly air, and he shivered involuntarily as he waited, with his eyes fixed ahead.

All along the line the musketry had faded, with only an occasional single shot now to be heard as the skirmishers of each side marked their territory. The Yankees would be anxious to discourage any close pursuit, while the southerners were equally determined to ensure that the enemy had actually gone and that there were no further unwanted surprises out on that muddy landscape. Out on the slope, Jenkins had finally halted and dropped to a crouch, and seeing this Daniel pushed himself to his feet and started forward, hearing his feet slopping in the mud as he settled into a suitable gait, his body hunched slightly forward and his musket held across his body. His eyes flitted from side to side taking in every detail that he could make out in the gloom. He was close to Jenkins now. He could see the boy clearly and he deviated slightly so as not to pass too closely and give any dallying Yankee too much of a target. He was drawing close to where the outpost trench should be, though it was hard to make out anything for certain in the mysterious moonlight. Off to the right there was a flash and a crack as somebody, whether friend or foe, saw a target.

Daniel halted and tensed, waiting to see if there was any further shooting before resuming his cautious way forward, finally coming to a stop and crouching again as more muzzle flashes and shots rang out away on the other flank. He waited, never taking his eyes from his front, eventually hearing what must be Jenkins' approaching footsteps in the mud, as he came up behind, audible in spite of the cries and groans that seemed to be all around them. He looked to either side, seeing the moving form that must be the boy to his right. He balanced his musket with his left hand before stretching out his right sideways, to bring him to a halt, aware of him crouching as he saw the signal.

They waited, still looking intently forward into the darkness, but out in front there were now shapes and forms that suggested that they were maybe just short of the captured forward line. There was the dim shape of a consistent obstacle of some kind out there, maybe the parapet of a trench, but they would not be rushing on to reach it. If the Yankees wanted to wait around and discourage the southern re-occupation of their own skirmish line, then the trench itself was the best place to do it. His eyes settled on another shape, for it had shifted, and then he heard the groan and realised that this was a wounded man who had perhaps regained consciousness and tried to move himself. Daniel continued to watch till he was satisfied, as far as he could be, that there was no threat there. He looked over towards Jenkins and signalled again, placing his thumb on his chest and then pointing forward, the sign that indicated that he, rather than the boy, would move. He waited for the acknowledgement before pushing himself to his feet and starting forward again. He glanced towards where the fallen man lay, seeing him twitch again, the movement just visible in the dim light.

The moans and cries were closer, indicating that this must be where the advancing Yankees had halted. The barrier that he had previously seen was close also, close enough to it to be confirmed that it was indeed the parapet of the trench line. Daniel saw a couple of shapes moving there and he froze, until one of them raised an arm and waved him forward. Alert to the possibility of an ambush he stayed low as he went forward, moving from tree stump to any unevenness in the ground, seeking any cover that he could find as he approached the trench. He kept his eyes fixed there, seeing the figure wave again and this time he recognised it as Matthew Hale. Daniel breathed a deep sigh of relief as he semi-straightened and signalled Jenkins forward, moving more briskly himself as he covered the last few yards to the trench. He was conscious of a whole chorus of pleas and groans from wounded men here, and he paused briefly at the edge, before jumping down into the position, stumbling immediately on an inert shape that lay there. He heard Hale's voice from a little to his left.

"Watch where ya step, there's a whole mess o' them along here." Over to his right he heard Kane speak.

"Slowin' down Daniel," he whispered. "We've bin here fer a while."

"Plunderin' dead Yankees must appeal more to you," Daniel hissed back, as Jenkins arrived beside him in the trench.

"Are they gone," he asked in a low whisper.

"Reckon so," Daniel told him, "but don't go dancin' around or you might find that their pickets ain't gone that far."

"There's southern boys here as well," he heard Winder exclaim, but before Daniel could reply he became conscious of another movement. He looked to see Ballard coming along the trench at a crouch.

"Settle here a while," he said as he came up to them. "Joe says the duty boys've gone forward to their places and once we hear from them we kin report back, so keep a good watch fer whoever they send back." Daniel shrugged and joined the others of the section as they settled along their stretch of the line. Behind them there were more noises and movements and Daniel squinted around seeing Jenkins start around also, raising his musket as he did so.

"Stay calm," he told him. "It'll be the details they've sent out for the wounded boys." He saw the boy visibly relax, as he turned to settle in his own place once more.

They waited for a further time while the orderlies worked around the ground to their rear. Along the trench a few men left their places to try to help the injured, taking the opportunity to relieve the fallen Yankees of anything of value while doing so, but without canteens there was little enough that they could do beyond making the wounded men as comfortable as they could.

At length, a few of the orderlies began to arrive around the trench line to begin the job of helping or carrying the wounded to the rear. As the earthwork emptied of its wounded, several of the orderlies began moving gingerly

254

forward from it to, seek more of the fallen and this went on for a time until Winder's voice came to them.

"See him there!" Daniel's eyes darted across, to take in the shape of a returning figure, distinguishable from the orderlies by his crouching, hurrying pace and by the musket that he carried. He came up to the trench line some yards to the left of where Ryan's section watched and waited. After the briefest of further intervals Thompson appeared along the line and gestured to the boy.

"Yo're young and spry," he told him, "so git yoreself back to the company. Tell Barnard that the Yankees're gone and the line and the outposts are secure." Jenkins scrambled across the dirt edge of the trench and made off.

"See how long it takes 'em to send our relief," Jones growled.

They waited for what was most of an hour, with the last of the outpost sniping having long since faded away, until they finally made out a loose rank of men approaching from the rear, visible in the moonlight, as still the orderlies worked out in front. The relief detail arrived, with Henry Bayfield in charge and, at his brief gesture, the men spaced themselves out along the line, while Thompson's section formed into a group and prepared to depart.

"Reckon this means double watches fer a while," they heard Bayfield tell Thompson. "Leastways till they all git themselves calmed down back thar." Thompson nodded, his movement also just visible in the moonlight, which chose that moment to dim and fade as more cloud crept across.

"Ain't a fair world Henry," he growled, before turning to his men and jerking his thumb to the rear, waiting in the dimmer light till all his section had clambered from the trench before following them away. The men moved away, stumbling over unseen obstacles in the now near to total darkness as they sloshed across the broken, muddy ground.

Back at the camp the off duty men were finally stood down to return to their fires, reviving what remained of them with more wood before seeking water canteens to wash the stink of battle and the taste of powder from their mouths. With this done most men made for their blankets, leaving only a few dallying around their fires to exchange comments about the brief fight. The camp was soon quiet, while above them the moon continued its game with the clouds and away in the distance and the darkness the cries of the remaining wounded, who had lain beyond where the toiling orderlies had reached, continued to come through the darkness.

That earthwork, up there with its flagpole on top of the higher plateau, was situated at the place where the Yankee line angled from running parallel with the railroad to stretch back south towards the river. It was called Fort Loudon, the men now knew, and it dominated the northwest portion of the defensive line. Although the fortification itself was squat and comparatively low, there was something solid and enduring about it. The stories had now begun to centre on the idea that here, especially after all othe coming and going of the previous week, the main attack on Knoxville would be launched. Here Alexander's batteries were now assembled in greatest numbers and here the effort of capturing the enemy skirmish line had been expended, but the time was continuing to pass and still there was no definite word.

Two days after the night skirmish while the men skulked in the rain and the mud of their camps, Otis Ballard was restored to the rank of corporal. The return of his stripes was not announced as assemblies were not held regularly along the lines, but Jessop had apparently used the ex-corporal's conduct during the night action as grounds for restoring the stripes. How Gilby felt about the matter was not known, but to most if not all of Company B it was no more than justice, and the news was discussed with satisfaction for the most part, it being regarded as vindication for Ballard, but also as something of a slight for the disliked lieutenant.

Further up the army hierarchy the generals, from "Old Pete" on down, continued with their routines, riding their lines in groups, to peer through binoculars at the Yankee works before departing again with their staffs trailing behind them, all of it no doubt enabling them to discuss and arrange and plan some more. With those binoculars they would certainly have seen the Yankees, still hard at work, strengthening their lines yet further. In all truth, a man needed no binoculars to see the enemy at work, but though their lines grew ever stronger there was still no word from the generals as to what they finally intended to do. Those "Tennessee slows" were, it seemed, just as much of a problem up here as they had been back at Chattanooga.

Chapter 11 Fort Loudon

A further duty was spent on the picket line on the Wednesday afternoon, where a brighter day had earlier given the members of Daniel Ryan's mess a chance to wash and even partly dry what spare items of clothing remained to them. The duty watch, later in the day, had allowed them to scrutinise the squat bulk of Fort Loudon once more, this time without the disadvantage of mist or low cloud since the stories of a pending assault on the fort had persisted through the morning. The place commanded that higher plateau that separated the city from the railroad, its approach marked by clusters of tree stumps. The rampart of the fort was crowned by a parapet of what looked like cotton bales that extended along the length of its walls, save for several embrasures presumably left for cannon.

It was known that a ditch flanked its external sides, but from their positions there was nothing that the southern pickets could see of this. What could be seen however was the rumoured line of approach, a break in the slope of the hill, a gully, which must be a blind area, or pretty near to it, from the wall of the fort. The covered route led up from the valley where the Confederate forward positions lay, towards the crest of the hill, emerging almost at the summit where the cleared ground commenced. Along there were situated the latest line of Yankee picket positions which covered the fort itself, and these offered visual support to those persisting stories in the camps. If the Yankees were unable to see an approaching column of attack until it was almost on top of their outposts, then here after all might be the key to breaching the defences and capturing the city.

Hardly had the opinion in the camps hardened on the place for the coming attack when further rumours arrived. Bragg had, after all, sent those reinforcements that Longstreet had repeatedly requested to support the assault. With them had come General Leadbetter, an engineer who, it was being said, had helped lay out the defences of Knoxville when the Confederate army had held the city. This might help or it might not, the boys told each other, but the day ended with no further word of an attack, while up on the heights the ant like figures of the Yankees could be seen, still busy making the job of capturing that earthwork a more intimidating prospect.

The following day came further developments. The morning arrived with renewed mist and rain, to reveal a commotion of some kind in the artillery positions. Horses, invisible in the mist, whinnied and snorted, while equally invisible vehicles, whether wagons or limbers, came and went, all to a succession of shouted orders. Word soon began to circulate among the infantry camps as to what was afoot. The guns that had been assembled and positioned here to the north west of the city to bear on Fort Loudon were, it was being said, limbering up and moving out, heading away to some place for sure, but the rumours said they were on their way on General Leadbetter's say so to another part of the defensive line, where a better prospect for success was to be had.

All through the day, with the mist now departed, the rumours were steadily reinforced by a sequence of observed facts. The artillerymen laboured with their train of guns, limbers and wagons heading away to the east, while the infantry waited in their camps and positions, speculating on what in the hell was going on. It had already taken well over a week since originally investing the city to do next to nothing, and now it looked like the minds at headquarters were changing once more, though whether it would lead to anything of importance was another matter. It was not as though there was a great range of choices as to where to attack, since the Yankees, by previously damming parts of the creeks that crossed the ground in front of their lines, had flooded vital approaches to the positions, limiting the options for attack. There weren't that many choices, but if that was the case, the men complained, why did there have to be such delay and confusion in making one? Late in the day the name

"Maybre's Hill" first cropped up in the stories. It was said to lie to the east, at the far north eastern part of the defence lines in fact, and this was where Leadbetter, the engineer, was said to be advising an attack.

On the Saturday morning as the rain continued to pelt down and the mist hung low over the landscape once more, further rumours swept around the camps. Whatever Leadbetter had said to "Old Pete" it had only led to a further bout of indecision, for according to the latest stories, the guns were today being brought back, though nobody could see whether that was true or not, the mist being again too thick for much of anything to be seen at all. The rumours persisted however. The general, it was being said, had gone out to look at the section of the line along to the east on Maybre's Hill and had taken his divisional and brigade commanders along as well as Leadbetter, to comment on the revised assault plan.

Whatever had been talked about out there could only be guessed at, but it had apparently led to the plan being changed yet again, and now, after nearly two weeks of yet another half-hearted kind of a siege, it looked like things were back to where they had been at the start. If there were to be an attack it would now be launched back where it had originally been intended, on Fort Loudon on that hill up there, the north western extremity of the city's defence lines. The further fumbling and delay was regrettable, for it had resulted in the Yankees being allowed still more time to beaver around, digging and chopping and shifting and, as a result, the defences were now stronger and more extensive still.

Midday had come, with news of final attack plans seemingly being completed, when Jeffers came around calling on the men to assemble, as still the rain fell. They came, emerging like moles from the shelters that had been burrowed into the sides of the rising ground, dirty, vermin-infested men who gathered with considerable reluctance, tearing themselves from their fires with a show of irritation, to form their ranks and await the officers' pleasure. Jessop arrived in due course, with Carson and Gilby in tow, as Jeffers called the company to order. Gilby, even in the rain and mud, was resplendently dressed, far surpassing the captain and Carson in smartness, though only the collar of his uniform coat was visible, marked by the symbols of his rank, with the rest of the garment covered by a tailored greatcoat of the same colour, to shield him against the rain and cold.

"At ease men," the captain called, as he took his place at the front of the double rank. "Everythin' but your ears that is," he added. The men relaxed as he looked along the bearded faces.

"We have orders," he resumed, "attack orders." A murmur of expectation moved along the ranks as Jessop paused. "Fort Loudon is to be attacked at dawn tomorrow and our brigade has been given the lead in storming the north section of the wall. That's the one straight ahead up there, that we've bin lookin' at for the last couple o' weeks.The attack is to be made, followin' a bombardment from our artillery to soften the Yankees up some. General McLaws is meetin' with Colonel Alexander, to work out the details of how the attack will proceed. The gunners will do as much damage as they kin to the fort and then support us when we go forward." As Jessop's words sank in, Daniel Ryan could feel his stomach and chest tightening in their all too familiar way at the prospect of what was now to come, while out in front, the captain continued to speak.

"We are to assemble tonight and will approach the fort by the gully yonder. The attack is to be made at first light and will go forward at the double quick. The brigade will be formed in column of regiments, with the Phillips Legion boys in first line. We will be in third line and our job will be to push the attack on, after the fort wall has been taken." Ryan felt a vague feeling of relief cross his mind at that particular detail, but the mercy of not being at the forefront of the attack was quickly lost as the captain continued to outline what was to come.

"The fort is guarded by a ditch on its northern and western sides," he went on, "but, after careful inspection, it has been established that it is not deep, three or four feet, according to the general's estimation and it will not delay or obstruct the assault unduly. Speed is to be the essence of this attack and we must not allow anything to stop us. We can get close to the fort by using the break in the slope. That will conceal us, until we are less than two hundred yards from the ditch. Once the Yankee forward positions are overrun, we will form and move on across the glacis and the ditch and be over the wall before the Yankees know we're on top o' them. The Yankees in the fort are only militia, local levies," Jessop uttered the word disdainfully, "they are home-grown Yankees, who'll skedaddle as soon as we show up on top of their wall. They are sittin' on stores full of shoes and winter coats. The place is full of rations, and all we got to do is push over that wall to git them."

Daniel's mind continued to race as he listened to the captain's words. It all sounded pretty simple, at least it did the way that Jessop was describing it. But everyone knew that one of the improvements that the Yankees had made over the course of the last week had been to strengthen their new line of picket trenches, placed along the top of the steepest part of the slope to spot and warn of any attack approaching the fort. The idea of getting quickly through that line and on to the fort without the Yankees knowing about it: seemed pretty unlikely to him.

Cannon also were of limited effect against entrenchments or earthworks. Only howitzers, with their high trajectory fire, could drop their shells into trenches or behind ramparts, but there were precious few of these weapons among the Confederate artillery and, with the tradition of unreliable fuses among southern shells, the chances of destroying a trench line or a fort parapet protected by a glacis and a counterscarp would not be that good. Porter Alexander however was a competent gunner, who demanded high standards from his men. Daniel recalled the shot that he had dropped into that house on Hanover Street back in Fredericksburg when it was being used by the Yankees for sharpshooting last winter. Alexander, it was said, had laid that gun personally, having supervised the loading of a reduced charge of powder, and had demolished the place with a single shell. If anybody could breach a fort's defences with cannon he could, so maybe there was a chance, though realistically no more than a chance, that a thorough pounding from his guns might damage the fort enough for the infantry, following up on the double quick, to break in without undue loss.

Out in front, the captain had finished speaking and the ranks were once more called to attention. Jessop turned on his heel and made his way off, pursued by the two lieutenants. With the officers gone, the men were dismissed to their shelters to grasp the opportunity of drying out at the fires, for they had received a good soaking from the persistent rain. But there was still not a sign of any rations issue.

Late afternoon had come when the company was called again. As the men emerged from their shelters they found that the rain had almost ceased, though the mist remained low and there was a cold edge to the wind, suggesting that the weather might be in the process of changing. This time the officers were waiting as the ranks formed, hurried on by Bayfield and Thompson. Called to order, they were once more stood at ease by Jessop, before he began to speak once more.

"The attack plans have been completed by the general, after further consultation with the engineers and artillery officers," he told them. "General Longstreet has decided that a prolonged artillery bombardment will be of limited effect and will serve to warn the Yankees of the coming attack. He has ordered that the fort be taken by a "Coup de Main." To you and me that means an almighty rush at the place, without too much time bein' taken by the artillery to reduce it. The Yankee forward posts will be stormed tonight and the fort itself will be attacked as planned, at first light.

The main assault will be signalled by three cannon shots. Then the gunners will have twenty minutes to do as much damage as they can and once their time's up it's forward, for us, at the double quick. When we get to the ditch we'll be below where the Yankees kin reach with their muskets and cannon, so then it'll jest be a matter of pushin' straight on up and over that parapet boys. You will be called to assemble with arms and ammunition only. Muskets should be loaded, but not primed and all other belongings will be left behind. Like I said earlier, the Philipps Legion will lead the assault with the Eighteenth, ourselves and the Sixteenth regiments following. When we go in our boys, from the Third Sharpshooters and the Twenty Fourth Regiment, will be stationed along the enemy outpost line, with orders to move up onto the glacis while the artillery boys are doin' their work, to pin down the Yankees on the fort wall till the assault force passes. We are to assemble tonight, so spend the time between now and then makin' yoreselves ready and get what rest you can....." Jessop paused, as though he was drawing breath to continue, and the silence lasted for a number of seconds before his next words came.

"Dismiss the company First Sergeant," he finally uttered brusquely, as though he had eventually thought better of whatever he had previously intended saying. At that he was gone, leaving the men to return to their camps to collect and prepare weapons and divest themselves of anything not needed. Ryan's mess re-assembled around their fire in due course to dissect what they had been told.

"If he was tryin' to make us think this'll be a straight on up and over attack, he didn't make much of a job of it," Kane growled. Ballard was even more scathing.

"The goddam general's gotta be stupider than jest about everybody else in the army if he can't figure out that three cannon shots and any kind o' a bombardment are jest as much of a signal to the Yankees as they are to us," he snarled. Daniel Ryan was equally critical.

"How in the hell do we occupy the Yankee outpost line without them knowin' that we've done it and figurin' from it that somethin's about to happen and where it's goin' to happen" he complained? A number of nods, grunts and further comments and complaints greeted his words.

"I sure as hell hope that the boys in the brigade 'specially them in Philipps Legion kin run like goddam march hares," Jones said, "cuz that's the only thing that'll save 'em in this attack." Even Winder, who tended to restrain himself from commenting too much on the stupidity of white generals, was as outspoken as the others of the mess.

"I surely don't know what Ol' Pete's thinkin' about," he told them. "As far as I kin see, unless everythin' that he hopes'll happen does happen like he hopes it will, he's ordered an attack that could turn into a damned brigade suicide." A silence followed his words. Nobody challenged what he had said and nobody added anything. It was unlike Eli to launch himself into such an outburst in the first place and anyway, when a man thought on it, there was little more to be said, as far as Daniel Ryan was concerned, on the entire matter.

The night grew colder still and as dusk came on the rain, that had continued to fall, had turned to sleet, persisting until it had formed a slushy layer on the ground, stubbornly refusing to fully melt, and chilling the feet of the shod until they were numb with the cold. What it must be like for the barefoot men, Daniel Ryan reckoned, must be grim in the extreme. Mist gathered steadily in the valley and, in the darkness, the Yankee artillery had begun a slow bombardment, sending their shells sailing over the forward positions of both sides, giving the waiting men another trial to endure. It soon became clear however that the missiles were passing over to burst somewhere to the rear beyond the Confederate camp areas, but as the time passed their smoke was in the air, invisible in the mist, but the stink catching in the nostrils and the throat.

The company was eventually called to prepare in the pitch darkness, with no moon visible through the mist and the banks of low cloud. The mess collected their stoppered muskets and ammunition pouches from where they waited in their stacks, covered in a shred of a gum blanket. The weapons were carried to the fires where they were warmed to clear the dampness that the cold of the night and the persistent rain and sleet had caused. The Yankee shells continued to come over, sailing through the air with an occasional fuse visible through the mist, glowing like a passing yellow star, with that ripping, tearing noise peculiar to shells, announcing their approach. As the men waited and watched, Jeffers moved around the fires with a bag of cartridges and percussion caps, passing handfuls of the paper cylinders and miniature copper thimbles to the men of each mess in turn. At length, from up on the hill, there came an outbreak of musketry, indicating, most like, that the foray to capture the enemy forward line was under way. The engagement was brief however, lasting only minutes before the musketry died away, leaving the darkness to the artillery.

Having donned ammunition pouches and completed the warming of their weapons as far as was possible in the continuing sleety rain, the men of Company B assembled in their files and were promptly moved off, leaving their camp area to move forward to pass through the main trench line and descend the ridge slope, then halting in the area south of the railroad line where the other regiments of the brigade were already assembling. Up on the hilltop the fort lay hidden by the darkness as the now assembled column began to move forward, trooping up to the gully to come to a further halt there. The men were stood down to wait in their company and regimental groups, but with no blankets or haversacks brought forward and fires forbidden, there was little they could do to make themselves comfortable, as the cold persisted and the time passed slowly.

A further shower of sleet pelted down as men shifted around in the restricted space with their still stoppered muskets slung on their straps, rubbing their hands and stamping their feet, while a growling tide of whispered complaints began to rise, shooshed regularly by the sergeants and company officers.

"Can't feel my damned toes," Kane growled.

"How goddam long till first light?" Jones muttered. "Reckon my goddam fingers'll be froze solid by then."

Ryan continued to shuffle in his place, stamping his feet into the mud as he did so, his musket clamped between his arm and his body and his hands thrust firmly into his armpits, sparing himself the chore of grousing as he contemplated what lay ahead. Attacking a prepared position was the worst kind of fight, unless they really could surprise the defenders up there, but how could that be possible, since the Yankee artillery had been demonstrating their preparedness for the last several hours by sending that desultory barrage of shells arcing over in a regular procession? So far they were still sailing over to explode well to the rear of the Confederate positions, with the flash of their detonations followed a second or so later by the ugly crump of the explosions as they had done at regular intervals over the preceding couple of hours. Even if they were doing no particular damage, it was serving to demonstrate that the enemy were awake and ready, and surprise was unlikely to be any part of the proceedings that were about to commence.

As he awaited the arrival of the next shell Daniel continued with his own sombre thoughts. There was no understanding the sense of this latest move that the general had apparently decided upon. Perhaps the only thing that might help would be the timing of the attack. Maybe, in spite of the picket line engagement, as the night passed the Yankees would think that nothing was happening after all and lower their guard, but this too he knew was a forlorn hope. Attacks often came at dawn and everybody on both sides knew that. Even without the earlier tussle to overrun the enemy positions, serving to warn them, it was a standard military practice for troops, when in the presence of the enemy, to stand to their posts before dawn. So, even with nothing else in the way of a warning, the Yankees would be on the alert up there when daylight came. The southerners had heard their bugles and drums, summoning them on every previous morning, so the coming dawn would be no different. In addition to that standard routine, the general was going to further oblige them with an additional warning of three cannon shots, which would signal whatever bombardment was to take place and then only the deaf or the dead would be unaware of what was coming.

Daniel felt a tide of frustration rising within him as he contemplated the whole damned foul up. The last shred of hope, he told himself, was speed. If they could indeed form their assault column without being detected in the darkness, they could maybe cover that shorter distance from the outpost line to the fort before the Yankees could do too much damage. But that fort would be a hard nut to crack. There were those cannon embrasures in the rampart, and the bastion shape of the wall meant that there would be almost no blind spots close to the ditch or the wall where men would be sheltered from the defenders' fire. Unless the sharpshooters at the picket line could keep the heads of the Yankee infantry well down behind their cotton bales, there could be hell to pay when the attackers rushed the fort. Speed therefore was vitally important. If the attack was slowed, or stalled at any point between the picket trenches and the wall, it would give the defenders extra time to concentrate their fire and bleed the assaulting column, disorganising it still further.

Try though he might, Daniel Ryan simply could not fathom what the general was thinking about. Longstreet's reputation as a general was as a methodical commander, who did not move until he was properly prepared yet, even after near to two weeks of waiting and discussing, this attack had all the features of a hastily put together piece of poor planning and inadequate preparation. It was discarding normal practice for such situations, gambling everything on the speed of the advance being sufficient to take the attackers up and over that wall before the defenders really woke up to what was happening. It was a long shot, a hope rather than an expectation, and the men of the assaulting brigades, Ben Humphries' Mississippians and "Tige" Anderson's

Georgians, as well as their own regiments, were the ones whose lives were being gambled on it. Daniel Ryan knew all too well the tension of pre-battle waiting and expectation with its fraught symptoms of fear. He always felt like this, but tonight it all seemed even worse, for somehow the prospect of this attack filled his mind with a sense of dread and foreboding which was more intimidating than anything he could previously remember.

Chapter 12 The Storming Party

The first hints of the coming day were at last visible away to the left as the men began to move again, deploying into their wide battle lines. The sleet showers had stopped and as the men shuffled upwards from the valley the mist had thinned, revealing glimpses of a sky that had partly cleared with a setting moon and a scattering of stars out to the west. As a result it now felt colder still and ice had begun to form on the sleet and mud beneath their feet. The crunching sound it made underfoot could be heard along the gully as they pushed into their places, while those first hints of the coming day slowly spread, low in the sky to their left.

The crash of the cannon came, not from the Yankee guns this time but from somewhere to their rear. Heads craned to watch as the shot sailed overhead, to crash down somewhere beyond the ridge crest where the fort lay, announcing the opening of the attack. Two more shots came, following at regular intervals after the opening discharge and then the valley was filled with sound as more cannon opened up, sending a succession of shells over the ranks of waiting infantry towards the Yankee lines. On the bombardment went, filling the pre-dawn with flame and noise as the relayed orders set the first rank of the infantry moving. The successive ranks followed and the procession of shivering men began to struggle up the muddy ascent while still the guns roared. The men slipped and slithered on the treacherous surface and even the sergeants were silent as the slope finally began to diminish, though up ahead there was still no sign of the rampart of the fort. Daniel Ryan shivered as he went, scarcely able to feel his feet in his shoes or his fingers as he gripped his musket butt with his right hand.

They must be close to the picket trenches now, but at least the ascent had so far been accomplished without mishap, but first there was the abattis, clumps of jagged branches distributed along the slope to halt and disorganise an advance.

270

Then there were the rows of sharpened poles facing outwards along in front of the trench line itself, but maybe in the darkness, with no signs of life from up ahead, they would be no more than a brief obstacle. Beyond the trench line there was the glacis to cross, open ground where only tree stumps remained, before they reached the ditch and the rampart of the fort itself. Daniel found himself profoundly hoping that what Jessop had said was true and that when they reached the fort itself the walls would indeed be too steep for most of the defenders to fire down on them. They would see, he thought grimly, for it was too late now to do anything about it.

Up ahead there were sounds of movement as the men halted and dressed their battle lines, each of them a regiment in width. Still the cannon thundered, while the men waited until finally the discharges ceased and the orders came, sending the wide column of men pushing forward on to the approach to the fort, tentatively at first, feeling their feet crunching on the lying remains of frozen sleet, but settling soon into a rhythm as they started across the open ground. From up ahead there were more sounds now, mutters and curses as the men behind pressed forward, only to find those in front stalled at the abbatis, beyond which those ranks of crudely sharpened poles embedded in the ground were just visible in the beginnings of dawn.

Ahead the men struggled and pushed on, not in a regular line now but as best they could, through the tangle of tree branches which caught repeatedly on the clothing and tore mercilessly at the skin. Seeing those in front struggle, Daniel hauled his cuffs down over his hands as far as possible, gripping the ragged edges with his fingers and pushing his musket out in front of him to keep the tangling, tearing strands from his face.

At last those in front were through the branches and the following ranks pushed on in their turn. Thankfully, as the Company B rank came up to them, they found that sections of the obstacle had been pushed and trampled down, with gaps now in places along their length. Daniel Ryan diverted slightly to his left to negotiate the tearing, scratching barrier through one such space, fending off the clumps with his musket as he went.

"Trenches!" The word came from just ahead and there was a falter in the advance. Dim shapes loomed from the darkness and the voices came again.

"Trenches, right here." An impression of those sharpened poles angled towards the attacking column came as a host of half- visible figures in the ranks ahead milled around them, pushing between the poles and jumping or stepping across the narrow pits beyond. Daniel followed in his turn, manoeuvring his way through between two of the poles and there immediately was the trench line. He was aware of crouching figures below him, as he took a last step and launched himself into a long, leaping stride that landed his leading foot in more icy sleet, which immediately gave way for his sole to crunch through the frozen slush into softer mud beneath. A steadying step with the other foot followed and the obstacle was past. He looked up, just as a succession of lights soared into the sky from out ahead. Flares from the fort, the idea flashed into his mind, as the ascending lights burst successively into dazzling brightness overhead. The whole tangled column of men on the open expanse of the glacis was suddenly visible in a great white light, unfamiliar and somehow unreal, as the host of men there tried vainly to reform into their ranks, pushed and harangued by their officers and sergeants.

Daniel Ryan's heart gave a wild lurch of fear. Nobody up there was surprised and, in this light, the approaching southerners looked exposed and vulnerable as they struggled to form, waiting now for whatever the fort and its defenders would inflict on them. With a piercing yell, the ranks moved forward, accelerating into a lumbering double-time pace as more flares rose into the sky and the first volley of musketry came in a flickering, pulsing line of orange flashes up ahead. As the smoke rose out in front more noises began to reach Daniel Ryan's ears. Shouts and curses rose as, in the advancing lines, men stumbled and fell, their bodies landing in the mud in a series of ugly squelches. Hardly had he registered the stumbles, cries and curses that had immediately followed the musket volley, when he felt his own leg snarl against what must be a wire, and he too pitched forward, his momentum having too readily anticipated where his next step should have taken him. He vainly reached forward with his left hand to break his fall, his musket falling from his grasp into the mud, splashing into it a split second before Ryan himself joined it there, uttering an angry profanity as he did so.

All around him men were stumbling from their places, most of them falling headlong into the sleet covered mud, while those remaining on their feet swerved and faltered in their efforts to avoid those who had finished up lying in their path. Daniel scrambled to his feet as all around him more men tripped and fell. It was wire sure enough, for he could feel a stretch of it with the fingers of his left hand, which like the shins of both of his legs stung sharply where the wire had snagged it. It was strung about knee high, between the stumps of the cleared trees, at almost an ideal height to throw an advancing rank of infantry into confusion. Daniel Ryan saw the next volley of musketry flicker along the rampart of the fort as he retrieved his musket and straightened up. Around him men collapsed, caught in the hail of bullets as they struggled in the tangling, snaring webs of wire, while those behind pushed forward, only to stumble and curse in their turn as they too fell victim to the enemy trap.

The sergeants were up among their men now, as still more musketry came with that tell-tale flickering of innocent looking flashes, growling and cursing at their men as they hauled and pushed at them to reform their lines and continue towards the fort, but the damage was done. Up ahead there were further yellow winks of musketry and more bullets were coming through, some of them buzzing past or overhead, while others found targets with their sickly wet smacks on flesh. On the men pushed, to find that the wires were stretched in a tangle of diagonals as well as in lines directly

273

across their path. The ranks still advanced, but as quickly as the men who had stumbled on the wire heaved themselves to their feet and resumed their shuffling run through the frozen mud towards the fort, more men fell on the next stretch of wire.

From an orderly formation, the company had in mere seconds dissolved into a chaos of stumbling, cursing men. Among them, their sergeants struggled vainly to restore some semblance of order, hurrying their men forward, aware of the need to cover the open ground quickly, only to find the chaos renewed a few yards further on. From the darkness up ahead there now came a brighter flash, followed by the dull thunderclap of a cannon and now canister swept across the glacis also, bringing whole clumps of men down with its iron hail.

"Move boys," Jessop's voice came through the smoke and noise and confusion. "Get on, for God's sake. We're dead meat if we wait out here." The men stumbled on, and now the rampart of the fort was clearly in view, marked against the lightening sky as a dark, ugly mass, whose parapet and gun embrasures were illuminated by the discharges of cannon and muskets. At last the wire entanglements were behind them and the men struggled to recover their line, as with their feet crunching and slopping in the icy mud, they double-timed towards the fort, whose dark, sparkling parapet now loomed starkly ahead of them.

To the east the sky was continuing to lighten, but by now all pretence of ranks had gone and the advancing men were little more than a crowd. From the right, still more men began to push across, jostling among those of Company B, obstructing their path and creating yet more chaos, as men lost sight of their sergeants and officers. On they pushed, until at last the ground fell away in front of them. The shouts from in front redoubled, but they were now from below where Daniel Ryan, his lower legs throbbing from the effects of the wire, had come to a slithering halt. This was indeed the ditch, but the muddy rim, where the Ogeechee Volunteers now

274

stood, was above the heads of the men who had preceded them.

A panicking thought seared through Daniel Ryan's mind, that if this ditch was deeper than the height of a man, how in the hell could anyone get up the other side, climb the additional height of that angled wall and cross the cotton bale rampart on top? From behind came a further jostling, double-timing mass of men and, as a result of the crowd pushing on from the rear, the Company B men were now being physically herded and manhandled over the slippery edge and down into the ditch, to land on and among the mass of men who already milled and struggled there. Many, including Ryan, jumped without waiting to be finally pushed and, mingling with the thunder of the guns, a chorus of shouts and curses of surprise rang out as they descended.

Daniel landed half on top of another man, who mouthed a loud curse as he did so. The breath was knocked from his lungs by the force of the landing as he squelched into the thick layer of icy mud at the bottom. All around him more men were jumping into the ditch, many of them landing on those who already struggled to cross to where the earth wall shone wetly in the growing light of the morning. Daniel struggled with them, pulling his feet from the clinging mud to flounder forward. He reached the mud wall to join those already there, some of whom had already begun scrambling their way upwards, digging fingers and feet into the packed earth of the wall only to slither back to the bottom after a bare few feet had been scaled. All around, mixing with the sounds of musketry and cannon, were shouts and cries of anger and dismay.

"We're stuck!"

"It's a damned trap!"

"There ain't no way up!" The shouts mingled with the groans and curses of wounded men and the beginnings of a battle yell that moved along the ditch.

Along the line there came the sudden blast of an explosion. Daniel whirled to see the flames as he heard the fragments whizz past. Jessop had been right. The walls were certainly too steep for anyone to fire down into the ditch without revealing themselves to the fire of the men who had been stationed on the glacis. They could not fire, they were not firing, instead, all along the wall, they were throwing shells, with their fuses lit, into the milling, crowded mass of men who stumbled and scrambled at the base of the wall. From over to the right there came a further blast of a cannon, sending a hail of canister balls and a pall of yellow smoke whizzing along the ditch. This was the bastion position they had seen from the valley below, built to extend out into the ditch in order to expose that stretch along the base of the wall to its fire. Around Daniel there were still more shouts, mingling with the cries and screams of those who had been hit and the curses and shouts of those who struggled frantically to find a way out of this apparent death trap.

"Up boys, up!"

"We gotta climb the wall!"

"The only way outa here is up boys!"

Some were stooping now, allowing comrades to scramble onto their backs, to stand on their shoulders, in order to get at least part of the way towards that rampart, now silhouetted clearly against the ever lightening sky, from where the dark shapes of shells, their fuses spluttering orange, continued to arc down into the ditch. Seeing them coming, some men scrambled to reach them as they landed, smothering them with wet mud to extinguish their fuses. Daniel saw several of the missiles neutralised in this way, but by far the majority of them exploded, either in the air above the heads of the trapped men or on reaching the ground. Up there to the right, that cannon muzzle appeared again, to discharge its hail of canister along the ditch, whose muddy bottom was now covered with the dead and wounded men of the stalled assault party.

Daniel looked upwards as he pushed himself into the muddy surface of the wall, seeing a few men up there balancing on some kind of a ledge where the wall was crowned by the rampart, as they tried to scramble the last few feet to the top. He heard a voice from beside him, Winder's.

"If we stay here we're as good as dead!" The black man stooped. "Up ya go Daniel, I'll be along."

Daniel slid the strap of his musket over his head, securing the weapon diagonally across his back, and jamming a foot into the side of the wall to give himself some initial momentum. He scrambled onto Winder's back, feeling the black man straighten as he perched there precariously and yet another hail of canister swept along the ditch. He levered upwards, trying to balance against the muddy wall as Winder reached his full height, before straightening his legs abruptly and springing upwards to push his fingers into the surface of the wall. He paused there momentarily, spread-eagled against the earth of the rampart only to find that, at this height, the mud had frozen and was covered in a layer of ice, against which his fingernails scrambled in vain. He began to slither downwards, struggling and flailing as he slid to the bottom of the ditch, landing almost on top of Winder as he moved hastily away.

Daniel scrambled to his feet and faced the black man.

"It's covered in ice," he yelled, "and there's no berme, so there's nothin' to grip up there."

"Lemme try," his companion returned and Daniel stooped, positioning his feet apart, and gripping his knees with his hands, struggling to keep his balance among the crowd of jostling, frantic men. He felt Winder's knee thump onto his back. Daniel gave him a second or two to steady and balance before pushing up to his full height, feeling the black man shift position as he did so. Then he gave a sudden thump and heave from his feet on Daniel's back, that pushed him violently downwards and expelled the breath from his lungs in a gasp. He looked upwards to see Winder hanging there, with his musket slung across his back on its strap, scrabbling vainly with both hands and feet for some kind of grip, as he too began to slide down the wall to the ditch, while still more shells sailed downwards, black ugly missiles illuminated by their spluttering orange fuses, to explode in the ditch. Winder landed half on top of him, with something between a thud and a splash. He began to pick himself up and the two of them exchanged brief looks while, all around them, groups of men pushed this way and that along the ditch, seeking somewhere, anywhere, where they could get at their enemy, while officers vainly screamed for their men.

"Company C, Sixteenth Regiment!"

"Sergeant Porter, for God's sake!"

"Company A, over here with me!" Daniel shook his head, as still more shouts came, turning once more to Winder as he heard his voice amid the chaos.

"There ain't no way outa here except the way we came in," he said. "We can't get up there."

"We've got t' think of ourselves Eli," Daniel told him, bellowing to make himself heard at all. "We can't get up there and we can't go back, cuz we'll be even better targets out there in the open. We're trapped here meantime and that means we're stuck with the shells, but we've got to get out of the way of the cannon," he gestured to the right, towards the angle in the line of the ditch, above where the cannon was blasting its showers of metal death along its length, "and that means that way." They began to move and as they did so Daniel Ryan was aware of Matthew Hale emerging from the crowd of jostling, milling men to join them. Still the shells came flying down, visible by their spitting fuses, to burst in the bottom of the ditch. Coming down too were bodies of men who had made it up the wall, only to slip while almost within reach of the top, or maybe they had been thrown back from the parapet itself by the Yankee defenders. They too landed in the ditch, crashing into the men who crouched there, men who now waited, trapped in the mud at the bottom, for death to come in whatever way it chose.

Ryan and his companions pushed and fought their way along, through the deep mud and struggling bodies which now virtually filled the whole length and width of the ditch, aware that more and more of these trapped men were seeing

278

that reaching that margin of dead ground under the reach of the cannon was the best hope of survival. But they were also able to see only too well that even if they could reach that section of the ditch, up on the rampart the defenders were still hard at work, tossing their spluttering shells, like grenades, into that portion of the trench. There were other things too coming down upon the struggling men. Muskets, with bayonets fixed, were descending like spears into the trapped mass below and rocks and then Ryan saw an axe, its blade flashing dully in the increasing light, plunging down into the crowds where it was almost impossible to miss.

Again the cannon up on the bastion crashed out and in front of them they saw a whole group of struggling figures swept like chaff along the ditch, to collapse like rag dolls into the churning mud. Daniel Ryan had never been this close to a canister discharge before and his flesh cringed at the blast of hot air, while his eyes watered and his nose ran with the stink of the powder smoke and the burning sawdust packing from the canister round. Ryan exchanged another brief glance with Hale.

"On," he yelled at the top of his voice, "it's the only way to go." He saw Hale nod briefly as he turned to face along the ditch once more, where the lottery of where a man stood or struggled when the shells and rocks and bayoneted muskets came plunging down, was, again and again, deciding whether he lived or died. Ahead of him he caught a glimpse of Ballard and Jones, struggling in the same direction, their heads bowed and their shoulders hunched forward, as though against a storm of rain. He pushed ahead once more, aware that Winder and Hale were at his shoulders, so close that he could feel an occasional breath on the back of his neck. On they struggled through the fire and the smoke and the chaos of an expanse of muddy slime that was now nothing more than a death trap for literally hundreds of men. They were close now, but here was the most dangerous part of the trench wall. Here the bastion that angled outwards from the line of the main wall towered above them, and here, in this last stretch of the trench within

279

the cannon's angle of fire, was the greatest danger. If they could not get below its angle there would be no protection from the next blast of the gun. Up above, in the almost full light, Daniel Ryan saw the dark muzzle of the cannon appear as it was pushed forward into the embrasure after reloading. It was too soon. They were short, a few vital yards short of that safer zone, below the angle where the cannon could bear. It was shockingly evident by the tangle of dead and dying who lay all around them that just those few tantalising yards farther on was the expanse of sheltered ground where a crowd of men now crouched, which the weapon's barrel could not be depressed far enough to reach.

"Down!" he bellowed, as he threw himself forward, while above him the muzzle of the cannon disappeared in a belch of yellow flame and a billow of dirty smoke. He pushed himself down into the tangle of men's limbs and mud, tasting the dirt as it engulfed his face, feeling and hearing the whoosh of hot air and the passing hum of those lethal iron balls just above him as he burrowed still deeper among the human debris at the bottom of the ditch, feeling others do likewise around him. Then up, he pushed with his hands on the prostrate body of a dead man, feeling the freezing mixture of mud and blood squash through his fingers as he looked ahead through the mud that dripped and ran down his face. He levered himself up to his knees and then to his feet, into the cloud of stinking smoke, wiping his mud-saturated sleeve across his face, seeing as he looked up towards the embrasure above him that it was silhouetted against the sky and empty. Even as he struggled to his feet he could visualise those Yankees up there, swabbing and loading and ramming as the seconds dripped steadily away until the next shot was ready.

"C'mon Eli, Matthew," he yelled. "Move now or the next one'll be comin'!" He pushed himself forward glancing around as he went. All around him other men were doing likewise, pushing themselves to their feet to resume the struggle to reach the sanctuary of the bastion wall, but, though his gaze lingered on those behind him for a further instant and he could make out a mud covered apparition that must be Eli Winder, he could see no sign of Matthew Hale. Ahead of him another shell plunged down into the ditch, but, though he winced as he awaited its detonation, there was no explosion. Maybe the fuse had been cut too long, the thought flashed across his mind, allowing the liquid mud to extinguish the fuse, or maybe somebody over there had got to it in time and had pulled the fuse from the charge, saving himself and his companions in the process.

Ryan pushed on once more, jostling in the crowd of struggling men now within a few yards of that angle in the wall where the canister from the cannon could not reach them. A crowd of men had jammed themselves into that vital ground, safe, to a precarious degree, from the enemy fire and here, perhaps because of the need for space along the parapet above to serve the gun, the shell grenades were fewer. Maybe the Yankees up above had been so pinned down by the fire from the men on the glacis slope that they did not realise the numbers of trapped men who had now pushed into that narrow safer zone beneath the bastion. Men pressed themselves into the frozen mud of the wall, while others pressed against them. The cannon crashed out again, filling the ditch to the east with more smoke and renewed screams, while all along this section of the ditch the eyes of all of the trapped men turned upwards, waiting for the next shell to come angling over the parapet and down into the crowd, where any further explosion would kill and maim a totally disproportionate number of those who sheltered there. Ryan joined them, straining his eyes for a black smudge with that tell tale yellow splutter of flame attached to it that could bring death in an instant. A few yards from him a fleeting glimpse of another flickering yellow light appeared over the rampart.

"Git it!" A dozen voices shouted the words, almost in unison, as hands reached up to catch the missile. Daniel saw it grasped and dashed to the ground, as all around the staring eyes of the men trapped in the ditch nearby turned to watch briefly before returning to the parapet above. A brief pause followed while farther along the ditch more shells plunged down to explode in more yellow blasts of smoke and flame bringing still more screams from the injured and dying below. Around Daniel Ryan the watch on the parapet continued, as necks craned and eyes strained, waiting for the next black missile with its bright spluttering fuse to come sailing over that parapet so near above them, but unattainable in the ice and mud of this frozen dawn.

Out on the glacis there were shouts and further down the ditch men were beginning to move, scrambling up the muddy side of the ditch onto the glacis, to run the gauntlet back across the expanse of tree stumps and wire to safety. Daniel took it all in as some of those around him also started to move, making for the wall of the ditch to take their chance out there. Suddenly a shout came from close by and he whirled to see the latest dark shape descend with its sparkling fuse, as hands reached up again to catch it. Daniel watched them, almost transfixed, not close enough to attempt to catch the shell himself, yet knowing that if it exploded he was well within range of its fragments. He saw the arms waver as those waiting to catch the falling projectile were pushed and jostled by those making for the wall and the glacis beyond. The shell plunged on down, brushing the fingers of at least one of those who tried to grab it, but the barging and pushing in the ditch was too much and it continued on its way, avoiding those vainly groping hands to reach the ground just feet away from him, as men stooped and crouched around it, scrambling to reach that all important fuse, but it was all taking too long. Daniel Ryan dropped to the ground again as all around him other men did likewise. As he pushed into the mud once more he was aware of being almost engulfed in a flash of brilliant light and a blast of deafening sound. He cringed as he heard and sensed the metal fragments flying around him, feeling a whizzing passing impact on the left side of his head and hearing a succession of wet tearing thuds as other fragments found targets among the trapped men, this being confirmed by the screams that rose around him. He stayed there for only a

282

second or two, knowing that he had to move again, pushing in as far as he could in to the part of the trench that was shielded by the wall of the fort.

There was a roaring noise in his ears as he scrambled to his knees, feeling the frozen slime soak immediately through the fabric of his pants as he wiped the mud from his face again with a sleeve that was already saturated with liquid filth. There was blood all around him, mixed with the mud and running in rivulets through it, though his own limbs save for the side of his head, aching and sore from his fall among the wire, felt no sharp pain of a wound. He looked around him as still more men pushed past, seeing fallen men, now two or three deep in places, and mixed among the bodies were parts of bodies. Daniel saw a detached hand lying incongruously in the mud, as still more men pushed past him making for the wall of the ditch to scramble up the muddy slope and move away out of sight.

All around him were the groans and cries of the injured, and as his eyes moved around them and the roaring in his ears only slowly began to diminish, he caught sight of Winder. He was there, just a few feet away, half-sitting and half-lying amidst a tangle of wounded, wedged against the wall of the fort and his gaze caught Daniel's.

"Looks like I got one," he ground out through clenched teeth. Daniel pushed himself up into a crouch and started across the ditch towards him, struggling in the thick, blood-stained mud past other injured, dead and dismembered men, among whom the living still crouched, unwilling to run the gauntlet of fire by climbing from the ditch to the glacis. But here the chance of death was scarcely less, for still the shells came sailing down into the ditch, while the desperate men there still watched, leaping like furies towards them as soon as they came into view. Daniel looked away, concentrating on his friend as he half-stumbled the final clumsy steps to where he lay. At last he was there and he knelt beside Winder, feeling the icy chill of the mud again through the knees of his pants as he did so.

283

"How bad, Eli," he asked?

"Bad," was the reply. "Reckon I got a bleeder." Daniel looked down towards where the black man's hands were gripped tightly around his right thigh a few inches above his knee, seeing the dark blood pulse out between his fingers with a hint of crimson in its colour now as the daylight grew stronger.

"I kin feel the beatin' in it," Winder gasped. Daniel moved closer to him, pressing himself finally into the muddy wall at the base of the fort. Glancing along he could at last see no sign of the far bastion, from which the cannon had been firing, as he reached towards his friend's leg.

"I can do that Eli," Daniel told him. "Let me get my finger on it." He pushed his hands down on Winder's, feeling the black man pull away.

"No!" Winder gasped, "no!" He gritted his teeth and paused before continuing. "Need to strap it. Got t' git somethin' to strap it with." Daniel nodded in acknowledgement, feeling embarrassed that Winder had had to tell him the obvious. He turned away, as his eyes scanned furiously around, seeking something, anything that would serve, a rope, a belt. His gaze came to rest on a bloodied and mud-plastered soldier who lay face down in the ditch a few feet away, and his eyes settled immediately on the man's belt. He lunged towards him, pushing his way through the throng of those who still lived and struggled in the ditch to reach the soldier and pull his body around, then fumbling with his fingers for the belt buckle. He wrenched and pulled, feeling the numbness of his fingers as he struggled to loosen the leather tongue. He cursed as it refused to come and he wrenched at it again with all his strength, until finally the buckle released, and he hauled the leather strap bodily from its loops and pushed back along the trench past more struggling men, to where Winder lay.

"Let's get it around," he muttered as he pushed the buckle of the belt underneath the outside of Winder's thigh. He pressed the tongue into his free hand while he reached down

284

the inside of his leg to pull the other end underneath, while his other hand, still grasping the belt tongue, steadied him in the jostling chaos of the trench.

He searched frantically under Winder's leg, groping in the icy mud with his numbed fingers. For a second his mind illogically cursed Winder. Couldn't he move the damned leg that few inches that would make the job of finding and fastening the belt so much easier? He dismissed the thought, recognising its churlishness and feeling a renewed twinge of embarrassment. He groped again, until at last he felt the buckle brush the backs of his searching fingers. He reversed their direction immediately, scrambling them through the mud and blood until he felt the thing brush again at their tips and he twisted his hand, pinching the metal buckle of the belt at last between his middle and fourth finger. He twisted the hand again, finally managing to grasp the metal in his fist and he pulled firmly on it, feeding it up around where he still held the leather tongue. He slipped the belt tongue through the metal channel at the rear of the buckle plate and pulled the thing tight, pausing then to position it just above Winder's other hand that still pressed on the wound. He turned to look into the black man's mud-plastered face.

"Now Eli, hold it there while I git somethin' to twist it." He glanced around. "There," he gestured with his head towards a bayoneted musket, almost underneath where he knelt. He reached down and pulled the weapon towards him, reaching towards the muzzle and the bayonet ring to loosen it from its place. Then a twist to the left and he eased the socket across the muzzle, only to feel it clog and jam in the mud and grit that plastered the barrel. He cursed again and twisted the bayonet in his hand, feeling it scrape and move, but so slowly and reluctantly. He bent down and spat on it before working his fingers among the mix of saliva and dirt to soften and loosen it. He twisted again, feeling it move at last and he wrenched frantically until at last the steel blade was free. He grasped it and turned to where Winder lay, manoeuvring the bayonet point towards the belt, pushing the blade underneath the leather and pushing it on until the angle in the steel, between the blade and the socket, rested under the strap.

"Hold it there," he grunted to Winder, "while I tighten it." He grasped the two ends and laboriously formed a knot, doubling it in case the saturated leather slipped, then grasped the bayonet with both hands and twisted it firmly, feeling his friend move and tense as it tightened. Tighter and tighter he pulled, feeling the leg tremble and flinch as he increased the pressure of the belt on the flesh. He twisted it again and Eli Winder looked at Daniel. Their eyes met for a second, but the black man said nothing.

"Easy Eli," Daniel gasped. "Reckon we got it." He was suddenly aware of how light it had become, to the point that when he looked around at what remained of the jostling crowd around them he could see it beginning to thin, and could now make out the details of individual men as they moved away to scramble up the wall of the ditch and take their chances at last on the slope.

"Look," he said, "the boys're goin' back. This won't last much longer and then we can try and get you some help."

Daniel saw Winder nod and then he moved his arm, loosening his fingers ever so slightly, holding his breath as he watched. Blood immediately welled out between Winder's fingers, but not in the same tide of crimson that it previously had. The black man nodded to him and he twisted the belt again, seeing the blood flow decline further as he twisted it once more, tightening it inexorably, until the flow had almost stopped. Now, one last twist and.... He looked into Winder's face, seeing a pallid look, an expression that looked like drowsiness cloud the black man's features. How could a man with a complexion as dark as Winder's look pale, he asked himself, but he was seeing it with his own eyes.

"Can you grip it Eli?" he said, aware that all around him the firing and shouting had almost died away.

"C'mon Eli," he entreated, aware that his own chances of escape were diminishing with every second that he remained in the ditch, but looking again into Winder's face he could see that there was no chance of him holding his own tourniquet in place, for his features had a look of semi-insensibility, suggesting that he was pretty near to passing out completely, most likely from the loss of all of that blood.

Daniel looked around him along the littered length of the trench. Men squirmed and writhed in the mud, their cries and groans gathering into an increasing litany of despair, as all around the gunfire died away. With the attack, and thankfully the slaughter too, now over and most of the uninjured now gone, it could only be a matter of time before the Yankees came down to inspect their work of killing and secure the men who still remained. Daniel could see those who had opted to stay shrinking from the hail of enemy fire which was now directed out on the glacis. They squatted there, singly or in groups, hunched against the fort side of the ditch, pressing themselves against the mud wall, dirt-plastered and wild-eyed as though afraid that the rain of canister and shells from the parapet would resume. His eyes moved on across the expanse of dead and wounded before gravitating towards a particular corpse, and he recognised Matthew Hale where he lay among a tangle of bodies, among whom all signs of movement had now ceased.

He racked his dazed brain, aware that his ears were still buzzing from the concussion of the exploding shell. Was this the end for him also? If he remained here with Winder, then the stockade was almost a certainty, living out what remained of this war as a prisoner, starved and abused by the Yankees, unless....? He looked around him, seeing the host of dead and wounded men who carpeted the bottom of the ditch. In some places they were several men deep and maybe, if the Yankees did not look too closely, there was a chance of feigning death, of maybe lasting out here in this mess of men and blood and mud through the day (his mind reeled at the thought), until nightfall when there might be a chance for him to escape in the darkness, back down that wire strewn glacis to some kind of safety.

It was a thin hope, his brain told him, but the alternative was to give up when the Yankees came and to join the dismal procession north, to whichever of their hell holes they chose for him. His mind pondered them, those much discussed places where men froze and died like flies or sickened from lack of decent food. Rock Island, Point Lookout, each of them, and others also, enjoyed a grim reputation and he had no intention of going meekly into them...., but then there was Winder. Without help he would die, and if Daniel was prepared to simply let him, then he might as well have let go of the bayonet and taken his chances on the glacis long before now. If he left Winder, whether as a fugitive or as a prisoner, he would certainly die, but what choice did he really have? He looked at his companion as he lay in the mud and his own blood, drifting in and out of consciousness, far too weak to take charge of his own wound. Ryan knew that the only chance he had of survival was if he stayed with him and help came from the Yankees, who must surely soon descend into the chaotic mess of the ditch and begin to render some kind of assistance to their fallen enemies.

Over to the left, towards the bastion that marked the corner of the fort, he heard a voice calling sharply.

"Out reb's, step out t' where we kin see ya!"

"Git yoreselves up here and leave the weapons down there!"

"Move reb's, else we'll drop a few more shells."

"Will ya take a look at the dead meat in that damned ditch?" another voice called. Around Daniel a scattering of the skulking men had begun to move. In ones and twos they were rising to their feet, raising their hands as they picked their way across, clambering over the tangles of dead and wounded, to begin scrambling up the wall of the ditch. Daniel hunched down, half behind where Winder lay, leaning against another twitching man as he tried to conceal himself. The time had come, his racing mind told him. It was now: surrender or stay? He pushed his head down behind Winder's back, feeling the cold mud again on his face as he tried to

288

merge himself into the carpet of dead and dying. He must stay with his friend. He knew that in his heart. Whatever it meant for him, be it the stockade or even a bullet, he must give Winder the best that he could in terms of a chance, even if it was only a pathetically small one, of survival.

Around him the scrambling and sloshing of those who now clambered their way to captivity mixed with the groans and cries of the wounded, until the wet footfalls faded and gradually ceased. Ryan was aware of further voices and of muddy footsteps above him, either on the scarp of the ditch or the parapet itself. They were obscured by the cries, sobs and groans of the men who lay around him, but they were there. It was the Yankees, it could only be the Yankees, out to gaze upon this scene from the pit of hell and survey the extent of their success. He pushed his head still lower and altered his grip on the bayonet as surreptitiously as he could, hearing his enemies close by, as he flexed the numbed, frozen fingers on each hand in turn for a brief time, before ceasing even that, not daring to move another muscle. His limbs grew steadily colder and after a further time, as still the voices came from close by, he began to shiver.

Daniel Ryan did not know how long it was until he heard the sounds of more footfalls down in the trench itself. It was full daylight and the sun was high, illuminating the scene about as much as was going to happen on this November day. He had heard the Yankees gradually move away, leaving the area where he and Eli Winder lay among the corpses and groans and entreaties of the wounded all around them. His body felt numb from the cold and he was now shivering uncontrollably, but he dared not look, for fear that this would be the end of his efforts to save his friend. It was the shout from above that told him that whoever had arrived in the trench, it was no longer the enemy, for it was a taunt, uttered by one of the men on the parapet, out of sight because of the angle of the fort wall.

"Plenty o' dead Johnnies down there for ya." A reply came, from somewhere along the ditch, but Ryan could not, in the continuing jumble of cries and groans from the wounded men all around him, decipher what it was. It could however mean only one thing; wherever they were, there were men down in the ditch. He wanted to look, but was still afraid to do so, for he knew that almost certainly it was the Yankees who had come to begin the work of removing the wounded and the dead. His mind raced as he considered what to do.

If he lay still it could be hours or even longer before help would come for Winder, and even if he could last through the day till darkness, what would he do then? He could not leave his friend, nor could he hope to carry or drag him from the ditch without being seen. He looked across at his companion as his own body convulsed uncontrollably, aware that he had not stirred for some time. On an impulse he raised his head from the mud and looked briefly along the ditch, seeing several figures now working among the tangle of fallen men while still more were arriving at the scarp to come scrambling down into the ditch, but they all wore Yankee tunics of drab blue. Ryan lowered his head again as his mind raced furiously. It could only be a matter of time, maybe only minutes, till he was discovered by these men, and there was liitle time left for him to make his choice.

He raised his head slowly once more, squinting over the limbs of the fallen at the labouring figures who were lifting the wounded from where they lay and passing them up to other men who waited on the edge of the ditch. There was nothing to do now but surrender and by doing so get help for Winder. He had begun to raise his arm when he saw the grey uniform: he promptly lowered his hand again as he focussed his eyes on the man. He was about ten yards away along the ditch, or maybe slightly more than that; an officer, a surgeon judging by the green facings on his uniform coat, and he was moving among the men in the ditch, apparently identifying those for immediate help. Daniel Ryan saw him stoop again to examine a wounded man before gesturing to a couple of the Yankee orderlies.

Ryan lowered his head once more and tried to think, aware that his mind was confused, likely as a result of the extreme cold. Could the presence of this man, here in the ditch, offer him any sort of chance of escaping captivity? He raised his head slowly and looked again. Certainly the man seemed to be working his way along the ditch towards where he lay with Winder, but everyone else working in the ditch seemed to be a Yankee, so what possible chance was there of escape in such a situation? He lowered his head once again as the thoughts jumbled around in his dazed mind, and then it came to him and in a way it was obvious. This man was an officer: he could decide. When he got close enough he would try to attract his attention and ask what he should do. It all seemed simple when he thought about it, but with so many Yankees working all around, would they not reach where he lay before this Confederate surgeon? He slumped down once more as his mind grappled with the dilemma. There was no help for it, however fraught this option was: the alternative was to give up and surrender, and he could have done that some time ago.

He looked again at the southern surgeon. He was closer now, crouching as he examined yet another wounded man, while all around others were raising their arms and calling to him and to the others who were at work.

"Here!"

"For the lord's sake help me!"

"Over here!"

"Water, please...!"

Daniel Ryan watched as the man straightened up again and in an instant, as their eyes met, he gestured to him. The surgeon seemed to blink before fixing his gaze on him and nodding. He began to make for where Ryan and Winder lay, but not directly, pausing instead to examine further men on the way before calling the Yankee litter bearers over to assist. Finally he was only feet away and as he crouched to tend to yet another man, he spoke.

"Where are you hit, boy?" he inquired in a tone that was almost gentle. Ryan took a deep breath and tried to answer, aware as he started that his chattering teeth would make talking difficult.

"I got a fragment' in the head," he tried hard to form the words, "but it ain't me, it's him." He gestured towards Winder's leg. "He's got a bleeder so I had t' stay t' keep the strap tight." The words were a garbled jumble of sounds, distorted by the chattering of his teeth that got worse every time that he tried to relax his jaw to speak, but the man seemed to understand. He moved Ryan's hand partly aside glancing at the tourniquet as he did so. Then he took a quick look at Daniel's head, fingering the semi-dried blood that crusted his scalp.

"You're walkin' wounded," he said slowly, "so that means they won't be lettin' you go no place." He looked straight into Daniel's face and seemed to ponder briefly, then he reached into the bag that he had brought with him and withdrew a pad of cloth.

"What's your name, private," he asked?

"Daniel Ryan."

"Well Daniel Ryan, I am Captain Henry Maskell, I'm on the corps surgeon's staff. Wipe your face with that," he said, passing him the pad, "and try to clean as much of that dirt off your face as you can. Get yourself a hat and wedge that pad on the wound underneath it, in case it starts to bleed again. For the next few minutes, you are my orderly. You'll carry this bag and pass me stuff and then, once these Yankees get used to that idea, I'm goin' to send you back to our lines with some kind of a message. They may allow it or they may not, if they don't it's the stockade, for you and maybe for me too, but maybe tryin' to help a man, who's passed up on his own chance to escape to keep his friend alive is worth it." He looked down at Winder.

"How do you know he isn't dead," he said, "and that you haven't wasted your time out here?" He reached down, took hold of the bayonet with one hand and felt under the hinge of

292

Winder's jaw with the other, holding his finger there for a few seconds, while Daniel Ryan tried to clean the blood and mud from his face and head, casting around, as he did so, for a hat.

"He's alive," he grunted, "there's a pulse there, looks like you weren't wastin' your time after all."

He gestured towards the leather bag.

"Pick that up," he said, "and bring it over here." He turned as Ryan lifted the bag, feeling his body continue to convulse with shivering as he did so. Then Maskell looked past Ryan.

"Orderly!" he shouted. Down the trench a Yankee looked up. Maskell beckoned to him and the man straightened up and started forward, picking his way through the tangle of dead and wounded as he squelched towards where the surgeon and Ryan crouched.

"We need a litter for this man," Maskell told the Yankee. "He has an arterial bleed and if he's goin' to live, he needs help and pretty quick." The man looked down at Winder.

"Ain't no need to go bustin' a gut over no reb' nigger," he growled. Maskell shook his head and sighed.

"Either do it, or I'll find out what your superior thinks about it," he replied in a resigned tone. He turned to Ryan as the Yankee shrugged and started away.

"See if you can find me a compression strap in there."

"A what?" Daniel Ryan stammered.

"It doesn't matter, pass the bag over here." He prowled through the contents, withdrawing his hand at last with a leather strap with what looked like a metal clip at one end.

"Take hold of the bayonet," he said, "while I get this on his leg."

By the time that Maskell had fitted and tightened the strap, two further Yankees had arrived bearing a litter made of fence rails.

"This man will live, if he gets prompt treatment," the surgeon told them. He turned to Daniel Ryan.

"Ryan get back to our lines and get me more clips, I've used all that I brought up." Ryan tried to keep his arm and hand from trembling as he saluted and turned away. The two Yankees looked at each other.

"Reckon he should be in the fort with the prisoners," one of them said. "Covered in all that shit he must 'a come up with the rest o' the reb's."

"This man is serving as my orderly," Maskell told them. "He's covered in all of that shit, as you put it, because he's been pulling wounded men out of this trench for the last hour. If you want to see a lot more shit you should take a look at each other." The Yankees exchanged more glances before returning to the task of settling Winder on the litter. Maskell looked at Ryan.

"Get on with it Ryan," he said. "I don't have all day."

Daniel Ryan started towards the wall of the ditch, feeling weak and unsteady as he tried to move, vainly trying to control the shuddering that racked him. His fingers and toes were almost devoid of feeling, as he stumbled across, striving to keep up with the Yankees who carried Winder and to avoid trampling on the men who still lay there. As he moved away, he looked back towards Maskell, but the surgeon had already returned to his work. His eyes wandered across to where Matthew Hale lay, but his face was now hidden by the body of another soldier, and among the tangle of men who lay around him there was no sign of movement of any kind.

He shifted his gaze up to the wall of the ditch to see that not all of the Yankees detailed to help the wounded had descended into it. More men waited at the edge and these were engaged in evacuating the wounded who were being passed up to them by those who worked in the ditch itself. Winder's litter was being carried towards where several of these men stood stretching their hands down into the ditch to grasp the arms of the wounded, the corners of blankets or the litter poles pushed up towards them. One man with a corporal's stripes on his muddy sleeves stood on a narrow ledge of earth half way down into the ditch and who was therefore able to assist in lifting the casualties up to those awaiting them. Daniel waited behind Winder's litter wondering, while several other wounded were passed up in this way, how he would negotiate the climb. Winder's turn finally came and the corporal on the ledge stretched towards the Yankees with his litter.

"What d' ya know," he growled? "A nigger who ain't figured out what side he should be on."

"This nigger's got a bleeder," one of the Yankees grunted. The man nodded and grasped the poles of the litter, while the two other Yankees pushed it upwards from behind. Daniel waited until the two Yankees stood on the edge of the ditch, with the litter ready to go, before starting to climb. He reached out his numbed hands, seeking holds in the wall of the ditch as he began to ascend, digging his toes into the mud to get some kind of purchase for his feet. The corporal on the ledge looked down at him

"Who's he," he growled?

"He's the reb' surgeon's orderly," one of the men at the litter muttered. "He's sent him back across fer clamps or somethin'," The corporal looked back towards Daniel and reached forward towards him.

"Orderly my ass," he growled. The other Yankee shrugged.

"That's what the surgeon said." The corporal looked at Daniel and his expression seemed to change slightly.

"Reckon you could use a boost," he said, as he reached his hand across to pull Daniel's arm, hauling him onto the ledge where he stood. He moved his other arm to rest his hand against the small of Daniel's back, upon which he braced himself and pushed him upwards.

Daniel tried to nod as he passed the man, but once again the movement was lost in the uncontrollable shivering of his body. He scrambled vainly towards the top, seeing other hands reach down towards him to grasp his tunic and belt, with which he was hauled bodily out of the ditch at last. He tried to nod to his helpers, as they pushed him down the beginning of the glacis where the muddy slope opened up in front of him. He cast his eyes around, finally catching sight of

Winder's litter and its two bearers, already on their way down the glacis. He began to shuffle after them, aware of some of the Yankees at the edge of the ditch watching him and seeing as he went the further tangle of dead and wounded men that extended down the glacis towards the captured Yankee picket trenches.

Men lay in groups and singly, some of them almost at the edge of the ditch, while others marked the line of the advance all the way back to the tree stumps and the wire, where still more dead lay tangled and trapped in the strands. It was a sight that Daniel Ryan found utterly appalling. These men had died because not enough had been done to prepare for this attack. The army had been here around this city for nearly two weeks, yet the generals had failed to put together any kind of a sensible plan. It had come in the end to an ungainly rush by a crowd of mortal, vulnerable men, into what had promptly become a trap, and they had paid the price for the neglect that had sent them out in the darkness and gloom into a devil's mixture of death.

Further down the glacis fires had been lit and there the Yankees were passing the wounded on their litters or in blankets to Confederate soldiers. Daniel passed a number of them as they returned, as he shambled slowly on down, struggling to balance as he took each ungainly step, picking his way among the dead and the dying where still more men laboured. He was aware that the litter bearing Eli Winder had changed bearers and was slowly moving away from him, but he knew also that he could go no faster. His eyes ranged across the slope ahead. All along this lower part of the glacis more bodies lay, more of them tangled in lengths of wire. Other men picked and prowled their way across the muddy wasteland of dead and injured, likely in search of missing comrades, Daniel's mind concluded dully, or maybe it was shoes or other necessities that occupied them.

It was as his mind coursed through these notions that he saw a figure appear over the steeper part of the slope, beyond the tangle of abbatis and pointed poles of the forward trench line. The man was plastered in mud, but there was something familiar about him as he started up the slope, though it was only as he crossed the picket trench line that Daniel recognised the way that the soldier was moving and saw that it was Ballard. He tried to raise his arm, but could manage only a clumsy sideways lurch with it. He called out, but his garbled shout seemed lost in the continuing chorus of talk among the surgeons and orderlies and the cries from the wounded who still remained on the glacis, but Ballard had turned and now came directly towards him through the throng of wounded and their helpers. The corporal was unencumbered by any weapon and he quickened his pace to cover the final stretch of corpse-littered mud to reach Daniel Ryan. He stretched out his hands and gripped Daniel's shoulders, steadying him and pulling him gently upright.

"OK Daniel," he growled, "I got ya." Daniel tried to speak but the words remained almost incoherent, distorted by the continued chattering of his teeth and the shuddering of his limbs. Ballard stepped to his side, still supporting him as they started down the glacis.

"We got a bit more'n five more hours to move these poor bastards," Ballard told him. "Word is it was Burnside that offered, not "Ol' Pete" that asked." Ryan pulled on his friend's sleeve and gasped and grunted at him.

"Did they get out?" He tried to say the words, but to his utter frustration they still refused to form properly, coming out as a collection of gutteral noises rather than any kind of coherent language, Ballard however seemed to understand.

"Don't try and talk," he said. "Isaac and Joe are back at the camp, Edwin's at the hospital, with shrapnel in his arm, but it was only a little piece, so we reckon he ain't too bad. Matthew and Eli are both missin' and so's Sam Jenkins. Jim Dellings too, that's the ones I know about."

"No!" Daniel, pulled his friend to a halt as he tried to form his words again. "Eli's there." He attempted to gesture with his arm towards the now distant litter, almost lost among the many others. "Hurt bad, but he's alive." Again his words were

297

incoherent, as his jaw refused to function and his body continued to shudder and convulse, but Ballard nodded. A brief silence followed as they resumed their way on down towards the trench line and the gully beyond, until Daniel tried again to speak.

"Matthew's back in the ditch." He felt the words coming slightly easier now as the shivering in him slowly diminished. Maybe the movement and exertion was helping him, making his blood flow, reviving him, at least a little, but as he spoke he could feel the emotion rising within him.

"He's back there Otis, in that god-damned hole. I wanted to help him, but I couldn't. I had to help Eli'. He was bleedin' too bad. I couldn't leave him to help Matthew." Daniel Ryan felt the tears well up in his eyes and start to trickle down his filthy cheeks, but at least the sounds he made were more like words, and he could begin to tell his friend something about the fate of their comrades.

"I couldn't help him Otis." He sighed deeply as the tears dribbled down his face, "so he's still back up there in that goddam ditch." He felt himself shudder again, but this time it was not the cold, it was something much more troubling than that. It was instead the acknowledgement of what had taken place back in the ditch. The tears continued down his cheeks, trickling into the corner of his mouth, tasting of salt and mud on his tongue as, supported by Ballard, he stumbled his way across the trench line and on towards the steeper part of the hill. He knew that there had been only so much that any one man could have done back there, but he also knew that he had made some kind of a choice in helping Winder and leaving Hale. In going to help one comrade he had forsaken another. Maybe it had simply been unavoidable, but he had still made the choice and the knowledge and recollection of it was forcing a bitter shaft of something that felt uncomfortably like guilt to course through his soul.

Ballard remained silent for a while, as though leaving Ryan to get over his remorse and compose himself, and as a result they were well down the crowded gully when he spoke again.

"Thar's more I didn't tell ya," he said. "Ruff got killed in the ditch and Preston too, and Jessop didn't come back neither." He looked at Daniel. "Carson as well," he added. "It's mubbee too soon fer any word of the colonel or the captain, or Carson either fer that matter, but they ain't back, so that means they're most likely either dead or wounded, cuz they weren't takin' hardly any prisoners back up there that I saw. Not that it matters much whether they're dead, crippled or captured. They ain't back and that's that." He looked again at Daniel Ryan as though to see if he understood. But even with Daniel's mind still numbed, and the shuddering in his limbs only slowly moderating, he knew well enough what all of this meant. He was sorry about Sam Jenkins. He was sorry about all of them, but there was something worse about Jenkins absence. If he was wounded then that was bad enough, but if he was dead then his family would have paid for this war with the lives of both of their sons; but the war was like that and it did not distinguish among those whom it swallowed.

It had always been that way, but then his mind moved on to focus on the other matter which also directly affected those who were still alive and with the company. If Preston was dead, or badly hurt, the regiment would likely come under Randolph's command, and that would be no worse and maybe even somewhat better than before. But with Jessop too being missing, whether dead or wounded, that was different. With the captain gone, seniority among the officers who remained would have been the main factor in deciding who took his place, but since Carson also was missing, that too was irrelevant. Replacement officers, like replacement enlisted men, were scarce now to the point of being almost non-existent, and all this meant that the new commander of what remained of Company B would, in all likelihood, be none other than Lieutenant Jefferson Gilby.

Chapter 13 The Price of Failure

Daniel Ryan spent the rest of that day in the shelter, cocooned in his blankets and situated as close to the fire as he dared get without his covers or limbs being singed by the heat. Ballard had cleaned and dressed the cut in his scalp and his lower legs were wrapped in crude bandages, covering the abrasions from the wire. His left hand, though not bandaged, bore a further gash from the same source. Rations had been issued as far as they went, and for their mess it meant a few handfuls of corn meal and some pieces of sorghum. The flour was cooked into a mash, supplemented by some acorns and nuts and berries from Kane's collection, and the whole mess was then baked in Thompson's improvised stone oven. The surviving five, with Jones having returned from the hospital, each got a small plateful of the bitter-tasting mix, but they devoured it as though it was the most sought after delicacy. Daniel felt it coursing around in his stomach, but at least his stomach now had something to get to work on. The shivering had gradually diminished, until by the late afternoon it had gone and feeling was returning to his hands and feet, though he still felt weak after his hours in the frozen mud of the ditch.

As the day moved towards dusk, Henry Bayfield had appeared and on producing a bottle of spirit from his shirt pocket, he had offered Daniel a mouthful. The others had looked on glumly as Daniel had sampled the contents, and Henry had seen them.

"Medicine like that goes to them that need it," he growled, "and, if what we're hearin' now is true, Daniel'll need t' make a hell of a recovery by the mornin'." He had risen to go without elaborating, pausing only to converse briefly with Thompson before finally departing. As Bayfield moved away, Thompson had come across to the fire, occupying himself for a while with arranging a few of the things that lay there that didn't really need arranging, indulging in his familiar game of acting as though there was nothing to report and letting the others of the mess stew for a time, before finally telling them whatever piece of news he had learned.

"Reckon there'll be marchin' orders by mornin'," he eventually began. His words were greeted by silence and continuing stares, while he amused himself by throwing additional wood on the fire.

"Will ya git on and tell us Joe," Kane rasped.

"Bragg got whipped at Chattanooga sure enough," Thompson told them. "Last week, Tuesday accordin' t' Henry."

"We pretty well knew that," Jones retorted.

"He's fallen back t' Dalton," Thompson resumed, after directing a long-suffering look of reproach at Jones. "The Yankees have started a relief force fer Knoxville, three or four divisions of them western boys, under that feller Sherman. Barnard says that they could be here in a couple o' days, but when they do git here we won't be waitin' around t' welcome them."

"So even if we'd a' took that fort and the city as well, we wouldn't have bin stayin' there long," Ballard growled. Thompson shrugged.

"We'd a gotten the stores up there," he said, "'n' then maybe we'd a waited around and let them come at us," he added. "Don't make no difference now. That waste o' good men up there jest became a bigger waste. Looks like "Ol' Pete's" mubbee left his brains down at Chickamauga Creek after all, or maybe they're back in Virginia," he added.

There was silence around the fire, though each of them could likely have made a good enough guess at what the others were thinking. Daniel Ryan occupied himself with his own thoughts and they were deeply pessimistic. Having waited for two weeks around Knoxville, the general had finally made his move and what a grim charade of military competence it had been. Yesterday their mess, having heard the plan for taking the fort, had pointed out its flaws one by one, and almost without exception, their comments had been borne out by the events of the early morning. If enlisted men

301

could see it, what in the hell was wrong with their damned generals that it took a trench full of slaughtered men to convince them that the attack plan had been wrong-headed from top to bottom? This campaign seemed to be going from bad to worse, staggering from one blunder to the next, and in the process bleeding away a never-ending stream of irreplaceable men from disease, privation and from these ill-fated fights that never seemed to gain anything any more.

It was almost as though the general was a different man, so lacklustre was his performance out here from how it had been in Virginia and now, if Thompson's news was true, they would be stuck here, chased about this God-forsaken stretch of Tennessee by the triumphant Yankees. It might indeed have been Braxton Bragg who had wasted the victory, won at such cost down at Chickamauga Creek, but the mutterings about their own generals, particularly about Longstreet himself, were growing among his men as it began to seem that since coming out here, he and some of his lieutenants had lost the edge that had distinguished them in Lee's army.

The service of the First Corps divisions out here was reaching a level of stumbling failure rivalling anything that had been previously attributed to Bragg, something that the men of the corps would never have believed before they had embarked on those trains back in Virginia last summer. Daniel's mind turned to the members of their own mess who had not returned. Hale they knew was dead. Jones too had seen him in the trench, lifeless and mud-plastered. As for Winder, there was at least a chance for him. He had been alive when carried to the rear on the litter, and maybe, just maybe, he would survive.

Daniel's mind turned then to Sam Jenkins, who was missing rather than confirmed as dead. The thought crossed his mind that maybe Jenkins, deep down, had not been so different from the other conscripts, and maybe he had found a way to escape the carnage in the ditch. Maybe, even now, he was being held in Knoxville or perhaps, even better than that, he was on his way south to Georgia. He immediately

302

dismissed the idea. The longer Jenkins had stayed with the company, the more he had come across as a sincere boy who meant what he had said about serving in the regiment till final victory. In all likelihood therefore he was either lying at some mud-soiled field hospital, whether in Knoxville or back here in the southern rear area, or still up there in that ditch, cold and lifeless, like Hale and Colonel Ruff and Preston and Jessop and Dellings and all the rest of them.

He thought first of Matthew Hale, only recently returned from his Chickamauga wounding, then of Dellings, who had seemed to pick up a wound in almost every serious fight they had gotten into. Then his mind returned to Sam Jenkins and Daniel once more pondered the boy's fate. He shuddered, and a flush of inward shame and embarrassment swept over him as he thought again of the boy whom he had ignored and excluded for the whole summer. He thought of the bottom land farm back in eastern Georgia, where the woman and the sisters that he now knew of but had never seen, struggled to scratch a living with no men folk now to help them. The hapless family would likely soon learn that their remaining son and brother would not be coming home either, just like the other boy Caleb those seventeen months ago at Malvern Hill, and it had been his, Daniel Ryan's, dismal lot to be present at the time of both their deaths. But missing, rather than dead, always offered an element of hope. Maybe the chance that he might have survived was slim, but it was possible and right now that chance, however remote, was that he was alive within the city, or better still away from this grim ordeal of blood and death and heading for Georgia. Even if that meant having to accept that he had done what conscripts tended to do and had turned his back on the comrades who had finally adopted him, it was very much the option that Daniel Ryan would have chosen to be the fate of Sam Jenkins and of his family.

It was all so damned pointless, another episode of the brutal progress of this war, as it ground on and on, extracting its ever-increasing cost in lives and blood. The depressing thoughts coursed endlessly through his mind. It was all down to the war, the war that they had entered so innocently nearly three years ago, but with the Yankees set to invade, what else could they have done but enlist to defend their homes and yet, had there been no other way? Had war been so inevitable that nothing could have been done to prevent it? Maybe so, and in that white heat of optimistic patriotism that had burned so strongly three years ago, was anyone of much of a mind to turn away from the prospect of war and look for another way? Daniel lay back and tried to put these sombre and depressing thoughts from his mind. It had all happened anyway, whatever anyone now thought, and the only thing to be done was to end the war, but with the standard of generalship that they had repeatedly seen out here in Tennessee, could that be achieved?

Now, for the first time since enlisting, Daniel Ryan was forced to confront the prospect that the south might not after all emerge victorious from this struggle. Out here the Yankees were maybe just too strong, yet in spite of the enemy threat, the southern generals seemed intent on making things worse, by throwing away whatever opportunities came their way. Maybe Virginia was the only place where things were different, the only place where the northern masses had really been fought to a standstill. If that was the true state of affairs, it all boded ill for the future, but having come this far there was nothing much for them to do now but fight it out, which would mean more death and more blood and more mothers and sisters left to starve. Daniel shook his head as he tried to dismiss this mournful train of thought. It did not do to think too much about it. All too many men had given in to it, leaving their places in the army and melting away into the woods and the darkness. Despair, given its head, could ruin the army, and without the army the people of the south were helpless in the face of the Yankee invaders. No, he told himself. They must hold fast. There were still friends to serve with and rely on and if they stuck together and stayed strong they could yet outlast the enemy. They too must be sick of this tide of blood and perhaps they would soon be ready to quit, especially if they saw that their adversary remained strong and united.

They did not leave the next day, nor the day after that: instead they waited in their muddy camps till the Thursday, before the artillery and supply trains were started away to the east. The infantry did not follow them immediately, but lingered until the following day, knowing they were going, ready to go, but dallying during those extra hours until the last of the daylight on the Friday, before breaking up their camps and forming their column of march on the muddy road as dusk fell and yet another downpour of rain began. As Daniel Ryan stepped away in his file, still limping on his half-healed legs, his eyes scanned around to the southwest in the last traces of daylight, eventually coming to rest on the distant ugly bulk of Fort Loudon, squat and immovable where it sat on its higher plateau, as it slowly disappeared into the descending cloud of rain and mist and the gathering darkness. Below its parapet, he reflected, another chapter of this whole Tennessee expedition had been written, but this one too had been recorded in the blood of the men of McLaws' brigades, and their blood, like that shed only weeks ago at Campbell's Station, had all been sacrificed for nothing.

They headed east as darkness settled over the land, following the route taken by the wagons and guns, moving ever further into this region of mountains and river valleys, yet conversely with every splashing step they took they were drawing closer to the Virginia line. Away to their front, beyond those mist covered ridge lines and mountain ranges, lay the Army of Northern Virginia, likely in winter quarters by now. The thought of it all filled Daniel Ryan with a sense of regret and longing. He wanted to be away from this misbegotten place. Even those ransacked and plundered counties of central Virginia which had seemed so desolate and depressing back in the days of late summer, now seemed like a prize, though so far it was all still a remote and unattainable one.

The march continued eastward, on roads that were often little more than sloughs of mud, with the infantry regularly getting saddled with their additional task of hauling wagons and guns through the worst of it. The labouring column stayed generally on the route of the East Tennessee and Virginia Railroad, passing through a succession of settlements and hamlets that gave an impression of depression and apathy that sat well with the mood of these initial days of winter. Strawberry Plains was passed, where the railroad crossed the river once more, with, as Ballard said, "not so much as a damned strawberry to be seen anywhere around the place." Then Bean's Station came and went, with various others in the files ready to make their own observations about beans when they found that there were none of those to be had either. Sarcastic humour was a familiar enough tactic that men regularly used to divert the depression and the ordeal of soldiering, and having done their best to make light of the hardships of a pretty miserable trek eastwards, the column finally halted close to a settlement named Rutledge. A camp was established and details were sent out to forage and requisition for the famished set of men who had seen their commissary wagons just once since leaving the lines around Knoxville.

The weather stayed cold and showery as camps were organised and the wagons began to return and rations were finally issued, but hardly had the standard improvements been commenced on their shelters and the re-establishment of regular rations issues been achieved, when rumours began to circulate that a further move was imminent. There were Yankees approaching, following along the railroad, not exactly in pursuit of the southern column, but more engaged in the process of satisfying themselves that their enemies had really gone. An advance force of enemy cavalry had therefore pushed well to the east of Knoxville and the word was that,

"Old Pete" was disposed to ambush it. For the army this meant retracing their steps along the road that they had just taken to get this far, but for some men at least, the fact that the general was showing his aggressive side was a welcome development, especially after all the dithering over at Knoxville. If there were Yankees back along the road in need of a whipping, then they were certainly up for the job, even if it meant that the usual trials of commissary inadequacy would be the likely result. They had come out here to whip Yankees, these men said, so the sooner they got to grips with these impudent blue-bellies the better, particularly since fighting Yankees usually meant a chance of plunder.

The following day, the Monday the march began in more heavy showers of rain, with the rude comfort of the camps abandoned and only the remains of the previous ration in the men's haversacks. The column toiled west, enduring the familiar waterlogged roads and being regularly called upon to leave their files to prise guns, limbers or wagons from where they had stalled in the mud. Evening came and the men were dismissed to bivouac, with the customary details immediately setting out in search of water and firewood. Fires proved difficult to kindle however, with almost everything collected to burn being saturated by the rain. Dry kindling of any kind was the secret, so any fuel gained from barns or other buildings was priceless, for it enabled the first fires to be kindled and fed, from which all of the others were started. Warmed finally at the end of this ritual, the men sheltered around their fires as the showers continued to come, eating whatever scraps of food remained to them. This done, the camp turned in, with most of the men of the company drowsing in the customary way with their elbows on their knees for such rest as they could get. They settled for these brief dozes through the night, taking turns to feed the fires with the wood they had gathered and dried.

The column was promptly formed just after dawn and the march resumed, with no sign of the commissary wagons. The day passed, in much the same way as the previous one, a laborious plod through the mud and showers of rain that eventually died away towards dusk, when a cheerless bivouac was set up. There was little in the way of food, and fires were forbidden, signifying the proximity of the enemy. The men huddled together for what warmth they could communally generate, most resorting to lying in the tried and tested formation known as "spooning," where each man settled with his knees pushed against the backs of his companion's knees and his groin against his companion's buttocks, while a further man settled in the same fashion behind him.

"It's a damn good job we're all keepin' our pants on," Vallance had quipped, reviving one of the oldest jokes about the arrangement, though there was little response from the others. "Spooning," Daniel Ryan reflected, was an, "in extremis" arrangement, and men forced to adopt it were usually in no mood for much in the way of hilarity on the subject.

There was little to be had of either sleep or comfort through the hours of darkness. The rain pulses had resumed towards dawn, nullifying the efforts of the men to warm themselves, and when the sergeants appeared at first light to rouse the company they found many of their men already on their feet, stamping around the saturated pasture, trying to restore circulation to their chilled limbs. Today, the camp talk said, would bring a fight. The column was promptly assembled and started on the saturated roads again, but the mood along the files was black. They were wet and filthy and for most of them, today was the third without food. As the morning drew on, the sound of skirmish fire began, crackling idly in the distance. The rain continued to fall as the column advanced, hearing the gunfire gradually increasing in its intensity out in front. By now the men were angrier still, especially as there were rumours coursing along the column that Kershaw's boys had gotten fed this morning, on plunder taken from the Yankees.

"How come they're first in line fer rations?"

"What's good fer gamecocks should be good fer Georgia boys too," were the general sentiments along the column. Perhaps it would have remained little more than anger among the enlisted men had they not been commanded by Gilby, who had been well enough fed by all accounts over the previous three days. True or otherwise, this notion increased the sense of injustice among those of Company B, with a rich chorus of cursing and complaint flowing among them, and the sergeants, likely reading the mood of their men, refrained from their customary censures and threats.

The column was halted by yet another delay on the road, with the men having to stand in the rain, their mood becoming more and more angry and savage. At length a mutter began, which grew into a sullen subdued chant as more men heard it and took it up.

"Bread! Bread!" The sergeants began to look around them as their sections successively joined the chant, but none of them made any move to subdue it. Gilby came down the column, his face dark with anger as he heard the men's voices.

"Bread! Bread!" Ahead the column began to shuffle forward, but the Company B files remained where they were.

"Bread! Bread!" The chanting continued as the men stood fast.

"First Sergeant Jeffers," Gilby yelled. There was a pause, before Jeffers approached and saluted.

"Sah!"

"Put a stop to this damned insubordination," Gilby snapped, "and get them moving again." Jeffers looked up and down the files, seeing and hearing before turning back towards the officer.

"The boys ain't ate since Sun...," Jeffers began, with a tone of unfamiliar uncertainty in his voice.

"Do as you're told, damn you," Gilby shouted, but his further pronouncements were interrupted and his expression changed as a procession of horsemen approached, heralded by the splashing thud of their hooves in the mud and the jingling

309

of their harness. The heads of everyone turned to look, as McLaws and his staff steered their mounts along the road. The general reined in, as Gilby drew himself to attention. Salutes were exchanged and McLaws looked around at the stationary column, as he lowered his gauntleted hand.

"I see these boys are hungry also," he said. Gilby flushed, but said nothing in reply, while along the files the chant had lowered to a mutter, but even with the general present, it did not die away completely.

"I hear you boys," McLaws called, as he turned in his saddle. "A man can't be expected to march all day and then fight on an empty stomach." He paused momentarily before raising his voice again. "We have obtained a supply of flour and a ration of it has been ordered up. It will be with you as soon as the drivers can get it here." The final voices ceased their subdued chant as the general raised himself in his stirrups.

"I reckon this fight can wait long enough for the men to get their ration," he called, as the beginnings of a cheer germinated along the column. McLaws raised his hat and called one of his staff to approach. A curt order was uttered and upon hearing it, the boy wheeled his horse and trotted back down the road the way he had come. The general meanwhile put spurs to his own horse's flanks and started away along the column, followed by the others of his staff, as behind him the cheers grew into a shout of approval.

McLaws was as good as his word, for in a matter of minutes the column was ordered over onto the muddy verge of the road, as wagons came straining up, their mules plastered in filth from their haunches down. Several vehicles passed on before the driver of the rearmost one, almost as mud-saturated as his team, pulled on his single rein, hauling the lead animal to the left, while the men moved and jostled aside to make room for the vehicle along the verge. The files dissolved; the men gathered around the wagon and a commissary sergeant appeared around the side with a grubby, canvas bag under his arm. The tailboard was lowered to horizontal and the sergeant clambered wearily up onto the board, turned back a tarpaulin that was roughly laid across the load and pulled the nearest sack closer to the edge.

"Don't you damn well spill none o' that," a voice called above the general melee of talk, to a chorus of grim laughter. The sergeant scowled in return as he clambered down into the mud and pulled his measure from the canvas bag.

"I ain't issuin' nothin' to a rabble like this," he growled. Jeffers stepped across and began pushing the men into a line.

"Ya see, boys," he intoned. "Ask and you shall receive. It says so in the lord's sacred scriptures so there ain't no arguin'. I don't recall no chapter and verse, but it's sure as hell in there some place." Daniel Ryan looked across as he moved towards the wagon to where Gilby had been, but there was now no sign of the lieutenant. It seemed, Ryan reckoned, that seeing his men being issued with their long overdue rations of flour was something that he felt no desire to witness. Up ahead the gunfire still grew, but for once, Yankees or not, the men of Company B had their minds on other things.

The march was resumed as soon as the issue had been completed, but with the flour safely deposited in haversacks and food bags there was a different mood among the men in spite of the fact that not a morsel of the issue had been consumed, save by those who were prepared to stuff raw handfuls of it into their mouths as they continued on their way. The column was eventually ordered from the road, moving off to the right through a stubble field and across a straggling stream, before pushing on into a saturated wood. On they floundered, to emerge at last into a further field as still the gunfire rattled and thundered, now away to their left beyond a substantial rise in the ground. The customary cloud of gun smoke was there in the sky, drifting away on the wind, as still more rose to take its place.

The men were eventually wheeled into line of battle and halted there, giving still more of them the chance to dip fingers into their stash of flour, grasping further handfuls of it to push into their mouths. Daniel Ryan refrained from doing so. The afternoon was already well advanced and surely it could not be long till darkness ended the brief winter day and, fight or not, they would be dismissed to cook and eat. Baked flour would go a lot further than handfuls of the uncooked ingredient, or so he reasoned as he waited and, glancing along the rank, he noted that the others of his mess had apparently concluded likewise.

"Goddam flour's jest extra weight t'carry unless they give ya a goddam minute to cook it and eat it," Ballard rasped. His remark, on this occasion, was greeted by silence. Possession, after all, Daniel Ryan concluded, was the greater part of the law and finally having the damned stuff meant the most.

There was no fight for the Ogeechee Volunteers that day. There was plenty of trampling around in the mud, manoeuvring to the north, in company with Kershaw's brigade it was being said, still further out beyond the flank of where the battle continued, marked by its musketry and artillery discharges and its sullen cloud of drifting smoke whose dirty white shade stood out against the overcast sky. They were seeking, the sergeants eventually told them, to turn the Yankee flank, but this was not news to men who had engaged in this kind of manoeuvre repeatedly in previous fights. The main part of the fight had, so the later stories said, been carried by Johnson's division with its brigades Tennessee and Alabama boys, those same ones who had fought with the "Blues" contingent at Chickamauga, advancing on either side of the road. The success of this flanking movement depended, like all others, on how well they had managed to pin the enemy, making him fight rather than withdraw, but as the winter evening gathered again, it became clear that there would be insufficient daylight remaining for their own brigades to engage.

Down towards the road, the shooting began to decline; until darkness finally ended the fighting and the marching, with word circulating that the Yankees were retreating back along the road towards Knoxville. The men were finally dismissed in the gathering dusk, having marched for much of the afternoon around this particular muddy corner of Tennessee, vainly seeking an enemy that was circumspectly pulling back, avoiding the flanking movement that McLaws' division had spent the final hours of daylight trying to execute. The buildings of Bean's Station, where the enemy had been positioned, were never so much as glimpsed and the company finally made camp in a field. Tomorrow, the rumours also said, they would go forward and bring the enemy to battle again, but in the meantime there were fires to be set in the dusk, surprisingly permitted in spite of the proximity of the enemy, with saturated wood, before the precious flour issue that McLaws had used to bribe them forward could finally be baked and eaten.

It was fully dark before fires could be got going, a process again made difficult by the lack of dry kindling, but enough was obtained for a single fire to be nursed into life. From this another was kindled, with a burning brand, and then another, until each mess had its own, blown into and carefully fed, until healthy, if smoky, blazes warmed the men and the cooking was able to begin. Isaac Kane added a touch of his customary seasoning to their own mixes, the resulting ramrod rolls therefore acquiring a measure of taste as well as bulk, and having eaten, the men turned in around their fire with their wet blankets at least warmed, and started on the process of drying in the glare and heat of the flames.

They were roused the following morning without drum or bugle. Instead the sergeants went pacing around their own sections, wakening their men brusquely to a cold, damp day. The company was formed with little delay, and moved in column back in the general direction of the road to resume the advance. Up ahead, a few of the men told the others, lay Blaine's Crossroads, known from their passing this way the previous week, only back then they had been going in the other direction with the Yankees doing the following.

The morning passed as the men trudged westwards on the slowly firming road. Ahead there was a spatter of skirmish fire, but it was minor compared with the scale of yesterday's shooting. Towards noon the column was halted amid further rumours. The Yankees were half way back to Knoxville said one story, the general was organising his columns to attack them again said another, the enemy had halted, but their position was too strong to be assaulted a third theory asserted. It was so often this way in the army with a wide range of gossip available and a free choice as to which of it, if any, was most likely to be true.

The regiment spent a further time halted and waiting on the road before being stood down, dispersing details going immediately into the surrounding woods and fields in search of more firewood. Camps were set up and what remained of the flour issue was baked and eaten while the men pondered the latest developments. Those Yankees, whoever they were, like the previous set on the other side of Knoxville last month, seemed to have eluded whatever "Old Pete" had intended for them and now, after a lot of muddy manoeuvring for little real result, they were halted and waiting again. Whatever the general was planning in the way of further marches or attacks nobody could tell, but the comments around the newly kindled fires were generally of the opinion that no matter what he had intended, he still seemed stuck with his "Tennessee slows," when it came to carrying it out.

Chapter 14 The Bitterest Enemy

The following morning saw no marching orders at first and it was getting towards noon when the column was finally formed and started back the way they had come, signifying that this latest march and fight, like all of the ones since Chickamauga, had yielded nothing of any importance. The files plodded eastwards, under a lowering sky and a rising wind, soon coming to the scene of the earlier engagement. The buildings of Bean's Station, particularly the prominent "T" shaped, brick-built hotel, still smouldered and the burial of dead was far from complete as the Company B files tramped through. Another bitter harvest of dead, Daniel Ryan reflected, for little or no result.

The renewed eastward hike proceeded as the weather worsened again, with further frequent showers of sleety rain carried on a northwest wind that found its frigid way right to a man's vitals. Those who still had blankets of any description wore them as cloaks, with gum blankets, if such a luxury remained, being worn on top. Even with these additional garments in place however, the wind gusted its way through with contemptuous ease as the ragged miserable columns headed east on roads that were steadily returning to quagmires of liquid mud which soaked its miserable chill through whatever shoes a man had. As for the barefoot men in the column, and there were still a considerable number of them, their ordeal, as far as Daniel Ryan was concerned, must be almost beyond imagination, even on the slightly less arduous margins of the road.

The withdrawal continued over the following days, with the column crossing the Holsten River, finally to halt near the settlement of Morristown where camps were set up, most of them situated along the railroad. Perhaps as a judgement on this latest dismal chapter of their soldiering, a further scattering of men had opted, in the course of the retreat, to turn their backs on the army and head for distant homes. The mountains and valleys of eastern Tennessee were, after all, considerably closer to Georgia than northern Virginia, and numbers of the disillusioned took full advantage of that fact. Whether they were going on those familiar "plough furloughs", where farmers took unofficial leave of absence to go home and provide for families who were often near to starving, nobody who remained could tell. This had been done on many occasions with the tacit approval of captains and colonels, but the likelihood was that many were leaving on a more permanent basis, through profound war-weariness. Whichever was true, what could be easily seen was the extent to which company rolls took a plunge as winter, in company with disillusionment, worked its course through the ranks. Company B was no exception to this tide and with the Georgia state line as close as it now was, this was not too surprising. Some messes clung stubbornly together however, taking an almost fierce pride in their endurance and damning the fainter spirits who had succumbed to the tide of depression which had swept through the whole division following the retreat from Knoxville.

Ryan's mess was one of those who stayed, labouring diligently to complete their shelter which replicated the final design from the previous winter on the Rappahannock River, attending to each feature of the building and finishing it with some care, for here, the camp word said, they would be staying, and this shelter would therefore be their home and their base. With winter quarters established, and more time to spend in them, the talk on what had transpired here in Tennessee grew and most of that talk was pessimistic. In common with the company as a whole, the mess views on the lately concluded campaign was roundly critical, but what during the earlier autumn could be attributed to Braxton Bragg's incompetence was now alarmingly closer to home. Bragg had surely mismanaged the battle at Chickamauga and its aftermath, allowing the Yankee army to escape with a licking when it should have experienced an annihilation. The siege which had seen little but the steady strengthening of the originally beleaguered Yankees could also be blamed on Bragg, as could the lack of a wagon train for Longstreet's force when it had departed from Chattanooga for Knoxville.

But the mismanagement had not ended there, even if the delay in reaching the crossroads ahead of Burnside's Yankees after crossing the Holsten River could be blamed on bad weather and the lack of transport. The events of the siege itself however and especially the abortive assault on Fort Loudon could scarcely be blamed on a general who was over a hundred miles away and had even sent further troops to strengthen the force around the city. No, even though the final abandonment of the campaign had become necessary on the approach of the powerful enemy relief force, the most disturbing feature of the events of the autumn and winter had been the succession of misfortunes that had taken place within the Army of Northern Virginia divisions, and the responsibility for these had to lie with "Old Pete" himself. He had allowed the rivalry to continue between Jenkins and Law, even perpetuating it through his supporting Jenkins and promoting him, a newcomer to the division, over an officer who had served and fought with it since it had been established. Perhaps this was a big part of what had hamstrung the effort to keep the supply route to Chattanooga along Lookout Valley closed to the enemy, for if officers as well as enlisted men did not serve whole-heartedly together, only trouble would result.

Longstreet had also allowed delays to cripple the advance on Knoxville and the investment of the city, marching his men and his guns around the town's fortifications only to finish up bringing them back again to their starting places, frittering away day after day, when the place cried out for a quick and decisive move in order to capture it without crippling losses. Worst of all, the attack on the fort, with insufficient artillery support, into a ditch full of frozen mud, had been of his devising. For all that he had delayed the assault for almost two weeks, not enough reconnoitring had been done in all that time. The extent of the defences had

317

become clear only when the attacking brigades had stumbled upon them in the pre-dawn gloom, and men had died in their scores on that slope and trapped in that ditch as a result.

That failed attack was Longstreet's failure and that had been the event that had turned many of his men into critics of their general. He was not the same reliable leader that he had been in Virginia, and around the camps many of his soldiers were already referring to their previously trusted general as "Slow Pete", and whether a man had taken to using the new nickname or not, it was clear that out here in Tennessee there was nothing special about Longstreet, nor, worryingly, about their other commanders either.

The land where the railroad meandered east of Knoxville between the Holsten and the French Broad Rivers was certainly fertile, with farms dotted around the various creeks and runs that fed the larger rivers which in turn eventually emptied their waters into the Holsten, which downstream would become the Tennessee. What was more, the area had hardly been touched by the war, and spared the heavy hand of military occupation and the systematic foraging and requisitioning that went with it, supplies were plentiful on the local farms. As a result, once the commissary details got themselves busy, the provisions began to flow in and the rations promptly began to improve. Morale among the men improved also, at least superficially, but the more discerning could see that beneath that part of the human spirit that could be satisfied by regular meals and warm camps lay the deeper parts of the man that wagon loads of pork, beef, poultry, flour and vegetables would not satisfy.

It had become clear to many of those who remained with the army, as well as to those who had left, that the war had changed. Out here things were indeed different and spreading quietly among the camps and messes was an acceptance that in Tennessee the struggle had swung progressively against the south, and that without much greater concentration of southern forces, and likely some banging together of generals' heads, further effort and sacrifice might well be futile or even wasted. Unlike Virginia where, according to such newspapers that could still be obtained around the camps, the war had again stalled in comparative stalemate, the balance in Tennessee and all the way west to the Mississippi had clearly gone the way of the Yankees.

Perhaps the victory at Chickamauga, back in the fall, had just been the latest opportunity to regain the initiative out here, but the Army of the Cumberland had been allowed to escape. Now the reinforced enemy was spreading his forces across the Tennessee-Georgia border and although Bragg was now gone and Joe Johnston was taking command of the Army of Tennessee there was little that he, or for that matter their own force either, could do once the enemy concentrated his strength against them. Look at how Old Pete had skedaddled his men promptly out of the lines around Knoxville, once the word had arrived of the approach of Sherman's army. Now Sherman was being said to have withdrawn once more, but even if this was true, their own force lacked the strength, the provisions, and maybe even the will, to push its way forcibly west once again and take those Knoxville Yankees by the throat.

That skirmish at Bean's Station had proved that even when faced by only a portion of the enemy forces in the area, they were not able to mount a decisive offensive to regain lost territory and re-establish themselves beyond the mountain country in the east of the state. As if that was not enough, the perennial weaknesses that tormented the Confederate armies had been gathering again as the time had passed. The campaign from Chattanooga to Knoxville and beyond had been a tale of shortage and want, initially in terms of provisions, but gradually the other shortages had mounted also. These included clothing (the Richmond uniforms now wearing out and no replacements were available) blankets, with only those who had managed to forage successfully back at Chickamauga still able to boast wool or waterproof coverings, and, most of all, as always, shoes.

319

The camps now held significant numbers of men who were excused any but housekeeping duties, with all the customary substitutes for shoes, home-made moccasins or sandals, carpet or cloth scraps tied around the feet, still leaving a proportion of the men barefoot. In the winter conditions the men's feet were seldom completely dry, but for the bare-foot men, further injuries, ailments and infections afflicted them, rendering some unfit for any kind of duty. It was true, Daniel Ryan reckoned more than once, that full bellies were good for the morale of soldiers, but they did not solve everything, and the other increasing shortages, coupled with the accumulating list of dismal experiences that had befallen Company B, since their departure from Virginia in the first days of the fall, was approaching a scale to disillusion the most philosophical of men.

In fairness to "Old Pete" he promptly did what "Marse Robert" had done the previous winter on the Rappahannock. He withdrew those men of his command with shoe-making expertise from their units and set them to work on the hides of the plentiful livestock which the area had contributed to the army's commissary details. Similarly, with a number of local domestic looms able to supply homespun cloth, any soldiers who had been tailors before enlisting or being drafted, were also withdrawn. Parallel cottage industries were set up, some to tan hides and fashion them into shoes, while others made tunics and pants. Within a couple of weeks these measures were producing significant amounts of clothing and footwear, but neither of them was ever manufactured in numbers sufficient to eradicate the problem. Late in the month, with the railroad east to Virginia open, a trainload of supplies had brought further clothing and several hundred pairs of shoes from Richmond, but even these had provided only a temporary solution to the shortages. Among the enlisted men, uniforms as well as shoes were wearing out almost as quickly as they could be replaced by whatever means the general was able to devise or utilise, and winter was now exerting its grip.

With the army now established on the south side of the river the men continued to improve their shelters and camps. Parties of soldiers ranged around the surrounding farms, requisitioning timber and cannibalising all but the most essential buildings for materials to improve, extend or furnish their shelters. The woods of the surrounding counties were steadily felled for building materials and for fuel, and over the course of those initial days that led up towards Christmas, whole villages of huts had materialised, most of them consisting of log or wood-walled tents erected over clay dugouts, where the men could gain more reliable shelter and warmth from the extremes of weather. As the days passed, the soldiers' expertise, gained over the previous winters, was visibly put to good use, and additional luxuries steadily appeared. Planked roofs multiplied, replacing or lining whatever canvas coverings had been initially erected. Chimneys made of stones caulked with clay also blossomed around the camp, most of them at the end of the shelters opposite their entrance, though some were built into those entrances or even into side walls.

While the army's enlisted men busied themselves on the job of survival, the officers resumed their own hobbies. The camps were not long established before rumours began to circulate of further serious dissension among the top commanders. Within days, this was confirmed by the departure of LaFayette McLaws, having been relieved of the command of his division by Longstreet, for reasons that nobody in the camps seemed able to discover. Hard on the heels of this, the Texas brigade commander Jerome Robertson, known to his men as "Aunt Polly", had been similarly relieved and had left the camps also, again for reasons that nobody seemed certain of. Even more curious was the case of the Alabama brigade commander and previous temporary commander of John Hood's division. Evander Law was being said to have submitted his resignation from command of his brigade and, this having being accepted, he had entrained for Richmond without delay. This was

321

widely regarded as the latest chapter of that protracted feud over command of brigade and division that he had waged with Micah Jenkins. Jenkins, as Longstreet's nominee, had got the command over Law, who had been favoured by the now departed Hood. But the three departures coming hard on each other's heels had served notice to the men of both divisions that all was still far from well among their own generals.

It seemed to many of the men that their time out here in Tennessee had fatally infected their officers with what they had previously referred to as the Tennessee disease, of jealousy and acrimony. Here, with these departures, was visible proof that their own generals, who had served together under General Lee without anything on such a scale as this, were turning on each other in exactly the way that the Army of Tennessee generals had habitually done and for which the newly arrived Army of Northern Virginia troops had held them in such profound contempt. It now looked as though nobody was immune from the "Tennessee Fever" of jealousy and incompetence, an affliction that infected the generals who served out here in the western army, for their own Virginia generals had obviously contracted the condition in their turn. They had turned upon each other showing a level of enmity that had increasingly undermined efforts of their men, sometimes, as out in the Wahatchie Valley at the end of October, bringing them to nothing. No, the Tennessee Fever seemed to be an illness to which anybody out here was susceptible, maybe even to the point that it now seemed as though only Marse Robert himself and precious few others were immune to its symptoms.

"Hell, ain't they got enough Yankees to fight," Kane observed disgustedly in camp when the events among the high command had gotten a further airing.

"Reckon all o' this fresh mountain air out here ought t' help 'em all git along, like they should," Ballard observed, "but there surely ain't no sign of that happenin'."

Even worse were the reasons that eventually emerged for the dismissal of McLaws and Robertson. In the case of their own commander, it was being said that his relief had been for failing to support the plans and intentions of the commanding general. Longstreet, whose friendship with McLaws had by all accounts gone back many years to their shared class at West Point Military Academy, had dismissed his friend for something that hardly anyone in the camp could understand.

"Goddam it," Edwin Jones had said when the news had gone around. "If he relieved everybody in this division who's belly-ached about his plans this fall, there wouldn't be nobody left in the damned division now."

With Robertson, the reason seemed different, yet equally ridiculous. He had been relieved, so the latest rumours asserted, for undermining the commanding general's plans by speaking of them with other generals in an unsupportive and uncomplimentary manner. The men scratched their heads further when they heard this, with Daniel Ryan concluding that Jones' sarcastic comment about McLaws' dismissal seemed to hold good in the case of Robertson also.

The best thing about Christmas was that by the time that it came, the men had had those valuable preceding days to make their camps as comfortable as they could realistically be. As for rations, as the south side of the Holsten River had turned out to be a rich source of food, Company B spent the days of Christmas week in camp, warm, comfortable and well provisioned. The remaining cavalry were picketing the river crossings to the south and west, with the infantry therefore being called upon to perform only routine duties.

The comparative tranquillity of the days around Christmas was temporary however. In the final days of December word began to spread of an enemy force having crossed the river and having begun to advance eastwards on the southern bank. The thrust had been intercepted by General Martin's horsemen at a minor tributary named Mossy Creek between the railroad and the river. The enemy had, as before, not pressed their advance and had been forced back, eventually retiring once again to the west. With the repulse at Mossy Creek the sense of urgency seemed to subside, and thereafter even the Yankees seemed content to leave things be, for the meantime at least. Perhaps even they, with their endless stream of supplies and replacements for everything, were finding the tougher winter going enough to make them pause.

Over the final days of the year the weather had turned steadily colder, with the temperature plunging, until good sense dictated that the men stay in camp as far as possible and keep a goodly supply of firewood on hand. The increasing cold however proved to be to the liking of at least one member of Company B, and that man was Lieutenant Jefferson Gilby, for the acting company commander promptly utilised the icy temperatures as a tool for chastising his men and maintaining his brand of "discipline," over them.

Company punishments had never been a prominent feature of Company B life. They had been used as minor sanctions for minor misdeeds, traditionally including extra duties, these mainly being fatigues, guard or picket duties, and all of these things tending to be periodic rather than regular features of company life. Gilby, from the time when he had first taken charge, had utilised his "discipline" options fully, greatly increasing the frequency with which such punishments were imposed. Now however, with winter settled over eastern Tennessee, the punishment of dusk to dawn guard duty became his favoured sanction. Aware that extra picket duty placed duty sergeants and corporals of the guard in a position to reduce the scale of the punishment by permitting time at the grand post fire rather than on the line, Gilby employed the picket duty option less and less, and the dusk till dawn guard duty more and more. Pacing the camp perimeter meant that the punishment could be more easily observed and therefore fully completed without any sympathetic NCOs being able to interfere.

So on most of the nights spent in camp, one or more men were to be seen tramping the camp perimeter with musket slung, serving their punishment even in the severest of winter conditions. From the last week of December onwards, the punishment took place in the bitterest of cold, which resulted in the feeling gradually leaving the toes, fingers, noses and ears of the miscreant, as the chill advanced through limbs. In the mornings, when daylight finally came, these sufferers had regularly to be helped to their mess fires, to begin the process of thawing and then warming their frozen limbs, a considerably painful process in itself. The lieutenant continued to impose the punishment without modifying it in any way in response to the extreme winter conditions, well aware that its severity had greatly increased but remaining inscrutable as he employed it, as though it was being done in the brief and balmy nights of midsummer instead of the longest and coldest nights of the year.

The enlisted men had responded to the increased punishments when they had been imposed. Such stouter shoes and warmer additional items of clothing as were available around the messes, including overcoats and blankets, were donated by comrades for the duration of the punishment, all to allay the effects of the bitter cold. Josiah too promptly established a habit, when the sufferers had finished their duty, of showing up with a measure of spirit procured from nobody knew where, for administering in a timely manner. All these measures however did no more than offset the effects on the unfortunate victims of the frozen temperatures that had settled over those counties of eastern Tennessee in those final days of 1863.

January came and the cold grew yet more intense. Outside duties of any kind became increasingly tedious for an insufficiently clad army, and Gilby's guard duties were now the extreme manifestation of this, becoming ever more of an ordeal, with those punished in this way being subjected to mental as well as physical ordeal. The pacing victim, in addition to feeling the bitter cold steadily penetrating his limbs, could at the same time smell the wood smoke and see the glows of the mess fires which he was forbidden to approach for relief. Such a punishment, in the conditions that then prevailed, seemed made for an officer like Gilby and steadily increased the resentment and loathing that virtually all the enlisted men, in addition to the company NCOs, now harboured towards him.

January advanced and the weather remained frigid, with the temperature descending to the point that there was now no suggestion of a thaw at any time during the brief winter days. The roads and trails were ridged with rock-hard frozen mud, and the trees and fields were clothed in white frost. The cold made the work of wood and water details more difficult, with trees clad in thick frost, and thick layers of ice which covered the creeks having to be broken through in order to fill canteens or buckets. The trains on the East Tennessee and Virginia line followed no such thing as schedules any more, with water butts and wood piles frozen and the tracks themselves regularly impassable due to frozen points on the line. The men, with increasing numbers of them short of warm clothing, coats and shoes, remained in their camps save for essential duties, amid rumours that the Yankees, positioned along the railroad towards Knoxville, had been reinforced and re-supplied and were stirring themselves, even now, for a further advance eastwards.

It was the middle days of the month when the men were assembled and told to cook three days rations, the age old signal for a move, before setting out from their camps.

McLaws' division was under the temporary command of William Wofford, and its brigades, together with Robert Ransom's infantry and a battalion of Porter Alexander's artillery, set out along the road to the west where the enemy base at New Market lay. The roads remained rock-hard and slippery with frost and ice, and the march was a sequence of slithering and stumbling accidents for both men and animals, in the iron cold. With ever fewer serviceable blankets, most soldiers were totally dependent upon their fires for warmth, and in spite of early bivouacking, these were hard to kindle and feed. Even when healthy blazes could be gotten going, fire warmth on its own had never been a recipe for sound sleep. If a man settled too close to the flames the side of him facing the fire began to scorch, but if he moved any distance away from it, the side that faced away from the flames began to chill and freeze. When the fire burned down its heat steadily waned in the bitter cold, but when additional fuel was added, the flames flared up and the heat increased to a level that forced the men to shift back to a more comfortable distance. The best that could be done was for some men to stay awake to feed the fire while others used what blankets and makeshift covers were available to get what sleep they could, with the men changing places at intervals through the night.

Daniel Ryan's mess, with their Chickamauga trophies, remained better off than most, but the bitter nights spent in march bivouacs on the road between Morristown and Knoxville were times when no one got decent rest. Camp rumours suggested that the enemy advance was two-pronged, with a northern force advancing from Strawberry Plains and New Market while a further force advanced towards Dandridge, a town to the south west on the north bank of the French Broad River. Jenkins' and Johnson's divisions, with further artillery, had been detached to confront this latter thrust, while their own force advanced along the railroad to face the Yankees there.

It turned out to be an ordeal of endurance rather than anything resembling a real fight, for the enemy had not pushed their advance along the rail line. Instead they simply manoeuvred around the frozen country for a few days before withdrawing again. To the south however, news soon arrived that some skirmishing had actually taken place, involving infantry as well as the cavalry, though this had been indecisive, with those Yankees also eventually pulling out. To make matters worse, as soon as the brigades began to move, still with only the bare minimum of a supply train, problems arose regarding the requisitioning of food supplies and, more pointedly, the delivering of those supplies to where the troops had marched, especially since this was required to be done over the most treacherous of road conditions.

It had always been the case that the Confederate supply services experienced their worst problems when the armies were on the move, and here in east Tennessee things, if anything, were worse than previously. The troops quickly exhausted their carried rations and with these gone there was nothing more to be had. Thompson reckoned it was down to the fact that they had accumulated just about enough wagons and animals to collect the stuff, but taking it to any place other than the main camps was beyond the capability of their makeshift commissary.

In spite of it all, orders came for a pursuit of the withdrawing enemy, but even as the long columns of men and vehicles started westwards the weather began to change. The temperature rose and the ice and frost began to melt. The roads quickly changed from hard ice to chilled mud and the familiar hardships of marching on quagmires once more emerged. The men and animals floundered on, with repeated hauling of stalled wagons and guns again a feature of the march. Eventually, with the enemy out of reach and no sign of anything like the required supplies, there was little more to be done. It became a matter of retracing their route back to their camps, with the land now lashed by sleety rain and the roads still treacherous, though this was now due to mud.

The winter continued, with periods of ice and snow punctuated by thaws when the roads and camps became expanses of mud, reducing the movements of even the most essential divisional services to a minimum on the difficult and treacherous ways. Times on outpost lines were reduced, so that men could return earlier to the fires at their grand posts and warm or dry themselves before resuming duty on the line. With shortages persisting, the soldiers remained around their fires as far as possible and, while this spared them the worst of the seasonal hardships, it gave ample time for boredom to establish its grip and for argument and dissent to ferment, and for plenty of further reflection on recent events and on their current predicament.

They were far from home and far also from where they had rendered almost all of their military service. They were in a strange country and had had to endure grievous further losses and a further trying chapter of privation and shortages. Worst of all their efforts and endurance had apparently gone for nothing, as the enemy, far from being dislodged from his foothold in Georgia, had confirmed his grip on the border country. As before Christmas after the retreat from Knoxville, for some men it was all too much and a further sequence of desertions took place, with the continuing nearer proximity of their homes in the deeper southern states perhaps providing the final temptation for them to get up and go. Two of Company B's most recent conscripts were among those to depart in this way, disappearing from the picket line into the darkness, thus confirming what the veterans largely thought of them anyway.

With ample time in camp, much of the talk inevitably dwelled on their troubles and the Company B camp was no exception. Times were hard and perhaps the worst of it all was the feeling, reinforced by Longstreet's turning as he had done on his subordinates, of unity being lacking, a concerning situation for an army in strange and far from friendly country. Men needed to be able to rely on their comrades and on their commanders and there seemed to be nowhere, save among their most trusted mess companions, that they could do this. The high command was clearly at odds, which was worrying in itself, for it implied that the generals' gaze was at least partly inward instead of being directed fully towards the enemy. As if that were not enough, in their own company they were now led by an officer who was almost universally distrusted and despised. Gilby ran the company on the basis of punishment even for the most minor infractions, and men got extra duties for transgressions that would previously have barely been noted, or at most would have prompted little more than censure from a sergeant.

There were plenty of enemies out there across those distant mountains, Daniel Ryan reflected, but worse than any Yankee, there was now a further insidious enemy at work here in their midst, and that was disillusionment and despair. These enemies did not face a man in battle, but threatened most when the camps were quiet and the spirits were low. Hope was what sustained men, especially in tough times, but the worst thing about this campaign in Tennessee was the extent to which it had undermined that buoyant spirit of optimism and faith in their own prowess that had sustained the units of the Army of Northern Virginia over the previous campaigns. Now, like never before, it had been weakened, undermined by the catalogue of depressing features that governed their present existence, and the camps reflected it.

Despair, though it deployed no cannon or small arms, was a worse threat than the enemies that did, for it eroded a man's willingness to persevere, sapped his resolve and weakened his spirit. Despair was truly the bitterest enemy of all and as that January ran its course, with word arriving in the final days of the month of the cavalry screen suffering a reverse at the hands of another Yankee column, despair grew still further. With the cold still clinging to the land, stern and unrelenting, the soldiers of the First Corps battled the worst threat that they had ever encountered, for this threat was within themselves, an erosion of hope and a feeling that no matter what they did, it might all in the end count for nothing. It was an experience that was new to them and they did not like it.

As though to confirm their plight, Matty Weald, whose chronic chest ailments had barely allowed him to remain with the company this far into the winter, emerged as the latest man detailed for dusk till dawn perimeter guard, on a night of heavy, sleety rain, as punishment for some minor neglect of army regulations. The men had rallied around, as they had grown accustomed to doing, donating shoes, warmest clothing and wool and gum blankets for the occasion, but the punishing of Matty in this way, in spite of the well understood state of his health, spread a still blacker mood among them.

This latest example of Gilby's vindictiveness reduced the company to a new and as yet unplumbed low, confirming the climate of meanness and cruelty that now governed it. They were now substantially in the charge of a young man who seemed to believe that authority rested upon rule and punishment, without any spark of humanity to encourage the loyalty of his men. A bleak and hard winter was being made even bleaker by the manner in which Company B was being administered, and this was testing and wearing down the men's endurance more than any extreme of the weather or action of the enemy.

The weather continued cold alternating with wet, and the men of the company endured both it and the regime that now had charge of them. The punishments went on, with dusk till dawn guards set on most nights and the hardship of it only lessened by that small measure of the generosity of the victim's comrades, who continued to send the unfortunates to their ordeal equipped with the best garments and blankets that were still available, and by the boy Josiah's persistence in his practice of bringing a taste of spirit to help revive the men so punished.

Cavalry probes excepted, the Yankees had made no further attempts to advance since the affair at Dandridge, suggesting that the winter weather had convinced them also that waiting for spring was the best option available. For the First Corps soldiers, Spring would also bring a resolution of the question of where their own future lay, and there were the usual rumours on this subject. The most persistent ones asserted that Spring would involve a return to the Army of Northern Virginia, but, with no definite word, the matter of surviving and sustaining spirit and body as the winter stretched endlessly on, was the principal test for the enlisted men of the Ogeechee Volunteers.

It was maybe true that the darkest part of the night came just before the dawn, but nobody expected the old saying to be borne out as profoundly as it was, for on another of those

331

bitter days, a morning when the frost was of a severity which had previously seen roll calls dispensed with, an assembly was called at first light by the drum roll. The summons prompted a chorus of curses among the men, as Jeffers, assisted as was customary by Bayfield and Thompson, moved from shelter to shelter to prod the occupants into activity. They stumbled from their dwellings to form, with the ice and hoar frost thick on the ground, but, as Daniel Ryan made his way to his place in the ranks there was already a mutter among the men who were there. As he reached his own place he looked over towards where Gilby would customarily be waiting to make an entrance, but he saw nothing of the despised lieutenant. The ranks complete, they were called to order by Jeffers and as they settled at attention, Daniel Ryan saw the flap of the company tent move aside to reveal instead the overcoated figure of William Boyce. Daniel Ryan gazed at him, recognising his familiar gait, as he made his way to the front of the assembled company, and immediately recalled the last time he had seen him, on the back of an ambulance wagon to the south of Gettysburg, covered in his own blood.

The captain's face looked pale and thin, pretty well as he had the previous year when he had returned from hospital after his Sharpsburg wounding. As he watched him take his place, Daniel thought there was a worn and still more haggard look about his features now, but he was here, real flesh and blood, with an unfamiliar officer, another lieutenant, following behind him. All along the ranks there was an almost imperceptible movement, accompanied by the tiniest of mutters, for there had been no inkling among the men of the captain's return, not even a whisper from the sergeants, an occurrence which was rare enough to be almost unheard of in a military community whose lifeblood was rumour.

As a result of Boyce's return, Gilby was now displaced and would revert to his previous status, and that realisation was like a gift from God to Ryan and likely to the whole of Company B. Even Jeffers seemed to move about his duties

332

with a faint air of jauntiness as, with the company assembled, he paced across to Boyce.

"Company is assembled sah," he reported in his formal tone. The captain nodded to him.

"Thank you First Sergeant," he replied, upon which Jeffers turned and strode across to his accustomed place. Boyce stepped forward and paced along in front of the ranks, spending several seconds looking at them, as though considering not only who remained and who did not, but also deeper things like spirit and bearing. He finally turned to Jeffers.

"I see First Sergeant that Privates Winder and Hale are among those who are no longer with the company." Jeffers cleared his throat.

"We heard that Eli made it t' the hospital, sah, but Matthew was killed in the ditch, back at Knoxville." Boyce nodded solemnly in response, before turning back to address the waiting men.

"I am glad to see you all," he began, "but I cannot help recalling the faces of the men who were in Pennsylvania last summer, who are now no longer with us." He looked around the camp and then his eyes moved on, to take in the hills and woods beyond, as though searching for something, before finally returning his gaze to his men. He gestured towards the new officer.

"I want to introduce Lieutenant Williams to you. He will be the senior lieutenant in the company. Be gentle with him." He glanced towards the new man and Daniel Ryan saw the suggestion of a smile cross the faces of both captain and lieutenant, while a further brief murmur coursed along the ranks as Boyce's face returned to its serious expression.

"We are in the middle of a difficult and dangerous campaign," he resumed, "in a country where our enemies are at least as numerous as our friends among its people all of this in the worst season of the year. We are alone here, with little in the way of reinforcements to be expected, and this means that we must depend on ourselves for our survival, on

333

ourselves and on each other, for by no other means can we be sure of reaching the end of this campaign in this unfriendly place. We must stick together to win through, but we are still the First Corps," he emphasised the last two words clearly, "of the Army of Northern Virginia, even while we are out here, away from where we have always served. We remain General Lee's soldiers and it is my belief that, in due time, we shall return to the rest of the army. Whatever enemies or difficulties we face, we must remember who we are and draw strength from it. We must sustain our resolve to stick together. We must be like a band of brothers, in order to overcome what lies before us. If we do that, no enemy can subdue us and no hardships can wear us down." He stopped and seemed to relax before speaking again. "I am told that the wagons have been delayed by the state of the roads and have not arrived again. There are therefore no rations to provide a breakfast." He gave a brief and rueful smile. "Some things do not change, unless Daniel Ryan here has something stashed away." Daniel felt himself redden as Boyce's eyes rested on him briefly and he shook his head in response.

"Nothing," the captain inquired? Daniel shook his head again.

"Hard times indeed," Boyce said. He returned his gaze to the ranks, scanning them briefly once more, before turning finally to Jeffers.

"Thank you First Sergeant, please dismiss the men." He stepped away as Jeffers shout rang out and the ranks were dismissed to return to their shelters and fires.

Daniel Ryan had divided his gaze between the newly returned captain and the newly deposed Gilby for much of the time that Boyce had spent addressing the company. The lieutenant had stood behind Boyce, and to one side, with an expression of utter impassiveness on his face. No sentiment of any kind had been discernible from his features, as he had seen his brief reign over the company brought to this abrupt end. But even as Daniel considered this development, other thoughts began to enter his mind. There was more to the captain's return than merely the supplanting and thwarting of Gilby, for to his surprise, as he returned to their shelter with the others of his mess, there was a difference now in the talk and the manner and the very look of the men around him, something that would be impossible to measure, but which was there nevertheless. Boyce's words had been simple, but had any other officer uttered them, the response would almost certainly have been one of cynicism Jessop had been a fair and capable enough replacement, but since his wounding they had had Gilby, and those weeks spent with him in charge had certainly been enough of a trial for the men of Company B, who had been through the mill in so many other ways that their spirit as soldiers and comrades had been undermined and perhaps almost lost.

Boyce however had returned. Not since the evening of that second day of the previous July at Gettysburg had they seen him, but his appearance at this time seemed to have somehow returned something of what they felt that they had lost. Maybe his arrival meant something more than just one field officer returning to duty after recovering from wounds. Maybe his return, and the simple brief talk that he had just given represented some kind of a turning point, even to these hard-bitten men. Boyce was no great stump speaker, relying more on quieter words and fair treatment of his men to retain their loyalty. Yet his simple address on this frozen morning, although containing little of the inspirational words that a skilled orator might have used, had already had an effect, reviving something that was almost like a ray of hope among the jaded, disillusioned soldiers.

Within a couple of days of the captain's return, Matthew Weald was gone from the hospital that had been set up to the north east of their camps, evacuated on a train, they subsequently heard, to a bigger, better hospital back in Staunton in Virginia's Shenandoah Valley. Maybe Matty's longstanding weakness of chest and lungs would have brought this situation about sooner or later anyway, but as far as the men of Company B were concerned, though Boyce's return may have ended his brief period of command, the departure of Weald somehow had the look of his being a final victim for Gilby, thus hardening, if that were possible, what the men of Company B felt towards their junior lieutenant.

Chapter 15 A Divided Country

The first half of February had been a quiet time compared with the previous weeks. The cavalry continued to hold the river line, picketing along the bank, but there were no major incursions attempted by the Yankees, who at last seemed willing to wait for spring. At the end of the second week of the month however, rumours began to circulate that the cavalry had been recalled to join the Army of Tennessee once more, around the town of Dalton some forty miles down the Western and Atlantic Railroad from Chattanooga, where it was assembling its strength for the coming Spring campaign. Cavalry, as everyone well knew, were vital to any army being able to function in the presence of the enemy. All armies depended upon horsemen, who were their eyes, their ears and their first line of defence. But, if their own cavalry were to go, would this not mean that the infantry would be compelled to do the same? Rumours abounded on the subject, suggesting for the most part that this move would herald the transfer of the infantry and artillery back to Virginia. Days passed, and as the third week of February wore on and no definite word came, that prospect began to fade, to be replaced by a further option. The most recent rumours now spoke of a different course of action, of staying in Tennessee by shifting or manoeuvring the troops that remained. The enlisted men passed the stories on, while they waited in a mood akin to resignation to see what eventually came to pass.

With the cavalry set to depart there was little the army could do about maintaining its positions in the area between the Holston and French Broad Rivers. The area was almost indefensible, with no features, save for the rivers themselves, that would delay or hinder the approach of the enemy. But leaving this region carried its own consequences and it surely meant an end of any idea of taking the fight to the Yankees by seeking to try to ensnare or ambush any advanced or unwary portions of the enemy forces. The situation was similar, in some ways at least, to those vital summer days in Pennsylvania when Jeb Stuart, with the best brigades of the Army of Northern Virginia's cavalry, had left his station around the fringes of the army. Without cavalry any army was blind. They had seen it amply illustrated back then, when Stuart and his men had gone a'frolicking and the consequences of it had been serious. Without horsemen to screen its outposts and scout the territory in which it moved and foraged, an army was left to grope around in a gloom of mist and ignorance while its enemy gathered around it. Sustaining themselves here in this advanced position in a country that was at least partly hostile, was out of the question without a substantial force of horsemen. From the general down to the meanest enlisted man, the army knew that it would not do, and as a result of the imminent departure of William Martin and his mounted units there was no alternative but to withdraw still further to the east.

To most of the men however this knowledge was not the acute disappointment that it likely was to "Old Pete," and maybe some of the other generals also. Disengagement and withdrawal would mean leaving the camps on which much effort had been spent, but remaining here might well mean simply being pushed out a little later in the year, once the Yankees organised themselves for further advance, so a voluntary withdrawal now was certainly preferable to an enforced retreat a little later. At the very least, going now would mean that the cavalry could screen the move prior to departing themselves, and the job of setting up fresh camps and likely defensive positions also, further to the east, could at least be undertaken without the risk of enemy interference. That, once accomplished, would at least restore some level of comfort for the remaining weeks of winter, with proper shelters and fires and, especially if they remained close to the railroad, a better chance of further suppplies.

With the rumours having already detailed the reasons for doing so, it was no surprise when the orders were issued and the camps broken up. The army made its way eastwards once

338

more, with the cavalry screening the move as predicted, prior to departing for Dalton. The withdrawal continued until by the following Tuesday, the columns had reached Bull's Gap, another of those minor settlements on the railroad, but this one nestling, as its name suggested, in a wide cleft in the mountains. Here, it was being said, the camps would be re-established, for here, with the mountains lending their impregnable fastness on either side, an army, especially one without cavalry, would be more secure.

The word now was no longer of withdrawal, instead it was of fortifying, with the troops set to work preparing defensive positions that commanded the roads while establishing a line of camps from Russellville, close to the Holston River, south eastwards to Greeneville, just north of the Nolichucky River. The mountains would be a substantial part of the defences, with imposing ranges obstructing the land between the two rivers, leaving only a few places where east to west roads ran. Here the army would be as safe as they could reasonably be anywhere in eastern Tennessee. Here, with their own movements now restricted by their lack of cavalry, the First Corps infantry and artillery formations could await the enemy, confident that they could be thrown back from these positions should they attempt an attack.

All this was fair enough, most of the men reckoned, but they were well aware that the campaign had now changed further. Their force under Longstreet, which had come out to Tennessee to dislodge the enemy from the southern portion of the state, was now able to do little more than hold its ground here in these eastern mountains, which were at best a backwater isolated from the main area of operations. They now skulked here, in uneasy security, suspended between the main theatres of the war in Virginia and north Georgia, and if a man wished to ponder the way things had changed for the worse since their arrival in Tennessee, there was ample on the subject for him to dwell upon.

As for misfortunes, in the course of the first week after establishing the new line, word began to circulate of Jacob

Morsby's illness. Morsby had been the Regimental Sergeant Major since the regiment had been formed and had survived all of its battles and privations, to the point that he seemed as close to indestructible as a soldier could hope to be.

"The Yankee bullet ain't been made that'll do fer me," had been his customary comment, when a fight was pending and though this had proved true thus far, typhoid had, by all accounts, now come close to achieving what the Yankee bullets could not. After a couple of days of further rumour, it was finally confirmed that Morsby had been evacuated by train to Bristol, and likely on to Staunton or Charlottesville. Hard on the heels of the news of his departure came the further rumour, also promptly confirmed, that Morsby's place would be taken, at least on an acting basis, by the Company B First Sergeant, Barnard Jeffers. "A bloody war or a sickly season," had been a longstanding saying among soldiers on the subject of promotion, and with Jeffers benefitting from the latter, it remained to be seen whether Bayfield or Thompson or a further nominee from outside the company would be shuffled up the ladder of rank to take his place.

With the cavalry largely gone, rumours began almost immediately of those Yankees from the north, up towards Cumberland Gap, extending their interfering and marauding southwards again. Infantry could not hope to patrol the range of territory that horsemen could, and incursions by opportunistic Yankee bands were not a surprising development. Reports came in over that initial week on the Bull's Gap line of raiding parties plundering, burning and even murdering in the counties to the north. As a result, orders were circulated that commissary details travel with an escort of infantry to dissuade such bands from interfering with their vital work. Thompson's section, in compliance with the order, formed the escort for one such foraging detail, which set out on the morning of the last Friday of February in a dismal cloud of sleety drizzle. They started off with Lieutenant Jordan of the brigade commissariat in charge, the officer riding out in front of the wagons and infantry on a horse on which the ribs could be easily counted. Thompson followed on after horse and rider, while the men moved on either side of the four commissary wagons whose mules shambled along with the long-suffering air that was typical of their breed.

They struck north eastwards, initially along the Rogersville Road, before branching off to the north after a mile or so, taking a further road that led up through the valley of fast-flowing Little Beaver Creek. The road generally followed the course of the creek, though the going on it became gradually tougher as it degenerated gradually from a road to little more than a rude country trail which had been reduced still further by the heavy rains and snows and the alternating freezes and thaws that had accompanied them. As the column moved on up into the hills the conditions became still worse, with the sleet starting to lie on top of the mud in a slushy layer which chilled the soaking feet of all, as they sank nearly to the ankles in the dismal mix, and formed an increasingly treacherous surface for the mules in particular as their wagons and their footing became ever more unpredictable. As they headed ever further upward, the men were regularly called upon to push, haul or steady the vehicles, as animals slithered and wagons lurched this way and that in response to the lateral as well as downward slope of the road.

In late morning they came up to the first farm. It was a small cabin of the kind they had become all too familiar with here in Tennessee, surrounded by a smattering of sheds and a barn which exceeded the house in size. Jordan directed the drivers to the side of the road beside a crude fence of tree boughs, whose rails spanned the distance between the posts in a topsy-turvy pattern, highlighted by their covering of almost white sleet. Over at the house, several figures had appeared at the door, sheltered to some extent at least by the overhang of the roof. Seeing them, Jordan turned his horse's head and started the animal towards them. Thompson, as he made to

341

follow, gestured to Kane and Ryan to accompany them. An old man had stepped forward from the group, which apart from himself consisted of a middle-aged woman and a younger boy, while the faces of two further children peeped around the half-closed door.

"Good morning to you all," Jordan called, raising his hand in what looked to Daniel Ryan like something between a wave and a military salute.

"Mornin'," the old man returned, with somewhat less enthusiasm than the officer's greeting.

"We are seeking provisions and are authorised to requisition our requirements," Jordan went on, while Daniel Ryan watched the reactions of the family. Somewhat to his surprise there was nothing in the way of hostility in their expressions, unlike on a considerable proportion of the farms they had come upon over the previous weeks.

"You Longstreet's boys?" the old man inquired. Jordan nodded, and removing his hat in spite of the sleet, he gave something resembling a bow, all while mounted on his horse.

"General Wofford's brigade, Army of Northern Virginia," he told them.

"If'n yo're northern Virginia boys, yo're far from home then," was the reply, "but yo're welcome to what we kin spare. Clara here'll see t' yore wants." The woman stepped away from the door and gestured with her hand towards the barn, which stood to the rear of the cabin. The lieutenant nodded to Thompson.

"Go see sergeant," he told him. Thompson nodded in turn to Ryan and the two of them started after the woman.

"We ain't got overmuch left by now," she said in a sing song tone, as they made their way along a muddy path around the cabin in her wake, "but yo're welcome to a share." Ryan and Thompson exchanged further glances.

"Sounds to me like we're among friends here ma'am," the sergeant said. "We'd bin told that the folks in this part o' the state were Yankee in their preferences."

"We ain't no Yankees," came the response in a tone that was a shade testier. "Thar's southern folks in this valley, even if others o' them around here ain't. We got two boys still servin' in Cheatham's outfit and Clay, our other boy, died last summer. That were over in Mississippi at some place called Grand Gulf." She turned to face them, as she reached the door of the store house. "You boys from Virginia sure enough?"

"We served in Virginia, up till last fall," Thompson told her, "but we're from Georgia, down Savannah way. Name's Thompson ma'am," he added, "and it's surely an agreeable thing to see some friendly faces around here." She nodded and gave a grunt of confirmation as she hauled on the door of the store.

It was dark inside and Daniel Ryan squinted to see as he followed Thompson through the door.

There was a smell of mustiness mingled with the odour of smoked meat. Barrels and sacks lay on either side and a few joints of bacon hung in a row from one of the rafters. The woman produced a small knife and reached up to cut the strings suspending a couple of them, balancing them in her left hand before handing them to Thompson, who promptly passed them on to Daniel Ryan.

"Which o' the other families around here would ya say are southern in their sympathies?" Thompson inquired.

"Not too many," was the reply. "On up from here you'll pass the Hassell, the Berry and the Morris places, but you boys better not be expectin' no welcome from any o' them. Over east o' here, but off the trail a ways, there's the Osburns. They got kin in the same outfit as our boys. That's the Thirty First Tennessee regiment," she added. "Then there's the Little's. They live out back o' here a step," she gestured vaguely with her hand. "They'd likely favour the Yankees too, but they keep themselves to themselves and anyway they ain't got no family. Next farm up this way, after the three Yankee ones, is the Duncans. They're southern thinkin' too," she assured them. "They got a boy in Forrest's cavalry and another one at home. Ned's crippled," she said, "on account

343

o' bein' shot in his back bone, year afore last, up at some place in Kentucky. Theirs is the last farm in this part o' the valley, that is unless you boys're thinkin' of headin' right on over t' Smoky Top Mountain, but, if you're set on doin' that, you surely won't be takin' no wagons along. The wagon trail goes the other way, the west fork that is. The folks up there are mostly Yankees. There's the Wendells and the Pearsons and then the Adams's. I ain't sure about them. They're another family that keep themselves to themselves." She looked around at them, making eye contact with each before continuing.

"We surely are a mixed bag up here," she continued, "but, so far, there ain't been no real trouble. We've had Yankees around over the fall," she eventually added, "so we bin keepin' our heads down and our tongues still, but that's the way it's bin for everybody. We've all had turns at stayin' quiet, dependin' on whose patrols are comin' around for vittles." Thompson glanced again at Ryan and then turned towards the door as White and Kane arrived, before looking back to the woman.

"Ya kin take a couple o' each o' those," she added, pointing towards the sacks and barrels, "but no more'n that, or ya'll be leavin' us short till we git in another crop."

"How did you keep your supplies out o' Yankee hands," Thompson asked her?

"Didn't keep it all safe," she replied. "Folks've been burned out fer that, or so we heard, but there's ways and there's places around here, though that would be tattlin', besides it ain't just the Yankees is it?" Thompson grinned at her.

"Well we're much obliged to ya ma'am," he told her. He turned towards the newcomers.

"So git haulin'," he told them. He gestured to Ryan also.

"Take what she gave," he said, "but we ain't leavin' these folks short, no matter what he says." He nodded in the direction of Jordan, snatches of whose continuing talk with the old man could just about be made out over towards the

344

cabin. The three of them began lifting the provisions and heading out of the door, picking their way along the muddy path back towards the trail where the wagons waited, with steam rising from the backs of the mules as they shifted and stepped in their harness.

The sleet had stopped. Daniel Ryan noticed the brighter sky and the better light as he emerged from the store. Overhead there was almost a glimmer of sun but its promise was brief, disappearing by the time he had reached the second wagon with the sack of vegetables he was carrying. Ballard was starting along the path with Petersen and Jones, to where Thompson waited at the door of the store, still in conversation with the woman. It must be fraught up here now, Daniel Ryan thought. Their own arrival here meant that this was at least the second change in occupation in a matter of months, and in an area with divided loyalties along the lines that the woman had described, this could be a threatening climate for each community in turn. He dismissed the thought, reflecting that none of it was of any direct concern to him, as he moved away from the wagon and, after a few further pleasantries between Jordan and the family and the handing over of the required bill of requisition, the detail resumed its journey.

The sleet had returned, though it fell less heavily as they approached the second farm, almost an hour after leaving the first. A wisp of smoke rising in a wavering trail above the trees gave notice of its proximity, and they rounded a slow bend in the muddy trail to see an arrangement of rude buildings similar to the previous one, with the cleared expanse of a field leading on to the farm itself, built of timbers caulked with clay. This time two women and a man, whose jaw worked on chewing tobacco, appeared at the door as the column of men and vehicles approached. They struck Daniel Ryan as being somewhere in middle age and their faces were stolid and impassive, giving nothing away. Jordan greeted them in the same manner as previously.

345

"Good day to you," he called. "We are gathering provisions for army use." The watchers glowered in response.

"Didn't reckon it was no social visit," the man snapped back, spitting a stream of tobacco juice into the mud at his feet as though to emphasise his disapproval.

"We are authorised to pay in Confederate currency or give a bill of requisition," Jordan told them, but this brought no reaction from the group, save for continued glowering.

"Each o' them's jest about as worthless as the other," the man finally muttered, but Jordan ignored the remark, waving Thompson on towards the stores and outhouses while he steered his horse on up to the cabin, presumably to occupy the family, while others of the detail sought out their stores. Ballard made for the smokehouse with Jones and White, while Thompson headed once again for the barn cum store with Kane and Ryan following. The sergeant operated the heavy wooden latch, before hauling on one side of the double door. Inside, a combination of smells similar to those of the previous barn immediately came to them, though considerably less in the way of provisions were to be seen.

"Looks like they were expectin' us," Daniel Ryan said. Kane grunted in agreement.

"Reckon they've been doin' plenty o' shiftin' on their own account," he said. Thompson nodded.

"Wouldn't you,? he muttered.

"Do we take it all this time," Ryan asked him, "seein' as how they're Yankees?" Thompson shook his head.

"Not all," he said. "It's still winter fer them as well, even if they are Yankees. You boys just haul and I'll tell you when we're done." They got to work, taking cobs of corn from a set of shelves and transferring them to a sack before heading to the door and on out towards the wagons, this time seeing Jordan making notes on a pad as the provisions appeared. Ballard was at the wagons.

"Looks like these folks had a poorer year than them at the last farm," he commented, "or more like they jest got better places to hide what they got."

346

"Hard times back around here now," Kane told him. Then he paused and sniffed and raised a finger before moving away, making his way around to the side of the cabin, before taking out his clasp knife and stooping towards a growing patch. Ballard watched him go.

"Herbs," he said. "He kin smell 'em a mile off. All I kin smell right now is the stink o' you boys 'n' them mules."

It took only minutes to gather their haul and load the wagons, though by now it was well past noon with maybe something over four hours of daylight remaining. Jordan too had begun looking at the sky and on Thompson's return, he called to him.

"We had better move on now, sergeant," Daniel Ryan heard him say. "I'd like to get as far as we can before we lose the daylight." Thompson nodded.

"Don't want to give 'em all damn day to get word around fer the others to hide what they got neither," he said.

"Can't be helped," Jordan replied. "Most of them'll have expected us before we ever started this way," he said. "Once the army goes any place, word gets around and it travels a damned sight faster than we can march."

With a wagon nearly filled with the supplies obtained from the Mellor and Hassell farms, Jordan now detached the vehicle, turning it around and starting it back down the valley towards the road, with Abe White and Charlie Thorne as escorts and Linus Cooper in charge. The other three vehicles with the remaining men of the section, having watched them start away, took a terse leave of the family before resuming their trek up the valley.

They arrived at the Berry and the Morris farms in the course of the next couple of hours, to experience a similar reception to that at the Hassell's. In both cases the houses were little more than cabins, each of them with a steeply sloping roof which extended beyond the wall at one end of the structure, providing something resembling a porch. Each time Jordan steered his horse towards this feature where the families stood watching the approach of the men and vehicles with stony faces, to call his now familiar greeting, though in neither case did he get anything in the way of a response from the residents. The Berry's, a middle-aged couple and a younger woman, said almost nothing in the course of the requisitioning, though as the wagons and their escort left with their haul of provisions, a brief shout followed them up the trail.

"Thieves!" The word rang out in a bitter tone, emphasising what the family's silence had already made clear to the southerners.

At the Morris farm a haul of vegetables and a couple of sides of bacon were assembled ready for loading onto the wagons while, from the porch, two women and a further man whom Daniel Ryan judged to be in his middle years also, together with two younger girls, continued to watch them. As the supplies were gathered, the lieutenant turned to the scowling adults with his pad and pencil at the ready.

"I am authorised to offer currency or a requisition for what you have supplied," he told them.

"D'ya mean that worthless Jeff Davis script?" the man added. Jordan hesitated before nodding.

"We ain't supplied nothin'. You rebels just stole it," the younger of the two women snapped. "Neither o' that paper's no good to nobody around here," she continued.

"Greenbacks is all that we kin use," the man growled. "None o' you's goin' t' pay us for anythin' you took. You rebels have bin comin' around here fer the last two years, with your phoney notes and yore bills o' requisition, 'n' both o' them's jest another word fer robbery."

"I will draw up a list of what we have taken and sign it for you then," Jordan said coldly, his tone communicating clearly enough that he was wearying of the exchange. The man promptly withdrew inside the house, while the two women returned to sullen silence as they watched the last of the provisions being lifted onto the wagons. As the detail moved off Daniel Ryan noticed that only one of the smaller girls continued to watch, with the rest of the family having retreated inside the cabin.

Evening was coming closer as the convoy pulled away, following the muddy road on up the valley as the drizzling sleet resumed. Thompson joined the enlisted men alongside the leading wagon, to be immediately accosted by Kane.

"He reckonin' on spendin' the night on the road, or does he know that the next farm's southern folks?"

The sergeant nodded.

"He'll likely want to make up his own mind about that, but I made sure he knew who took what side on each o' these farms," he said.

"He'll overnight at the next place," Ballard said. "Even officers like him ain't such a damned set o' fools that they'd to want to spend the night soakin' wet 'n' freezin' to goddam death up in these woods, 'specially if they kin git a roof over their head and a good fire to sit at jest as easy."

As on the previous farm there were three adults and two children on the Duncan place, all of them watching from the doorway as the foraging party approached in the misty, gathering dusk. The cabin was a slightly larger version of the previous ones, with a built-on extension at one end and the same type of extended roof providing an overhang for a rudimentary porch at the other. The barn was a measure larger and there was a smokehouse on its farther side. Once again there were no animals to be seen, indicating that this family, regardless of any southern preference, had also set a limit to what they were prepared to supply to the army. The two women greeted them cordially enough and the old man, who turned out to be nearly deaf, added the occasional shouted greeting or comment to whatever talk was continuing between the women and Lieutenant Jordan. As for the children, there was a girl, whom Ryan reckoned would be around ten years old, and a boy whom he guessed would be a year or two older, though he still had very much the look of a child about him. There was no sign however of the crippled boy "Ned," of whom the Mellors had spoken. As on the previous

349

properties, the children, while watching every move the soldiers made with wide staring eyes, said nothing, leaving the conversation entirely to the adults.

When the prospect of staying overnight on the place was mentioned by Jordan, the women voiced no objection.
"There's space in the barn over there," one told them. "Ya'll be snug enough there. There ain't no room in the house fer so many and besides, we wouldn't be wantin' no stayin' on guests. Reckon we could spare a bite o' supper." Daniel Ryan grinned inwardly at her tactful reference to the men's infestation. Out in the barn would do well enough, he reflected. It looked spacious enough and would be warm once a fire was built and dry also, providing accommodation no less comfortable than their camp shelters. Wood was taken from the pile outside the house and once a fire had been started with drier kindling from the barn, it was fed gradually, until a crackling blaze was going just in front of the entrance close enough to gain shelter from the barn but not exactly inside, thereby preventing the building from filling with its smoke.

The men had been settled around their fire for a time, awaiting the promised supper, when one of the women appeared with the girl at her side, each of them carrying dishes. A large plate of sliced up ham was presented to Isaac Kane by the woman, while the girl pushed the other dish of steaming potatoes, into Daniel Ryan's hands, both of them receiving a loud chorus of thanks from the group. Jones and Ballard immediately reached for their mess pans, settling them on the fire before getting to work, spreading slices of the meat on them to fry. The woman and the girl dallied, seemingly wishing to satisfy a measure of curiosity, as the ham began to spit and sizzle.

"Which outfit are you boys from," the woman asked them.

"We're Georgians," Ballard told her. "Wofford's Georgia brigade. That's General Longstreet's Corps, Army of Northern Virginia."

"Would that be General Lee's boys?" she inquired. Ballard nodded.

"Surely is ma'am." The woman nodded.

"We heard there was some o' Lee's boys around here," she said. "My husband, and my brother're both in Bedford Forrest's cavalry. Last we heard they were over around Chattanooga. That's away west of here, but that were last fall."

"We know where Chattanooga is, Ma'am," Thompson told her. "We were there last fall too at least we were there for the fight down at Chickamauga Creek and for a while after it." The woman nodded.

"We don't get much word from Gus or from Billy," she said, "but they don't seem to spend hardly any time any place, before that Bedford Forrest's got them all headin' off some place else."

"That's soldierin' for ya ma'am," Kane told her as he prodded the sizzling ham.

"Reckon I'll go get your greens," she said, starting to head for the door. "You just go right ahead and serve up that other stuff, rest'll be along directly," she added as she disappeared around it into the gloom. The girl however did not immediately go. She waited around the door of the barn, just about inside, but not quite on terms with the group of soldiers, though several of them nodded or winked in her direction as their casual talk resumed, before disappearing in her turn towards the house.

"It was Forrest who wanted to shoot ol' Bragg, when he let the Yankees get away, after Chickamauga," Jones said.

"Reckon he's one o' the more fightin' generals out here," Kane added.

"Stewart's boys spoke well of Cleburne too," Daniel Ryan put in.

"Trust Daniel t' blow the horn fer the Mick," Jones returned.

They parcelled out the ham onto their plates and had just completed the operation when the woman returned carrying a

351

second large dish, which contained corn and beans. There were exclamations of acknowledgement as she re-appeared with the girl following on behind her, and briefly held the dish out for them to admire.

"These'll put some meat on your ribs," she said as she passed the dish to Ballard.

"We're surely much obliged to ya ma'am," he told her, "and to your folks. Reckon any man'd do pretty well by hisself if he got himself set up around here, with a fine lady like you. I tell ya ma'am, it's somethin' o' a surprise t' me to find yore man's off soldierin'." Her face flushed as she let go of the dish, and her flush deepened as a chuckle moved around the group in response to Ballard's remark.

"I'm sure you're all very welcome," she said. She paused uncomfortably for a second or two, until Ballard took her hand.

"Beggin' yore pardon, ma'am," he added, "'n' meanin' no disrespect, o' course. Name's Otis Ballard, from Bulloch County, Georgia and I'm mighty glad to make yore acquaintance." He turned to the others. "This here's Joe Thompson. Joe's a sergeant, so he helps to run this here army. These others are Daniel Ryan, Daniel's a foreigner from some faraway place name of Ireland, Isaac Kane, Edwin Jones, Abe White 'n' Luke Petersen," he gestured towards each of them as he spoke, "they're Bryan County boys. These," he turned at last to the teamsters, "they're mule drivers, so that means they're little damned use to nobody." A further chuckle went around the barn as the corporal concluded his introductions.

"Beg pardon agin, ma'am," he finished, a shade sheepishly. The woman flushed again and gave a small curtsy as she smiled around the group.

"I'm Milly Duncan," she said. "Milly's's short for Melissa and I'm surely glad to meet you boys too. This here's Winifred, she's my daughter, but around here we call her Winnie."

She delayed a little longer to converse with them while still the girl again looked on. Yes, the Yankees had been

352

around here back in the fall, she told them. Not the whole Yankee army, just some cavalry who had come around to help themselves to vittles and stock. The family reckoned that some of their neighbours, she spoke the word in a disparaging tone, had told them who were southern thinkin' folks along the valley, because, a few days after the cavalry had been here, they had had militia boys comin' around also. Some of them were even from around there, she added, but they had still taken what they wanted from their neighbours barns and smokehouses.

"Weren't very neighbourly," Thompson remarked.

"Way it is around here now," she went on. "Reckon the Yankee folks up here weren't too pleased when the southern boys was in charge neither, nor when they came back around again after the Yankees all skedaddled." By now Kane was dishing up the ham, and seeing this the woman excused herself and left, carrying the empty ham dish with her and gesturing to the girl to follow, as the vegetables were passed around the group for each of them to help themselves. There was still no sign of Jordan who, being an officer, had clearly ingratiated himself sufficiently to be invited to enjoy the hospitality of the house.

"Hope he don't leave any critters over there," Kane said as they worked on their meal. "It'd surely spoil our welcome."

"By the time they find any he'll be well gone," Ballard told him.

Having finished the meal and licked their plates, they settled for the night. Jones retrieved a few more logs from outside, placing them near the fire to dry out before being burned. Kane was then dispatched by Thompson to take the first watch of guard duty and he retrieved his blankets and musket, slinging the latter by its strap, before making his way from the barn.

"Daniel'll relieve ya in a couple o' hours," Thompson told him and he grunted in reply. The others settled themselves, comfortable in the heat of the fire, with blankets being unrolled to air and warm before use, luxury indeed compared

353

to a typical winter bivouac, Ryan reflected. Within minutes, the barn was quiet, with the men either drowsing or already asleep and only an occasional snore or a subdued movement among the mules, which had been brought in and settled in the vacant stalls at the far end of the barn, to disturb the peace of the place.

Breakfast arrived early and maintained the high standards set by the previous evening's meal. A large dish of hashed up bacon and potatoes, with slices of corn bread on a further dish, appeared shortly after first light, brought by Milly Duncan, who set the dish down on a barrel, gesturing to the yawning men to help themselves before taking her leave. The tin plates promptly re-appeared and the food was divided up by Kane, as Jones appeared from his stint of guard duty.

"Jordan's lookin' fer ya," he told Thompson, upon which the sergeant heaved himself to his feet and started for the house. Ballard passed Kane's plate to him.

"If we stay around here much longer we might not have any further use fer you," he told him while the others smirked.

"Let's see if yo're showin' that kinda disrespect when it's supper time back in camp," Kane growled in reply as he took the plate. The food disappeared quickly, and finished with plate licking, they gathered their belongings and made their way outside. Thompson re-appeared and resumed his interrupted breakfast as the others busied themselves.

"What did he want," Ballard inquired?

"We ain't goin' no further up," the sergeant announced. "He reckons the wagons're full enough fer the state o' the teams, so we're headin' back, once we're loaded up and ready. Them further up farms'll jest have t' wait their turn." Ballard nodded.

"Ain't that clever stuff fer an officer," he said.

The sky remained grey and there was a chilly wind, though thankfully the sleet and rain held off as they attended to the wagons. The drivers occupied themselves in leading out and hitching their teams, while the Company B men attended to the loading of the provisions the Duncans had laid out, spreading and fixing the worn tarpaulins over the vehicles when the loading was done. Jordan finally appeared as the last of the mules were being harnessed, pulling his coat collar around him and fastening the top buttons as he came. One of the teamsters was already leading the officer's horse from the barn, saddled and bridled, ready for the lieutenant to mount. He passed the bridle to him before heading back to his own team.

The family assembled at their door as the detail left, with the girl beside her mother, though her face was impassive as she watched the departure. They moved away on a road that though free of the previous day's sleet, was covered in a layer of liquid mud, which made it little less treacherous than the sleet had done previously. Down the trail they plodded, taking their time on the slippery surface, getting no greeting and seeing no signs of life of any kind at the Morris, Berry or Hassell farms as they passed by, though further down, the Mellor woman came to her door to wave. The contrasting receptions all seemed to confirm the way things were up here, Daniel Ryan thought, for in truth it was a divided country, with neighbours, if not exactly at each other's throats, sadly afflicted nevertheless by the politics and divisions of the war.

Chapter 16 Neighbour Against Neighbour

As the winter drew to its close and the spring approached, the hauls gathered by the commissary details declined. With the spring ploughing and sowing season almost here, the winter stores on the various farms were down towards the barest minimums required to see the families through until their early crops could be harvested. In spite of this, the rations delivered, as the first days of spring arrived, stayed reasonably regular and though fresh meat was decidedly rare now, preserved meats, principally bacon, was still to be had, and flour also stayed available, as did some vegetables. The commissary wagons came creaking around every few days, with a reasonable enough ration for that day and sufficient on most occasions for the one that followed. There was therefore less to complain about on the subject of food, and morale around the camps was reasonably sustained on that matter at least.

On other matters however there was little enough to be cheerful about. Longstreet had spent some of the time away from the camps and from his Russellville headquarters. The general had been away in Richmond, proposing, it had been rumoured, ideas for offensives, provided the army could be reinforced. But failing substantial reinforcements, there seemed little to justify the First Corps units remaining here, isolated, as they were, in this corner of eastern Tennessee. Among the common soldiers, who awaited decisions on all of this high strategy while pursuing their routine daily duties, there was little enthusiasm for remaining in Tennessee. Perhaps what had happened among their officers out here, from Old Pete down, taken together with the defeat around Chattanooga and their own repulse at Knoxville, had set too much of a complexion of failure upon this Tennessee campaign. This mood seemed to have settled in the minds of the men, for there was a feeling of discontent about their continuing presence here and this was sharpened by the prospect of having to remain still longer. This mood of discontent had spread itself through the camps along the Millersville-Greeneville line and had become deeper and more profound, as the final weeks of winter had run their course.

During the previous winter in the lines around Fredericksburg there had been this kind of defeatist talk. Men back then had begun to speak of the war as, "a rich man's war, but a poor man's fight," and such talk was back again now, only out here now it seemed more widespread and profound. Too often on this campaign, men's lives had been wasted for no good purpose, which spread pessimism and bitterness widely among their comrades. In addition, there was a persistent feeling of being marooned here, with their generals at odds, in an apathetic, if not openly hostile, region and this had its own effect on morale. Disputes and fights were more common in the camps as men took out their disillusionment and the anger which arose from it, on each other. To all too many of those who occupied these east Tennessee camps, the lives of the men who had fallen since their arrival in Tennessee, had simply been wasted by the damned fool actions of all too many of their generals. It seemed to Daniel Ryan that their own moods of resentment and sometimes open anger, stemmed largely from this notion of wilful, pointless waste.

In the Ogeechee Volunteer Rifles every mess could all too easily recall the faces and names of the men who had come west with the regiment back in September, that seeming eternity ago, who were no longer in the ranks. Many had been wounded and had gone home, some of them permanently disabled by their injuries, but too many of them also were now in the ground. It all followed the pattern of death and injury that had prevailed for the last two years, with just one exception, and that was the difference between success and failure. In Virginia, while losses had also been grievous, there had at least been the achievement of repeatedly repulsing the Yankees when they attempted their drives on Richmond. Out

357

here however, following on that initial success, there had been a distinct absence of any kind of achievement to counterbalance the price paid by the army in blood.

The regiment had paid its part in that continuing price with its own casualties. Too many good men gone for ever, too many friends and brothers ground away by the remorseless fires of this war, and still the Yankees came on. Perhaps the losses would have mattered less and also the endurance of hardships, if the war had been going better, but it was not. The Yankees, as a result of the last year's fighting, now made their camps in the northern counties of Georgia. They controlled the entire length of the Mississippi River and had overrun whole segments of the southern states' coastline. Only in Virginia had they been stalled and repeatedly thrown back, but Virginia was only a part of the whole war. Being sent out here to Tennessee had shown the men of the First Corps, if they had not already known it, that the struggle was a lot more than just Virginia. Out here in the west, away from Virginia, a man was compelled to look at the war as a much larger struggle, and even though a great victory had been won back in September, great expanses of territory out here had been steadily lost over the past two years and almost none of what had been lost had ever been regained.

Out here the spaces were wider, the distances so much greater and this seemed, time and again, to have favoured the Yankees. Out here too the southern leadership was too often divided and at odds with itself, something that had simply never seemed to get to that pass in Marse Robert's army in Virginia. Defeat had been the result. That final lost battle at Chattanooga in November, had served to reinforce in the minds of those who survived, that in spite of all of the valour and resilience of the southern soldiers in the face of the incompetence of their leaders, the prodigious Yankee war machine was inexorably grinding onwards out here in the west, increasingly raising the spectre of defeat for soldiers who had not known such sentiments back in Virginia.

Was it all down, in the end, to General Lee? This too was debated and discussed extensively in the camps. Until this dismal winter the disharmony that seemed so widespread in the western army had not been a similar factor in the Army of Northern Virginia. There had been jealousy among generals and others too, in the east, but somehow Marse Robert had always managed to smooth things over and restore the focus of the army to the job of confronting and defeating the enemy. Their own predicament out here seemed to illustrate very clearly how different things could be away from the "Old Man's" guiding hand. There was a resilience, a greater unity of purpose in his army that was absent out here, in spite of what the captain might think, and many men were now openly voicing the view that the only solution for them would be a return to Virginia.

Two weeks after their first journey along the Little Beaver Creek trail, Thompson's section traversed the locality again in the course of a foraging expedition further up the valley. They headed away, this time in pale March sunshine, though the wind remained cold and the variable cloud banks indicated that rain might not be far away. The creek was noticeably higher with snow melt and rain from the mountains, but the verges and the hillsides that flanked the trail were brightened by little splashes of colour from early flowers that spoke of better things to come. The Mellors greeted them cordially enough, especially since the matter of provisions was not mentioned this time. Jordan again had charge of the detail and he kept his conversation to general matters, though that would change, Daniel Ryan knew, if the so far untouched farms further up the valley, did not yield sufficient in the way of food.

"Word's been goin' around that the Yankees are on their way round these parts agin," the lieutenant was told. "Their militia boys've bin seen up a little north o' here and from what we bin hearin', some Hawkins and Grierson County boys've bin with 'em." Jordan was a shade dismissive of the news.

"Our patrols haven't reported any Yankees this far south," he told them. "If they're from up around the Cumberland Gap area, they'd be a long way from home down here. Truth is, I don't think they'll come this far south, not as long as we occupy these parts with the numbers that we have." Daniel Ryan, detached by a few yards from the main group, felt Ballard's elbow in his ribs, as the lieutenant finished speaking.

"We don't occupy nothin' around here," his friend murmured. "Without cavalry, we jest come callin' around now and agin." Daniel acknowledged the words with a brief nod. It was true. Only cavalry gave the army the mobility that enabled it to spread its authority and influence wider areas. Without it, they were powerless to administer or protect these remote valleys. Yankee horsemen could therefore range through these counties with impunity, and what these people were telling them indicated that the enemy militias were well aware of that fact.

The persisting rumours of incursions by the Yankees had made it unwise to detach wagons to return individually when sufficient supplies had been gathered. This trip they would be staying together, which meant that the requisitioning would only begin when they commenced their return leg. They resumed their trek along the slowly ascending creek trail, passing the intervening farms of the Hassells, the Berrys and the Morris's. They did not pause at any of them, aware enough of the sentiments and aware also that there was no need to antagonise them further, at least not on this leg of the journey, but they had barely negotiated the bend in the trail which led on from the Morris farm, when Daniel Ryan became aware of a figure moving through the shadows in the woods on his side of the road. He watched the movement briefly, soon deducing that the person was making almost no attempt at concealment, for he quickly recognised the figure as the younger of the two girls from the farm that they had just left. He signalled across to Ballard and gestured towards the girl, who had now drawn closer to the trail.

"Reckon I'll wait and see what she wants," he told his friend.

"Don't drop too far back," the corporal returned. "They could be lookin' to set somebody up fer their Yankee friends t' bushwhack." Ryan nodded and shortened his stride until he was moving at a virtual snail's pace, with the wagons and their escort slowly creaking away up the trail. He went on watching the girl as she continued to approach, heading through the woods on a diagonal course towards the road. Ryan increased his pace again on seeing that the girl, unless she changed her course or pace, would arrive at the trail a short way ahead. At length she reached the side of the trail and stopped there, watching Ryan intently as he approached. She was wearing the same pale brown dress as before, with a darker smock over it, which gave her an older, almost matronly look, in spite of her child's years. Up ahead the wagons and escort were still in view, but the girl paid them no attention, keeping her eyes on Ryan as he came up. When she spoke it was in a thin, nervous tone.

"Are you rebels goin' on up to Winnie's house," she inquired. Daniel nodded.

"How do you know Winnie, little lady?" he inquired gently.

"I know her from Reverend Buntain's school," was the reply. "We're friends in the school, but we can't be friends at home, because her family's Jeff Davis folks and my folks're for Abe Lincoln." Daniel nodded again, recognising, in this child's simplistic description, yet another aspect of this sad and divided country where families were pulled apart by the politics of the war, with even children unable to maintain friendships as a result. It was a damned shame, he told himself.

Beside him the girl spoke again.

"Could you tell Winnie somethin?" she asked him. He nodded again, gravely. "Tell her," she went on, "that I said

361

that she and her folks better be extra careful cos there's Lincoln milishy boys gonna be headin' through this valley and they'll be lookin' for rebels." Daniel eyed her quizzically.

"Do you know when the militia boys'll be comin' around here?" he asked her. She shook her head emphatically, making her curly hair swirl around her face and head.

"I heard my ma talkin' to Mrs Berry yesterday," she said, "but they didn't say nothin' about when the milishy were comin' they just said they were comin'. Winnie's my friend and I don't want nothin' happenin' to her, or to her folks neither." Daniel looked at her for a moment or two longer.

"Do your folks know you've come out here to warn Winnie and her family?" he asked. Again the girl shook her head, with the same mannerisms as before, making her curls flutter around her face as she wrinkled her features. She looked, Daniel Ryan thought, as though she had just smelled or tasted something nasty.

"Reckon I'd get a switchin' if they knew where I was," she said, "but I ain't tellin'."

"Maybe you'd better be gettin' back then," Ryan told her, "so your folks don't figure out that you've been out here talkin' to us." She nodded gravely and turned back towards the woods. There must be a path of sorts Ryan thought, though it was impossible to see anything of it from here on the trail.

She turned as she reached the edge of the trees.

"You'll tell Winnie what I said." Her voice was insistent almost anxious in its tone. "Tell her it was Harriet that told you."

"I'll tell her," Ryan replied. "You get on home, Harriet." She turned to leave and, after a final moment of hesitation, started away, with the browns of her clothing soon merging into the shadows of the wood. Daniel Ryan watched her go, and as she became less and less visible in the shadows he scanned the woods carefully, remembering Ballard's warning, until having seen no sign of any movements or activity, he returned his eyes to the trail.

Up ahead, the convoy of wagons and infantry had moved on out of sight, though he could still faintly hear the rumbling of the wagons on the muddy surface. Ryan started after them beginning to double time gently, hearing his feet slosh and splash rhythmically in the mud of the trail until, on rounding a further bend, he caught sight of them once again. He slowed to a brisk walk as the distance between them slowly reduced, until he could hear the mutter of conversation among some of the men and the creak of harness, while the endless splashing of hooves and feet in the mud continued without pause.

"News," he said to Ballard as he came level with him, "but how useful it might be ain't certain." The corporal gave him an enquiring look.

"Yankee militia," Ryan told him, "supposed to be headin' for this valley."

"Better tell Jordan," the corporal said. "He kin decide on it, Lord help us, cuz we won't be doin' nothing about it till he does." Ryan nodded and moved on up the column of wagons and plodding infantry, getting comments as he passed.

"In a hurry, aintcha," White rapped. Daniel nodded.

"Can't spend the whole day hangin' around here," he said. As he came up past the leading wagon, he drew close to where Thompson walked with his tireless rangy stride.

"Got news," he said, as he came abreast of the sergeant. Thompson raised his eyebrows.

"Little girl from the last farm came after us," he told him, "wanted to warn the Duncans up ahead that there's Yankee militia aimin' to come through this valley, lookin' for southern families. She's friends with the little Duncan girl," he added. Thompson seemed to ponder briefly before answering.

"Better tell him," he said, nodding towards the lean swaying rump of the Lieutenant's horse.

Jordan too had pondered briefly, in his turn, before replying to Ryan's report.

"May be nothing more than rumour," he said, "or local gossip." Ryan said nothing for a moment or two, but when the officer remained silent he steeled himself, glancing at Thompson who had come up with him, and getting the briefest suggestion of a nod from him.

"There's been rumours around the camp about this," he said. "Ever since the cavalry were recalled and we fell back."

"Rumours are just what they are," Jordan retorted. "We can't tell anything definite from rumours and even if all of it is true, there's nothing of it that we can use, not without some idea of when it's all supposed to happen."

"The least we can do is pass this on to the family," Daniel Ryan told him.

"That could be just spreading the rumours," Jordan commented almost wearily, "but I suppose we at least owe them a warning, just in case it might be true."

The Duncan adults said little as Jordan, flanked by Ryan and Thompson, passed on what the Morris girl had said.

"We bin hearin' that kind o' thing fer weeks now," the old man said laconically, after the news had been shouted into his ears by Milly Duncan. "Ain't bin no sign o' no militia so far around here. We've had a few pilferers and stragglers from either side like we told ya, but we can't afford to let this kinda talk spook us into anythin' like leavin' this here spread. This is all we got and we'll be holdin' onto it so long as we kin."

"The word came from some of your neighbours," Jordan told them, "but we can't say whether it's a fact or a rumour." The two women had said little, but there was a pensiveness about them thereafter that suggested to Daniel Ryan that they at least were taking the news more seriously.

The family acquiesced to the detail overnighting in their barn once again, though Ryan thought he detected a shade less enthusiasm than on the last trip. The fare also was more meagre than on the previous stay, consisting of a thin cross between soup and stew, with a few pieces of bacon to be found among the sweet potatoes and greens that made up by far the greater proportion of the meal. They ate it gratefully enough and with the required elaborate thanks to Milly Duncan, who served it and to Winnie who assisted her.

It had rained during the night but now, as the detail prepared to depart after a breakfast of corn bread and bacon, the sky had cleared and the sun was above the trees that clothed the mountains to the east. Its light made the trees, on which the dew or the remains of the raindrops still lingered, sparkle and glitter with thousands of tiny pinpricks of light, and looking around at it all, Daniel Ryan thought that it gave the farm and its setting a natural beauty that he had not noticed before. On a morning like this it was easy to see why people would want to stay here and yet, however beguiling theses surroundings were today, the reality was an altogether grimmer and more threatening one.

Jordan waited beside his horse, overseeing the preparations to leave until, with the task complete, he turned to the family.

"If you believe the story of the Yankees presents a risk for you," he told them, "and you decide that you want to leave, we can escort you down to a safer place on our way back down." Milly Duncan looked at him for a moment before she shook her head.

"Where would this safer place be?" she asked. Jordan remained silent and did not meet her gaze.

"Where could we go?" she persisted. "Where could we shelter and what would we eat? It strikes me that there's too many folks been forced out of their homes by this war and none of them, as far as I ever heard, were any better for it. This is our home. It's all we got and we can't afford to leave, just because of a story, so as long as we can stay here we will. We keep to ourselves up here and bother nobody, so there ain't nobody got any reason to harm us. Sure they can steal our food, but that's been happenin' on and off for the last two years," she said pointedly.

Daniel Ryan listened to her, sympathising with her reluctance to consider leaving. Leaving would mean becoming refugees, dependent upon the charity of relations, or worse, of relief committees. But he knew too that it was maybe naive for anyone to assume that staying put would mean being left in any sort of peace, especially in this family's situation, for the war had changed things and was still changing them. Up here, as in so many other places now, people were labelled. They were either Union or Confederate, Yankee or rebel, loyal or secesh, Abe Lincoln folks or Jeff Davis folks. The titles did not matter, but what did was which side they were perceived to favour, for with the order of things slowly changing again in these counties, this family, with boys who had served or still served in the Confederate army, would be regarded, by some of their neighbours at least, as enemies. Jordan nodded slowly as the woman fell silent.

"I understand ma'am, but we shall be back tomorrow on our return journey and, if you should change your mind, my offer still holds. In the meantime we will take our leave." He raised his hat gravely to them. "I wish you all good day and trust that you will be left in peace." He replaced his hat before turning towards his horse to mount up, a task which he experienced with some difficulty, as the animal seemed to Daniel Ryan a shade reluctant to remain still enough for him to easily do, for it shifted its hind quarters round in an arc, causing him to shuffle several times in pursuit. Finally in the saddle, he turned once more to the assembled family and raised his right hand to the brim of his hat.

"Good day to you all," he called gravely, before waving the detail into motion. The drivers flicked their reins in succession and the wagons squeaked into motion. Daniel Ryan looked around as they moved off, seeing the family watching from their tiny porch surrounded by the natural beauty of their home. It was almost idyllic, he reflected, but more than that it was all so vulnerable. There was nothing now but an old man and a crippled boy to stand in the way of whatever lawless and vengeful forces were ranging through the mountains to the north and, if the Yankee families down

366

the trail were to be believed, were coming this way. Maybe they would change their minds by tomorrow, but as this farm was all that the family possessed he doubted it, though how long they would be spared here was a question that had no answer. The war and its consequences, even in these remote counties, might bring their time here to an abrupt end before many more Spring days like this one had dawned over these picturesque mountains and valleys.

The Duncans did not change their minds. When the detail passed on the return leg, almost a day later than they had said they would, the members of the family were employed on various chores around the place. Jordan halted the detail briefly and exchanged pleasantries with them, but the idea of leaving was pointedly absent from the conversation and with the wagons reasonably well-stocked from the Wendell, Pearson and Adams farms, provisions were not mentioned either. It left the option of a further foraging visit so there was no reason, Daniel reckoned, to shake the tree every time they passed it. They spent the night at the Mellor farm, ensconced in their slightly smaller barn and served up with boiled bacon, corn bread and cabbage, which disappeared promptly from their plates.

As March ended the talk around the camps intensified, with two contrasting theories being persistently pushed in the ever-circulating rumours. Some men spoke of reinforcements coming up on the railroad to strengthen the corps for a thrust northwards towards Kentucky, to cut the supply lines of the Yankee host poised around Chattanooga, a foray that would hopefully pick up recruits as it went. Thus strengthened, they could maybe finally shift the balance of the war out here in the west. In contrast, the other course of action, supported by its own crop of rumours, suggested the much more modest option of a return to the Army of Northern Virginia.

The men of Company B considered the stories in turn as they arrived in their midst. A few favoured the idea of a bold thrust northwards, for without something like that the war out here was facing still more disappointment and adversity for the south. For others however, when they considered the alternatives, Daniel Ryan and his companions were among them, the idea of a return to Virginia was their preferred option, for this excursion westwards, having commenced with such high hopes, had been a trail of disappointment and reverses. When all things were considered, the difference seemed to be Lee, for out here in his absence things had just not been the same. They had arrived in Tennessee seeing themselves as somehow different from these feuding, defeat-prone westerners, yet as time had passed it had not been as they thought. Who was to say that whatever offensive was attempted out here would not simply follow the same kind of doleful pattern as the events of the previous fall and winter had done?

It was all very dispiriting and disillusioning and maybe the best thing to be done was to accept that it had been ill-fated from the start and get back to concentrating the efforts in Virginia. With Lee in command there, the prospect remained of fashioning the stroke that might yet convince the Yankees that they could not overcome the south and they should therefore let it be.

To Daniel Ryan there was one further factor, for one of the worst things about this whole Tennessee misadventure had been the events of the more recent weeks, where with the arrival of the armies, neighbours had turned on each other. Divisions among local people had been exacerbated to the point that the peace of different communities had been fractured, bringing hardship and sometimes even death to simple country people who had asked for nothing more than to be left alone to grapple their living from nature in these difficult uplands. His mind turned repeatedly to the Duncans up there on their remote farm, threatened by so far unseen enemies, with their predicament and their fate a direct example of what the war meant in these divided regions.

It was into the final week of March when Thompson's men again provided the escort for a further commissary expedition along the Little Beaver Creek trail once more, amid persisting rumours both of further incursions by the Yankees and also, for the Army of Northern Virginia units at least, of an imminent departure. In response to the rumours, Boyce assigned the whole of Thompson's section to escort the three wagons with Jordan once again in charge of the detail, and they set out in conditions hardly less muddy, but appreciably less cold, than on their previous sweep of the locality.

Several piles of ashes, with a set of blackened timbers protruding from each of them, was all that remained of the Mellor's farm when they arrived at it. Of the family there was no sign and a brief inspection of the place revealed no clue as to where they had gone. Maybe, Daniel Ryan speculated, the fact that there was no sign of any of them meant that they had concluded that departing was the sensible course and had gone of their own accord before any of the threatened Yankees had actually arrived, but they were gone and there was no way of knowing for certain the circumstances of their leaving. With nothing worth foraging, no further time was wasted, and Jordan ordered the detail under way once more.

The Hassells were at home as were the Berrys and the Morris's. All three families, by Daniel Ryan's reckoning at least, displayed more defiance in their manner than they previously had, taking their objections and resentment almost to the point of obstruction. Only the paltriest provisions were obtained from their farms and as the afternoon drew on, Jordan once again ordered the detail onwards from the Morris place.

Daniel Ryan felt the tension inside him grow as they departed, knowing that the biggest question of all, along this trail, was about to be answered, but the absence of the only other pro-southern family from this valley and the destruction of their home, as well as the cockiness of the Yankee ones, had given plenty of grounds for concern. He had seen the little girl looking at him during their time at the Morris farm. The child had risked something to warn her friend and her family, but the talk that took place was with the sullen, almost sneering adults of her family.

"Rebels are on borrowed time around here now," one of the women had snapped.

"Ya'd be best stayin' mannerly anyway, at least till we're well gone," Ballard had growled in reply.

Up the trail as the Duncan place drew closer, further warning signs began to appear. A smell of old burning came to them, suggestive maybe of what they would find. The detail ground on at its customary crawl, a pace that troubled nobody in normal circumstances, but which Daniel Ryan found exasperating today.

They came at length to the farm to find, as at the Mellor's, only burnt out ruins, while at the roadside, maybe fifty yards distant from the ashes of their home, they came across the three females of the Duncan family, together with the boy Thomas, in a crude camp just off the road. There was no sign of the old man nor of the crippled boy Ned. Jordan spurred his horse ahead and dismounted promptly, while the vehicles and escort laboured up. By the time that they reached the group, the two women were relating to Jordan what had taken place.

"It was militia," she told them, "Ezra Farley's boys."

"Who's Ezra Farley," Jordan wanted to know?

"He's a preacher from up north," she told him. "He came through here with his men on Monday and they robbed us of just about everythin' we had left." She paused, to wipe her face with a corner of her shawl, before continuing. "The worst of it all," she went on, "was that Nathan Berry and Simon Wendell were with them. The two of them just hung around and watched, while the others took everything they could set their hands on." She turned away and wiped the sleeve of her shawl across her eyes again. "I'd never have believed that our own neighbours would have helped a bunch of thieves like them to rob us like that, but they did even worse than that. Once they had done with us, they headed down the trail t'ard their own friends, but then they came back up here the next

370

afternoon, that was the day before yesterday, and said we'd been harbourin' rebels, so they ordered us out and set fire to our house and barn. They left Ned inside and stopped us from getting back in there to where he was. Every time we tried to get to him, they pushed us back and when pa tried to stop them they shot him, just like that. We begged them, but all the time Farley just stood there, tellin' us that rebels were unclean in the eyes of God. He ain't a real minister o' the lord, but people took to callin' him "Preacher." He kept callin' out that this was the judgement of the lord on rebels, but what, in the name of Jesus, has burning our home and murdering our kin got to do with God?" She had been calm, almost matter of fact this far in telling the story, but now she almost shouted those final words, with her voice breaking as her emotions rose, after which she fell silent and quietly began to weep, Ryan heard her sister's sob also. He saw her shoulders convulse as Milly Duncan turned to embrace her and they clung together there, with the tears running down the cheeks of them both, while the soldiers stood and looked, seemingly at a loss as to what to do in this situation.

"They kept us out there," Milly Duncan resumed, as she composed herself, "while Ned burned to death inside and Farley kept yellin' and callin' out bits from the bible. We had to stand there and listen to Ned's screams as he tried to move himself, to get away from the fire....." She broke off again and then both women were sobbing bitterly once more, while all around them, the faces of the circle of watching and listening soldiers were grim and taut with anger. Jordan fumbled in his pocket and produced a handkerchief which he passed to Milly Duncan, but Thompson almost pushed him aside as he stepped forward to embrace both women, placing an arm around the shoulders of each of them.

"Yo're safe now," he told them gently as he patted their shoulders. Ryan had never heard the gruff and laconic sergeant speak or behave in such a way and his mouth almost fell open in his surprise. Thompson had a voice like a horn and he did not hesitate to use it, but here it was gentle and almost soothing, as he spoke to the two women.

"We'll see ya get out o' here safe," the sergeant continued, "ain't nobody goin' to lay a finger on any o' ya now."

Over at the makeshift shelter the two children waited, with expressions of fear on both of their faces. Their lives were just the latest to be turned upside down by the intrusion of the war. Jordan stepped forward to take charge again and promptly summoned Thompson to consult with him. The two of them spent several minutes in conversation and upon the conclusion of their talk, Thompson returned to the group.

"We're headin' back," he told them. "With Yankees around here, it's too big a big risk to head on up.

We could easy get bushwhacked up there, or cut off if they come back on to this trail." Jordan too had returned to inform his drivers and he then detailed several of the section to load onto the wagons the sparse possessions that the Duncans had managed to save, before having the vehicles laboriously turned on the limited open ground around the ashes of the farm.

Jordan dispatched Ballard, together with Ryan, Kane and Jones, to scout into the woods, for a, "stretch" to seek for signs of the renegades. To Ryan this seemed a fool's errand. Those who had done this would have been unlikely to remain around the place, especially since there were further pickings to be had by staying on the move. Being mounted, they would also have stuck to the roads and most likely have headed east, across the creek if they were staying in the area, away from the railroad and the main concentration of Confederate camps. Jordan however was the officer, so they obediently trooped away, separating into a rough line as they pushed forward, before turning to move in a curve through the woods, parallel, as near as they could ascertain, with the trail below. Having spent upwards of an hour on the task, Ballard recalled them.

"Reckon we spent more'n enough time on this damn fool idea," he told them, before directing them back towards the road. They reached the trail further down, not far from the

372

Morris farm. Daniel Ryan saw the thin tendril of smoke rising above the trees and moved to take a long look down along the last stretch towards the buildings before they started back again.

The sun was sinking lower in the sky and the air had grown chilly by the time they sighted the remainder of the detail, advancing at their customary pace. They halted, allowing the wagons, which now carried the Duncans as well as provisions, to approach, upon which Ballard reported to Jordan, who wheeled his horse from the trail to hear. The lieutenant heard him out without comment, nodding briefly when he had finished, before moving on.

Ballard walked with Thompson for a time before returning to his place to the rear of the wagons. The corporal made no immediate comment, though Ryan and the others looked at him inquiringly.

"He wants to overnight back here at the Morris place," he told them eventually, "so Joe says, but there's still a good hour and a half o' daylight. He could find that doin' that's a different thing on a Yankee place, than on a Confederate one. If them militia," he growled the term contemptuously, "are any place around here, stayin' this far out fer the night could give them all the chance they need to git word, swing back this way and bushwhack us further down the trail."

"Maybe Joe, or all of us, can talk him into movin' on," Ryan said, "and get farther down the trail before we have to lay up," but, even as he said it, he knew how unlikely it was that Jordan would agree. Maybe at least the comforts of barn would weigh too much on the commissary officer's mind, making him willing to disregard whatever risk prevailed by staying there. Maybe there was no best option in a situation like this, he thought, when it came to deciding whether to stay or to move on. If the enemy were still in the locality they might know already of their detail's presence, and would therefore have a choice of bushwhacking options. But were they still around here and did they know? It was impossible to say, but one further thing had to be considered. There were among the families who lived along this trail a number of people who would likely be perfectly willing to warn or inform whatever Yankees might be around here of the presence and the movements of the southern group, giving to the enemy the advantage of choosing not only their course of action, but their time and their method of carrying out whatever they decided against Jordan's detail. In this remote valley, though the Yankee irregulars of this man Farley might be the main foe, there was certainly more than one enemy.

To their dismay, events transpired in exactly the way that the escorts had feared. Jordan halted the wagons at the Morris farm and instructed the teamsters to unhitch their animals, before detailing the men of the escort to set up camp.

"Spring may be comin' on," he had told Thompson, within earshot of most of the others, "but a night under shelter is still better than one on the road." Ballard and Cooper had approached them both and there had followed a discussion among the four of them, the result of which was a confirmation of the lieutenant's previous order. Ballard had returned in a bad humour to take charge of the setting up.

"Didn't see sense then," Ryan muttered briefly.

"Goddam officer's brains are in his butt," the corporal rasped in return. "Reckons the goddam mules shouldn't be inconvenienced none. If what could happen does happen, them mules'll get a goddam bullet, same as the rest of us."

"At least we got him to post pickets," Linus Cooper added sarcastically, "so they won't catch us in our blankets, but to my way of thinkin', that ain't gonna help us much."

"Maybe the Yankees're gone," Kane said. "Renegades like that'll keep on the move and, if these are doin' the same, there ain't no harm in stayin' here. Besides these varmints don't like the idea of tanglin' with regular troops, cuz they know they'll most likely get whipped."

"Do you want to bet your damn hide on that?" Ballard growled in return. Kane shook his head and said nothing more.

A substantial enough supper was put together from the haul on the wagons, with the Duncan women taking charge of cooking it and Isaac Kane reduced, in consequence, to a role of observing and muttering in the background. They ate at the barn as darkness came, ignored by the Morris family who remained in their house with the door firmly closed. Thompson and the two corporals had organised the escort into watches and had included the teamsters in them, which had pleased the latter not at all.

"It's your damn necks as well as ours," the sergeant had told them brusquely, and there the matter had rested. They would serve watch about, for two hour shifts, picketing the perimeter of the farm until first light, when they would get moving once more.

The Duncans settled to one side of the barn for the night, with the soldiers unrolling their blankets on the other, in order to give everyone some benefit from the warmth of the fire. Jordan occupied himself for some time by arranging for a screen to be set up, extending some element of privacy to the family. The lieutenant completed the task with extravagant gallantry, inquiring solicitously of them, once the setting up was complete, if the arrangement would suffice, while the men going on sentry duty shrugged and left him to it.

In the last of the dusk the first group including Ryan, Jones and Kane commenced their initial watch, with Ballard in charge, using the fire just inside the double door of the barn as their post. There was little stirring in the course of the first hour of duty. Daniel Ryan completed two circuits of the farm perimeter finding that the noises of the night were confined to the quiet gurgling of the creek out beyond the screen of trees and undergrowth on the other side of the trail, and the nocturnal sounds of the forest on the near side, where night hunters would doubtless be abroad in search of prey. Ryan found himself hoping that none of these carried guns. He consoled himself with the thought that militia would not be well disciplined and therefore a night approach should be unlikely, but there was no guarantee of anything like this and he eyed the dark trail keenly in the course of his rounds.

He had commenced his third circuit, which began with a patrol towards the house before turning beyond the building and making for the paddock and smokehouse. It was as he began to move away from the cabin that Ryan became aware of the girl, Harriet. He looked around to see her, crouching in the lee of the house where the timbers crossed and formed a concealed place. He stopped and for several seconds the two of them looked at each other in the faint light from the fire over at the barn.

Eventually the girl spoke in a whisper.

"Is it you," she asked? Ryan nodded.

"It's me," he told her in a low voice.

"Shshshshsh......." Her face took on a look of fright. "If ma finds I'm talkin' to you she'll take the skin off o' my backside. I came to warn Winnie and her family. The milishy are on their way back. Mr Berry got word to them about you after you left their place. They were headin' over on the road that goes to Kingsport, but now they've got word, pa says they'll be comin' back to kill you all. They know all about you now cuz Mr Berry rode over to -" Ryan held up his hand to stop her.

"Can you come on over and tell the lieutenant what you just told me?" he whispered. She shook her head violently in the same manner that he had noticed in their previous encounter.

"No!" she whispered fiercely. "I have to get back, before they see where I've been. Tell Winnie and her folks. Tell her I'm sorry about all of this." She looked at him for a second or so more and then turned and vanished around the corner of the building.

Ryan pondered briefly on whether he should continue his circuit of the farm before reporting what he had learned from the little girl, deciding almost immediately to cut short his pacing and alert Ballard. The corporal's reaction was equally prompt. He roused Thompson who, in turn, woke Jordan, with the activity involved in it all ensuring that by the time the lieutenant joined them at the fire almost everyone in the barn was awake. Ryan repeated what he had learned from the little girl, while the others listened as they stood or squatted around the fire. When he had finished there was a brief silence.

"A brawl with them boys is somethin' I'd be pretty happy about," Petersen growled.

"We are not up here looking for trouble," Jordan snapped. "This is a commissary detail and the safety of our supplies comes first." Ballard sniffed.

"If what Daniel tells us is right, then we don't have to look fer no trouble," he said. "It'll be along directly, no matter what we do." Jordan looked at Thompson.

"We'd better get moving at first blush," he told him. "If the Yankees are coming from the direction of Kingsport, they'll have the creek to cross to reach this trail, but where they'll cross, and how they'll approach we have no way of knowing. They have the advantage of local knowledge, but if we get going early and put a good distance -"

"They'll cross at the ford just this side of the Berry place," Milly Duncan's voice came from beyond the group of listening soldiers, but she stepped forward towards the fire after she had spoken. Several of the men shuffled aside to make a space for her.

"The creek ain't high enough to need fordin' for a lot o' the year," she went on. "Most o' the time you can just wade across nearly anywhere, but it's higher now, with the rains and the snow melt. But it ain't just the water depth that makes the ford the place to cross, it's the banks as well. There's only a few places, where the banks are flat enough to get a wagon or even a cart across and Berry's Ford is the best on this stretch." She drew herself upright. "They got wagons with them, so if they're comin' back up here from the east, that's where they'll cross." Her gaze rested on Jordan after she fell silent, but it was Thompson who stepped towards her.

"How far from here?" he rapped in his business tone, which, Daniel Ryan noted, was substantially different from the one he had employed that afternoon.

"Two miles," she said, "maybe a little more."

"Do they all have horses?" he persisted. The woman nodded.

"We can be past there an hour after sunrise," Jordan put in, "then it's just a matter of keeping ahead and getting back down to the Rogersville road as soon as we can." To Daniel Ryan's surprise, Joseph Thompson shook his head. He did it gently, in an unostentatious way, he was disagreeing with an officer after all, but his dissent was unmistakable.

"That'll put the Yankees in charge o' things," he said. "They're mounted, so they'll be able to move a lot faster than we kin, with most of us on foot. Even if we're past the ford, they'll just follow on after us and pick their time and place. They'll bushwhack us whenever it suits them, 'specially if some o' these local Yankees lend them a helpin' hand, by takin' shots at us from behind every tree along the way." Jordan looked at him with what, Daniel Ryan reckoned, was something between irritation and uncertainty on his face.

"What else can we do," he said?

"We kin git some men down to that ford damned quick," Thompson replied. "If the Yankees are already there, then whoever we send kin fall back slowly towards the rest of us and that at least gives us a good warnin' and the chance to git ourselves set, but, bein' militia, I don't reckon these boys'll move by night. They ain't real trained fightin' men, 'specially if they're pickin' up local Yankees as they go, so that means they'll likely lay up till dawn. If some of us head out now and get to the ford first, they kin maybe hold there, till the rest of us come up, then we got the chance to bushwhack them, instead o' the other way round."

"That sounds a lot like looking for trouble," Jordan put in, "and, like I already said, that's not why we're up here."

Thompson paused before responding, still a measure tactfully, Daniel Ryan thought, undoubtedly aware of the

378

delicacy of trying to tell an officer, even a commissary officer, what to do.

"If we leave them be," he said. "They'll be huntin' us and we'll be tryin' to run, only we can't run nowhere near fast enough to get clear." He turned to Milly Duncan.

"How many of these varmints were there?" he asked brusquely. There was a pause while she pondered and considered.

"Twenty, no, more like thirty, perhaps a few more," she told him. Thompson nodded to her and then turned to Jordan.

"If we hit them a good lick at the ford, then that'll stop 'em in their tracks and give 'em some good scratches to think about. Maybe they'll decide that they got better things to do, easier pickin's to go for, rather than come after us, in case they get scratched some more. At the very least, if they do come on after us, they'll come careful and won't be pushin' on, in case they get hit agin." He paused, as though inviting a response from Jordan, but it was Ballard who spoke next.

"What Joe says makes good sense to me," he said. "I'm fer hittin' these Yankees hard and once we've done that, they likely won't bother us no more."

"If we don't do somethin' to get 'em off our backs," Cooper said, "they kin jest follow us on down that trail, like Joe says, pickin' us off as it suits 'em, or pin us down and wait us out. I'm fer takin' a lick at 'em, if we got the chance. That gives us the best chance o' gittin' clear." There was a mutter of assent from all around the group as he finished, but Daniel Ryan, even though he saw the sense of Thompson's view, found himself wondering how much of the men's agreement might be more about getting a chance to serve out some retribution to these murdering Yankees, rather than being solely about saving Jordan's wagons.

The lieutenant looked from Thompson to Ballard and then on to Cooper before he finally replied.

"All right," he said at length, "let's get some men down to that ford. Who do we send down there, you sergeant?"

379

"Me, or Otis or Linus, it don't make no difference," Thompson told him. Jordan paused again, while everyone else in the barn waited and the fire continued to crackle gently. Finally he gestured to Thompson.

"Pick an advance party sergeant and move out as soon as you're ready. Night's no time for running wagons on a trail like this one, but the rest of us'll be on the way at first light and we'll be with you as soon as we can -" He was interrupted by Ballard.

"With the Lieutenant's permission, I'll mubbee take a couple o' the boys and go knock on the door o' these Yankees here, to get our hands on whatever guns they got. That way, if they want to follow on down after us in the mornin', to help their murderin' militia friends, at least they won't have nothin' to shoot us in the back with." Jordan glanced again towards Thompson, who gave an almost imperceptible nod.

"See to it then corporal," the lieutenant rapped. He turned to Cooper.

"See to getting loaded up and ready to go. Leave the teams meantime, but we move out as soon as it's light enough to see."

"Who ya takin' Joe?" Ballard inquired.

"The mess'll do well enough," Thompson told him, "and one o' these here ladies, to show us the place." Ballard nodded.

"Luke, Charlie!" he snapped, "let's go pay these Yankee folks a visit!"

Chapter 17 Retribution of a Kind

The eastern sky was beginning to lighten, showing the first vague smudge of a horizon along the tree covered ridge crest, as Milly Duncan directed the four of Ryan's mess off the trail and down a brief diagonal slope towards the creek. At first it was too dark to see much, as it had been for the last portion of the hurried hike from the Morris Farm down the trail to the ford, for the moon had set, leaving the landscape in comparative blackness. The woman had not seemed troubled by this however, for she had guided them confidently to the ford, answering on the way a succession of questions from Thompson about their approaching enemy.

"They say he's not a real ordained preacher, but one o' them lay preachers," she told them. "He's supposed to be from Kentucky and some folks say he had a church out west, in Iowa or Kansas, before the war. Last year we heard he'd arrived in Tennessee. He's got a band of men and they've been ridin' around the counties up north o' here, lookin' for southern folks to rob and drive off and, if they made any objection, they got killed. There's bin stories of Farley's men hangin' folks, or burnin' their homes down around them, as well as shootin' them."

Having reached the place, the four of them spread out to briefly reconnoiter the area before coming together back on the trail as the night turned to pre-dawn greyness around them. Thompson had then waded across the creek and had headed on up the slope of the far bank, his progress just visible in the growing light as he went to inspect the trail beyond the ridge line. He was gone for ten minutes or more and when he returned, his first order was to Edwin Jones.

"Get across to the top o' that there ridge, Edwin," he told him. "Up beyond there the trail leaves the trees and goes on a stretch, across some open meadow, so if you set up at the top there, you'll git a good sight o' anybody comin' and we'll be able to see you signal. You'll be in the trees and close enough to git back here afore anybody sees you. They won't be expectin' an ambush. As far as they know they're the ones who're aimin' to do the ambushin', so we got surprise on our side. I jest hope the rest of our boys get here before the Yankees do." Jones nodded and departed without comment, as Thompson turned to Kane and Ryan.

"Choose yore ground," he said. "I'd pick some place where you kin get back to the trail under cover, jest in case we got to git away in a hurry."

Milly Duncan had watched them from up nearer to the trail as they did their inspecting and preparing.

"Do any of you have another gun?" she called softly, as they made to separate. The three of them turned and shook their heads, almost in unison.

"Extra weapons is extra weight to a soldier ma'am," Thompson told her. He gave her a long hard look. "We got some idea what you must be feelin'," he said, "but maybe you shouldn't be in too much of a hurry to shoot down boys that include some o' your own neighbours."

"They are not my neighbours any more," she retorted. "They watched what happened and they did nothing, so they are damned Yankees. They took their side back at our farm and now I wouldn't flinch from shooting every last one of them."

"I surely don't blame her fer that," Kane muttered to Daniel Ryan, as they turned away and started along the bank seeking places to settle. Ryan nodded.

"If you're set on joinin' in with this fight, maybe you can see if Otis has any extra guns when he gits here," Kane called back to her. "He'll maybe have whatever he gets from them Morris folks, back up the trail there." The woman nodded and Ryan and Kane separated, as Ryan caught sight of a possible place near the top of the little slope.

It was a partly fallen tree that had attracted him. It lay at a curious angle, wedged against the lower branches of a neighbouring trunk, its branches stretching in crazy directions with the buds of their new leaves formed in their clusters, in spite of its predicament. Enough of its roots must still be in the ground to maintain something of its growth, Daniel deduced, as he levered himself across the lower part of its main trunk and stepped along behind it to reach the point where he could rest and comfortably aim his musket. He settled behind the tree trunk and pulled several cartridges from his pouch, laying them along the flattest part of the trunk. These would be his subsequent shots, saving the vital second or two that it would take to scramble them from his pouch once the fight was joined.

He looked up at the far approach in the early morning light.

Out to the east there were clouds near the horizon, lit up by the rising sun, but this light would serve better, he thought, since they were looking somewhere south of east and they would be spared the handicap of any dazzling sunlight to spoil observation and aim. His mind went back to other ambushes over the last two years, to the previous summer back in Virginia, when a small group of them had ambushed that column of Yankee cavalry near Ashby's Gap in the Blue Ridge and had held them there just long enough for help to come. He shook his head ruefully. Of the five from the mess who had fought together that day, only himself and Ballard now remained. Fitzpatrick was dead, buried up in Pennsylvania, Jenkins too and maybe Winder were also gone.... He pushed the thoughts away, trying to banish the dismal losses of the past year and of the war as a whole from his mind, but still the recollections came.

There was that other time too, up in Maryland the previous fall, when the Yankee militia boys had walked naively into their ambush. Mick Daley had saved Daniel's life that sultry day. He thought of Daley, also wounded up in Pennsylvania. He had not died, instead he was in a hospital back in Virginia, so they had heard, recovering from two wounds, either of which might have killed him, but Daley was tough and it would take more than... He tried to halt this train of thought,

383

dismissing the memories from his mind to concentrate instead on what he was doing, as he settled to begin loading the Enfield, slowly and methodically taking exaggerated care with each step, keeping the doleful images of lost comrades at bay, until, with the weapon ready, save for a cap in place under the hammer, he rested it against the tree trunk, and with the help of full daylight, looked around at the ground on both sides of the creek.

On the positive side, the immediate bank on this side was slightly higher, allowing the southern group to take up positions that enabled them to shoot down on any enemy on the far side, even one in cover, provided they could be kept on that far bank. On the negative side, the approach trail on the far side loomed much higher than this side, meaning that they had to try to get the Yankees down to the creek side without suspecting trouble. In addition, if they had to withdraw, cover was not continuous on this side. There was a sparser margin between the screen of trees along the creek itself and those that bordered the trail, which would have to be crossed exposing anyone who was pulling back to the fire of whoever remained on the far bank.

He caught a sight of Thompson as he passed along the closest portion of the creek, as though assessing it for some deep tactical purpose. There was however one fundamental truth about the whole situation. Four of them could not possibly delay an enemy of any strength for long. On their own, they could barely check the renegades before having to withdraw. It was the same as last summer. They were too few to achieve much without help. If the Yankees did not arrive within the next hour or so, they would at least have the remainder of their own group here, to add their weapons to the ambush.

That vital first volley, when they would spend their advantage of surprise, was all important. They must hit the Yankees as hard as they could with that volley, for after that it would be a straightforward fight, only then the enemy would have the advantage of numbers and mobility and maybe of weapons too. Their own group would have a maximum of a dozen muskets, or maybe slightly more, and that was counting the teamsters and Jordan himself, so they must make those first shots count.

There was only one further factor and it was the one that Thompson had mentioned earlier, at the improvised council of war back in the Morris barn. These Yankees were not trained or experienced soldiers. They were militia led, it seemed, by a religious crazy man, which could mean it was some kind of local force, used to keep a neighbourhood or area under control, but lacking in the real skills of soldiering. If they suffered a real surprise and lost some of their number, especially their leaders, in the first shots of the coming ambush, they might not stay around to make a fight of it. The term, "Militia" was to some extent at least, a derogatory one, used by veteran soldiers to describe these amateurs. They wore uniforms, but did little more than patrol around a local area, intimidating local people, requisitioning their supplies and often stealing from them, but avoiding any real fighting. These were likely no different, except to the extent that they had returned to kill the people of this valley after robbing them. They had shot an old man and had burned a crippled boy alive, just because he had served in the Confederate army. For that they would get no mercy, the mood back in the barn had made that amply clear. This coming fight had an edge to it, for a grudge now existed among his comrades towards these Yankees and their leader, their having seen this happen to a family who had done no more than offer hospitality to a southern commissary detail. No, he thought, these boys had it coming and, if the men of their section had a say in it, they would certainly get it.

The noises on the trail behind him came as the sun was not far clear of the trees on the eastern horizon, but still only visible as a brighter patch behind the distant clouds. It was an approaching rumbling of wheels, as Thompson appeared on the approach to the creek, coming up towards the trail to meet the arriving detail. Daniel also moved from his place, stepping out onto the approach to see the wagons and the remaining men of the escort arrive, aware of Milly Duncan coming up the approach after Thompson. Her face wore a grim expression, a clear enough indication, Daniel Ryan reckoned, that she still hankered after that gun. As he followed the slope of the approach up towards the trail, he saw Jordan reining his horse in beside Thompson, who gave a brief salute, which the officer returned with an air of casualness.

"Well, Sergeant Thompson," he heard Jordan say, "and how are things down here?"

"Quiet enough," Thompson answered, "no Yankees yet, but I've got a man out a piece on that side keepin' a watch fer them."

"I've been giving this whole thing some more thought," Jordan resumed, as he dismounted. "This could easily be something of a waste of time now. We were probably right to send your detachment on ahead, as a precaution last night, but now here we all are and there's nothing to be seen of any Yankees. This whole thing is only the word of a child and we now have the option of moving out and being well on our way back, before anybody gets here, if there is anybody to get here at all." Ballard had come up from the rear and had heard the final part of the lieutenant's comments. Daniel saw him lower his eyes and shake his head slowly. Thompson was staying calm however, Daniel reckoned, you could tell it by his tone as he answered.

"That's all up to you lieutenant," the sergeant said. "If you reckon it's best to go, all that you need to do is give the order. But if we do hand this ford over for anybody to use and the first ones along to use it are these militia then we are in trouble. One or two Yankee farmers with rifles can hold us up any place they like, all the way down the trail, makin' us halt and send men off into the woods to chase 'em off, or maybe jest killin' our mules or pinnin' us down, so we can't go no place anyhow. That could happen anyway, but, if we have to keep on top o' all o' that and, at the same time, keep lookin' over our shoulder for these militia boys, then they got us between a rock and a hard place. Let's fight one enemy at a time and, if we hit the first one hard enough, word could get around and any others might not even trouble themselves to come our way at all." Jordan pursed his mouth, as though to make it clear that he was thinking, and Daniel Ryan found himself inwardly cursing as the seconds passed. It was bad enough being stuck in this position, he thought, without the added handicap of a greenhorn officer, inexperienced in real soldiering, who would rather manoeuvre them all into an even tighter fix.

Jordan finally seemed to make a decision of some kind, for he straightened up and looked Thompson in the eye.

"The word of a child is a pretty thin reason for delaying this whole expedition," he said. "The girl may have been mistaken, or she may have exaggerated. She may even have been lying, put up to it by her Yankee family, to set us up for some different kind of approach by these varmints. Given the choice that we face, I can see your point, but if it is a risk to go on it is a risk also to remain. Taking it all into account, we will stay here meantime. Deploy your men on this side...," Thompson gestured with his thumb to Ballard, who immediately moved off, "and we will start the wagons down the trail," Jordan stopped as he saw the sergeant's expression.

"You have something else to suggest, sergeant?" he said, with a tone of annoyance in his voice.

"We've only got a handful of men," Thompson began, "so, whatever we decide t' do now, we should put everythin' we've got into it. If the wagons start off without the rest o' the boys, what happens if they git bushwhacked down the trail by the farmers, with nobody there to chase 'em off? As far as these militia Yankees go, if we aim to hit 'em hard and get them off our backs by doin' it, yore teamsters give us three extra guns..." Jordan's face furrowed in thought again, as Daniel Ryan's irritation gathered. This was all taking too much talking and deciding. Maybe there was a risk in staying, but there was a worse one in going and then getting held up on the trail, giving whatever Yankees came along the chance to choose their moment and their ground. There was no reason to suppose that the approaching Yankees suspected any trouble and, all other things being equal, here at the creek ford offered the best chance of striking them hard enough to drive them off. Again he saw Jordan's features change to his "making up his mind" expression.

"Very well sergeant," he said. "We will conceal the wagons a little way down the trail and they will stay, along with their drivers, for the time being, but if no enemy appears soon I am sending them on their way and the remainder of this detail, your escort, will shortly follow them." He turned and moved away, leading his horse to the other side of the trail, before hitching its reins to the tailgate of the rear wagon. Thompson shrugged and looked at Cooper and Ryan.

"Well he surely ain't no Stonewall Jackson, is he?" he growled. Daniel looked around as Ballard returned.

"What if he's right?" Cooper said. "Maybe the kid could have lied or been mistaken." Thompson eyed him briefly and then turned to Ryan.

"That is your call Daniel," he said, "and maybe all of our necks depend on it. Was that kid lyin', or was she mistaken?" Daniel pondered for a second or two, well aware of the importance of his answer.

"No, Joe," he said. "By the best I can judge, she was tellin' the truth." He paused briefly, as a further thought came to him. "There's one other thing we maybe need to think about," he said. "It's possible that the Morris's back there saw the signs, or overheard what we were doin', and have sent or took word to the Yankees." At that Ballard gave a half-cough, half-chuckle.

"Nope," he said. "They won't do that." The other three looked at him.

"Ya might not o' noticed in all o' the fuss around here, that you're a musket short in yore ambush Joe. I left Luke Petersen back up there at the Morris place. He's still up there with the whole crowd o' them collected in their parlour.

They've been there since we knocked on their door, jest as you boys were movin' out. Luke's keepin' them all company, fer the time bein', with one o' the two pistols I took off o' them in his belt. He'll make sure none o' them goes wanderin' off any place else. Luke's surely ornery enough, 'specially about Yankees, to make sure they'll stay home when they're told." Thompson grinned briefly.

"Jest as well somebody's gotten some horse sense around here," he said. He turned and looked at Jordan, who had begun directing the wagons down the trail beyond the ford approach, and shook his head.

"Mr Ballard!" The voice belonged to Milly Duncan, who had waited over on the other side of the trail while the soldiering exchanges were in progress, but now, with these weightier matters seemingly dealt with, she had seen her chance.

"I was asking earlier if there was another gun, one that I could borrow?" Ballard looked at her.

"You sure you want to go involvin' yoreself in a fight Ma'am?" he inquired. "Wouldn't you be better off stayin' up at the wagons here with yore kin?" The woman furrowed her face in response, with her disapproval clearly indicating her reluctance to let the matter lie.

"When the Yankees come," she said, "the more guns we have on our side the better. Mr Kane said that you might have got guns from the Morris's...?"

Daniel saw Ballard look inquiringly towards Thompson and, on getting a brief shrug in return, he turned deliberately and started away, moving on down to where the last wagon had just halted. He stepped up onto one of the spokes of the nearest of the front wheels and reached inside, rummaging under the tarpaulin at one of the front corners, and retrieved a large Colt revolver from where it had lain. He balanced himself on the wheel and reached down again with his other hand, this time withdrawing a leather bag. He stepped down and brought them both over, looking searchingly at Milly Duncan as he approached.

"You ever shot a pistol before ma'am?" he said, as he showed it to her. She nodded.

"I have fired a gun before," she said sarcastically. "It surely isn't difficult, even for a woman?" Ballard shook his head.

"One like this?" When she remained silent, he smiled grimly at her.

"This here's a Colt Forty Four and it's surely a man's piece. No offence ma'am, but it's got a kick like a mule. Took a fowlin' piece and a shotgun off o' that farmer up thar and that was fair enough, but I'm sure I don't rightly know why he had t' have two o' these buried in no woodpile, next t' his fireplace, cuz ya don't go huntin' possum, or nothin' else fer the pot, with these." He looked back to the woman. "Some o' the cavalry boys, that use this kind o' piece, reckon that the regulation charge o' powder's far too much. They couldn't aim the damned thing, when it had a kick that just about broke yore damned wrist, beggin' yore pardon, ma'am. Lot o' them've cut the powder charge back, by near to a half, and they reckon it's still got plenty o' stoppin' power and nowhere near as bad a kick. It saves damn powder as well," he added. He held the pistol out towards her. "If yo're set on joinin' in this fight, I'll load this one with the smaller charge, so ya'll have a fairer chance o' hittin' somethin', mubbee even whatever yo're aimin' at, and less o' a risk o' damagin' yoreself, when ya fire the thing."

"I'd be obliged to you Mr Ballard," she said.

"One more thing ma'am," Thompson turned to her again. "What does this preacher, this Ezra Farley look like?"

"Him!" Her tone was disdainful. "You can't hardly miss him. He's small and really thin and wrinkled. He has red hair, really bright red, and a red beard, a longer beard, that comes down to here." She pointed to her own collar bone.

"Obliged." Thompson thanked her as she moved away, following Ballard and the Colt. The sergeant turned, shaking his head as he did, towards Ryan and Cooper.

"Like she said, another gun's another gun," he said. "She might even hit somethin' with it and even if she don't, she'll be no worse 'n them." He gestured towards the three teamsters now gathered around Jordan, who was instructing them earnestly about something or another. The sergeant placed his hand on the shoulder of each of his companions in turn.

"Let him play with his wagons," he said, "and she kin do the same with that horse pistol. The rest of us have got work to do." He turned to Cooper.

"Send Silas over," he told him, "and see yore boys're settled." The corporal moved away, calling out for Norton as he went. Daniel saw him emerge from a thicket and start in their direction. Cooper pointed him on and he came up to Thompson.

"Got a job for ya, Silas," the sergeant told him. Norton looked at him without expression. When a sergeant had a job for you, Daniel Ryan reflected, it was not often good news.

"When they git here," Thompson told him, "and they come on. I want you to mark down this Ezra Farley. Lady says he's little and thin and he's got a long, red beard, but he'll likely have some kind o' officer's straps or sech on his coat as well. He is yours Silas and I don't want to hear no more from him." Norton nodded.

"Shootin' an officer's maybe somethin' I could git to enjoy," he muttered, glancing towards Jordan as he turned to depart.

Daniel Ryan moved away also, heading for the place he had selected earlier. He looked briefly back towards the approach before moving into the trees. You would really have to know about this place, he thought, for it was shielded from the trail by the screening trees and the slanting course it took down towards the water. He glanced back to where Milly Duncan still dallied with Ballard on the near side of the trail, and shuddered. Women toting damn great cavalry pistols and all to settle scores with their murdering neighbours, he

391

thought: what a damned mess this war had made of everybody's life around here.

His mind turned to the brief instructions that he had heard Thompson give to Norton. The latter was long since acknowledged as the best shot in the company, with an instinct for hitting what he aimed at. Daniel grimaced slightly. By giving this, "preacher" to Norton, Thompson had, unless the good Lord decided to thwart it in some miraculous way, condemned the man to death, for Norton would kill this Ezra Farley with cold efficiency. Daniel set his face grimly as he pondered on it. The man had it coming for he had committed cold-blooded murder back up there at the Duncan's farm, and in various other counties as well if even a fraction of the stories about him were true, but now it was settled. Whoever else lived or died around this creek ford today, if this Preacher Farley steered his horse down that far approach, along with the rest of his militia renegades, then these trees and the sky and the waters of this valley would be the last things on God's earth that he would ever see.

The sun was higher and the clouds had separated, allowing longer spells of its light, when Jones finally moved, descending first below the crest of the approach and then waving his free arm until, with his signal acknowledged by Cooper, he started back. The men on the near side watched intently as he descended the trail on the far side of the creek, and splashed his way across, seeking out Thompson as he came. The sergeant moved down close to the water's edge to meet him and Jordan appeared with the three teamsters, each of them holding a carbine. The lieutenant waved the three of them off into the trees and brush before stepping over to where Jones now stood with Thompson, drawing his pistol dramatically as he approached. The three of them conversed, just a few yards below where Daniel Ryan waited behind his fallen tree.

"It's them," Jones told them, "headin' this way. They're all mounted and they got two wagons with 'em, but, by the way they're comin' on, they ain't actin' like they're expectin' trouble."

"How many?" Thompson snapped.

"Maybe thirty, hardly more'n that."

"Get some cover," Thompson told him and Daniel saw him move away into the trees and brush. The sergeant turned away also, starting towards where the three teamsters had settled in a group, while Jordan brandished his pistol for the rest of the men to see.

"Let's be ready," he called, "and make your shots count." Thompson looked back briefly, before shifting his eyes back towards where the three teamsters crouched in the brush. Daniel Ryan could just make out the sergeant's words, but Thompson's voice was like that, audible in the middle of a full scale fight.

"We hold our fire," he told the teamsters. "Nobody shoots till I tell 'em. We let 'em cross the creek, all the way over fer the leaders. That way we kin serve it up t' them good with our first volley. The first one's the best one. It's loaded best and it's the only one we'll be able t' aim without a cloud o' damned powder smoke in the way, so we make it count." He glared at the three of them before moving off into the bushes and trees. The near bank was now quiet as all along the creek bank around the ford the men settled in their places. Here and there a musket muzzle protruded gently from the brush, while the attention of the waiting men shifted back towards the crest of the approach on the opposite bank.

They waited and watched, but for a few further minutes there was nothing to see or hear. The woods along the creek told only of the nesting chants of spring birds, their chirps and trills carrying above the steady flow of the creek. The sun came out again, illuminating the valley in bright yellow light, but still there was not a sign of the enemy. Daniel selected a cap and settled it on the musket nipple, before easing the hammer back down from half cocked to wedge it in place. He sighted his musket, estimating the distance to the far bank of the creek. It would be well under a hundred yards, he thought, as he stretched out his hand to adjust the slide on the rear sight of his weapon, point blank range for a rifled musket. But now other thoughts began to intrude, as his mind started to entertain all the things that might still go wrong. What could be keeping the Yankees? Had they been warned at the last minute? Could one of the locals have got wind of the planned ambush and managed to get across to alert the approaching militia? If they had been warned then the whole situation had changed, for they could ride in whichever direction they chose and make their approach on their own terms, with the advantages of surprise restored to them.

Still apprehensive, his eyes detected a movement at the crest on the opposite side. He squinted to look, just as the sunlight faded again and in the less dazzling light, he began to see them, crossing the top of the ridge in succession to begin their descent among the trees towards the ford. Daniel watched them come, noting the manner of their approach. They were arrogant and confident that was for sure, he thought, as he watched more and more of them cross the ridge crest. There was no suggestion of a pause, no thought of halting up there, nor of sending scouts ahead to inspect the ford and its surroundings. Instead they were simply coming on, with an almost casual air about them.

Daniel scrutinised their dress, noting the breeches that many of them wore, dark in colour, and their tan coloured leggings, at odds with their faded blue tunics and the black slouch hats that they wore on their heads, rather than those little kepi caps with which regular Yankee cavalry, as well as infantry back east, were issued' A few of the approaching riders had no uniforms at all, so these, most likely, were their local, more recent recruits. But it was their cocksure manner that struck him most, for they moved with a confidence that spoke of men at ease, as though they thought that nothing could happen around here unless they made it happen. Well, Daniel thought grimly, they were about to get a world of enlightenment about that.

His eyes flickered back up the far bank as he saw the two wagons, drawn by horses rather than mules, appear over the ridge crest and start down the approach, followed by the tail of the enemy column; but the leaders were now approaching the water's edge. Daniel watched them pull successively on their bridles, slowing their horses as they arranged themselves into an order for the crossing. On the near bank there was not a movement and Daniel held his breath as he moved his musket to sight on and track a rider about seven or eight from the front of the column. He scanned along the leading riders. Out in front was an officer, or at least he looked like an officer, for he had a bearing of authority about him as he pulled his horse to one side of the approach, on the last few yards of the far bank. Daniel saw the red beard and he stiffened. So this was Ezra Farley, the man who reckoned that burning crippled boys alive was the work of the God-fearing. Well, he thought, he was about to see some smiting done, if Norton permitted him to live long enough to see it begin, and whether it was God's work or not would make little difference. Almost automatically his right thumb gripped the hammer of the Enfield and he eased it back, feeling and hearing the successive clicks, as inside the weapon's lock the notches on the tumbler engaged the jaw of the sear, these sounds being matched by others as those close by readied their weapons also.

The leading riders were in the water now, urging their horses on as the spray splashed up around them, having slackened only modestly the pace at which they had approached the creek. Daniel squinted along his sights, aiming for his chosen Yankee's chest, noting a thick bushy beard of brown just above his aiming point. His target too was entering the creek shallows and the leaders were almost over, when Thompson's shout came.

"Fire!" The bank all around erupted in smoke and noise, as perhaps fifteen weapons discharged, almost in a single sound. Daniel felt the kick of the Enfield and had a split-second image of the Yankee pitching backwards from his horse, just

395

as everything was smothered in the evil-smelling powder smoke. He grabbed at the first of the cartridges that he had left on the tree trunk, biting the flap and the bullet away in an instant and scrambling the paper cylinder to the musket muzzle to pour the powder in. He worked at his reloading with furious haste, aware that the Yankees would now be heading for cover. As he rammed he recognised the crack of a pistol nearby, which must be either the woman or Jordan, discharging their weapon's successive chambers into the slowly drifting smoke. They couldn't possibly be seeing anything of the dispersing enemy, Daniel thought, and he felt his irritation begin to rise again as he replaced his own cap and brought the Enfield up, seeking another target on the far side as the trees and the scattering jumble of figures slowly swam back into view. He sighted, looking.., looking...., till...., there. He pulled the musket in as he took a brief deliberate aim at a crouching figure at the edge of the water and squeezed the trigger, hearing the loud report of his shot and feeling the recoil again punch into his shoulder. A scattering of shots were now ringing out from either bank, but with nothing like the same concentration of fire as for the first volley.

He was able to see only snatches of the creek area through the drifting smoke as he furiously loaded his own third shot. Down along the water's edge there was something resembling chaos, for the head of the Yankee column had been blasted away by that first volley of musketry, leaving a succession of blue shapes and horses struggling in the creek. Others lay in the water, beginning, in one or two cases, to move and drift on the reddening tide. The far bank also was a confused mess of riders, some attempting to retreat up that narrow congested path, while others still seemed to be trying to descend the slope; or maybe they simply had no idea, in the smoke and noise and confusion all around them, what was the best thing to try to do.

The wagons too had stalled on the approach. Unable to turn, they simply sat there, with their drivers nowhere to be seen, obstructing the trail, about half way between the ridge line and the creek. All the confusion and congestion on the approach was now preventing the escape of many of the horsemen nearer to the creek, for the way was now substantially blocked to those frantically trying to escape the continuing fire from this side. Seeing this, some of them were seeking to steer their horses off the approach trail into the brush. Daniel could see them pushing their way among the bushes and trees, seeking a way to free themselves from this chaos of dead and dying men and screaming horses.

Now was the time to pile it on, he thought, while these damned murdering greenhorns were stunned and confused and getting in each other's way. He completed his reloading and looked again for a target, feeling no thought of remorse or pity as he sought to kill again in this group of trapped, milling men.

He sighted on another rider who had turned his horse from the trail into the brush, but had succeeded only in pushing into an area where the scrub, even with only the buds of its new leaf covering, was almost too thick for even a horse to force a way through. It was almost too easy he thought, as he squeezed the trigger, feeling the renewed thump of the recoil, and glimpsing the figure toppling from the horse into the brush, as the smoke billowed around him. Daniel grasped another cartridge and bit at the flap, looking around to see the men nearest him all biting, pouring, ramming and replacing caps. He glimpsed a couple of muskets coming up to aim and felt a surge of satisfaction as the killing continued. This would teach these murdering renegades, he thought, for the real war had come to them at last. They had tangled today with soldiers, instead of helpless women and cripples and old men and they would not soon forget it, those that lived anyway. Reloading completed, he swung the musket up in search of a further target.

Down at the ford the jumble of milling riders had at last dispersed. A few had got away along the bank of the creek, with one or two even running a gauntlet along the shallows of the water itself, splashing their way to safety away from the killing zone, milking the fragile advantage of presenting a faster moving target to their assailants. Others had finally worked their way back up the approach, threading their way past the hopelessly stalled wagons as Daniel Ryan aimed and fired again. The whole farther bank was rapidly clearing of the enemy, until with hardly anything left to shoot at, Thompson called on them to cease firing. The musketry died only gradually, but eventually the valley began to clear of powder smoke, revealing the extent of the killing.

At the ford itself there were maybe a dozen Yankees lying among the carcasses of several dead horses. Around half of them lay motionless save for the tugging of the current on the ones who lay in the shallows, while others twitched or wriggled. Two of the enemy had been washed downstream, though one of these had now been brought to a halt by a fallen branch, while the other continued to drift down, moving at the whim of the current. Daniel saw the man's body turn lazily over before it moved out of sight behind some thicker scrub on the near bank.

All the way up the far side were the forms of more men and horses. Here and there blue clad figures darted from tree cover to tree cover, struggling their way to the crest and relative safety. Daniel looked to his left on hearing a musket cock, to see Norton taking aim for a final shot. Then the report of the discharge echoed around the valley, sending more smoke drifting along the near bank. Daniel squinted towards the far side, getting a brief sight of a blue shape rolling down the slope for a few yards before coming to a halt, almost invisible in the mixture of new and old grass. Half way up the approach trail the wagons lay where they had stopped, abandoned now by their drivers. One of the horses, harnessed to the leading vehicle, lay in its traces, having been struck by a stray shot, or maybe somebody on this side had failed to deduce that there was no need to kill the teams to prevent these wagons from going anywhere.

The whole scene was a tangle of death and destruction and Daniel Ryan wondered inwardly if the carnage would have been significantly less if the southerners had not known of these men's recent deeds. Thompson and Cooper were already down at the water's edge and Daniel Ryan, having reloaded once more, moved to join them, seeing Ballard also on his way. Thompson was signalling to the others to move forward, and all along the sloping approach men emerged from cover and started forward to the ford. Daniel saw that Petersen was now among them, returned from the Morris Farm, but then Luke was one of those who could smell a fight. As he moved towards the creek, Daniel heard Jordan's voice. He looked downstream to see him heading for Thompson, calling to the sergeant as he went.

"Wait! Get them back here! Now's the time to get moving, while they're on the run." Thompson turned to face him as he arrived at the shallows.

"First we better clear 'em off that ridge," he said, a shade indulgently, by Daniel Ryan's reckoning, "else they could settle up there and once they git organised, they'll start pickin' us off, while we're movin' out." Jordan stopped at the water's edge and let his arm, still holding the pistol, drop to his side. Around him, the southern line went splashing on over and on reaching the far side they began moving up the bank, diverting this way or that as they reached the thicker patches of scrub and trees.

Some altered their course to reach fallen Yankees, pausing to relieve them of anything of value. A couple of them stopped around the wagons, until Thompson angrily shouted and waved them on. Daniel Ryan pushed up near to the approach, passing the body of a thin man with a long red beard who lay on his back, his head tilted slightly to the right and his mouth wide open. There were several wounds on him, but the one that most likely counted was the neat hole to the left side of his forehead, almost certainly Norton's shot, from which a small trickle of dark blood oozed down into his right eye before continuing its way down the lean features of his face to drip onto the dirt of the trail. Daniel eyed him momentarily before moving on up the slope. This preacher's ministry was over and now there would be the matter of accounting to his maker for his own actions.

Daniel diverted his path several times to inspect more of the dead, seeking shoes first and foremost, but to his disappointment all the fallen Yankees that he scrutinised were wearing boots, utterly impractical for infantrymen. He heard Thompson call irritably to them to adopt skirmish order as they approached the crest, and they paired off, moving alternately save for the three teamsters who kept on moving independently. They were calling to each other almost like schoolboys as they sought further pickings, having seemingly taken to this idea of killing and plundering Yankees. Daniel halted near the top and allowed Ballard to pass on, but there was no sign of life or activity along the crest. He saw his friend pause and he began to move, coming up on his right to gaze through the last of the trees at an empty pasture beyond.

"Looks like we whipped 'em good," Ballard said, and he grinned at Daniel. "Servin' it up to scum like that does ya good don't it?" Daniel nodded.

"Be better if they had real shoes," he said.

Thompson did not delay. Leaving Kane and Thorne at the top to keep watch, he promptly started the others back down towards the creek. On the far bank they saw a small group of blue figures moving around among their fallen, watched over, at some distance, by Jordan and Jones.

"Hell," Ballard growled, "prisoners is the last damned thing that we need." Thompson had re-crossed the creek just behind the others, who now gathered on his approach. Jordan stood slightly further up the bank and he waved his pistol towards the captured Yankees.

"We have no time for tending to wounded, so you will see to that yourselves," he called out to them.

Further up on the approach Daniel Ryan saw the figure of the woman, Milly Duncan. He had not seen her since before the fight had begun. She looked dishevelled with her face

400

streaked on one side by powder smoke as she started to descend towards the group of Yankee wounded who had been collected on the near side of the creek. She still carried the pistol, Daniel noticed, though how much she had actually used it in the fight he did not know, but she clutched it in to the side of her skirt as she picked her way down the approach. Daniel had just passed her as he followed Ballard on up towards the trail, when he heard her call out.

"Nathan! Nathan Berry!" Daniel looked around, as one of the Yankee walking wounded turned on her call. He looked at her.

"Milly!" he returned, "I'm sorry about Ned. I swear I never knew he was still inside, not till it was too late..."

"Where in the name of God did you think he was!" she screamed, while all along the bank of the creek men turned and looked, alerted by her voice.

"You know he hardly left his bed this last year and a half." Still, she moved towards him until he seemed to notice the pistol that she held down by her side. He started back as she raised the weapon and pointed it straight at his face.

"Murdering filth!" She screamed the words from only a few feet away from him, as she squeezed the trigger of the Colt. The discharge cracked its distinctive tone, which echoed along the valley, causing a spray of blood, and darker things also to shoot from the back of Berry's head as he pitched violently backwards, from the impact of the ball, then to splash into the shallow water at the edge of the creek. Milly Duncan turned and looked around at the watching soldiers with a wild expression still on her face.

"Will somebody git that damned piece off a' her," Daniel heard Thompson shout. He started towards her, but she began to lift the pistol again, swaying the barrel towards the remaining Yankees she stepped away from Daniel, only to lurch straight into the arms of Jones who had promptly slung his musket on its strap in order to free his hands. He grasped her waist with one hand and her pistol hand with the other, jerking her away with her own momentum helping in prising

401

the weapon from her fingers. He tossed the pistol to Ryan and then deftly moved his hand around her other side, supporting her there in something between a grapple and a hug.

"Wouldn't trouble me none if she shot 'em all" he said, as he tightened his grip.

"He knew!" Milly Duncan screamed the words into his face as she struggled in his grip. She sobbed between breaths as she continued to speak.

"To all of those other Yankees, Ned was nothin', just a reb' cripple, who they wouldn't trouble themselves to save, but Berry stood there and watched, when he knew he was in there, and Wendell knew as well. They'd been neighbours, raised and schooled together, and still they let him burn. God damn them forever, if I could find that Simon Wendell I'd finish him as well." She screamed the final words at the top of her voice, then fell silent. Jones still gripped her, and as she slumped down a little in his arms, he relaxed his hold slightly and spoke to her.

"Don't you worry about it any, ma'am," he said. "You surely finished off that other damned renegade good enough."

Daniel carried the warm pistol by its barrel, up to where Ballard stood and handed it to him.

"Maybe she shouldn't ever have gotten her hands on it," he said, "that shot could've ended up anywhere after it went through that Yankee." The corporal shrugged as he flicked open the cover on the right side of the weapon, revealing the rear of the revolving chamber. He spun it slowly with his fingers, peering at the cap at the base of each chamber as it turned.

"Whad'ya know," he said softly. "That there shot were the only one she fired." He looked at Daniel Ryan. "So once she got a hold o' this piece she jest bided her time," he said, "waitin' fer a chance at any o' them boys that she knew."

"Nobody's off collectin' any flowers for the one she got," Daniel observed drily.

"But a woman," Ballard said. He shook his head, "gives ya a creepy feelin', don't it?"

402

They had quickly finished their preparing and had gotten moving again. The other Duncan woman had spent a brief time washing and dressing a wound in Vallance's upper arm, but with him the only casualty, Daniel Ryan pondered on how cheap and complete their success had been. The enemy had been seriously beaten, and dispossessed of their supplies and plunder, almost without loss. Where they would go from here was anybody's guess, though Ryan considered it unlikely that they would wish to tangle again with the southern detail.

On Jordan's orders, the two Yankee wagons had been retrieved from the opposite approach, with the dead horse cut loose from its harness. They had been manoeuvred down the last of the approach, across the ford and up onto the trail. Three further horses had been rounded up, and the most docile looking one of these had been harnessed to replace the dead one, again on Jordan's order. Thompson had shaken his head.

"He should know," he muttered to Cooper, Ballard and Ryan, "or his damned drivers should be able to tell him, that saddle horses're too skittish to pull in a team." Daniel looked at the animal which seemed a placid enough creature as it waited in its place, but time could prove it different, as Thompson had said.

"What does he know," Ballard had added. "He ain't no more of a stock man than he is a soldier. He's a damned book keeper and that's as far as he goes."

"Let him do what he damn well pleases," the sergeant had finally pronounced, "I ain't wet-nursin' him no more."

The Yankee prisoners were left behind, along with their wounded, and Thompson, in spite of his pronouncement, had ordered them relieved of their boots, socks, pants and belts, and spoke briefly to them before departing.

"If I smell a hide or a hair o' you," he growled at them, "what she did to that other critter will be nothin' to what I'll do to you. Yo're alive by that much," he gestured with his finger and thumb about a half inch apart and said nothing more.

"I'd shoot 'em now and be done with it," Ballard told him loudly, as he passed on up the approach, "or let the lady loose on 'em."

"Whether they git a bullet or not's up to them," the sergeant had rasped, half in Ballard's direction and half towards the group of Yankees. He had then waved to Kane and Thorne to return, and they watched them descend the approach and wade the creek. There was no sign of the militia that had got away, but while that might mean they had made off in confusion, the chance remained that they could be heading downstream, looking for a chance of revenge.

Up on the trail Jordan had retrieved his horse and as the escort positioned themselves in their places, the convoy lumbered finally into motion, with Milly Duncan, having rejoined the others of her family, seated in one of the vehicles, staring stolidly ahead. Edwin Jones, whose sawmill job at Eden Station had included wagon driving, had taken the reins of one of the captured vehicles, while Silas Norton was seated on the driver's bench of the other, following down the trail after the three commissary vehicles and their mule teams. The remainder of the escort spaced themselves out along the column as before, with those at the rear of each of the captured vehicles craning their necks to inspect their contents.

With the roads drier, they made better time than on their previous return journeys, arriving within an hour at the Berry farm. As they approached, Daniel wondered what might transpire here, since this family, more than any other, had been involved with the militia raids and with their return to the valley of Little Beaver Creek. It was possible also that the Yankee survivors had circled around and gotten here first. Jordan had ordered a scouting party forward while the rest of the detail waited. Cooper, with Kane, White and Petersen in company, had trodden warily forward, to poke around the various buildings, until having inspected the place and found it deserted, they had signalled the wagons and escort forward. As the convoy trundled past, Daniel Ryan looked towards the door of the house which now stood open, as though confirming the absence of the family who had lived here, Yankees maybe, but now chased from their home also by the intrusion of war.

"Reckon we'll burn it," Petersen called, as he waited near the house, "like their damn Yankee friends did up the valley."

"And they paid fer it," Thompson called in reply from his place beside the front wagon. Petersen grinned before turning and making for the barn, disappearing briefly inside once more before re-appearing and jogging across to the house, carrying a burning handful of straw.

"Will ya leave it Luke," Cooper growled at him, as he disappeared into the house. Within seconds he re-emerged and started along the trail in the wake of the wagons, while, as Daniel continued to look, thin wisps of smoke began to drift from the open door of the farm and the barn. Petersen saw him watching and looked back also.

"What a shame," he sneered. "Looks like they got a fire."

The vehicles and their escort drew steadily away, as Daniel switched his gaze to the hunched figures of the two women in their wagon just ahead of where he walked, seeing not so much as a sideways look from them. He glanced rearwards as Petersen resumed his place. Shaking his head he returned his gaze finally to the front. What a damned shambles this whole neighbourhood was in now, he thought, divided by the politics of the war: their differences had grown into informing on each other, with the consequences following on from that. Some of them, as a result, had now taken to killing each other, and now a succession of families had been burned out. His mind turned to the little girl who had given him the warning: Harriet Morris, the child who had tried to spare her friend and her family, but whose warning had simply led to more killing, including more of her own neighbours. To Daniel Ryan it was a miserable chapter of tragedy, suffering and hatred, and it now engulfed this valley.

405

But there was one more step in the whole dismal sequence of events, for if the rumours and stories that had swept the camps before their departure were to be believed, their own divisions would soon be gone from here.

It had all derived from that. The Yankees along this trail had surely gotten wind of it before it had even been ordered, and knowing that the southern occupation of this region was indeed, as one of them had said, "on borrowed time," the chain of events here had begun. At the end of it all, the army would indeed be going, and having now suffered a share of destruction and death, this valley would be left to whatever Yankees chose to come and occupy it. Safety for families like the Duncans and the Mellors, the latter maybe still clinging on somewhere along Little Beaver Creek, even though their farm lay in ashes, might well be a fleeting and temporary thing. As for the increasing numbers of refugee families like them, their fate would likely be to be thrown on the generosity of whatever relations they had further to the west, or at worst, to be an additional burden for one of the relief committees, organised for the most part by churches in the various counties. Either way, their time on that farm in the Little Beaver Valley was almost certainly over. They, along with the Mellors, and to some extent at least, the Berrys, were now dispossessed and homeless, a state in which all too many people had now finished up, as the war had intruded into their neighbourhoods and their lives.

Chapter 18 A Footprint of Blood

Those final days of March decided the matter, for by the time that the foraging detail returned to the Company B camp, the news was already going around that locomotives and rolling stock were being assembled on the Virginia and Tennessee Railroad. This was an indicator in itself, but what virtually put the lid on the whole matter was the news that almost all would be coming up empty. Their purpose therefore, could be none other than to transport the First Corps divisions back where they had come from. There would be no reinforcements for an offensive out here, west of the mountains up into Kentucky. Instead, this region would be left to a tiny local force, for the Army of Tennessee formations had also been recalled. Longstreet's infantry and artillery would be going back east by way of Bristol and Charlottesville, journeying on to Gordonsville to the south of Culpeper.

This would leave them just a couple of short marches from where the rest of the Army of Northern Virginia remained in winter quarters on their now familiar station, south of the Rappahannock and Rapidan Rivers, awaiting the coming onslaught of the enemy. This would begin once the spring warmth had dried the roads sufficiently to allow the colossal convoys of wagons and guns, necessary for any army to move, but especially one with the prodigious amounts of supplies and equipment that the Army of the Potomac possessed. As for the Ogeechee Volunteers, together with the rest of their brigade they would break camp the next day, the start of the month, burning what they could not carry on the fires that simultaneously fried their rations for the succeeding days. The march would be to the railroad, most likely at Greeneville, where they would meet the trains that would take them east once more.

In the chill of that Saturday evening the men of Company B gathered round their fires at the entrance to their shelters for the final time. A gusty wind blew around the camp, sending periodic showers of sparks, from the various fires sweeping around the groups of sitting or lounging men. Thompson, now the First Sergeant of the company, on the same acting basis as that by which Jeffers held the Sergeant Major's post, was initially absent from Ryan's mess, being briefed along with the other sergeants, by Boyce, presumably on details of the move. The talk among the remaining four was largely on the campaign that had begun with such high hopes, but which was now ending with something that resembled another inglorious skedaddle back to where they had come from. Though the circumstances of their going were far from auspicious, according to the comments that were going around the camp, it was pretty clear that a return to Virginia met with near to universal approval around the company. A common saying among the infantry was that all eastern Tennessee lacked of being hell was a roof over it, and this fairly reflected the views of the mess. Having vented their opinions once again, there was a silence around the fire, which was prompting Daniel Ryan into thinking of his blankets. Then Kane spoke again.

"Did he or didn't he do fer them, Otis?" Ryan's ears pricked up at the words, for the subject had evidently changed, though he was unsure of what was now being talked about. Ballard looked across at Kane initially, before nodding briefly.

"Most likely he did," he said quietly. With the corporal's reply, the beginnings of understanding slowly began to dawn on Daniel Ryan and he too turned to gaze at him, but there was a further pause before Ballard continued.

"Seems like he never jest left 'em to it," he said. "I told him to wait, till he heard the sound o' firin', or till two hours after sun up, whichever came first. Mubbee Luke was the wrong man to leave in charge of a family o' Yankees, but there weren't too many choices about that."

"Does Joe know?" Jones asked. Ballard nodded again.

"He knows as much as you or me," he rapped abruptly, "but what we know ain't the same as what we maybe think." Daniel heard him emphasise the final word.

"But, if it's true, it's plain God-damned murder," Kane hissed, aware that other fires were within easy earshot. "It makes us no better'n them damn Yankees that we bushwhacked up there at the creek."

"Do you know what he did Isaac, like really know?" The question came from Thompson, who had returned unnoticed, and now the heads of all of them turned to face him. The First Sergeant stepped closer to the fire and looked around them all before settling to sit and allowing some time to pass before he spoke again.

"If you know," he eventually continued, "then speak up, but, if you do know then that makes you a helluva lot smarter 'n the rest of us around here, on account o' the fact that there weren't nobody else around to see what happened up there on that farm." He looked at Kane and then on around the others of the group once again, and seeing that there was no reaction to his words, he shrugged and stretched his hands out towards the flames as though to warm them.

"I took that pistol off o' him," he eventually went on. "It had just one load left, so he likely fired five and that don't take account o' whether he fired his musket as well. When I asked him what he'd been shootin' at, he said he'd lamed the Yankee and then killed his horse afore he left the farm, so there weren't no way, either ridin' or walkin', that he could go off and warn them militia boys. He said the other three loads were fired at the Yankees at the creek." Daniel Ryan looked around his companions, clear at last, about it all.

"I never saw no horse on that there farm," Kane growled. "If they had one, it was pretty well hid." Thompson shrugged.

"Lamed?" Daniel Ryan said quietly. Thompson turned towards him.

"Luke says he shot the Yankee in the foot," he said. Daniel shook his head, while from the other side of the fire it was Jones who spoke.

"Reckon a man's gut's a helluva sight easier target than his foot," he said quietly, "'specially with a damn great horse pistol like he had."

"Ain't it the damn truth," Kane added. "Maybe I'm too damned suspicious fer my own good," he went on, "but I don't see him as the kinda man who goes around shootin' no Yankees, farmers or not, in the foot." Daniel Ryan felt a shudder of guilt and regret wash over him as the enormity of this latest dismal episode fixed itself in his mind. As if the firing of the Berry farm were not enough, there was now this. If five shots had been fired up on the Morris farm, those were enough to have dispatched not just the man, but the rest of his family as well.

"That family had kids," he eventually said, "and if one o' them hadn't spoke up, on account o' the fact that she kept some idea of friendship and sympathy, for her friend and her kin, alive in her mind, them militia could easy have caught us on the trail and cut us down." He shook his head. "So he's, we've, most likely gone and killed her family, and maybe not even stopped there." Nobody spoke for a few further moments, and as the seconds passed Daniel Ryan found himself wondering if this was partly because nobody really wanted to talk about the fact that, because however much they might disapprove of it, they were all implicated in Petersen's suspected brutality.

At length Thompson turned towards Daniel Ryan.

"Sometimes you sound like John used to. Yankees or not, you wouldn't a' shot them folks and I reckon I wouldn't neither. I don't reckon any o' us around this fire would a' done somethin' like that, but that don't mean that everybody in this camp thinks like that. This war ain't how we want it," he told him. "We all know that only too well by now. The war's what it is, and what it's become, and that's what we're all stuck with. We've seen it happen along the way since we joined up. A lot o' the boys, maybe all of us, started off thinkin' that lickin' the Yankees would be an easy enough thing, but now we know it ain't. When they've come

410

plunderin' and killin', like they did to that family back there, there's bin plenty around here that reckoned the thing to do was to serve the same thing up to them, or maybe even worse. Maybe some of us have preferred not to admit it to ourselves. This whole damned struggle's a more worthwhile thing to go on spendin' yore time and sweat and blood on if ya kin convince yoreself that somehow we're in the right. We like t' think we're stayin' kinda decent about it all, with the idea o' the war bein' jest between fightin' men on each side, but, too many times it's turned out a damn sight worse'n that. We git the war the way it comes, not how we want it, and we got to live with that, cuz, whether we like it or not, we're all a part of why it's turnin' out the way it is."

"But if he killed him.... them," Ryan snapped, as he looked over his shoulder in the flickering light of the fires, across the camp towards the fire on the far side, where he knew that Petersen sat with the others of his mess.

"Weren't nobody saw what he did," Ballard said. "Ain't nobody kin say he did this or did that, when nobody but him was there. I left him up there and maybe that was my mistake. I did it cuz I reckoned he was the best one to put a skeer on them Yankees, so's they wouldn't want to think about goin' off t' warn their militia friends. No matter what we think he might o' done, and most likely did do, there ain't no proof. Anyways, even if he did do it, all he was doin' was gittin' even with the same damn Yankee that sent them militia back up to the Duncan place to do their own killin'." There was silence around the fire, until at length, the five of them began to move, signifying that the conversation was at an end. They stretched out the thin remains of the blankets that they still possessed to warm and air at the fire, ready for turning in, as a further chilly gust of wind blew through, making the flames of the fires all around the camp whip this way and that, with a hint of more rain on it for good measure.

In his own blanket shortly after, Daniel Ryan found himself unable to sleep, as his mind wrestled with this latest revelation. As if it had not been enough for the militia to go

411

marauding up that trail, doing their own killing and burning, their own expeditions there had added yet another episode of murder, burning and tragedy to the lives of the people who remained there. As far as the man Morris was concerned, Daniel had little sympathy for him. He had turned the militia on his neighbours, likely knowing what that meant, but now, as a result of it being Petersen who had been left behind to prevent them warning the militia, that little girl had ended up fatherless or likely even worse, for if Petersen could lie about "laming" her father, rather than killing him, who could say where those other pistol loads had gone? His mind continued to turn over the doleful episode, while the wind still gusted around the camp, making the wooden boards of the shelter roof rattle and the frame creak and move slightly. It seemed that nothing good had come from any of this chapter, for it was yet another example of the long established fact that the armies seemed to spell misery and trouble wherever they arrived.

They had come out here to save this final part of the state of Tennessee from Yankee occupation, with all that that entailed, yet now they were leaving the place, and leaving it to the enemy. As if that were not bad enough for their own people in this divided region, the presence of Longstreet's men through the autumn and the miserable winter, had simply brought more suffering and death. Among the local people it had bred further grudges, and from those grudges would grow a desire for revenge, and from revenge would come still more grudges and feuds, and these would likely smoulder on endlessly, long after the departure of the soldiers, likely disfiguring this region for years to come. All in all, he thought, the sooner they were out of Tennessee the better, yet all that that would achieve would be their own departure from the ugly continuation of violence and death. If the war out here looked much blacker now than it had at the end of the previous summer, its cost to the people who lived in these counties where the armies had grappled had been worse, for it had set in motion this grave and tragic set of events, dividing

412

neighbours and spreading its tide of misery and loss ever wider, blighting the lives of these people probably for years to come.

The march began at sunrise and the regiment left its camps for the final time, promptly taking the trail that led down to join the main road to the railroad. They marched at ease, with the barefoot men, as usual, using the grass verges along the sides of the trail, and as the march proceeded, Daniel Ryan noticed that there were still bloody footprints from some at least of the shoeless men, on the trampled, remains of dead grass where the new growth had only just begun. If he could not replace his own shoes fairly soon, he thought grimly, he would soon be joining them.

They joined a road that was already crowded with soldiers and vehicles, though from the time that they joined it they could see that the army was sharing it with still more refugees. Family after family picked their way among the soldiers and wagons, having left their unseen homes to the enemy, carrying only as much of their belongings as could be loaded on a cart or a barrow, for few of them had animals to haul anything larger. Children walked the muddy road together with the old men and the women of their families. The smaller of them clutched at the hand of a mother or other older relative, as they gazed with staring frightened eyes at the great column of soldiers with whom they shared the road, perhaps vaguely aware that these men were part of the reason why their lives had been turned upside down. Along the column, some men reached into haversacks for parts of their ration, passing fragments of bread or cooked bacon across to the families as they passed. Other soldiers however, looked away, as though not wanting to rest their eyes on some of these grimmer results of their own divisive presence, or ponder yet again on the ill-fated campaign that had brought them here.

As the rail line drew closer the road grew steadily more congested. Waiting guns and wagons obstructed the way,

413

forcing the infantry and the dispossessed families to form into single files on either side of the road in order to pass. Delays were increasingly encountered, with the column halted under an again clouding sky, for whatever obstruction had blocked the way to be cleared. As the soldiers waited, the groups of displaced people continued to pass, with yet more groups of them joining the procession on the road from the side lanes and trails, till the muddy thoroughfare was nearly choked with the groups of refugees gradually forming an ever more substantial proportion of those using it.

When, in the later morning they finally reached the railroad, they found that the whole area along the line was crowded, predictably with soldiers, but the various military units who had assembled there for trains were far from having the place to themselves. Tents and rudimentary shelters were also to be seen, set up in clumps of dirty white canvas, where numbers of the refugees had also halted and settled themselves, some of them at least because they were likely aware there was nowhere else that they could go that would be safer or more secure than here.

A few helpers moved among the groups, carrying food and water around the makeshift camps as well as around the junction itself, but as Daniel Ryan took in the extent of these, he acknowledged that he was seeing here in this part of Hawkins County the manifestation of the consequence of the war that had troubled his attempts to sleep the previous night. These people would not starve today, the helpers would likely be able to see to that, but all that this trickle of help was doing in reality, was postponing the day when hunger and disease might well claim them. Seeing their numbers and the scant amount of sustenance that was here for them, Daniel recognised that the survival of many of these people, particularly the weaker ones, might well amount to a grim race between the early harvests of the coming summer and the ravages of hunger and disease.

The Ogeechee Volunteers endured yet another wait in the passing showers of a spring day that stayed resolutely chilly and changeable, while trains came and went, much as they had done back in September in Virginia. When, in the late afternoon, the men were shepherded across to the track and onto the latest line of just-arrived cars, they cheered loudly and spontaneously as most of their predecessors had, venting at least some of the frustration they felt about their time out here. Loaded and waiting, the men had begun to sing, while the families camped along either side of the railroad had looked on with expressions of sullen bewilderment on many of their faces as the strains of, "Carry me back to Old Virginny," moved from car to car. The singing had persisted until the locomotive whistle screeched mournfully, and the train finally jerked and wheezed into motion, whereupon the song finally gave way to a renewed bout of cheers and whistles.

"Tennessee," Daniel Ryan thought, as the car on which he had settled began to gather a degree of momentum. It moved past and then away from the shelters of the refugees, whose pale faces turned towards the departing train gazing without reaction at the cheering soldiers on the sequence of slowly passing cars that moved within feet of the nearest of them. The faces of Winder, Hale, Jenkins and Dellings, and even Jessop, swam into Ryan's mind, but he knew that they were just the closest, the most familiar, of the many who had paid with their lives for this expedition which was now at an end. As for east Tennessee, these farmers were welcome to it, but the trouble about it all was that what had gone on here over the previous months had changed things, and likely those changes would be lasting and profound.

The armies had left their footprint on this land as they had in Virginia and plenty of other places also, and that footprint, like those of the barefooted soldiers on the grass back up the trail, was of blood. Whatever hard-scrabbled parcels of land that these mountain folk had owned or farmed or made their homes on around here previously, were now lost to them.

415

Whatever lives these people had managed to fashion for themselves in these harsh highlands had gone also, and having dispossessed and impoverished them, the war was now leaving them to their destitution and loss. Its soldiers and its struggles were moving on, but they were far from finished. Spring was already here and within weeks or maybe even days, wherever the armies next chose to concentrate their strength, they would begin to manoeuvre once more, commencing the next inevitable chapter of the destruction that continued to range unchecked across this land.

Epilogue

The men eventually set up their camps around Mechanicsburg at the end of the third week of a changeable April, not far from the same railroad town of Gordonsville to the south west of Orange Courthouse, from which they had started out the previous fall. They arrived after a stop and go journey across the mountains, to find that rations of bacon and corn, in adequate quantities compared to much of their time in Tennessee, began to arrive almost immediately. On only their second day in camp, there came a further boon. Mail, seemingly redirected from Tennessee, also arrived. This included a letter for Daniel Ryan, which he recognised from the handwriting as being from Martha Bennett. He returned to the mess fire and settled there, before tearing it open. It would likely be the latest chapter of routine Eden Station news, he thought, for he had exchanged letters with Martha periodically since he had left with the regiment.

He started to read, noticing immediately that the address was not the familiar one in Eden Station, but rather a more formal street, with a number, in Savannah. Daniel turned his attention rapidly to the text, learning from Martha's opening sentences, that Hal, her husband, had died. He stopped reading, as a wave of regret washed through him. Of all people, Hal Bennett had been the one who had helped him to find something of a life after first arriving in Georgia. He had extended to him the opportunity to settle in Georgia, giving him a job and a place to stay in Eden Station. In many ways the Bennetts had behaved like a family towards him, treating him more like a member of their household than just an employee. Daniel shook his head slowly before returning to the letter, becoming aware, as he pondered this news, that Hal's death maybe represented a further milestone in his separation from the little Bryan County town that he had called home for more than two years.

417

Since leaving Eden Station with the Ogeechee Volunteers two years ago this very month, his contacts and ties with the town had slowly but steadily withered away. It was well over a year since he had last been in the place and that visit, rather than being the exercise of any sort of choice, had been as part of a regimental detail in search of winter provisions. As for the prospect of any return to Bryan County after the war, there had always been such an option of resuming life in the employ of the Bennetts. Hal had made the offer prior to Daniel's original departure, and had referred again to it last winter when he had briefly returned. But Daniel's preferred notion of a life after the army, had not lain back in Georgia. Until last summer it had consisted of an agreement, albeit a fairly vague one, with John Fitzpatrick, to seek to settle elsewhere, away in the great vacant spaces far to the west, but how and where had never been decided. The army and the war had come first, but with victory in that war proving increasingly illusive, specific plans to do anything after the struggle had ended had seemed a distant notion.

What the arrival of this letter was doing was finally closing the door on any lingering option of returning to Bryan County, and for a brief interval as he fingered the pages, Daniel let his mind dwell on this, for it marked the ending of what had been his remaining prospect, as the idea of striking out westwards had ended with Fitzpatrick's death at Gettysburg last summer. Both of his realistic options had now gone, and as he confronted this, a brief feeling of unease about his future entered his mind, but he promptly stifled that train of thought in the way that he often put unwelcome thoughts aside. He would not think about it now. There was no sign of the war ending any time soon, and thus what he did after it had done so, remained a matter for the future, and therefore something of lesser relevance now. For the meantime at least the army and the friends that he had made and now relied upon, those who had survived, were his future as well as his present.

He had known that Hal had been ailing. Even on his last visit, more than a year previously, the physical difference had been striking, but somehow he had not thought of it in terms of death. Soldiers died, often in dismaying numbers and circumstances, but somehow, especially since he remained absent from Eden Station, there had been a kind of assumption that life there would be going on much as it had before, but here was written confirmation that it had not. He returned to the letter, finding it confirmed that Martha Bennett had now left the town, giving up Hal's hardware store which she could never realistically have managed on her own. She had gone to live with her daughter, Susannah, and her husband, in Savannah. She was well and he should not worry. Hal's death had in many ways, been a mercy, she said, for he had continued to decline and in his final weeks had been unable to leave his bed. She hoped that Daniel remained well, and if he wanted to write, he should send his letters to her new Savannah address. He reached the end of the letter and sat on for a further few moments, before folding the pages and pushing them into the little leather wallet that he used for personal items. He would see about replying later, when he had had a chance to think some more about it all. For the moment he had no words that seemed adequate for the passing of the old man, who had been a true friend to him when he had really needed one. But for the foreseeable future, life was the army, which had a habit of giving him plenty to do and would no doubt continue to do so, especially when the now imminent campaigning season got under way.

Those Yankees in Virginia, so the now more plentiful newspapers were saying, had spent this winter the same way that they had spent the previous one. They had re-organised and strengthened and re-supplied, making ready for the spring and summer struggles, even though all that their organising and reinforcing in the previous years had resulted in was, at best, in stalemate. This was maybe the measure of the southern army's achievement however, for stalemate meant

419

that each year the larger and infinitely better supplied Yankee force had been defeated and frustrated, and as a result, it was little nearer now to reaching its objective than it had been in the opening months of the struggle.

This time however, the Yankee papers seemed to think that things might be different. This time the entire Yankee host, east and west, would be under the command of one man, and that man would be that same western general whose name had kept cropping up, as this war had dragged on. The man who had most recently supervised the final discomfiture of Braxton Bragg out at Chattanooga. "Sam" Grant seemed to be regarded by the enemy as their victory talisman. Newspapers, even Yankee newspapers, had been hard to come by up in the mountainous country of east Tennessee, but even though men had seen little or nothing of it in print, the news, the previous month, had still spread quickly, for Grant had been summoned to Washington to be promoted and placed in command of all of the Yankee armies. The soldiers of Company B had remained unmoved, preferring to do what soldiers tended to, taking each day and event as it came. They would wait and see, regarding such news from so far away, rather than jumping to any kind of conclusions.

Now, however, they were back in Virginia and not only were the papers more plentiful, but the returned troops once again had a direct stake in whatever the new enemy general did, and by the press reports that they had seen, he seemed intent on basing himself here in Virginia to spend his time with the Yankee Army of the Potomac, therefore confronting directly the Army of Northern Virginia, as though he recognised it as his principal enemy. As for Grant himself, the view was common among Longstreet's men, that out in the west against a divided Confederate command, he had maybe done well enough, but in Virginia things had always been different, for there was no trend of Union success in Virginia, as the men never tired of reminding each other. The campaigning would resume soon enough, and when it did, they would all see how the new man fared when he faced

Robert E. Lee and his re-assembled veterans of the Army of Northern Virginia.

The time for this confrontation was now close, for April had reached its third week and their journey from Tennessee had been far from smooth. The units of the First Corps had first journeyed to Bristol, on the Tennessee Virginia border, where they had remained in hastily established camps for nearly two weeks before moving on into Virginia at the end of the first week of April. Then they had been further delayed around Charlottesville, to guard against a reported thrust by the reorganised Yankees up the Shenandoah Valley. When that threat failed to materialise, they had been moved on here to Gordonsville, but had not gone all the way east to rejoin the rest of the army below the Rapidan River. Rumours now spoke of a smaller enemy thrust, a manoeuvre east of the Blue Ridge around the upper reaches of the Rappahannock River, to gain the flank of the Army of Northern Virginia. This would be a more limited offensive than the one spoken of at Charlottesville, but one still capable of dislodging Lee's troops from their positions further down the river. "Old Pete's" returned divisions were therefore being stationed here, a few marches to the west of the other corps: close enough to be able to promptly support the army, but far enough west to meet or discourage such a flanking development.

The weather remained cold and the spring late in coming, as the troops waited in their camps, back at last on familiar ground, ruminating on the latest news of officer appointments in their own formations. The divisional promotion had been confirmed for Joe Kershaw, a competent officer, loved by most of his South Carolinians, and sufficiently appreciated by those of the other three brigades for them to welcome him as the divisional commander, for he was seen as a soldier's general. Randolph had also been confirmed in command of the Ogeechee Volunteers, and for the most part, the men seemed content with him as commander. Though seen as being far from perfect, he was sufficiently experienced, and maybe able to satisfy the expectations of his men in terms of battlefield leadership. That, above all, was the important thing, for incompetent leadership in a fight was a thing that was likely to be fatal for soldiers. In addition, as far as Company B was concerned, Randolph harboured no notion of favouritism for Jefferson Gilby, which the men saw as a significant advantage. As for Gilby, he remained on the roll of Company B, wearing the same supercilious expression habitually on his features and maintaining the same vindictive attitude towards his men. Held in check by Boyce, he nevertheless remained a threat, and the enlisted men knew that they could never completely lower their guard while he remained as a company officer.

That company had been joined by a further sprinkling of men, but these were seasoned veterans rather than further conscripts, for in response to the regiment's generally reduced numbers, the disbandment of yet another company had been authorised. The officers and men of Company E were therefore dispersed among the four companies that remained, marking the end of the regiment's Tennessee campaign in the same way as the disbandment of Company F had marked its beginning. The main further change had been the elevation of Otis Ballard to the rank of sergeant. With Morsby still absent, and Jeffers and Thompson also confirmed in their places, the company required a further sergeant and Ballard, likely much to Gilby's disapproval, had been chosen for the vacant place, confirming that Boyce at least must have a high enough opinion of the corporal. He inherited Thompson's section, which included the members of his own mess, who ribbed him, though more circumspectly than they had, on his being promoted to corporal, the previous year. Sergeants, after all, were men of some importance in the army.

Perhaps surprisingly, a new surgeon had arrived for the regiment. Oliver Gilmore had joined on their arrival at Gordonsville and the most notable feature about him, as a first impression at least, was his age. His hair, what remained of it, was snow white and his weather beaten face had more wrinkles than a prune, at least that was Ballard's observation, for promotion had done nothing to reform his liking for sarcasm. He was said to be in his sixties, an age, Daniel Ryan reckoned, when he should be at home swinging his grandchildren on his knee, but the Confederacy was conscripting sixty year olds now to carry a musket, so maybe Gilmore was lucky to that extent at least.

The new surgeon had introduced himself to his duties by touring the camps, taking time to inspect the individual messes, checking on the men and their shelters, offering advice on ways of staying healthy. Ballard inevitably had his own view on this.

"Eat well," he had pronounced gravely, to the others of the mess, mimicking the serious tones of the new surgeon. "A good diet is the foundation of good health," he had continued, warming to his subject. "In this goddam army, who is he kiddin'? Avoid those Yankee bullets," he had resumed, before starting to give his own advice, though in the same grave tones of the surgeon. "They have proved to be extremely bad fer a man's health, and stay clear o' those damned shells too, that's my best medical advice." He had concluded by waggling his finger at his audience. "If ya follow these simple things closely, you'll lead a longer life." Even he had to admit however that the new surgeon had at least begun his tenure by demonstrating much more of an interest in the well-being of the men than his predecessor had ever done.

Both divisions had been bruised by their Tennessee experience, for it had cost too many of the comrades who had embarked on the trip there last fall, and for no tangible result. Most men, while acknowledging the cost in comrades and friends, tried to look to the future. At least, they told each other, they were back now with "Marse Robert", and if one thing had emerged above all others over the previous seven months, it was that a man seldom noticed the comparative blessings in his soldiering life until the day that he didn't have them anymore. Virginia was not their home, they were all from much farther south than that, but the fraught episode that

423

had just ended had proved, to most if not all of them, that the Army of Northern Virginia was where they belonged.

They waited in the camps around Mechanicsburg, but nobody thought that their stay there would be for very long. With no sign of any enemy move after all, along those upper stretches of the Rappahannock, they would most likely be called upon soon enough to rejoin the rest of the army further east, where the other corps had wintered. No, the men told each other, with no enemy threat to counter here, further delay would be more to do with the provision of rations, than for any greater tactical reason. Here, upriver from the other corps, rations had been fairly regular and that, as far as the enlisted men were concerned, was good enough reason for delaying here, as long as the war allowed it to continue.

If rations had been more regular, other things were in serious shortage. The numbers of barefoot men had been steadily increasing again, and Daniel Ryan's own shoes were on the verge of disintegration. Clothing too was short and virtually all of the men were ragged, with many of them wearing whatever items of non-uniform pants and in some cases tunics also, that they had been able to procure unofficially, for regulation replacements were no longer to be had.

It was the evening of the third day after Ballard's promotion had been confirmed, that Thompson arrived at the fire, seeking out Daniel Ryan. It was when the new First Sergeant beckoned to him to come that a dart of understanding crossed Daniel's mind, for he had been in this situation before when corporal's vacancies had come along, as they inevitably had done in the army. Having left the fire however, they did not pause anywhere for a quiet word, as Daniel had fully anticipated that they would, making instead for Boyce's tent. Upon their arrival there, Thompson rattled the pole with a coin and, since the call to enter was immediate, Daniel Ryan's misgivings mounted as he followed his friend inside. The tent was lit by a single lantern, and he squinted as his eyes began to adjust to its light. Boyce was on his feet behind his table and he waved them to approach, gesturing to his trunk which sat in front of the table.

"Sit please Sergeant, and you also Private." Thompson arranged himself on the trunk, and having seen him settle himself, Ryan perched a buttock on the remaining space. Boyce continued to stand and seeing this, both of them made to get once more to their feet, being prevented by the captain's further gesture. When they had settled once more on the trunk, the captain addressed Thompson.

"Is our friend here aware of the nature of our business, sergeant'," he inquired.

"Not yet, captain," Thompson replied.

"Maybe he thinks that," was the thought that flitted across Daniel Ryan's mind at the comment. On the other side of the table, Boyce pursed his lips and nodded briefly, as his gaze turned again towards Daniel Ryan.

"You are aware, Daniel that there is a corporal's vacancy in the company," he began, "and I am aware that you have twice previously turned down such a promotion." Daniel Ryan returned the captain's gaze.

"There's enough who hanker after the stripes, captain" he said, "without havin' to bother them that don't."

"Surely there is more to it than that." The officer's response was prompt and curt.

"I do my job," Daniel replied, "without looking to tell others what to do and, by doin' that, create a distance between myself and my friends." Having said that much he hesitated and Boyce looked at him, turning his ear towards him, tacitly inviting him to proceed.

"Between ourselves sir," Daniel continued. The captain nodded slowly.

"There's also others, who I wouldn't want to be dealin' with any more than I had to." Boyce nodded and then slowly turned his head towards Thompson.

"I see what you mean sergeant," he said slowly. "Perhaps we are wasting our time, as you suggested." He returned his eyes to Ryan, who felt a tinge of embarrassment as he met the officer's gaze once more.

"You mess with Sergeant Thompson and with Sergeant Ballard also," Boyce resumed. "Would you say that they are any less your friends because they have been promoted?" Daniel paused briefly before shaking his head.

"I still count both of them as my friends," he said, "in spite of everything." Beside him he heard Thompson chuckle at the remark, with Boyce too allowing the suggestion of a smile to cross his features.

"And do you think that you would make such a poor corporal that your friends would no longer count you as such," he inquired?

"Who's to say on that, captain?" Ryan countered. Boyce turned away, pacing briefly across to the other side of the tent, before turning and pacing back, to finally sit down on the folding chair.

"Regarding the other matter," he resumed, "you would remain in Lieutenant Williams' platoon, so your dealings, as far as they go, would be with him, but I will not press you further. If you are set against accepting the stripes, you will most certainly not be compelled to take them against your will, but I will put one more thing to you, before we leave the matter where it is. It is my view that the good of the company would be best served if you were to accept this promotion. I believe that you are the best available man and, on consulting the sergeants, all three of them think likewise. It therefore comes down to the simple question, of whether you are prepared to accept this step, for the good of the company." Daniel Ryan looked straight back at William Boyce, as his mind turned over his words. The captain was certainly showing that he was willing to twist his arm on the subject. Maybe he was, after all, being stubborn in continuing to resist this step. Did Boyce really think that his accepting a couple of stripes would make any real difference to Company B? He had never thought of it in any other way than simply not wishing to complicate things within the mess, yet Thompson and Ballard had both accepted promotion, and nothing, of any substance, had changed. He was aware of the captain looking at him and Thompson also. He sighed softly, as the answer came to him.

"I've always tried to be as reliable as any in the company, captain, but not because I was looking for anything like this..."

"Precisely!" Boyce put in, "and for that reason, as well as others, you are the man best suited for it, if only you will agree to do it." Again Ryan hesitated.

"Fer the lord's sake Daniel," Thompson growled from beside him, "we ain't got all day. D' ya intend doin' it or don't ya?" Daniel looked around at his friend for a few seconds and finally shrugged.

"The way you put it, how can I refuse," he said? Boyce looked at him.

"You've managed it this far," he snapped, "but if you feel your friendships would be less at risk, it could be arranged that you are placed in charge of another squad instead of simply inheriting Sergeant Ballard's."

"I wouldn't want that, captain," Daniel answered. "There are worse men than them around." Again Thompson and Boyce exchanged looks, and the sergeant chuckled once more as the captain rose to his feet.

"In that case, that will be all," he said, "corporal."

On the way back to the mess fire, Ryan had accosted Thompson, stopping him and turning to face him.

"Answer me one question," he had said. "Why me and not Isaac, or Edwin?" His friend had looked at him briefly.

"If there was to be one word for it," he had replied, "that word would be Maryland."

"Is that all there is to it?" Ryan had persisted, as they resumed walking.

"They're friends, and they're both good soldiers, same as you are," Thompson said. "You know that, jest like I do, but there was that one time, when they didn't stick and you did." He looked squarely at Daniel, "makes a difference don't it?"

The other three were still at the fire when they returned. Kane looked around as they approached.

"Did he, or didn't he?" he asked. Thompson looked at Ryan briefly before nodding.

"He did," he said.

"Hallelujah!" Jones intoned.

"Jest one thing that worries me about all o' this," Kane muttered.

"Worries you?" Ballard interjected. "What in the hell have you got to worry about?"

"What worries me sergeant, is how in the hell privates like me and Edwin here, are goin' to be able to git in so much as a word, in this mess full o' the highly promoted."

"Keep servin' up the vittles like always," Ballard told him, "and ya'll git along jest fine."

Though the weather remained cold for April, the roads were drying. Everyone knew that the movements would very soon begin and though the coming campaign would bring the chance to make good some at least of their shortages by giving them the chance to gain plunder from the Yankees, it would also bring its trials and hardships. Once their familiar adversaries of the Army of the Potomac moved south across the Rappahannock River once again, the struggle would be renewed for those vital miles between the two capital cities of Richmond and Washington, which had cost so much effort and blood over the previous three years. At least, the soldiers told each other with some irony, here in Virginia there was that one important difference from the way things had been in Tennessee. Back here, with the old man in charge, at least their own officers would be spending their time fighting the enemy, rather than turning on each other, and that would mean that the energies and abilities of everyone would maybe go where it was supposed to, towards giving the enemy, new general or not, that final licking that might just convince them at last to let it be.